Discipline with a Bullet

Robert D Coates

authors
On Line

Visit us online at www.authorsonline.co.uk

An Authors OnLine Book

Copyright © Robert D Coates 2006

Cover design by Siobhan Smith ©

All rights reserved. No part of this publication may be reproduced, stored in a retrieval system, or transmitted in any form or by any means, electronic, mechanical, photocopy, recording or otherwise, without prior written permission of the copyright owner. Nor can it be circulated in any form of binding or cover other than that in which it is published and without similar condition including this condition being imposed on a subsequent purchaser.

The moral rights of the authors have been asserted.

ISBN 0 7552 0237 6

Authors OnLine Ltd
19 The Cinques
Gamlingay, Sandy
Bedfordshire
SG19 3NU
England

This book is also available in e-book format, details of which are available at
www.authorsonline.co.uk

To Clare.

For her love, patience and encouragement.

Robert D Coates, BEM

Robert Coates was born in Bath, Somerset in 1939. one of six children having four brothers and one sister. Educated(?), as he puts it, at Oldfield Boys and West Twerton Secondary Modern Boys Schools, Bath.

He joined the Boys Regiment Royal Artillery, Hereford, April 1954 at the age of 15 and completed 25 years Regular Service. He then survived 20 years in HM Prison Service, just, as a Health Care Officer, retiring from the Service in 1999.

Married to Clare, they have four grown-up kids, one granddaughter and one recently arrived grandson. They are residents of Pontardawe, 10 miles from Swansea, his Mother having retired to Pembrokeshire.

Contents

Chapter 1	The Shiny Star	1
Chapter 2	Home, or is it?	50
Chapter 3	Hannah Jenkins	60
Chapter 4	Knife Attack	91
Chapter 5	A Misunderstanding	131
Chapter 6	You're Under Arrest	177
Chapter 7	Fighting Fit and Fit to Fight	199

Chapter 1

The Shiny Star

It was a bitterly cold early December morning in 1913, when a tall blonde distinguished-looking man with a large walrus moustache, the same colour as his hair, walked towards Wellington Barracks gate for what he thought would be the very last time.

Although only thirty-seven years old, he had just completed twenty years of regular army service and was on his way home.

He could hear the crack of hundreds of boots, almost as one, worn by his now ex-battalion comrades, being brought to attention, ready for inspection by the Commanding Officer of the Coldstream Guards, prior to their turn for Public Duties at Buckingham Palace and the Tower of London.

The private soldier standing sentry at the barracks gate stood to attention as the lance-sergeant, for that is what he was, approached. They had known each other for almost five years.

"Cheerio Walter, don't stand around too long, will you?" he said, smiling at his little joke.

"Oh thanks Sergeant, thanks Taff; you off then?"

"Steady now boyo, it ain't Taff until I'm though the gates, OK?"

"Sure Taff, um Sarg I mean. Not being nasty but I hope I won't be seeing you again 'cause then I might get promoted eh? Good luck anyway! Got to go Taff, RSM's on his way. Cheers mate."

Walter did a smart left turn and marched off towards the Guard Room. The soldier straightened his back and reached up and adjusted the forage cap to the correct position on his head.

The peak of the cap almost touched the bridge of his nose, making him lift his head so that his sight was not impaired. The position of the peak was peculiar to the Guards and their mode of dress.

If a cap with the peak in that position was worn by a soldier in another regiment, the culprit could be placed on a charge and punished according to King's Regulations.

In the centre of the forage cap, one inch above the seam connecting the peak to the cap, was the Shiny Star badge of the Coldstream Guards.

He had been a member of the Battalion and more proud to serve in it than in anything else in his life. The Coldstream Guards had been his family for twenty years. Now he was about to leave it and during the last two or three weeks his thoughts had gradually turned towards his own real family, old friends and hopefully a new settled life.

It was a freezing snow-covered street that the lance-sergeant stepped on to on that dull, dim morning but he still showed the light tan and fitness from his years in India, South Africa and the Middle East.

He was immensely proud of his service to the Crown but he was very reticent when he was asked about his role and experiences during his service.

The medal ribbons on his uniform showed the campaigns and battles he had marched to and fought in with the Coldstreams.

The wound stripes on his uniform and the long service stripes showed the experience and hardship he had endured. There was no need to ask about the service he had given to the Crown, it was there on his uniform and in his appearance.

His hard, stoic facial expression warned people off and he looked as though he had given the orders, not taken them. He would be the wrong man to cross but given the chance, he might be a great and everlasting friend.

There had been so many changes since he had sailed to the Indian continent: he was still surprised to see the number of trams, horse and motor cabs passing up and down the streets.

This was London. The Great Depression was just beginning, people were finding work more difficult to come by. The low paid workers were not so easily able to provide for their families. Their future looked grim and would never be the same for them as it had been in the recent past.

Where would new work come from? His mates and one or two of his officers said he was mad to leave the army now. Why didn't he re-engage for another few years? Life in the army for the regular soldier was becoming more bearable and better pay and conditions were in the offing.

There were still a good number of overseas postings on offer, but mostly as an individual, not with his company or battalion. That was one of the reasons he had decided to take his discharge.

He was a company, battalion, regimental soldier and he was leaving the Guards: he did not want to serve with another regiment of any description, even if offered promotion to go there.

On his return to England, he had been posted to his Battalion's Training Company at Pirbright, put in charge of a platoon of new recruits and ordered to train them to the regulatory standards of a private soldier, according to King's Rules and Regulations and the Guards Training Manual.

He didn't enjoy that job because he felt like a nursemaid and it entailed learning King's R and R and the GTM, as they were called, off by heart and he didn't consider that soldering.

Later he applied for the position of Officers Mess Sergeant at Wellington Barracks, which had recently become vacant, and his application was accepted even though it was only a temporary measure until a permanent candidate could be selected.

So he served the remainder of his contracted service in the officers mess. It taught him about the life of a Guards Officer in barracks and about the way they were addressed, approached and served, not that he didn't know most of that already; he had served under them long enough.

He had said to himself and his friends on more than one occasion, "I don't mind the soldiering and I don't mind the Officers Mess but I've had enough marching up and down outside 'Buck house' all day. I need something new every now and then, so I have to give Civvy Street a go."

A new motor taxi cab stopped near him; he'd never been near one before.

"How far is it to Paddington Station?" he asked the driver.

"Too far to walk, mate! Where you going anyway?"

"Bristol, if I can get a train today."

"Jump in, I'm going there to pick up a fare; some geezer, who's a nob, no doubt."

"How much is the fare to Paddington then?"

"Don't let that little item worry you mate, I said I'm going there anyway, didn't I? So just 'op in and we'll be on our way, eh?"

The ex-soldier, for that was what he was now, was amazed: no one had ever in his whole career, or his life for that matter, ever offered him something for nothing, not even a word of thanks.

As they drove through the London streets, the cabbie pointed out the sights and places of interest and reference, a free sightseeing tour. Crowds of shoppers and tourists thronged the pavements; cars, trams, buses, taxis and horse-drawn carts, the roads. It seemed like chaos to most visitors and tourists.

But in the end, it was organised chaos: with the aid of vehicle horns and raucous shouts of cabbies and others, everything seemed to sort itself out, the cabbie sitting calmly behind his steering wheel until the road was clear.

The now ex-soldier had been to London quite often but he and his friends were usually one of the sights, carrying out Public Duties at the Tower of London or Buckingham Palace.

As they drove slowly past Buckingham Palace, he noticed the Royal Standard flying above the Palace. The King and the Royal Family were in residence.

He was pleased he wasn't part of the guard that day, because the lance-sergeant in charge of the sentries and the guard room would have to be on his toes and it would be unlikely that he would get any sleep until late the following day, and only then, if he was lucky and not given any other duties, when the Dismounted Guard arrived back in barracks.

The men mounting the guard would have been up at five o'clock in the morning and wouldn't have been back in barracks until one o'clock the next afternoon. Normal duties wouldn't be finished until about five o'clock, then they would be dismissed to their barracks until the next day. All would be too tired to go out, even if they had been given a walking-out pass. So most stayed in barracks bulling their boots, cleaning their kit or pressing their uniforms and going to bed as early as possible, ready for the next parade in the morning.

It was unusual to watch other guardsmen doing those duties from the spectators' side and for a minute, as he watched, he became critical of the soldiers mounting the guard.

He realised what a fine spectacle they were to the watching crowd. Then, shrugging his shoulders as he realised that that drill and duty were not going to be part of his life anymore, he began to look out for more sights of interest that he hadn't had the chance to see whilst he had been stationed in the capital city.

When they arrived at Paddington Station, he attempted to press a shilling into the taxi driver's hand.

"No you don't mate, thanks. You're going to need it the way things are going. It looks as though you've done enough for this country already, besides there's the nob I'm taking to Whitehall, and that'll cost him a pretty penny, you'll see. Be on your way and catch that train, see your family and have a proper life. Good luck mate!"

The cabbie grinned and the soldier touched his cap and with a friendly "Thanks" went on his way.

The taxi driver's new fare was a tall and well-built man with white hair peeking from below his bowler hat. He had a large grey moustache and wore a monocle in his right eye, which gave his eye a fierce piercing appearance.

He wore a long black coat, pin stripe trousers and highly polished black shoes. Another man, accompanying the first, entered the cab; he was dressed in army uniform and wore the rank of captain, his cap badge showed him to be an officer of the Tenth Hussars.

Neither of the strangers looked at the soldier, so he turned his back to the cab as it was driven away. He didn't realise, as the taxi driver did, that the nob and himself bore a striking resemblance to each other.

The eleven o'clock train from Paddington to Bristol was the slow train, although the soldier didn't know it. The ticket collector had only pointed him in the direction of platform ten and not given him any further information to assist him on his way.

There were six or seven third and second class coaches and one first class Pullman coach. "Must be for the nobs," he said to himself, using the cab driver's disparaging name for the wealthy, as he peered through the windows of the coaches, looking for a spare seat.

There were no corridors in the coaches of the trains during the early twentieth century, so a seat had to be found before the train left the station. There were no seats in the third class compartments for which he had a ticket and the one or two left in the second class coaches were reserved for those affluent and experienced enough to book on an earlier occasion.

The soldier alarmed and frustrated realised that the next train to his destination wouldn't be until three o'clock in the afternoon.

As he turned away, dejected and angry with himself for hanging about in barracks, not really wanting to leave his friends, someone called out: "Hey you! Sergeant! There's a spare seat here, do you want it?" He turned towards the man who had called to him from the first class Pullman carriage.

"Thanks very much sir, but I've only a third class ticket and I couldn't afford a second class, let alone a first class one."

"It's all right Sergeant, my friend hasn't arrived and he's going to be too late; the seat has already been paid for so you might as well use it, hadn't you?"

The soldier could not believe his luck, twice in one day he'd been offered something for nothing. "Thank you sir, it's most kind of you, thank you very much."

He stepped into the Pullman and was immediately taken aback and amazed at the opulence of the furnishings. He had never ever seen anything like it before, not even in the ships' cabins that he'd seen the army officers occupying on the long journeys abroad.

As the train left the station the gentleman said, "Here, sit opposite me, you'll have a good view during the journey. My name is Major Richards, late, very late, of the Devonshire Regiment, retired I might add; and you are?"

"I'm Jenkins, sir."

"Are you going far, Sergeant?"

"I'm on my way to Bristol, sir, to see my sister who lives there. I've been given two weeks discharge leave and my two weeks annual leave."

"Leaving, eh?"

"Yes sir, I came back from the East almost ten months ago and I decided not to re-enlist because I've done twenty years regular service and it's about time I went home and saw my mother and sister and hopefully get a job. Besides that, there are too many senior NCOs in the Guards and it'll be years before I'll have a hope of getting further promotion!"

The major looked at the three stripes on the soldier's arm, "But you are a sergeant already, aren't you?"

"No sir, with respect, I'm a lance-sergeant. In any other regiment, other than the Guards, I would be a corporal, and, as you know, like any other regiment we have lance-corporals. Lance-corporals wear two stripes, a lance-sergeant is equivalent and paid the same as a corporal but wears three stripes. We can also use the Sergeants Mess but a corporal can't. Confusing ain't it, sir?"

"At times Sergeant, at times."

The soldier felt confused and a little embarrassed: he'd never been this close to an officer in his life, except on parade. If an officer spoke to you then, it was either to give an order or tell you off. If an officer wanted to speak to the soldiers it was rarely as individuals and it was usually on parade. Mostly it was either the Sergeant-Major repeating the officer's instructions or the company as a whole being given a pep talk just before a battle.

In all the years in the battalion, he'd never been spoken to by the battalion's Commanding Officer or the Regimental Colonel, on parade or at work in the Officers Mess, not even when he was in hospital in Malta in 1903, whilst he was recovering from one of several occurrences of malaria, which he had contracted during the Ashanti expedition of 1895 and 96.

Jenkins was one of thirteen men and an officer of the Coldstream Guards which was part of a composite company, in an expedition made up of three regiments of Foot Guards.

The expedition, led by Colonel Sir Francis Scott, arrived at Ashanti on the African Gold Coast at the end of December 1895. From there the force undertook a three-week, one hundred and fifty mile march through dense jungle to Kumassi, the King Prempeh's stronghold.

King Prempeh was captured along with his family, and all the apparatus used for torture, human sacrifice and sometimes cannibalism was destroyed. The King was removed, eventually to the Seychelles. Many soldiers became ill with swamp fever, dysentery and malaria during the expedition. Some died during the march from these illnesses. Others, unable to recover due to little knowledge and little treatment, died later, whilst being treated in hospital in Malta.

Jenkins had recovered enough to return to his battalion which was shipped back to England in October 1902.

Then he was detailed to return to Malta as part of King Edward VII's escort to Malta in 1903, the King's first visit to the island.

Towards the end of the King's visit, a recurring bout of malaria put Jenkins back in hospital, where along with many other sick and wounded soldiers, he was visited by Queen Alexandra who presented him with a red and gold tin of chocolates from the late Queen Victoria, a present for all the Queen's heroes. Although Victoria had passed away, these tins of chocolates were still being presented to 'Private Soldiers' serving abroad. He treasured that moment for the rest of his life.

Yet Jenkins was amazed and for the life of him couldn't understand why this retired officer was even looking at him, let alone talking to him, almost like a long lost friend.

His old mates he'd left behind would never believe him if he told them where he was at that time, unless they saw him sitting there. Even then they would still find it hard to believe.

The gentleman began to tell Jenkins about his service under the Colours.

"Well, Sergeant, I was once a Colour Sergeant, serving with the Devonshire Regiment, D Company, Second Battalion, in 1899, during the first battle of the campaign in Natal, South Africa.

"We were near Dundee and the battalion was advancing in columns towards Talama, along a valley road. I was in command of our skirmishers high up on the hills surrounding the valley.

"We were short of officers and NCOs even then, or someone else would have been in charge."

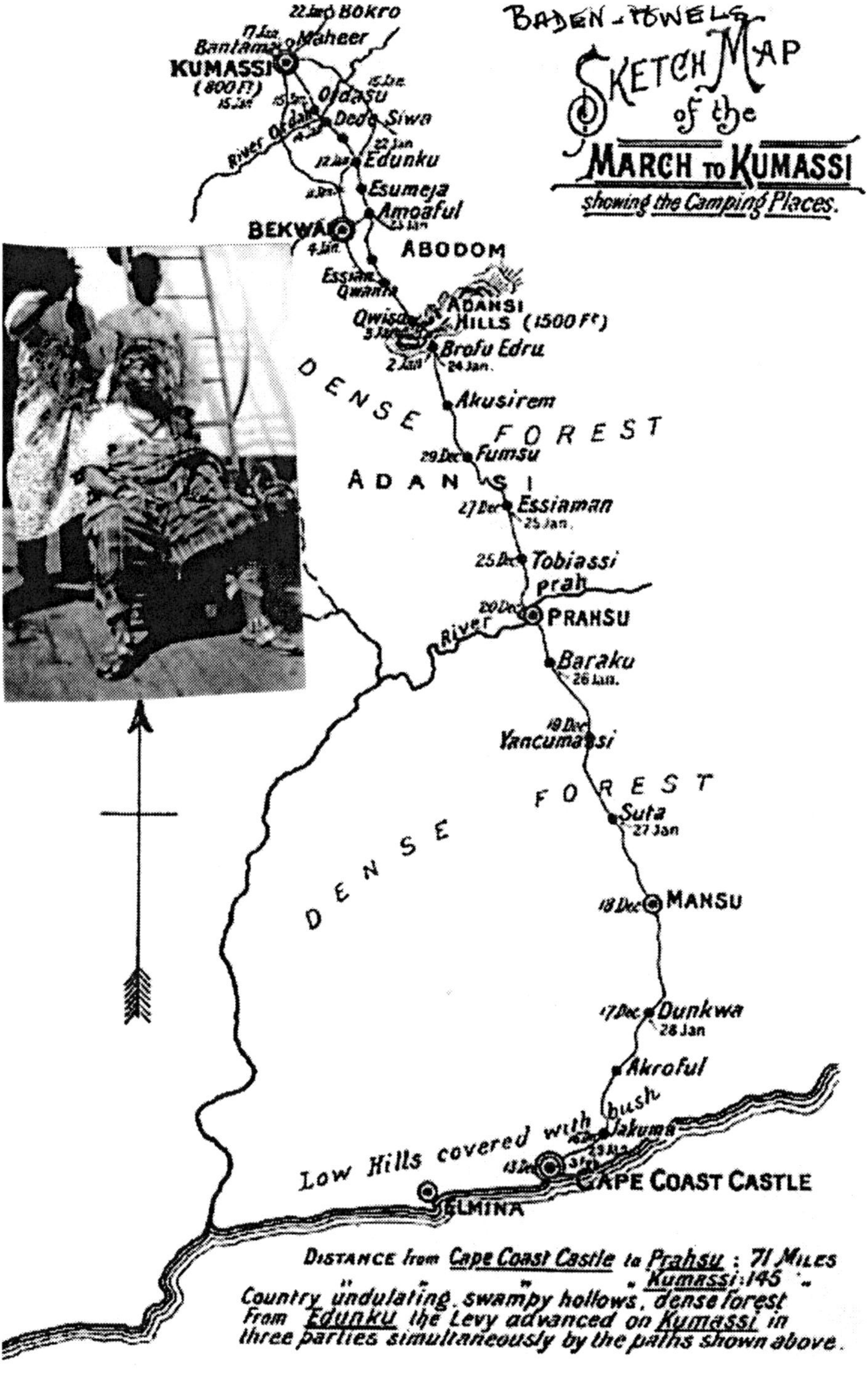
Baden-Powell's
Sketch Map
of the
March to Kumassi
showing the Camping Places.
Bokro
Maheer
Bantama
KUMASSI
(800 Ft)
Ordasu
Dede Siwa
River Ordah
Edunku
Esumeja
Amoaful
BEKWAI
ABODOM
Essian
Qwanta
Qwisa
ADANSI HILLS (1500 Ft)
Brofu Edru
DENSE FOREST
Akusirem
Fumsu
ADANSI
Essiaman
Tobiassi
prah
PRAHSU
River
Baraku
Yancumassi
DENSE FOREST
Suta
MANSU
Dunkwa
Akroful
Low Hills covered with bush
Jakuma
CAPE COAST CASTLE
ELMINA
Distance from Cape Coast Castle to Prahsu : 71 Miles
" " " " Kumassi : 145 "
Country undulating, swampy hollows, dense forest
From Edunku the Levy advanced on Kumassi in three parties simultaneously by the paths shown above.

He nodded, noting the sergeant's unasked question. "What happened to them all?"

The major went on, knowing that most soldiers liked war tales and he liked telling his tales as well to those who would appreciate them. "The Boers who, as you probable know, were very skilful at ambush and hit and run tactics, virtually left us, the skirmishers, alone but came in behind and attacked the column, where of course were all our officers commanding their battalions, companies and platoons.

"The Boers were crack-shot riflemen with their Mauser rifles, as you must already know?" He indicated the campaign ribbons on the soldier's chest. "Anyway, by the time we had taken Talama, forty-one officers and men had been killed and one hundred and eighty-five wounded.

"The Boers' tactics had always been to make casualties of as many officers as possible, though they tried to be less conspicuous by dressing down, even marching close to the men, often in the ranks. General Pen Synas VC was in command and directed the battle. As you might have heard he was one of those killed."

Richards went on, "There were only two young second lieutenants, 'ensigns' I believe you would call them, left able to command in my company. So, as a senior man I had to take charge of the skirmishers.

"Later, officers were posted to us from other battalions and I was promoted to lieutenant, a battlefield promotion.

"A year or two later I became Battalion Quartermaster. I admit it wasn't a job I easily took to. But with captain's pay and later a promotion to major, it wasn't a job to be sniffed at though, was it?

"I left the Army in 1905, and was lucky enough to receive a very good pension and an inheritance, which is why I now live at the Royal Crescent, Bath.

"I only hope you will have as good a life as myself in the future but it does look as though prospects are getting harder everyday doesn't it? Have you noticed that, so far?"

"No, sir, can't say I have, anyway not since I came back to England. I've been training recruits for a few months and then I was the Battalion Officers Mess Sergeant for the last few months until my discharge, which is today.

"So since coming back to England ten months ago I've been pretty busy, instructing recruits in the A to Z of soldering and running the officers mess."

The major smiled, "You've a novel way of putting things, Sergeant, maybe I'll be able to use it to liven up my stories."

8

During their journey to the West Country, they took to reminiscing about their careers and the campaigns they had both taken part in. Then both realised they had taken part in the same Talama battle on the same day.

The soldier, who was a private at the time, had been later mentioned in despatches.

Some months prior to the campaign he had been recommended and accepted as the brigade commander, Brigadier Paterson's, batman and bodyguard, and was with the Brigadier during the Talama battle.

During the action the Brigadier asked Private Jenkins to adjust his horse's bit and bridle. When Jenkins moved round toward the horse's head, he was hit in the shoulder by a sniper's first bullet. The Brigadier dismounted, it seemed with the intention of helping the soldier but was badly wounded by another bullet from the Boer crackshot. Jenkins immediately went to the aid of the Brigadier and although hit again in the thigh, managed to drag the Brigadier into the cover of the now-dead horse; they had to remain in that position until several snipers had been located and driven off.

Help finally arrived and Patterson and Jenkins were taken to a field hospital; later the Brigadier died under the surgeon's knife.

During that action one Boer sniper had accounted for at least six of the brigade headquarters' staff, two officers, three non-commissioned officers and Private Jenkins. After the war it was recorded and confirmed in Boer army reports of that battle that the same sniper had shot Patterson and Jenkins.

As the train travelled towards Reading, through the lush green fields, past woods and forests and through towns, the soldier realised just how much he had missed this beautiful West Country life.

A smartly dressed Pullman steward arrived and asked Major Richards, "Would you like an aperitif, sir?" glancing at the sergeant with disdain.

The major asked the soldier if he would like a drink; he nodded, dumbstruck.

Here he was in a Pullman carriage, sitting at an immaculate table set for a meal with silver service and was being asked by an officer if he would like a drink. He felt as though he was in a dream, only his best mates had ever offered him a drink. Never an officer. Retired or otherwise.

"Beer all right, Sergeant?"

He stuttered a thanks of sorts, "Yes sir, ale would be very nice – if they've got any," he added.

He was duly served with a glass of golden beer. When it arrived, the beer was drunk in almost one long swallow. He glanced guiltily at his host.

"It's all right Sergeant, it looks as though you enjoyed that; we've plenty of time you know, so you will have another, won't you?"

"That felt like nectar sir, thanks; the best beer I've had since coming back to England – but you will allow me to buy you a drink, sir?"

Jenkins couldn't believe what he just said: he suddenly realised that if the major said "Yes", he didn't know whether or not he would be able to pay for the drink, whatever the cost might be.

"Not now thanks, later perhaps," the major replied.

The sergeant couldn't get over the officer's generosity. He was also very relieved as he wasn't too sure if he could afford to buy the drinks, because his pay and bounty money wouldn't arrive at his local bank for a few days. At this moment he only had enough to pay for lodgings and food for a week so he had to be quite careful.

During his military service, he had made a great effort to save a few pounds a year, because he knew that one day, if he was still alive and fit enough, army life would end. He would then be responsible for his own welfare. Not like a lot of soldiers, they nearly always drank their money away, not expecting to live past the next battle or campaign.

By the time the train reached Swindon, the soldier was as relaxed as he would allow himself to become. He was still wary of the officer's intentions but he was soon able to talk more freely and began asking questions about the country and people since he had boarded the troop ship at Southampton in 1888.

Major Richards continued to direct him to points of interest, the Swindon railway engineering yards for instance, where railway engines, coaches and everything connected with the railways were built and repaired. The works were huge and at that time employed several hundred men, many of whom could be seen working on the engines and coaches.

"A good job if you could get one," Jenkins said to himself. "But I doubt if I would fit the bill!"

An hour later as the train arrived at Bath, Richards pointed out the peculiar, one-walled Sham Castle, then the magnificent Bath Abbey and the City of Bath across the River Avon as the train passed alongside it to the station.

No, he, Major Richards, had never understood why Sham Castle had been built like that and no one, it seemed, was about to tell him.

He explained that next to Bath Abbey were the Roman Baths. Historically the Baths were known as Aqua Sulis during the Roman occupation of Britain. During that period, Bath had been one of the Romans' major strongholds in the West Country.

He also pointed out the direction of Lansdowne, to the north-west of the city, where he had his home in the Royal Crescent. The Royal Crescent – the name didn't mean anything to Jenkins but it sounded a pretty rich man's paradise, he thought to himself.

Richards, he could tell, was proud of his home and city. "Perhaps I'll go and see it one day, maybe."

The train arrived at Bath Spa Station and came to a stop at platform two: the major stood up and offered the sergeant his hand.

"It's been a pleasure meeting you Sergeant, and thank you for your company, it made this usually tedious journey very enlightening and entertaining, most enjoyable."

The sergeant shook the proffered hand and replied hesitantly "No sir, it's thank *you*, thank you very much." He couldn't think of what else to say.

"Sergeant, if you ever require any assistance looking for work or getting a job, I have lots of contacts in this neck of the woods and further abroad; please write and let me know – I'll see if I can help."

He offered a small card to the flabbergasted sergeant and all Jenkins could reply was a mumbled, "Thanks, sir."

The major stepped out of the coach and walked towards the ticket collector. As the sergeant watched, he turned, raised his hand in a salute, and disappeared down the steps towards the station exit.

As the train pulled away on its next leg of the journey towards Bristol, the steward quietly approached the sergeant, "I see you met the Lord Longford, then, sir?"

Jenkins looked at him in astonishment, "What? Who?"

"Major, the Lord Longford of Kingsholm and Gloucester, a very kind gentleman, eh?" The sergeant sat down with a bump.

His whole outlook on the world was changing so rapidly he thought he was dreaming.

"Fancy another beer on me, sir?" said the steward. "Looks as though you've had quite a shock, eh? Y'know the title was awarded to the major's ancestors by Richard II and the major told me that it is recorded in the Doomsday Book of 1068. Interesting, eh?"

Doomsday Book? Richard II? Jenkins was still recovering from the shock as he took from his top jacket pocket a red and gold tin, six inches long by three inches wide. It had once contained chocolate. He hadn't a clue what the Doomsday Book was or when Richard II was on the throne.

The tin was the gift from Queen Victoria to all private soldiers who fought in the Boer War. On the Queen's instructions, the boxes were only to be given to private soldiers. Any remaining boxes were to be destroyed. He was lucky then he was still alive. Three months later he was promoted to lance-corporal.

It now contained ten hand-rolled cigarettes. Although he wasn't a regular smoker he did enjoy the occasional one each day. If he was tired or stressed, it would give him time to think and get his thoughts in order. As the train arrived at Bristol, Jenkins took out a cigarette and lit it, then put the major's card under the cigarettes for safe keeping. Home, or was it? Jenkins stepped off the train at Bristol Temple Meads.

Chocolates for Victoria's Heroes

Lifting his kit bag up and across his shoulder, he strode off towards the station's exit.

He was amazed at the changes that had been made since his departure from Swansea and his journey through Bristol Temple Meads station many years before. The station roof and buildings seemed to have grown upwards and outwards. Every building and platform was massive compared to the tiny single-storied waiting-rooms and the two arrival and departure platforms he remembered during his journey to London. It was the day after he had enlisted at the Swansea army recruiting office and been told to change trains at Bristol. It was his first time outside the Welsh Borders.

He handed his ticket to the waiting porter at the exit. "Where's the nearest tram stop then, mate?" he asked.

"Not far, just across the square and around that corner," came the reply. "Just a couple of minutes walk."

"OK, ta." Jenkins thanked the porter and headed in the direction the man had pointed out.

He felt very strange not to be with any of his friends or marching in a section or platoon. It felt weird to be alone after all this time.

A tram arrived. "This going to the docks?" he asked.

"Yes mate, via the centre," the conductor indicated the sign on the side of the tram. "All stops to the centre and then the docks. Where about in the docks are you going?"

"Guinea Street near Wapping Road and Redcliffe Parade. That OK?"

"Sure, jump on, it's a nice long ride, cost you three pence though."

"I reckon I can manage that," Jenkins replied.

It was almost an hour later that Jenkins got off the tram. Seeing and watching all of the hustle and bustle of the town and the arrival and departure of the numerous passengers together with the train journey, had tired him out.

He looked around for a street sign to confirm his surroundings. There were none but the docks were to his left and his front. He could see massive cranes towering over the buildings near the docks.

The road was fairly busy. "So this must be Wapping Road," he thought.

The tram conductor had told him when to get off the tram, but hadn't bothered to tell Jenkins where he was.

He looked around: there were plenty of three-storey houses and a couple of shops on the same side of the road on which he was standing. Three hundred yards further along on the same side there were rows of warehouses five storeys high. He could see men busy pushing large wheelbarrows backwards and forwards across the road, loaded up when they went into a warehouse, empty when they came out. He realised the men were unloading a small ship, which was tied up and low down at the side of the dock.

He noticed a pub on the corner of the street close to where the row of warehouses started.

"A good place to start," he said to himself, thinking, "always get information here," as he pushed open the door to enter.

He had to take off his cap and duck under the low arched doorway. It was difficult to see into the room which was dark, dingy and damp, with the pungent aroma of alcohol and pipe smoke pervading everything. Smokey, flickering oil lamps placed haphazardly around the room gave the place some vestige of light.

There were half a dozen men of varying ages and builds sitting at tables around the room; a couple were standing at the bar. The bar stretched from one end of the room to the other and consisted of nothing more than half a dozen large empty beer barrels, stood on end, supporting four or five wooden table tops. Crude but practical.

The bartender was in his late fifties, perhaps early sixties, had matted, greasy greying hair and was wearing spectacles with one cracked lens. The shirt he wore was stained with beer and he was reading a paper as he slumped his fat belly on to the top of the bar. The customers were either doing the same or chatting or playing cards.

Nearly all looked up when they realised it was someone in a uniform, but went back to their games or papers when they saw it wasn't the black of the police.

"What can I get you, son?" the bar tender enquired.

"Just a glass of mild ale, mate, thanks, and a little information if you will."

"Surely," the barman replied. "What is it, a place to stay, or a good woman?"

"Neither thanks. I'm looking for Guinea Street. The tram conductor told me it was somewhere near here, but not exactly where. Any ideas?"

"Yes Sergeant I have. Finish your ale and I'll get someone to show you, all right?" he replied. He nodded to someone behind Jenkins's shoulder. His smarmy smirk, which was meant to be a smile, went unnoticed by Jenkins.

He was thinking to himself, "Nearly there, nearly home at last!"

He tossed sixpence on the bar, "I'll have another before I go barman please." He drained his glass and passed it back for a refill. He was beginning to feel comfortable and contented: he turned towards the men at the tables and nodded a greeting to the one or two closest to him.

They raised their glasses in acknowledgement as he continued to survey the room, out of habit, mentally checking the stature and attitude of the various individuals. He wasn't expecting trouble; he never did but he always sized up people and the situation as he'd been trained to do. It was going to be a habit he would never get out of.

"When you're ready, mate?" A hand touched him on the shoulder; he turned and looked at the questioner.

"OK! Let's go," he replied.

He thanked the barman, emptied his glass, picked up his kitbag and followed his new guide out of the door.

"Guinea Street, ain't it mate?" the man asked.

"Yes, number 31, do you know it?"

"Sure I live a few streets away myself; follow me, eh?"

As they walked along the road towards the warehouses Jenkins could smell the river and he felt the tiredness slipping away.

The man guiding him looked big and slovenly from the back. Jenkins could smell his sweat and the oil that pervaded his clothes. He was walking quickly but was favouring his left leg and although Jenkins couldn't see, he could hear the man dragging his boot as he limped along.

When they arrived at the warehouses, Jenkins was aware of a corner on the other side of the road. The man in front turned across the road and headed towards the corner, which led into a lane between two of the three storey houses.

The lane was made up of cobbled stones; it had been raining earlier during the afternoon and it made the cobbles quite slippery. He noticed the lane began to rise towards a light from a house on the next street, running parallel to the one he'd just left.

As they arrived at the next junction the light flared up, blazing directly into his eyes, blinding him. As Jenkins raised his hands to block out the light, he felt something strike his left knee and then a blow was delivered to the back of his right knee. He went down on his right side and as he did he felt kicks to his kidneys and lower spine. Then blows to the back of the head and neck rendered him unconscious.

The beating had only taken about thirty seconds and he knew almost nothing about it.

The attack was very professional and extremely efficient.

Hours later, the soldier and his guide were found halfway down the lane in a shallow overflow ditch. Both were so badly beaten it was days before Jenkins regained consciousness and his faculties and was then able to speak to the nursing staff from his bed in Bristol Royal Infirmary.

His guide, 'old Limpy' as he was known, died without regaining consciousness.

The only way the police had been able to identify the Sergeant was from the laundry marks sewn into his trousers, shirt and underwear, as was the normal practice with all military ranks of his day. His name and last four digits of his army number were discovered in that way. His kitbag, jacket and hat were missing, presumed stolen, as was the little money he had left from his last army pay-day.

The police contacted Army Records office and found that he had been discharged from the army on the day that he had been found in the alley.

Technically he was still in the army as he was on discharge and annual leave but the Colonel of the Army Records Office asked the Bristol Royal Infirmary authorities and the police to continue to take charge, treat and monitor him until he recovered.

When Jenkins was able to talk, he was unable tell the police anything after his arrival at Bristol Temple Meads. He seemed to have forgotten everything from the time he had stepped off the train at Bristol Temple Meads station until he recovered consciousness.

What little money he had and almost all his personal belongings had been stolen. His discharge papers, letters, photos and the bank account number and details had been in his jacket pocket. His whole life was in that jacket and kit bag; the only thing he had left of his previous life and service was the red and gold chocolate tin, which he had inadvertently slipped into his trouser pocket whilst he'd had a smoke in the pub. The thugs who robbed him hadn't thought it worthwhile taking it, or missed it in their hurry to get away.

The doctors at Bristol Royal Infirmary insisted he stay in the hospital for a least a week to allow the bruising to subside, the wounds to heal and his right knee to regain some strength before he put any weight on it.

He did as he was told and whilst lying or sitting on his bed, did his own form of exercises, not just for his knee but for his back and neck.

The Colonel-in-Charge of Army Records had been informed of the robbery and assault and he forwarded a duplicate set of discharge papers and reimbursed the soldier with the money he had received on his discharge.

Although he didn't know where to start, the only thing Jenkins had on his mind was his mounting obsession for revenge on the attackers.

He didn't know where or when, but his and his assailants' paths would cross one day and there would only be one outcome.

A hospital visitor heard of his plight from the nursing staff. She was from the Salvation Army, a Mrs May Andrews. Normally Jenkins would have no truck with any religious group but when the lady spoke to him she seemed so genuinely kind and wanting to help, that he listened and accepted all that she had to offer. Clothes, a few shillings, accommodation and meals.

After two weeks in the hospital, Mrs Andrews took him by taxi to the hostel she had found for him.

He still couldn't remember why he had journeyed to Bristol but he knew that one day when he did remember, he would find out who beat him so badly and why. He knew it was to rob him but why did they try to kill him?

When he did eventually find the murdering thieves, it would be the time for his revenge.

He didn't tell Mrs Andrews because he knew she wouldn't approve; there didn't seem to be an ounce of anger in her.

He began to remember the other people who had shown him kindness, the taxi driver, the Major and the steward, but, after leaving the railway station, Jenkins didn't remember a thing until he woke up in Bristol Royal Infirmary.

May, as she insisted he call her, also helped him by recommending him for a job at the home of the Harbour Master as a gardener.

The Floating Harbour Master, his full title, was responsible for all the shipping that berthed at the Floating Harbour in Bristol Docks, most of which was local and arrived via the Severn and passing up the Avon to Bristol Docks. Prior to and during the early 1900s it was a very busy waterway and shipping area. Cargo was brought up the Avon from as far afield as America, Canada and the West Indies. Closer to home were the smaller transports from Ireland and even from Newport, Cardiff and Swansea along the Welsh coast. These Welsh ships usually brought in coal, steel and sand from the industries all over Wales.

Mr David Roberts had been born and brought up in Wales and knew all the local ships' captains and many of their crew members. He had moved to Bristol Docks when he been offered and accepted the position of Floating Harbour Master. He had worked and trained at Swansea Docks for many years before the Bristol position became available. It was the sort of position that would only be offered once in a lifetime, he therefore had no qualms in accepting the Bristol Docks Board's offer.

David Roberts was small, rotund, round red-faced and a jolly character who didn't have a bad word for anyone. His wife was built in the same mould, always smiling and chattering.

The four children Jenkins saw running around the house and garden seemed to be the happiest kids he had ever seen. But he did admit to himself he hadn't seen that many children close up since joining the army.

Roberts showed him the work he wanted done and told him that other jobs might become available if he turned out to be a good, conscientious worker, who took a pride in the job. Mrs Andrews agreed with Roberts and hoped he, Jenkins, would continue to get well and stronger. She gave him her home address and that of the Salvation Army establishment near the city centre.

The work would be for just twenty hours a week to begin with, for which he was to be paid one pound ten shillings. It was a start and Mrs Roberts said he could have soup, bread and tea every day that he went to work on the gardens.

"Perhaps it will lead on to other things," she said. "Better things?"

About the same time he realised it was his family, his sister, mother, father and brother he needed, although he hadn't seen any of them since joining the army. He didn't even know if they were still alive or where they were. He told himself he'd have to do something to find them and soon. He tried to remember the address of his sister, then realised it was her, Jenny, that he had come to Bristol to see before he had been attacked.

Mr Roberts and his family had a house just below Clifton, the garden had been well kept, but Roberts began to find he had less and less time to work at it. It was almost two acres square, with lawns, flowerbeds, fruit and vegetable patches laid out in meticulous patterns. Apple, pear and cherry trees were dotted around between the various patches of flowers and lawns.

When he saw the garden and house Jenkins knew that he was going to enjoy this work. He had often worked in his grandparents' garden as a young lad and always enjoyed it, especially at the time of picking the fruit and going to the harvest festival.

He tried hard to get out of going to chapel almost every week until his mother gave him a solid clout and told him to get going. After that he always made sure that he got into chapel before his parents arrived, especially at the time of the harvest festival or the Easter and Christmas Services. These were his most enjoyable days in chapel.

It was almost the end of February when he remembered where he had been going on the day he had been attacked. His sister's house near the docks; what was it? Ah yes, Guinea Street by Wapping Road. He realised he had the address all the time, scratched into the lid of his cigarette tin, as he often called it.

When Roberts came back to the house from the harbour, after Jenkins had been working on the garden for a couple of weeks, Jenkins asked him a string of questions about Bristol, the docks, Wapping Road and Guinea Street. Roberts answered him as well as he could and then asked Jenkins the reason for all the questions.

"Are you intent on leaving my employment; aren't you happy in your work here?"

"Oh no sir, I'm extremely grateful and I feel well suited to this job, I'll be happy to stay as long as circumstances allow and that you and your wife are happy with my work. I have to look for my sister and her family who are living somewhere near the docks. That was the reason I came to Bristol when

I left the army, after that I had intended to go on to South Wales to see my mother and father who live near Swansea. I'm Welsh you see."

"Well, I never would have guessed," Roberts said mockingly.

Jenkins hadn't realised that his South Wales accent was beginning to return. He'd picked up a flat nasal army accent and never noticed it during his service.

"How long is it since you saw your family, then?" Roberts enquired.

"More than twenty years I should imagine and I shouldn't like it to be another twenty. I think they, my Mam and Dad, must be well into their sixties by now and I really should be getting down to see them, shouldn't I?"

"All right, all right," Roberts retorted. "I'll try and get someone to show you around, this time someone who I can trust, as well as yourself. Don't worry just give me a couple of days and we'll soon have you at your sister's place. I would imagine she'd be wanting to see you too, wouldn't she, eh?"

"Well I hope she does," Jenkins replied, "after all the trouble it's taken to get this far!"

A few days later, Mr Roberts called Jenkins into the house.

"I've got someone to show you around, Mr Jenkins, and would you imagine, he's from the same neck of the woods as you and I. The Swansea Valley. Near Clydach to be exact."

As he said this, a small wiry, black haired man turned towards Jenkins holding out a knarled dark-skinned hand blackened by working with or handling coal and oil, which had become ingrained over the many years of using such materials.

He introduced himself as 'Jones the ship', a peculiar way of identifying himself, but Jenkins realised straight away that this chap must be working or living with a lot of other Jones's: it was the Welsh way of identifying different family names, such as 'Jones the milk', 'Williams the coal', 'Evans the bread'.

In the army, especially the Welsh Battalions, soldiers would be identified on roll call as '347 Jones', the next would be '952', next '045' and so on leaving out the name and using the numbers only.

Jones the ship lived in Bristol but worked a collier between Swansea and Bristol calling in at almost all the Welsh Ports along the coast. He usually worked five or six days a week depending on the weather and often had plenty of time off. Mr Roberts had known him for years and at one time employed him on the Swansea Docks in a variety of jobs. He could turn his hand to almost anything and was a useful chap to know. He seemed to know everyone and most people knew him. He always knew about everything that went on in and around the Bristol Dock area. Most days he worked in the ship's engine-room as a stoker, the reason for the blackened, knarled hands.

He looked at Jenkins with pale ice blue eyes, the skin around the sockets reddened with continual rubbing with dust-encrusted hands.

"How's it going Taff?" he said, grinning and pretending to lean back to look at Jenkins' height. "What lighthouse did you escape from then, mate?"

Jenkins grinned back and took the proffered hand, "Pleased to meet you to Dai, where do you say you come from?"

"The Swansea Valley; do you know it then?"

"I should say so; I'm from Pontardawe."

"Aye it's Clydach meself," Dai replied. It was only two or three miles along the Swansea Valley to Ponty as the locals called it. "What a bloody small world it is, ain't it?" Jones said in Welsh. "How's your Welsh then, still speak God's own tongue?"

"No, sorry, I've been with the English too long: I still know it but haven't spoken a word since I joined the Coldstream Guards almost twenty years ago. There aren't many Welshmen in the Regiment, worse luck. Could have done with a few more in many a fight."

He went on to explain why he needed help in finding his sister and family and after that he aimed to find the people that robbed and nearly killed him. He told Jones as much as he could remember, up until the time he got off the train and he woke up in the hospital. Until the minute he met Jones.

Dai Jones could hardly believe his ears, especially about the railway journey, but he said robbery and beatings and sometimes murder were a regular occurrence in and around the docks area of the city. It never had been safe to go there alone. But as he knew the docks and a lot of the stevedores, sailors and warehouse workers, they should be all right when they started to ask questions.

"One thing though, Taff," he said, "you'll have to grow shorter, everyone there will know that a six foot six ex-soldier was done over and robbed a few months ago and he had white hair and a bloody great moustache. He grinned again, "I've got a idea about the height and you'll have to see about the hair, all right? You'll have to sort out another jacket and shirt but I can't see anyone having a pair of trousers as long as that, can you Mr Roberts?"

Roberts smiled took a puff on his pipe and said, "Tell you what Dai, I'll get the clothes from the lost property at the docks office, if you show me how you are going to shorten him."

"Simple, I remember you used to use crutches when you hurt your leg after last year's accident. You've still got them I see, over there by the umbrella stand. There you are, Taff, have a go with them."

Jenkins picked up the crutches from the stand, took hold of the handgrips and put the rests under his armpits. He leaned forward to take up his weight on his arms, and realised the crutches were at least a foot too short as he fell on his face in front of the laughing onlookers.

"That's OK, Taff, we'll be able to lengthen and adjust them so that when you lean forward on them you should look at least nine inches shorter, if you can work at it. We'll have plenty of watching and waiting to do so there will be lots of time to sit down and rest. Will that be OK, mate?"

"Yes that'll be fine: when do we start? I've wasted too much time already so I ought to get going and do something, one way or another."

Dai Jones replied: "It's Saturday tomorrow, we have to coal the ship, so I'll come to the house on Sunday if you want, unless you'd rather me come to your digs?"

"Here will be fine, gives me time to sort out the crutches and clothes and if Mr Roberts doesn't mind, I can leave that stuff here."

Roberts nodded his agreement.

"Right then," said Dai, "I'll see you Sunday about nine-thirty and we can get started."

They shook hands all round and Jones said as he left: "See you then, Taff." He winked and smiled at the thought of Jenkins trying to use those short crutches, and as he went through the garden gate he laughed out loud.

A young couple sitting on the bank in the lane looked up at him thinking he was deranged or perhaps drunk.

"Don't take any notice," the young man said to his lady companion. "He'll be gone soon."

Dai Jones was still laughing to himself as he passed out of their sight.

"You can go too," Roberts said to Jenkins.

"No thanks sir. I'll put a couple of hours in while I think about what's been said and what's to be done."

Jenkins had been out of hospital and working for almost three weeks when Dai Jones came to take him on his first search for his sister. It was a Sunday, quiet at ten in the morning, with very few people walking the streets. They heard congregations at the various chapels and churches they passed, singing their hymns, and in one a prayer being said, as they walked towards Wapping Road. It suddenly reminded him of his home chapel and the Welsh congregation singing their hearts out: he realised then just what he had been missing all these years.

The walk to Wapping Road was about three miles from the Harbour Master's house near Clifton. It took them just under the hour to reach and arrive next to the warehouses that Jenkins had first seen on his arrival at Bristol Docks.

It came as a shock when he realised where he was and they decided that he should use his crutches and take up his disguise straight away, because there almost certainly would be someone on the look-out for strangers in the area. It would have been difficult to recognize Jenkins anyway. His hair was a greasy light brown colour and had grown until it was overlapping the collar of the old overcoat that he was wearing. He'd shaved off his moustache and felt naked without it. He hadn't been clean-shaven since a boy and hardly recognized himself as he looked in the mirror after he'd completed his shave. The sleeves of the coat had been lengthened but were still an inch or two short of a proper fit. It was also covered with various oil stains and was ripped strategically under both arms, enabling Jenkins to lift them comfortably. Even then, for an overcoat, it was almost a foot too short. The cap covering most of his hair came from the lost property office at Mr Roberts' Floating Harbour. It had once belonged to a seamen from the Merchant Navy, Flinders, a stoker: at least that was the name inscribed on the inside hatband.

"I'll bet the loss of this cost him a penny or two," Jenkins commented to Dai Jones.

"Perhaps it did but he could afford it see, he was a stoker wasn't he?" Dai replied.

Jenkins still wore his army issue trousers and boots. The trousers, although they'd been washed, were still bloodstained and muddy from his exertions in the garden during the past week. Both Mrs Andrews and Mrs Roberts had offered to wash his clothes but he had refused them both, preferring to do the job himself as he had always done in the army for all those years, except in South Africa and the Far and Middle East. Here the dhobi wallahs followed the troops on military campaigns and to their camps, cleaning their laundry and boots for a pittance. If some of the soldiers were crafty and lazy enough, the Indian boys would even carry their equipment on long marches. Dhobi and boot wallahs also waited on the officers and did all the menial work that was always available. In their own way they were very skilled and loyal to the officers and men they served.

Jenkins took the crutches and leaning heavily on them walked with Dai Jones along Wapping Road. By the time they reached the warehouses Jenkins was sweating like he'd never done before, even in battle.

"We'll have to stop for a bit, Dai," he said.

"Come on just a bit further; we'll go into that pub!" Dai said, as if giving Jenkins an order.

Jenkins looked at him as though looks could kill. "OK," he said angrily. "Go on then, I expect I'll need a drink by the time I get there."

They went on until they arrived at the pub door: Jenkins had cursed all the way.

"Been in here before, Dai?" Jenkins asked.

"No, don't think so: there's that many round here I'd never remember if I had anyway, 'cause most of the time I've been thrown out, drunk."

As they entered the pub Jenkins didn't need to duck below the lintel, as he had on the previous occasion he had made a visit to this pub. Then the realisation came to him, this is where he'd spoken to the barman and been directed to Guinea Street on his first day in Bristol.

"Dai," he whispered, "I've been here before, mate. I can't remember what happened but this is where I came for my first drink on the day I arrived. Watch yourself; don't say anything out of order."

"OK, Taff," Dai replied. "We'll have a pint or two, see the layout of the land and who's the boss around here and then we'll go and look for your sister's place, all right?"

Taff Jenkins nodded in agreement and went to a vacant table near the door and sat down with a sigh of relief.

Dai came to the table a couple of minutes later. "Mild was it Taff?" he asked, as he placed a pint of flat-looking beer in front of Jenkins.

"Thanks. Cheers Dai, thanks a lot," he said as he downed half of it in one go.

They took their time drinking the rest of their beer and gradually Jenkins' memories began to stir. He recognised the barman with the cracked glasses, dirty shirt and smarmy smile, having a short conversation with Dai, who the barman seemed to know. Occasionally he glanced over towards Jenkins but showed no signs of recognition.

"Did he have anything to say then, Dai?" Jenkins enquired.

"Not much, matey, just how was my family and job going. No! He didn't ask about you," Dai went on before he could be interrupted. "But there's one or two characters I don't like the look of. I've seen them before and I don't fancy my chances with any of them. I think they're part of one of the gangs that run all the crooked stuff around the docks here abouts."

"OK," Jenkins said. "Let's finish our beer and then go find my sister."

They took their time, trying not to make themselves too obvious.

When they left it was as if they hadn't existed; no one took the slightest notice as they stood up, chairs scraping along the floor. Remembering his crutch disguise Jenkins followed Dai Jones towards the door. Outside the weather had changed: it had started to drizzle quite heavily.

Dai said to Jenkins, "Just our bloody luck, we'll be soaked in a minute; we'd best get a move on or we'll never find the house. What number did you say it was?"

"31, Guinea Street. I think it was up that lane across the road, at least I think that's where he was taking me. You know, the old feller they killed when they attacked me and him."

"Yeh, that's right, Guinea Street runs alongside this road behind that row of houses, but starting to go up the hill towards the end, that's where the higher numbers are. Do you reckon you can manage those crutches up that slope?" Dai said, pointing to the lane.

"Don't you worry old son, I'll make it, no bother."

It was 'no bother' but he hadn't sweated so much since his Africa days.

They reached the corner of the lane and Guinea Street, and stopped for a minute or two trying to get their bearings. The street looked a mile long, but luckily they had arrived approximately in the middle. Checking the door numbers on the opposite side of the road they found the odd numbers to be on the same side as they were standing. Looking at the numbered door immediately to their left they saw it was number 71. Without a word they started off downhill, looking at the 'two up two down' terraced houses.

Most were clean, neat and tidy; one or two had been turned into hovels, seen by the filthy windows, curtains and rubbish thrown into the front gardens. As they approached the houses beginning with the numbers 40, Jenkins began to have misgivings with his unannounced visit and his appearance. He felt like a tramp and he thought Dai looked just as bad as well. Would he frighten his sister and have the door slammed in his face? Or would she recognize him? And give him a chance to explain his long absences and what he was doing, dressed like some hobo?

He didn't have much time to worry because Dai turned towards him pointing to a house that was a wreck. Burnt out.

Before he could say a word Dai said "I'm sorry mate, look, 33 that side and 29 the other, there's been one hell of a fire I imagine."

Jenkins sat on the wall in front of the house: he felt crushed as though he had been hit by a truck. He couldn't think or say anything: he tried to believe what he was looking at.

Dai said sympathetically, "I'll ask the neighbours what happened, eh, Taff?"

Whilst Dai went to talk to the neighbours, Jenkins went into the burnt-out shell of the house. The whole of the building had been gutted and the connecting walls to the houses on each side had collapsed, exposing their contents and badly damaging them as well.

Making three families homeless.

As he wandered around the building looking for some shred of evidence that his sister had lived there, a policeman entered the property.

Addressing Jenkins quietly he said, "What's this then, looking for something to nick, mister?"

"No! I bloody well ain't, I came to find my sister, who as you can see ain't here anymore," Jenkins retorted angrily. "I don't suppose you know what happened here, do you? Coppers are usually the last to know ain't they?" he went on sarcastically.

"Don't take that tone with me mister and I'm sorry to say I do know what happened that night last December." He took a deep breath, as if remembering the horror of that night's event. "Because as a matter of fact, me and my mate were the first to go in and get some of the people out, while it was burning. Two men and a little girl. The fire brigade arrived too late; by the time they did the house had collapsed and the ones each side were on fire as well. They found the bodies of two women in the house, in the kitchen. A wall had fallen on top of them, so they were both able to be identified, as it seemed they were overcome by smoke, rather than killed by the fire itself.

"The gas people came and from the evidence, it looked as though the fire was caused by a gas explosion in or near the gas cooker.

"Look lad, I'm very sorry but all five died, the three we got out, in hospital. So there wasn't anyone to give evidence to say exactly how the fire started. The next-door neighbours heard a bang, smelt the smoke and ran for their lives themselves.

"One chap claims to have heard screaming and shouting just before the explosion but that is the only witness we have who heard or saw anything.

"I'm really sorry if you were related to any of them. You did say your sister lived in number 31; is that true?"

"Yes she did, with her seven year-old daughter and her husband. I know she was married about eight years ago to an English bloke named Harris, I think, but that's all I know. We had very little contact, me being in the army so long."

"Where are you from then? Somewhere in Wales I know but where exactly?" The policeman wasn't unfriendly and was trying to show some sympathy for Jenkins' obvious shock and loss.

"About ten miles out of Swansea, a place called Pontardawe."

"I don't think that place was ever mentioned during our enquires, not by any friends or neighbours anyway. But if you were to go to the Wapping Road Police Station you will be given all the help and information that they have, to find your sister if she isn't one of the two ladies found in the house. Ask for Detective Inspector Hazelton: you can say PC Green sent you. Look! Walk down this road to the end, about two hundred yards, turn right and it's about a hundred yards along on the right. You OK lad?" Green asked Jenkins.

"Yeh I'll be right in a bit, thanks constable. Come on Dai, let's go and find this Inspector Hazelton. If he's there today."

He looked at the policeman, question unasked, who nodded, "Aye, he'll be there son, he's on duty all day."

They walked on down the road, Jenkins still using the crutches. Neither said a word until they found the Police Station.

Dai spoke first, "Listen I've got to tell you Taff, mate, I'm absolutely gutted for you; I couldn't imagine something like that happening to anyone, not in a hundred years." It was the first words he'd spoken since he'd seen number 31.

"All right Dai, thanks mate: let's go in and see if we can find out anything."

Neither had been in a police station before and both felt a little uncomfortable as they approached the desk sergeant. Jenkins explained their reason for going to the police station and asked for Inspector Hazelton.

Hazelton appeared from his office on hearing his name mentioned and eyed his visitors with some suspicion. "Well me lads, what can I do for you then?" he asked in a slow, rich, Somerset accent; something Jenkins had never heard before. Although Bristolians and Somerset-born people were all around the docks and the areas he had been moving around in, he had never heard anyone speak so slowly as the Inspector.

Jenkins explained who they were and why they had come to Guinea Street, then been told it had been his sister and her family that had been killed in the fire. The detective went to his office and brought out the file about the fire.

"First! I've got to ask you, do you have any identification? Otherwise I'm not allowed to divulge any of this information because this case isn't yet closed, even though a little girl and lady's body have been identified and there has been a funeral for them. No relatives and only a few friends and neighbours attended; it was terrible sad. A few members of the Salvation Army attended as well and they laid some lovely bouquets for them."

"Look Inspector, if one of them was Mrs Emily Harris, she was my sister and the little girl my niece. Before she married, about eight years ago, she was called Emily Hannah Jenkins and was born in the Memorial Hospital in Clydach near Swansea. She lived at number 8, Graig Road, Alltwen, Pontardawe near Swansea until she married this Harris bloke. Where is he anyhow?"

"If he's one of the two blokes who died that night he's still in the morgue waiting to be identified," replied Hazelton.

"What?" said Dai. "The poor bastard."

"No need for swearing," Hazelton retorted, then, "Have you got any ID?"

"Well I've got my army discharge papers that I received yesterday. I lost the originals when I arrived in Bristol in December. Two or three blokes attacked and robbed me about ten weeks ago, when me and this old chap called Limpy went up to Guinea Street to find my sister's house. I ended up in hospital for nearly a month and this old fella Limpy died after the beating he took. You must know about that, eh, Inspector?"

"Yes, I do know and for the life of me, it never dawned on me or anyone else, that the two incidents might have been related. They might be," he added, as Jenkins produced his duplicate discharge papers. Hazelton wasted no time reading them and handing them straight back to Jenkins.

Dai Jones had gone to sit on a bench waiting for the outcome of the interview. "Hey! What's happening, Taff? We going or staying? I've been told to take you home for tea when you're ready, to meet the missus and kids, you know."

"He won't be long now but I would like him to come in tomorrow or early next week to make a statement: that OK, Mr Jenkins?" said the detective.

"Right, I'll see what I can manage. One final thing, do trams run past here from Clifton, because it's a difficult and long walk from where I work," Jenkins said, continuing with his pretence of finding it difficult to walk. "I'll come and see you when I can, all right?"

They shook hands, both realising they had gained an immeasurable amount of information from the interview.

"Let's go and get a bollocking from the missus for being late, because that's exactly what we're going to be; it's nearly two mile to the top of Prewitt Street, all uphill," Dai laughed, imagining the struggle Jenkins would have getting to the house. He'd be knackered.

On the following afternoon Jenkins returned to the police station and, with Inspector Hazelton's guidance, made a formal statement about the assault made on himself and the old man, Limpy,

from the time he got off the tram until the time he felt the first blow, and then what had happened after recovering his senses whilst in hospital. He also mentioned his visit to his sister's house which really had no actual bearing on the incident he had been involved in. The Sergeant thought perhaps it might be better mentioned, in case one incident had a bearing on the other.

Jenkins decided to take the remainder of the afternoon off. He would make up any hours missed from the garden later on in the week. As he waited at a tram stop he was still mulling over the statement and reflecting what little he had known about Limpy and how he had almost forgotten the man who had been beaten to death alongside him.

A lady's voice said quietly, "There won't be another tram for another ten minutes, you know, if you're going into the City Centre."

He almost jumped out of his skin at the lady's first words, then realised who it was. He turned and saw the smiling face of Mrs May Andrews.

"How in hell… sorry!" realising she was in her Salvation Army uniform. "How did you get there without me seeing you?"

"Oh! you poor dear, did I give you that much of a shock? My, you've gone pale," she said mocking him. "Did you think I was a ghost or something worse? Never mind, have a sip of this, it'll liven you up a little. Now Taff – I can call you Taff, can't I? – it's only for medicinal purposes; go on, have a sip, please!"

She had produced a small silver whisky flask. "I often have a nip myself," Mrs Andrews continued, "especially when I have to console a relative or close friend of someone who has passed away in awful, sometimes horrible, circumstances. Often there isn't anyone I can turn to, to express my fears or feelings, so this helps a little. Oh! have no fear, I'm not a raging alcoholic; actually I don't like the stuff but it gets me out of the doldrums, as they say, and then I can get on with what I am supposed to be doing. I don't suppose God will mind either, will he? Besides, when I go to meet him, he'll tell me so, won't he?" She stopped, breathless.

He looked at her in amazement and gently took the flask from her outstretched hand. He watched her in her embarrassment; she had said much more than she had ever intended to. Continuing to look at her with a little suspicion he unscrewed the cap of the flask and took a tentative sip of what he thought might be watered down whisky.

It wasn't! He gagged and almost choked as he swallowed what he later found out to be almost one hundred percent proof smuggled Irish whiskey.

Mrs Andrews laughed, "I thought all you big he-men soldiers were supposed to be drinking men, aye Taff?"

Jenkins managed to force a smile, "What potato field did that come out of? Now that's why the Irish are always smiling, ain't it?" He went on, "Yes most soldiers are heavy drinkers but not all, I'm one of the 'not all'. Beer I can manage mostly but not the spirits. How on earth do you drink that stuff?" he asked.

"With a lot of practise," she smiled.

The tram eventually came and deposited them at the City Centre. By the time it did, they had become firm friends, exchanging pleasantries and little jokes: telling each other about their own army and the campaigns and battles they'd been involved in.

When they arrived at the City Centre, May, for that is what she asked him to call her, was trying hard to drop the formality between them, asked if he would like to visit the Citadel, the Salvation Army meeting place.

"Just for a cup of tea and a sandwich. I won't try to convert you," she said. "You're probably too far gone for that I would imagine."

When they arrived at the Citadel, she pointed to a small room. "You can take your coat off and put those horrible things over there," she said, pointing to the crutches. "They don't suit you anyway!"

"They hurt like bloody hell though," he replied, then he recoiled away from her in mock terror when he realised what he had said and where he was. "I'm awful sorry, Mrs Andrews," he said, reverting to a more formal attitude. "It's just me and the way I've been living over the last twenty years with all the bad habits and swearing I've picked up. I'm really sorry if my language offends you. I will try to curb it especially when I'm near or talking to you, is that OK?"

"It's still May and don't worry about a slip of the tongue, Taff: it'll happen a lot more in years to come I should imagine, should we be friends that long, eh? I do hope we are friends, Taff. We are, aren't we?"

"Course we are, May. Aye, I hope we stay friends too, honest!" he replied a little hoarsely.

In her uniform of the Salvation Army, May looked a lot older than her thirty-five years. Jenkins thought to himself, "She must be getting on a bit, about forty-five I would guess." Why her age suddenly came to mind, he never quite understood but when May removed her bonnet he realised he had guessed wrong and perhaps she was a lot younger. How much younger?

He never found out, because it never came up in their conversations, although he began to realise how attractive she actually was. After that day at the Citadel and during the next few weeks, they would often be seen together, going for walks around the City Centre and the docks area.

She took him to visit his sister's family graves. They were in a cemetery at the bottom of Guinea Street, across from the docks on Wapping Road. The flowers on the graves were still fresh and he guessed that the person who put them there was standing next to him.

May realised that he knew about the flowers but neither said anything until Jenkins said casually, "I'll be down sometime soon and see them all again: it'll be OK then, won't it?"

May nodded. "Fine," she said.

He talked about his Welsh chapel upbringing, his family and especially the demise of his sister and her family, whom he had never met.

May told him of the loss of her husband and her own parents and relations, where she was born and brought up just on the outskirts of Bath. And about a small village called Twerton and a strange little school called Twerton Parochial Juniors, a religious school run by Church of England nuns. They were very strict and often punished the children severely for anything that might be construed as a misdemeanour, for instance if a child was late for school or a class, he or she might be made to stand in a broom cupboard for the rest of the morning or afternoon. If anything more serious occurred, then a couple of cuts with a cane would be administered by the head teaching nun.

May left school at thirteen and went to work in the local bakery, making the bread and cakes and serving in the shop. The baker, Mr Anderson, was an ardent Salvationist, who over the four or five years that May worked for him convinced her that the Salvation Army was the way for her. Her upbringing and natural aptitude in wanting to help people, especially those unable to help themselves, gave her the energy to go out with the other members of 'The Army' and eventually become a full-time officer trying to follow in the steps of William Booth, the founder of the Salvation Army.

May married the baker when she was nineteen but he died two years later. He was almost fifty at the time but she was glad to have spent those last two years of his life with him and the Salvation Army. Now the last thirteen years of her life had been spent as a Salvationist working for the people of Bristol.

When she came to know Jenkins, May decided the Salvation Army would still be her life's work, but 'Jenks', as she began to call him, might become her man.

William Booth

"It's a pity you won't be able to stay and maybe join another army," she said to Jenkins. He looked at her in surprise. "Don't worry Jenks. I do know that you'll be moving on in a few months time – no, no, don't protest – I know you'll have to; you must go and find the rest your family no matter what; they won't be around forever, you know! Now drink your tea and when you're finished we'll go for a walk, all right?"

May went on to tell Jenkins of the vow that William Booth had made when he first set up the Salvationists with his son and a friend in 1878. It went:

While women weep as they do now, I'll fight:
While little children go hungry as they do now, I'll fight:
While men go to prison, in and out, in and out, I'll fight:
While there is a poor lost girl on the streets, I'll fight:
While there remains one dark soul without the light of God; I'll fight.

I'll Fight to the Very End.

"I believe this with all my heart," she said. "And nothing will ever turn me away from 'My Army', do you understand?"

"Yes I understand, May, but as you said, I do have other aims in life especially during the next couple of months."

He didn't tell her his first task was to track down the men who had attacked him, because he knew that she wouldn't approve and would probable tell him to forgive them. Which he never would. It didn't matter what they had done, of course, but as they were both of different opinions on what was right and wrong, he decided not to argue or refer to the subject again.

May went on: "We're two soldiers fighting in our own way, for our own cause; you have stopped fighting and must one day return to your own family and way of life. I, on the other hand, have to stay here and Fight the Good Fight for Right and Justice that the many poor and deprived will never have."

Although he visited Detective Inspector Hazelton at least once a week, nothing of any consequence had come to light and the Inspector said they would have to be very lucky to get a break and find new evidence; it really didn't look as though anything was forthcoming. But a lucky break did come.

It was in April 1914. Jenkins and Dai Jones were wandering around Bristol City Centre; they'd had enough of the docks and as May was at a prayer meeting on the other side of the city they decided to kill some time looking at the shops.

Jenkins and a few shillings and had decided to try and buy a second-hand suit, or at least some trousers. He'd got used to looking like a dock worker but as he hadn't any spare clothes was beginning to feel ashamed wearing rags all the time. He was mostly embarrassed to be seen in them when out with May. Even Dai Jones looked well dressed standing along-side him.

As they wandered round the City Centre, they realised the shopping area they were in contained all the expensive shops and stores. Not being able to see any cheaper clothes or afford the things they saw, they began to look in the shops in some of the side streets and then the back streets of the city. Eventually Jenkins found what he had been looking for, a second-hand and charity clothes shop. They both rummaged around the old worn and often dilapidated clothes that were in the shop. Some were on hangers and others thrown in large piles, trousers in one pile and jackets and overcoats in another. After much cursing and debating, Jenkins picked himself a dark grey suit, that was once light grey. The trousers were a little too short but perhaps Mrs Roberts could lengthen the legs.

"If she would, that is," Dai said, laughing at the sight of Jenkins in his frayed and almost-grey long johns.

Next door to the second-hand shop was a pawn shop; three faded gold painted balls were suspended over the door of the shop, looking as if they would fall any second. There wasn't much of interest in the window, which, although broken on the side nearest the door, was secured with a wooden panel and new steel bars.

"They don't put much of value in these pawn shop windows," Dai said with a knowing wink at Jenkins.

"Let's take a look; you wanted a ring for your missus's birthday, didn't you? Just a cheap one you said?" Jenkins retorted.

"Aye, suppose I'd better get one or I'm dead, ain't I? Well you know what she's like and you've seen her in action!"

Neither of the men had ever seen a pawn shop before, let alone been in one. Jenkins was also getting tired of the crutches and needed a rest. So they went in.

The owner was a small, ridiculous looking little man. He was sitting on a stool in what looked like a steel barred cage. Either side of the cage was a wire mesh fence attached to the wall at both ends of the long counter and to its front edge.

The man was wearing a black jacket and, except for the grey ashes of a huge cigar, a white waistcoat. A black, greasy, trilby hat, which along with his black horn rimmed spectacles covered a small, pale, wizened face. His eyes seemed to be in a permanent glassy stare through the grease-smeared glass of the spectacles. He was well into his sixties and to Dai and Taff it looked as though he had been in that seat forever.

"What've you got for me then, boys? 'Aven't seen you in here before, 'ave I?" he asked.

Jenkins replied, "No mate, just having a look to see if you've anything that Dai's missus might like," he lied. "You do sell stuff, don't you?"

"Course I do, if'n it's been 'ere longer than six monfs and the owner don't come back, I'll flog it. First come first served, got it? Anyfing you like then boys, go on 'ave a good look: do you a fair price for anyfing that takes your fancy, OK?"

Some of the pawned items were in a glass case on the counter, behind the wire mesh.

"Go on, 'ave a good butchers, lad," he said when he noticed Dai looking at framed photographs.

Dai pointed out to Jenkins a number of the photographs. "Hey Taff, people will pawn anyfing these days, won't they, boyo?"

Jenkins nodded in agreement but continued to examine as closely as he could all the other items in the shop. Not seeing anything that might be of any use but wanting to stay a bit longer he turned back to Dai.

"Let's have a look in there then, Dai!"

"What's he got that's so interesting, then?" Dai pointed to the glass case.

In it along with all those gold and silver things were photograph frames, some still with their photographs.

"People must be really on their uppers to bring things like that in for money," Dai said.

Jenkins gazed at the photographs, some of individuals, some of families: most of the frames were made of silver, others of tortoiseshell. Pictures of large and small families, younger and older children; all were represented.

One small, silver framed, family photograph caught his eye, a mother, father and two children, photographed in front of a large stone cottage, which in turn stood in front of a small cliff. The number of the house could be seen clearly on the door which framed the family in the photograph.

"Yessi Christ!" Jenkins blurted out. "Dai!" he whispered, "that photo there!" he said pointing at the photograph in the middle of the case. "That's my family back home. What the hell is it doing here?"

He went to the shop owner, "Where did that photograph come from? The one in the centre of the case, the one with the family with two kids." He didn't give the man time to reply. "Who brought it in?" he demanded.

The old man shouted back, "Hey you! Don't come in 'ere shouting and demandin'; it was 'ocked fair and square. No problem, no fuss, and the geezer got a fair price as well, cause it is good solid silver, that frame. In fact 'e didn't 'ock it, 'e sold it to me, if'n it's any of your business. Why! do you want it, sonny?"

Jenkins said, "Yes! I want to have it, pop; how much are you going to sell it for then?"

"Don't you pop me sonny, show us your money and you can 'ave it for free shillings. 'Ave you got free bob, then?"

"No I haven't, but tell me who brought it in, will you?"

The owner replied, "I can't do that, the bloody man will be back, wreck my business and maybe kill me."

"Does he come in here regular then?" Dai asked, trying to calm the situation that looked like getting out of hand. He didn't fancy being pulled by the police or worse than that, a gang of the old man's friends appearing. He didn't like the idea of going home and explaining to his wife why he'd told her he was going for a walk and ended up needing stitches. She would give him a few more if that ever happened.

Dai continued angrily: "Look mister, that photo is of him and the rest of his family; it was taken in South Wales and that's his mother and father, his sister and himself. If you get it out of the case and have a good look, you'll see it's him. 'Ow old was you Taff, when that was taken? Seven or eight, eh?"

Jenkins said "Look the house is number five and it's called Graig Road, in South Wales. The address might even be written on the back; will you have a look? Please!"

"I'm sorry mister, but I can't. Gimme free shillings and you can 'ave it wive my blessing, but wive-out the money I can't give you it, see?"

"Look, Jaccob," Jenkins had noticed the man's name on a pad of receipts near the old man's hand.

'Jaccob Purkinji' had come to Britain from Poland in 1880 to escape persecution from the anti-Semitics of the country. Now he virtually lived in his shop, so nothing escaped his beady eye's attention. "A penny is a penny," he would crow to his equally thrifty, scruffy, miserable son, as he pocketed the interest of some poor soul's loan on a valuable treasure.

"Jaccob! Will you tell us if the man who sold you this photograph comes here regularly?"

"Yeh! I can tell you that; 'e comes in one or two times a monf, sometimes more if'n 'e's got some good stuff."

"How do you know if the things he brings to the shop haven't been nicked, then?" Dai said almost bringing the conversation to an abrupt halt.

"Oi! there ain't no reason to say fings like that, mister. If'n you say fings like that anymore, you can get out of 'ere right now and you can stick your askins. I ain't saying noffink more: go on git out of 'ere!"

Jenkins said, "Dai shut up will you? Jaccob, it's OK to call you that, ain't it?" Jaccob nodded. "Look, mate, my sister, her husband and daughter were killed in a fire a couple of months ago, so we are wondering how that photo came to be in here; can you tell us, please? We're certain it used to belong to my sister. We only came here on the off-chance and we ain't the coppers and I never expected to see that picture here, so will you give us a bit of help? Will you?"

"All I can tell you is that picture and a load of over small bits of jewery and dem brass candlesticks was brought in by two or free blokes about two weeks since. I bought 'em, no questions asked. It's my livin', ain't it?" he said defensively. "I never ask if'n the gear they bring 'ere is nicked and them that's buying it don't ever ask. As I says, dem blokes comes 'ere two or free times a monf, all right?"

"Yeh, thanks, but can you tell us what do they look like? Please!"

"No I can't, just like dockers I spect. One 'as a docker's badge in his coat fing," Jaccob indicated his own jacket lapel. "You know, in 'ere."

"What sort of badge?"

"Can't say, dunno, only see'd it once!"

"Anything else you can tell us, then?"

"Yeh!" came Jaccob's reply. "They wus all wearin old uniform jackets, wive one or two badges on. All different, OK?"

Jenkins raised his eyebrows and turned and winked at Dai. "Well, that's a turn up for the book, ain't it Dai? Thanks very much Jaccob, thanks! Now can I put a deposit on that photo frame and if I come in next week I can pay you the rest, OK? I've got a shilling, will that do?"

"Aye, that's OK," the old man said as he slid a grimy thin hand under the front of the cage.

"Aye, and I'll have a receipt too," Jenkins said.

"What's the matter wive you? Don't you trust me or somefink?" Jacob replied, scribbling on a receipt form and pushing it under the wire.

"Course I do Jacob; now don't you let that frame go to anyone else, will you, 'cause I got a few mates I could bring back as well, OK?"

Pocketing the receipt Jenkins nodded to Dai, "OK, let's go, Dai, it's a long walk back to the lodgings and we've got lots to think about, eh?"

"Yeh," Dai replied. "If I'm late tonight, the missus is going to give me such a hard time for the rest of the week, I'll be glad to be back on the boat shovelling coal."

As they started the long walk home, Jenkins felt the crutches a lot easier to use and he started whistling. For the first time since he'd left the army he felt a sense of relief, the anxiety he'd known over the last few weeks was gradually diminishing.

On the Monday afternoon, when he'd finished his daily stint in the garden, Jenkins paid a visit to Inspector Hazelton and told him of the discovery of the photograph frame in the pawn shop.

The detective raised an eyebrow quizzically. "Oh yes, and where might that shop be, then?" he asked in the broad Somerset accent that sounded so slow to Jenkins.

Jenkins explained the reason for his and Dai's visit, what street the pawn shop was in and the name of the proprietor, a Jaccob Perkinji.

"Good God! I thought that old bugger had kicked the bucket years ago. It's been nearly five years since I last heard that name, so he must have kept his head down and his nose clean, otherwise someone in Bristol Central would have turned him over. I thought they had closed his shop and put him out of business ages ago. Do you know, he's turned seventy-five and it doesn't look like the old sod will ever turn it in. I'll tell you what Taff, I'll telephone my boss at Central Station and have a couple of CID lads pay him a visit, OK?

"Now describe the photo frame and it's picture as accurately as you can with all the details you can remember including the number of the house in the picture. If we are very lucky we might get some clues of who has handled it from the frame and glass itself."

"How are you going to do that?" Jenkins asked.

"With something called fingerprints, something that absolutely everyone has. It is thought that no one else in the world has fingerprints that will match another persons exactly!" Hazelton went on, as if giving his favourite lecture to police recruits. "Over the last few years the art of reading and examining peoples' fingerprints has been developed to a very high standard. Photographs of fingerprints of those caught committing criminal acts have been used in courts of law to convict criminals whether they be burglars or murderers or anyone else. Anyone who has handled an object or put or used their hands on a smooth surface, be it round or flat, can be identified by their fingerprints, unless the culprit's hands or fingers are covered, of course. For example, by not wearing gloves, then he or she is almost certain to leave a fingerprint, or even a palm print or part of one, at the scene of a crime. It is almost impossible not to. They can be identified from one fingerprint alone if the person who made it has been in our custody. I know this technique has been used for a number of years now, since before 1900 when it was first recognized and the technique invented. It's not fully developed, but along with new developments, those people committing crimes are going to find it very difficult to get away without being convicted for their criminal activities. Right, Taff, end of lecture.

"What do you reckon? We may get to a solution to your case; it may take some time but we'll get there in the end, especially as we're treating old Limpy's death as murder now. I know you can't identify those killers but there is evidence to connect you and them, even if they don't know it yet. I'll leave it at that now, Taff, but if anything comes to light, I'll let you know as soon as possible. See you then!"

He held out his hand; Jenkins took it and felt the firm friendly grip.

"Thanks Inspector, thanks. Hope to hear from you soon. eh?"

With that they left the police station and Jenkins went to see May, to tell her what had happened over the last couple of days, whilst Dai Jones went home to face his wife's wrath.

Jenkins went back to his lodgings feeling a lot happier at the way things were developing. He had a feeling that there might be light at the end of this very long tunnel.

When he went to work the following day, Mr Roberts gave him some more good news. "How would you, Mr Jenkins, like to work for Mr Roberts as a Floating Harbour Master's Assistant? An FHMA."

It was a grand title, Mr Roberts laughed, but no one would know what an FHMA was except Jenkins and himself, at least until people working on the docks got used to seeing him around.

"You can throw those crutches back in the corner now and just use one of my old walking sticks, if you want to. That's if you want the job, Taff, my boy."

Jenkins was pleasantly surprised. Whatever the job was to be, it would definitely suit him; it was exactly what he was looking for. He could keep his eye out on the comings and goings of the gangs on and around the docks and get to know the people working there, without causing too much suspicion.

The other thing was to be called 'Taff my boy'! Made him realise that there were still good people in this world, amongst all the viciousness and evil that pervaded the country. His friends were beginning to outnumber his unknown enemies but he hoped it wouldn't be too far in the future that he would find them, tackle and help remove them to a prison society that they belonged in.

It was the beginning of May when Jenkins would start his new job, although he promised Mr Roberts that he would spend as much time on Roberts' family garden as possible.

"Ah!" said Roberts, "that's if you've time. I'm a really hard taskmaster where the harbour is concerned. Don't worry, there will be plenty of work for you to do, and by the way, you'll only be able to take a lunch break when there's time and nothing else to do and that'll only be for half an hour!"

"Don't you worry, Mr Roberts," Jenkins grinned at the portly Harbour Master. "It'll be fine. I don't mind hard work as long as there's a point to it. Just like the garden, eh? What do you think of it this year, then?"

"Mr Jenkins, it's grand!" He always reverted to a formal tone when he was happy with something or someone; he liked to show them some respect no matter what the situation was or how 'low' in the system they had started or become. He hated the word 'class' because he had started low down on the rungs of education, employment and 'class' himself and he knew he would never be able to beat the system of wealth, education, ownership and the gulf of the classes.

"Everything seems to be coming on very well and Mrs Roberts is well pleased; she asked me to pass on her thanks for your excellent work."

"Well sir," – it was the first time he had called anyone sir since he left the train in January – "I would like to help out at least until the autumn season, just to see if anything I've planted comes to a decent crop. Mrs Roberts should have some nice vegetables this year and the flower beds look like they'll be a pretty picture. Anyway, what time I've got to spare I'll use it here, if you're both agreeable."

"Certainly Taff," Roberts replied. "That's a very kind offer and as you've offered your help, perhaps you'll take some of ours?" He went on before Jenkins could voice any protest. "As you already know, we have a solid-built coach shed next to the house." He paused, eyeing Jenkins, waiting for a reaction. "It's stone built, well roofed and quite warm, even without a fire. There are a couple of windows that are in need of repair and the doors rattle a bit, but if you would like to make a few repairs and do it up, it could make a nice little home for you. Hang on Taff!" Roberts held up his hand stopping Jenkins's protest. "There's an old blacksmith's forge there, that could be converted and made into a decent-sized fireplace, with a gas fire maybe. I think there might have been a chimney there at one time, if so that could be sorted out, couldn't it? There is gas lighting already installed and perhaps when the Harbour Company comes up with the money, I can have electricity installed in both buildings, not just the house."

"But sir, I don't have any money or furniture; how am I going to fit it out?"

"You don't have to worry about that either, because the coach house is where we store all our spare furniture, beds, tables, chairs etcetera. I'm sure you'll be able to make use of some of it, and, if not, it can go up into that little attic in the roof, all right, Taff? Look! Don't say another word, Taff. Mrs Roberts and I have discussed it and we're both satisfied and agreed that it'll be of use and help to you, as you have been to us, all right? Oh, by the way I saw your friend Mrs Andrews this morning, looking fine and chirpy she was, asking after you she was too. How are things going with you now? See her very often do you?"

Taff Jenkins had rarely been embarrassed, but he was by the time Roberts had finished asking questions. As he did so Mrs Roberts approached and realising his embarrassment said "Mr Roberts" – she always addressed him in this manner – "Mr Roberts, leave the lad alone and come and have supper."

Jenkins turned away as if to leave. "And you too, Taff, there's enough for everyone!"

There was no way Jenkins could say no, because she moved behind them both, as if herding them into the kitchen.

During the weeks he had been in Bristol, after leaving hospital, he had, with the help of May, written two letters to his parents in the Swansea Valley, to his old home address. He explained the circumstances in which he had left home and eventually joined the army, the different countries where he had served, and about one or two of the campaigns he had been involved in. He didn't mention that he had tried to find his sister or that she had died: he thought that he should tell his parents about her and her family when he eventually got back to the Swansea Valley.

He told them that he hoped it would be very soon, once he had settled down to his work and the civilian lifestyle, which, at the time he took his discharge he had found to be very difficult. He hoped they could understand how he felt, but it wouldn't be much longer before he would be coming to Ponty to see them.

He also spent as many hours a day as was possible on his new abode, especially with the help of Dai, May and Mrs Roberts. The repairs required and damage to the building weren't as bad as first thought and Dai was pretty handy with a trowel, hammer and saw. So it was only a week after they started to work on the building that Jenkins was able to move into his new home.

In his letters to his parents he wanted to say he had missed them a great deal. But he didn't, thinking they would call him soft or sloppy.

May asked him, "Why they would think you soft?"

"Well that's the way things are in the Valleys; men are men, boys are boys and the women folk make sure we stay that way. We look after them, then they'll look after us. See what I mean?"

"No not really," May replied, as Jenkins signed the letter 'From your son Richard', the name his mother called him.

His mother never approved of anyone calling him Dick as most of his old friends at school and those in the army did, even if she hadn't heard them using it. His father always got a tongue lashing from her if she heard he was misusing her son's name.

Three weeks after he had written and posted the letters, they were returned to Mr Roberts' address with 'Not known at this address' scribbled on the front of the envelopes. To say he was disappointed was the understatement of the year for him. Dai was the unfortunate individual who bore the brunt of his initial disappointment and anger. "Bloody hell!" he shouted. "I'm going to have to go home bloody soon, Dai. I've got to find out what's happened to them, haven't I?"

He took a deep breath, trying to control his anger and frustration. "You'd have thought someone would have told me what was happening, they could have written to the army or something. They have plenty of friends and we've a tidy few relations, surely somebody could have let me know what's been going on!"

Dai said, "Come on, Taff, you haven't been home in nearly twenty years, have you written to them at all in that time? Yes? Once or twice it was? When was that then Taff? When you were in Africa?"

Jenkins replied, "All right Dai, yes, it was in South Africa about ten years ago and the time before that I suppose was when we were going out to South Africa before the Boer War. My God! I never realised the time was passing so fast."

"Well it's gone Taff; what are you going to do about it now?"

"I'll have to get home and see what's happened to them, won't I? Christ! I haven't started my new job yet and I'm going to have to ask old Roberts for time off before I've even started it. What do think he'll say, Dai?"

"Look, Taff, don't start worrying about that now, wait till you start the bloody job: he thinks the world of you, likes the way you act and get on with things. Now try and relax; perhaps your friend Inspector Hazelton can find out what's happened to them. You know Mr Roberts has got a telephone down at the Harbour Office; when you start work there next week, perhaps he will telephone the policeman for you: it might be better coming from old Roberts in case Hazelton ain't there."

"Hey, thanks Dai, that ain't a bad idea, mate, you ain't so dumb as you look, are you? You little sod, thanks, I'll do that first thing Monday morning."

Jenkins started his new job at the Floating Harbour on the following Monday. He was quite pleased with himself; he would be working outside and the weather was beginning to warm up. His main job was to act as Mr Roberts's runner, to and from the ships that entered the harbour. Later when he had gained more knowledge and experience he would learn to allocate a berth to the visiting ships according to their size and cargo and especially draught (the amount of water each required under its keel before the ship ran aground). He would board each new ship entering the harbour for the first time and explain the procedures for entering and leaving harbour, escorting the ship's captain or his nominated officer to the Harbour Master's office and introducing him to Mr Roberts or his deputy.

It was a three mile walk to the Floating Harbour but Mr Roberts usually caught the local tram that ran to and past the FH, as he liked to call it. And two or three times a week the FH van which delivered various items of stores around the dock area would have to make a drop-off in a store nearby and the driver would make a prearranged call to Roberts's house and take him to work. On the first and subsequent days of working at the FH, Roberts arranged for the driver to pick up Jenkins as well whenever he himself used the van. After work was a different matter, it was usually a tram ride or a walk home.

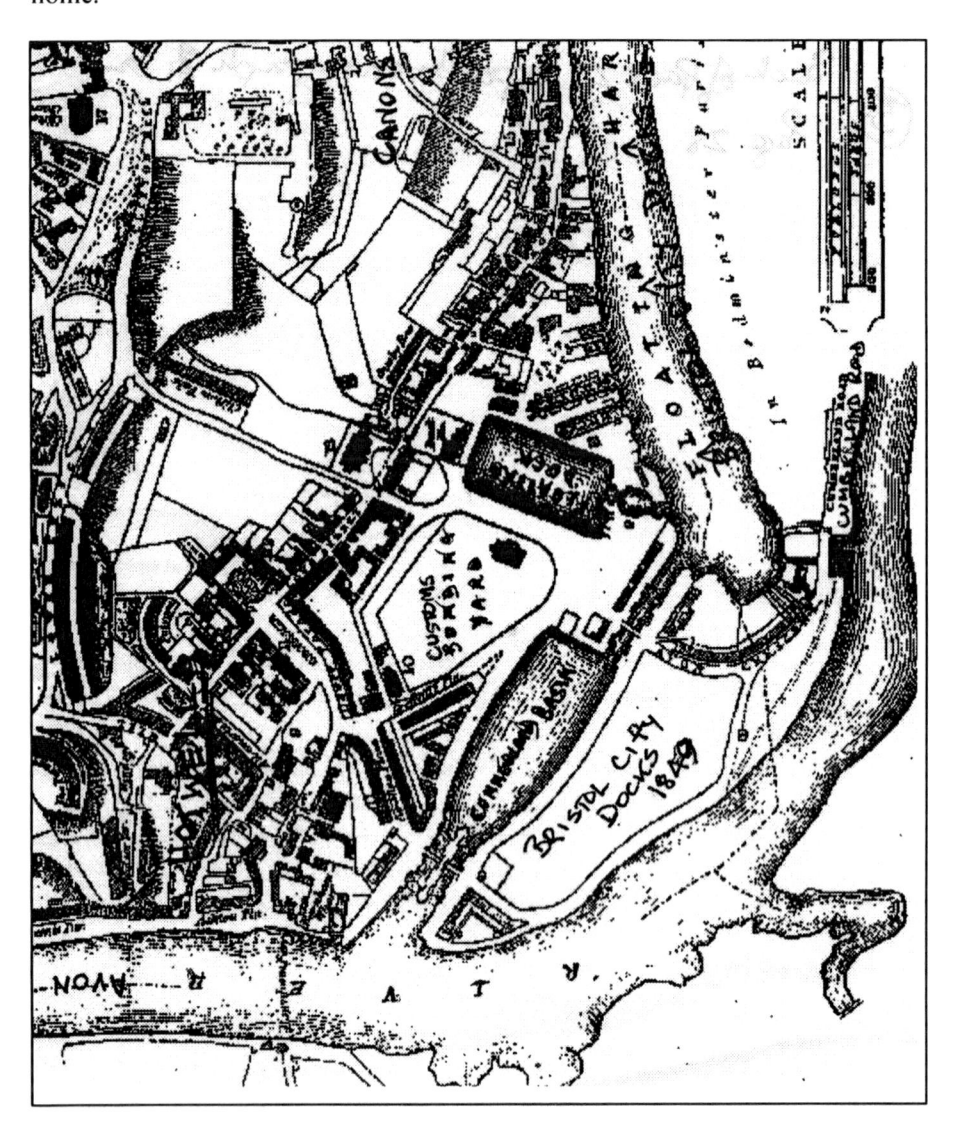

Gordon Peters was a completely different character to the Harbour Master in his appearance, attitude and demeanour. He was a very tall, stooped, thin, sallow-faced, morose man, completely humourless and without any kind of pity for anyone. It was said that a few years back, two or three ten year-old boys were running along the edge of the docks. Peters was sitting outside the Harbour Master's office eating his sandwiches and reading his newspaper.

One boy tripped over a hawser lying on the ground and fell over the side of the harbour wall. The boy was floundering around in the watery mud, the tide having gone out, and was screaming that he was stuck and sinking. The two other boys ran to Peters begging him to help, to do something.

"Throw him a life belt," was all he would say. "You've plenty of time before he sinks." He continued to sit and read his paper.

A boy did find and throw a life belt, and two stevedores hearing the boy's cries went down an iron wall ladder, waded into the mud and dragged the boy out. From that moment on no dock worker anywhere on the docks ever spoke to Peters again, except when it was business in the Harbour Office.

When Roberts and Jenkins arrived at the FH Office, on Jenkins's first Monday, he was a few yards ahead of Mr Roberts, who had stopped to pass the time of day with another dock worker: it was Mr Roberts' way. He always stopped and had a word for anyone that he knew. If he had the time and he would often go out of his way to have a chat with someone he knew that might have a problem, either personal or to do with the Docks business. He dealt with everyone in the same calm and matter-of-fact manner. If he had any enemies they could all be counted on two fingers and although he wouldn't have believed it if anyone told him, one of them was Gordon Peters.

Peters had applied for the job of the Floating Harbour Master twice before Roberts had been recommended and his application accepted. Peters was never told why his application had been turned down but on seeing the jovial little Welshman, he seethed with rage and indignation and cursed the day that Roberts arrived to take 'his' job from him. He vowed that one day he would have Roberts' position and see the little man go back to Wales with his tail between his legs.

He was envious of the Harbour Master because of the position in local society that it gave the holder, also the marvellously furnished, rent-free house that went with the job. He had to stay in his rented unfurnished two bedroomed private terraced house in the poorest part of Bristol. He had a miserable slattern of a wife and five screaming girls all under the age of ten years, none of whom ever gave him a minute's peace, especially when he wasn't working. He sometimes pretended to go to work on a Saturday or Sunday just to get away from them all.

Jenkins waited for the Harbour Master just outside of the office door. "It's all right Taff, you go on in! I'll be there in a couple of minutes, just having a chat with Joey here."

"OK Mr Roberts," Jenkins called back and entered the office.

There wasn't a lot of light and the place smelt musty and damp. About three feet inside the room, a counter ran from side wall to side wall, cutting off three-quarters of the office: this made a small reception area. A couple of desks were situated one either side of the room, each one facing the outside wall. A large six-foot desk was placed at the furthest end of the office facing the counter. Behind the desk stood a huge dark red leather office chair, worn almost brown in patches by years of wear. It looked as though it belonged in someones mansion house, which in fact it had, years ago. It was one of six, sold to a dealer five years before, who in turn made a tidy profit, selling the chairs to the dock management committee for their offices.

As Jenkins entered the office, Peters, a Deputy Floating Harbour Master, who was sitting at a desk, turned towards him and said in a rude yapping type way, "What the bloody hell do you want this time of day?" It was seven-thirty in the morning. "We're not open yet, get outside and wait."

"I'm here to start a new job, Sir!" emphasising the 'Sir' with as much sarcasm as he could muster.

"I said wait outside, now get out!" Peters realised it was the new man he had heard was being employed. "I said get outside mister! Wait until I call you in, can't you do as you're told?"

"OK mister, I'm going. I'll wait outside until the boss gets here".

Peters couldn't contain himself. "Listen you ignorant oaf, *I* am your boss: don't get lippy with me mister or you won't even start the job, do you hear me? Now get outside and wait until I call you."

As Jenkins turned to leave, Mr Roberts walked into the office.

"I see you've met my assistant Mr Peters. Yes, Mr Peters, this is Mr Jenkins." He hung on the word 'Mr'. "Mr Jenkins, this is Mr Peters, the 'Deputy' Floating Harbour Master; he is my deputy along with Mr Worrell, my other deputy. Do you see?"

"Yes, sir! Mr Roberts, you have two deputies and one assistant, the assistant being me, is that correct, sir? Am I to assist your deputies as well, sir?"

"No, no, certainly not, you shall have enough to do, as they do, without you running after them as well. All right, Peters?" He had dropped the 'Mr'.

"Yes sir, certainly, my apologies Mr Roberts; I didn't think, sir!"

"There's no need to apologise to me Peters, I think it's Mr Jenkins who deserves your apology, don't you? It wasn't a very civil way to welcome a new worker, was it sir?"

Peters turned to Jenkins "My apologies, Mr Jenkins," he intoned grudgingly. "I misunderstood!"

"Accepted, sir. Thank you!" Jenkins replied, a huge grin spreading across his face.

Peters was furious. He thought he'd found a lackey at last, a skivvy who would save him the hours of embarrassment, trying to talk to the dock workers who refused sometimes to give him lucid or sensible answers to some of the questions he had to ask. He often wondered if it was it entirely the incident with the kids, that people didn't trust him and sometimes refused to talk to him. Or was it the likes of Roberts and his cronies going behind his back and spreading vicious rumours about him and his family?

What they didn't know was one day he would make his fortune, then he would be giving the orders that they wouldn't like. No one knew he was gradually taking control of all the illegal trading and theft that was going on in and around the docks. He already had one little but rough and vicious gang in his pocket, who would do anything he asked, as long as the price was right. He had made a written statement under oath, to a Catholic priest and deposited it with a 'friendly' solicitor in case the gang turned on him. Even if he met his demise by accident or intentionally, the statement would be handed to the police and exonerate his family from any criminal proceedings. So even then, the gang members' futures and careers would still be in his hands and until then they would be at his beck and call. His wife would never know about his second career and his future wealth. She wasn't in his plans. Hopefully she wouldn't be around when his plans came to fruition. In fact he knew she wouldn't be.

Jenkins began his new job with a little excitement and great enthusiasm. He wore his second-hand suit and a shirt he'd been given by Mr Roberts, although it was without a collar, and he felt quite clean and tidy. His hair had grown a little longer and was no longer blonde and eye-catching and was covered by the old seaman's cap. He still used the walking stick as suggested by Mr Roberts, so it was very unlikely that he would be recognised. If he was, he'd have to take the appropriate action. But Roberts said recognition wasn't very likely here, because the gangs didn't like to operate too near this part of the docks. It was usually in the area surrounding the dock gates, nearest the city. That was the place where visitors or strangers were sometimes attacked and robbed and the thieves could disappear into the alley ways and back streets before help arrived.

The area where the ships docked was patrolled by Dock Police. If a particularly valuable cargo was being unloaded, the police patrol would often be doubled at the request of the ship's owner, captain or the Harbour Master himself. There had been numerous attempts to smuggle items into and out the country through all the British ports, including Bristol, so the Customs Service Officers were always around, searching and observing: sometimes their officers would be in disguise.

Jenkins was a quick learner. At first the jobs and tasks he was given were not difficult, usually carrying messages or packages to various offices or ships that had docked recently. After the first week he was asked to accompany the van drivers whose jobs were to deliver sometimes particularly large numbers of packages or parcels to the outlying port offices and stores. Then he felt he was actually escorting the drivers as a form of security, because the drivers seemed to be quite nervous on particular days with unusual loads.

During that period of time Mr Roberts had been in touch with Inspector Hazelton and asked on Jenkins's behalf if he could contact the Swansea police to make inquires and help to establish the whereabouts of his parents or if anything had happened to them.

Jenkins had also been to see May Andrews on a couple of evenings, after finishing either working in the Roberts' garden or at the Floating Harbour.

When he showed her his letters had been returned, she promised to ask her friends in her 'Army' to try and find out what had happened to his family. She told him that the Salvation Army had companies all over Britain and sometimes could make more subtle enquires than the police, whose approach was often heavy-handed and off-putting to the person being asked a question.

He got to know a few of the dock workers but made sure he didn't ask too many obvious questions when he spoke to them. Usually it was about work or football or which was a decent pub to go to. Nothing he hoped that would arouse any suspicion.

There was one old man that Jenkins often had a chat with during his lunch break or little spare time he might have during the day at work. He was known as Mudhog Jack; no one knew his last name or where he came from. He spoke with a broad Devonshire accent and was about five foot four inches tall. He wore a filthy pair of old seaman's boots, dirty, muddy, old brown trousers and an old red jersey, which someone said was only held together by its holes. His grey beard covered almost all of his face and his grey eyes peered at anyone who approached with deep suspicion through dirt-covered spectacles.

Mudhog's name was given him because he almost invariably, after a ship left the harbour and the tide had ebbed, went into the mud searching for anything that had been lost or deliberately thrown overboard. Sometimes he found small items of value, twice gold watches, another time a solid silver crucifix about nine inches high, the sort used on church alters.

He told Jenkins that he often found other items but refused to say how he'd disposed of them. He also said that there was so much thrown overboard, he wondered if there was anything left inside the ship to help keep it afloat. "Still I'll take anything they don't want, I'll make something out of it, the bloody wasters."

After a couple of weeks, their talks became more amiable and Jack began to talk more freely about his knowledge of the people and gangs who operated in the area. Jenkins didn't press him too hard though, because he knew that Jack would give more information voluntarily if he was trusted, rather being ask too many questions.

During the first week of May 1914 the Harbour Master called Jenkins into the office. May Andrews was sitting in Roberts' office chair, he was standing to the side of his desk. The deputy Harbour Masters had been ask to leave before Jenkins arrived.

When he entered the office and approached the counter Roberts said, "Come in lad and take a seat."

He went in and sat in Peters' chair. Looking at May, Jenkins sensed that it wasn't going to be good news that he was about to hear.

May stood up and walked forward a few steps to stand in front of him. She looked smart in her navy blue Salvationist uniform, but it made her normally pale complexion look almost white with the strain of what she was about to tell her friend. She spoke, a slight quaver in her voice. "Jenks" – it was her pet name for him – "Jenks, I'm really, really sorry to have to be the one to tell you this awful news." She continued quickly before she had time to change the words she had already rehearsed. "I'm sorry to say both your mother and father have passed away. Your father almost ten years ago, and your mother just last October."

She stopped, watching Jenkins face. There was no expression, no movement. He stared past her at the office wall. He felt cold twinges running down the side of his head, then face, like pins and needles.

Then May went on softly, "I'm sorry Jenks, the details are pretty sketchy, because your mother had moved somewhere into Swansea, to be near one or two of her friends and her older sister. I'm afraid that is all I've been told."

He looked at May and in a cold bleak voice said. "Thanks, May, thanks Mr Roberts. I'll go outside for a bit if you don't mind, try to clear my head, is that's all right, sir?"

"Certainly Taff, certainly my boy, go ahead; we'll see you when you're ready." By then Jenkins had left the office.

As he left, Peters approached and seeing the look on Jenkins face retorted, "Bad news I hope, Jenkins."

He raised his arm, thinking he had gone too far and Jenkins would hit him. To his amazement, Jenkins walked past him shouldering him out of the way without reply or even looking at him.

It was as if Peters wasn't there.

What none of them realised was that most soldiers or ex- soldiers took the news of someone's demise in a completely different manner to most other people when they saw or heard of the death of their close friends, families and loved ones. It was against all their training and experience to allow their grief and feelings to be shown to their friends or in public, because no matter how bad things became, life had to go on, either in battle or in the face of adversity. In private thoughts might turn to tears but not to the extent that anyone would hear or know about. Later in their lives, as they mellowed, their emotions would change and sometimes they might let their feelings show, whether it be in anger or sorrow, but eventually they would change. But times hadn't changed enough for Jenkins.

When Jenkins had left the office, he had heard Peters speak and knew that one day he would remember and when he did, he would retaliate. It would happen, he could guarantee it.

He decided to go for a walk for a few minutes to let his emotions settle down; because he didn't show them, it didn't mean he didn't have any, no matter what anyone else thought.

"Jesus Christ!" he said out loud, almost shouting at himself. "Six bloody months, what the bloody hell happened? Someone could have told me she had gone!"

When he got back to the office, May was outside, sitting on a bench situated against the wall. He went and sat beside her.

"Jenks! have a nip?" She offered him the little flask as she had done once before.

"OK, thanks, May love."

May did notice the word 'love' but didn't say anything. She supposed it was an expression of his friendship, not that he would make anything of it nor should she expect him to either. He took the flask then sipped the whiskey that was her favourite tipple. He still wasn't used to, or liked, the stuff but it brought him back to the world of the living.

"But I think I'd rather have a cup of tea," he said, smiling at her as she pretended to be offended at his tea, rather than her nips of whiskey.

Jenkins went home early that day.

Later, Mr Roberts told Jenkins to take a week off in the near future, so that he could go and visit the graves of his parents and at the same time try and find out what had happened to them and the rest of his family. Roberts gave him a week's pay in advance and arranged for Dai Jones's skipper to give him passage on his vessel to Swansea, where he'd be able to get a train home. At least to where his home had been.

The days went by. Jenkins hadn't seen Dai for a couple of days and he was beginning to get anxious. The waiting was unnerving him a little, in a way that had never happened in the army. He began to worry that something had happened to Dai, because although most of the time the weather had been fine, except for a couple of squally showers, the weather in the Bristol Channel and along the South Wales coast often changed quickly. Storms arrived without warning in that area, especially those that came in from the Atlantic.

The ship that Dai worked on, the *Welsh Lass*, and her skipper, had plied the same route for over twenty years and Dai had stoked it for nearly fifteen, so Jenkins told himself to stop worrying and being stupid. He found out later that the ship was due to dock in a couple of days' time, on the Friday.

The skipper, Tommy Redone, would unload, coal-up and take on a new cargo to unload at Cardiff or Newport, and Swansea. He would be sailing on Monday 11th May at midday.

Jenkins, although anxious, got on with his work at the harbour and in the garden, with a little help from the Roberts family, including a couple of the children.

He did find time though to talk to Mudhog Jack and one afternoon over a tot of gin, that Jenkins knew that Jack would appreciate, began to gently prise information from him about the gangs that operated on the harbour and in the docklands.

Jack was careful not to say anything too readily over the two or three days, while Jenkins waited for Dai. They would sit on the harbour steps, Jack drinking most of the gin that Jenkins provided, and talk about the docklands, as Jack called them.

Jenkins gradually obtained the information about the dock gangs that he was looking for. Most gangs used to target strangers or the smaller cargo boats. Some would kill, if they thought their actions would be reported or discovered. Others used snatch and grab tactics, usually on young women or old people, men or women. Sometimes if there was enough of them, they would overpower even the biggest, strongest of men.

One of those gangs wore red silk scarves. Another, seamen's caps with two small silver buttons on the left side. A third gang wore the same type of cap with three slightly larger brass buttons on the side.

There were several other gangs but Jack didn't like to divulge the information too readily, especially when he realised there might be a good few drinks in it, and knowing his 'friend' would provide them.

"Come on Jack, don't go to sleep yet, mate, we've got a half bottle of gin to finish yet; aren't you going to help me drink it?"

"Yes, give it 'er, then I'll have a kip, OK? Give us the bottle!" Jack took a large swig from the bottle. "Eh! I've just remembered, there's another crowd, a gang of three or four or maybe five." His speech was beginning to become slurred and difficult to understand. "You know! Them bastards that done me over for that pocket watch I did find."

"When was that then, Jack?"

"You know, about six months ago, aye six months now, before your time, wonit?"

"Come on Jack! Have another drink and tell me who they are, will you?"

"OK, OK, gimme time to fink, can't you, Taff? I know it was that lot that call themselves 'The Commodors', ex-train guards, and an ex-prison guard I fink." He stopped and then remembered something else. "There are four or five of 'em in that gang I reckon and they're the worst bunch of the lot." His head had become a little clearer and as he remembered what they had done, he became angrier. "I'll get them swine," he shouted.

"Hey! not so loud Jack, we don't want everyone to hear, do we?"

"OK, OK, Taff. I'll tell you 'ow you'll know 'em. By the jackets that they wear! Like a bus and railway ticket collector or a train guard, one wiv an old postman's jacket and there's another wiv an army jacket but he's a new bloke I fink, it's still got the old brass buttons on it. I ain't seen 'em for a couple of weeks either. Somebody said they'd gone up to Wells or somefink like that. Can't remember really."

At that Jack took another large swig of the gin and then felt that he couldn't stay awake any longer. He held the bottle up and saw that there was a tot or two left, put it to his lips and emptied the bottle. He dropped it without noticing where it had gone, rolled on to his side on the stone steps and went to sleep.

Jenkins went into the office to ask Mr Roberts what his next task would be. He saw that Gordon Peters was sitting at his desk with the window partly open. He didn't give it much thought as he went to speak to Mr Roberts, but as he left to carry out the task Roberts had given him, he saw Peters watching Jack through the window.

The look he gave Jenkins as he passed worried Jenkins a bit. "What was Peters game?" he thought to himself. It was a sort of smirk as if to say, "Got you, your secret's out mate!"

When Jenkins left work to walk home with Mr Roberts, old Jack had disappeared, perhaps to a little hovel, a cabin he called his home. It was about two miles away across the docks; no one ever went there, Jack never invited anyone. He seemed to be a lonely old man, Jenkins being the only person he even talked to in months. But nobody seemed overly surprised when occasionally he would sit and have a drink and a chat with someone that he came to like and trust. Up to a point and as long as they would provide the drink.

The following Monday Dai Jones came to his house and walked with him to the harbour.

The *Welsh Lass* was the small cargo ship that Dai Jones worked on as a stoker. Her cargo on the return trip to the Welsh ports was about two thousand tons of sand. It was her usual cargo on her return trip to her home port. Her skipper and owner was Tommy Redone and along with Dai Jones there were two other seamen aboard her; one helped Dai and the other was the general dogsbody.

Dai introduced Jenkins to the skipper, who preferred to be called 'Captain', which of course he was. That was the only formality on the ship and there was a great deal of laughter and joking as long as the work was done.

The captain asked Jenkins about his experiences of the sea and ships.

"Only as a passenger on troop ships; we didn't do anything except keep our bunks and selves clean and tidy. Otherwise it was on deck all day if the weather was fine and, if not, below decks out of the way."

"Well, Taff, you're going to have to work your passage this time; it'll only be for a couple of days, until we dock and unload the cargo at Swansea. Is that OK?"

"Sure, sir, that'll be fine. What will I have to do?"

"Well, Taff, we need a decent cook in the galley. Can you cook?"

"Yes I can, sir, but I only do it for myself, you know a few spuds and sausages and the like; I don't know much more, except perhaps eggs and toast."

"You'll have a job making toast on this old bucket but the rest should be OK. Manage that then?"

"OK, sir."

"'Captain' will do Taff. Now Dai will show you the galley and where the makings are. Tell you what, if the galley fire's still in, get it going and make the crew some tea. We've got time before we sail and it'll give you time to settle in, all right boyo?"

The *Welsh Lass* left harbour right on time with the high tide. Jenkins had settled into the galley and he would sleep there on the next two nights. There was a small bunk opposite the galley range so he definitely wouldn't be cold during the night. The blanket provided by the captain was adequate, if not clean. But he knew that he had fared a lot worse during his time, so he had no reason to complain.

His first attempt at cooking a meal on board was an excellent effort, at least that's what the captain and his little crew said. Boiled potatoes, tinned beans and sausages, because that was the only food aboard. To make it more appetising he added a touch of margarine and pepper to the potatoes, just to add to their flavour.

After he had cleaned the galley and the pots and pans, he lay on the bunk and thought about his family and home. He was beginning to become a little apprehensive but also began to feel a surge of excitement for what he was about to discover.

It took the next two days and nights for the *Welsh Lass* to chug along and arrive at Swansea, after docking at Cardiff and Newport to drop off a few light crates of engineering equipment for the dock cranes that were being repaired. That's what Dai said anyway! He never seemed to bother at the rate of knots that the old ship kept up. As long as he and sometimes one of the other crew gave him a hand keeping the fires stoked up and the engine oiled he would whistle and dream the whole day away. He didn't have to work on deck no matter what the weather but when he did go topside he couldn't help but admire the coast of Wales and the ever-changing colours of the sea and land as they came together.

Dai took Jenkins up to admire the view and as they chatted about their lives in general, they both admitted that there was too much missing to live in Bristol for the rest of their lives. They would have to 'go home' sooner or later.

"I don't know how the missus and kids will take it, though," Dai said dreamily as he went below to his fire and engine.

Jenkins sat on an upturned bucket peeling potatoes, thinking to himself of the last time he had to peel spuds. It was when he was on jankers (punishment) as a recruit in the army, twenty years before. Two weeks of spud bashing for being absent from parade one morning, and having to do punishment parades at reveille and last post. He knew then he would never do another day's spud bashing or punishment parade as long as he lived and he didn't, although once or twice he came close. But here he was: unbelievable.

The *Welsh Lass* docked late on the Wednesday evening and Dai said they'd be better off staying on board overnight, if the skipper didn't mind.

"There won't be many trams or trains going our way at this time of night and besides we won't have to rent a room, will we?"

"But aren't you going to stay with your Mam tonight then, Dai? There's no need to stay on board, I'll be OK, honest."

"Well!" the skipper said, "I'll need two of you on board to see the sand is unloaded first light tomorrow morning. Dai's done it plenty of times before. It's only to see the unloading is done properly by the crews on the dock and I'll feel a lot happier knowing who's on board ship tonight."

"Yeh, that's fine, skipper. I can't get any copper until you pay me my wages tomorrow, after you've been to the bank. Besides if I go all the way to my Mam's, it'll cost me to come all the way back tomorrow." Turning to Jenkins, Dai went on: "So not to worry, we'll have a bottle of somefink to drink and a game of cards, then get our heads down, all right?"

Jenkins thought that a great idea and went to get a tin of corned beef and some bread.

The next morning, after the sand had been unloaded, they went to Swansea High Street to meet the skipper. He had just left the bank and was walking along the street towards them. A young man left the bank, walking about ten yards behind the captain, who had put a white bag under his right arm. As Captain Redone approached Jenkins and Dai Jones, the man, who was wearing a seaman's navy blue cap and a navy blue jacket, started to run. Within the seconds that it took the man to reach the captain, Jenkins had seen the runner and anticipated the danger. He pointed and shouted a warning but knowing it was too late started to run towards the captain, who hearing the warning shout, half turned, realising that danger was coming from behind. As the captain turned towards his attacker, the man smashed into him with his shoulder. Redone never had a chance to brace himself for the cowardly attack but Jenkins did. As the attacker reached to snatch the white bag from under Redone's loosened grip, Jenkins shouted and hit the man across the right forearm with the walking stick he always carried.

The man, screaming in pain, fell to the ground. Dai Jones catching on to the situation, dived on top of the attacker, trying to hold him down. But the man was too big for him and struggled to his feet, throwing Dai off with his good hand.

Hearing a loud shout, the three turned towards what they thought was more danger. It was two policemen about fifty yards away: they'd seen the incident as they turned the corner and thought that the captain and his 'crew' were attacking the thief.

The thief, seeing the policemen, turned and ran off down a side street, and, as he did so, Jenkins saw two other men appear from a shop doorway and run off with him.

It didn't take the policemen long to realise the situation and that the incident had been an attempted robbery.

"How much were you carrying, sir?" one asked the captain.

"Seventy-five pounds," the captain replied. "If he'd got hold of that lot, it would be the crew's week's wages, food, coal and oil stocks for the next week. But thanks to Taff Jenkins here, he didn't get anything, except perhaps a busted arm and a lot of pain, I hope!"

He held out his hand to Jenkins, "Anything I can do for you Taff, just ask won't you?"

"That's all right, captain. I would have done the same for anyone and especially you. You're holding Dai's bloody wages and that's the only reason we came to meet you. Bloody lucky weren't we?"

The policemen, after listening to their version of events and that of onlookers, said if they wanted to make statements, they should go to the police station, near the Swansea railway station. The Desk Sergeant would help them out.

"I think we'll be OK now constable, we'll get this out of sight and the lads can get on their way."

He counted out Dai's money, who shoved it into his trouser pocket.

"And here's a couple of quid for you Taff: if it hadn't been for you none of us would have any money now."

Jenkins tried to protest that he didn't want a reward.

"It's not for that mate, it's for the best meals we've had on that bloody boat for months, eh Dai?"

"Aye skipper. He'll make a blinking good wife for some filly won't he?" Jenkins cringed and almost blushed with embarrassment.

"Come on Dai, let's go home, eh?"

Chapter 2

Home, or is it?

About an hour after the attempted robbery, they made their way to the High Street railway station in Swansea, the main station for trains to West Wales, and towards Cardiff, Newport and England. The train they wanted was the ten thirty, travelling north-east along the Swansea Valley. It called at St Thomas, Glais, Pontardawe, Ystrafera, Ystradguinlais, and then stopping at all other stations on its route to Hereford.

Dai suggested they stop off at Glais and see his Mam first; there they could have a cup of tea and Jenkins could get his thoughts together and decide on his next move.

Dai's Mam, as he called her, lived in the village at Glais, just across the River Tawe from Clydach. She lived in a little terraced two-up two-down cottage, with a privy toilet in the back yard. A widow and in her late sixties, Mrs Jones was a small, plump and jovial lady.

Speaking in her native Welsh, "Dai," she cried, "where have you been, boy? How are the children and Mira? Are they coming? I expected to see you two weeks ago. Who's this then?" she asked, just pausing to take a breath. "Come in, come in!"

Jenkins was still unsure of himself in his natural language but hopefully, after a few days back in his homeland and with people he knew, it would become more natural and he would get back to his own fluency, in the language of his birth. Almost all conversation was in Welsh and would be until they got back to Bristol. Jenkins understood it well enough, but needed to practise the vocal element of the language, which he was very happy and proud to do. He knew then that he was on his way home.

They were ushered into the immaculate kitchen, with its polished, black leaded range and kettle hanging on its chain above the open lid of the fire.

"Pnawn Da Mr?" She waited for Dai to introduce his friend.

"Mam this is Taff Jenkins, my friend from Bristol, the chap I told you about the last time I was home, remember?"

"Of course I remember, I'm not that far gone. Don't you be so cheeky, boyo, I'm still capable of giving you a clout for your bother." The gentle affection in her voice, showed how pleased, almost ecstatic, she was to see them both.

"Pnawn Da, Missis Jones," Jenkins said, taking her tiny hand.

"Come and sit down Taff, have a drink: cup of tea is it?" she asked, smiling as he ducked under the parlour doorway. "Come and tell me about yourself."

He told her about his family and Alltwen just along the valley, about his friends whilst he was there, even about the chapel he and his family attended almost every Sunday. Then he went on to say why he had joined the army.

"Nothing untoward," he said. "I just needed to get away for a new start because I didn't fancy going down a pit or on the steel like my Dad. Everyone round the valleys and working on the coal or on the steel are worn out by the time they're fifty and I wanted to see a bit of the world before that happened to me, so I joined up."

"Well, what's it been like, all this gallivanting and travelling and fighting?" she asked.

She was so full of questions that Dai said, "Come on Mam, give Taff a chance, he won't know where to start if you don't slow down."

"All right, all right," she replied and sat back in her chair waiting for him to have his say.

Jenkins went on to tell her about his life in the army, about the journeys he'd been on to North and South Africa, about the campaigns and battles that he had been part of and or witnessed. About his meeting with Queen Alexandra in a Maltese hospital in 1905 where he had been recovering from a re-occurring tropical illness and then in 1907 when he had gone back to Malta as part of King Edward VII's Escort during the review of the Army at the Marsa Parade Ground and later at the Malta Royal Opera House where he had to stand behind the royal box for over three hours, listening to Puccini's La Bohème.

Mrs Jones became very excited as he told her of his close proximity to the King and his consort Queen Alexandra. Her questions came like machine-gun fire, she could hardly draw a breath between each one. The strangest question he thought that she had asked was, "What did the Queen's scent smell like?"

He couldn't tell her the truth, that he wasn't standing that close, so he said, "Like fresh oranges and lemon's, beautiful!"

Mrs Jones clapped her hands with excitement. She couldn't stop herself. "Did she speak to you, did she?"

"No, but the King did!"

"What did he say? What did he say?" She was almost delirious: both Dai and Taff thought she was going to have a seizure.

"Only 'Good Morning, Private'!" Taff replied.

"Is that all?" She was so thoroughly deflated, that she gave Taff a withering look of disdain and went into the kitchen. "To get the dinner ready!" she said.

By that time he thought he'd said enough. It was past midday and he wanted to catch the one-thirty train to its next stop at Pontardawe. From there it was only a very short walk to his old home. He hoped to find answers to a few questions, for example, when his mother and father had passed away and where they were buried. Also where other members of the family might have moved.

Before he went, Mrs Jones insisted they have a bowl of 'cowl', lamb and vegetable stew, that had been kept hot in the range oven. She had been expecting Dai and Taff for the last two days and knew after a couple of days on the ship they would need a substantial meal inside them when they arrived in Glais.

The 'cowl' along with a thick slice of home-made bread was the best meal they had had since they sailed from Bristol, Dai said.

"So my cooking's not good enough for you then, eh?" Jenkins said pretending to be angry.

"No mate, it's fine, as far as ship's food goes, but not as good as my Mam's, is it? You've got to admit that, Taff."

"OK, but *you'll* have to do the cooking on the way back to Bristol, boyo."

After the meal Dai said he felt a good long sleep would be better than the walks that were ahead of them. "A tidy few miles, I'll bet?" he said to Jenkins, grimacing at the thought.

"Don't worry, there's plenty of places to have a rest once we get off the train, and I ain't in the army now, so there's no rush, is there? Besides it don't get dark till gone seven o'clock tonight, so what we want to do should be OK. What do you think Dai?"

"Fine, fine, mate. Let's go, eh? We'll be staying the night, Mam, if that's OK?" Dai turned quickly towards his Mam, nodding towards Jenkins. "Just in case we're disappointed! Me and him."

As they walked down her garden path on to the narrow road that led to the local station, they both turned and waved to the diminutive lady seeing them off, as if they'd be doing it for years. She waited in her doorway until they disappeared from sight.

They made it to the station just as the train arrived. Its arrival and departure was exactly on time, which pleased them and the other waiting passengers. It chugged along the narrow gauge railway at almost twenty miles an hour. Jenkins, seeing the view for the first time since leaving home, began to remember the good and bad times of his childhood and youth that he had spent on this local journey. It didn't take long; within ten minutes they were alighting at the Alltwen and Pontardawe station.

Jenkins stepped out on to the little platform, looking across the River Tawe at the church. It's steeple was the first thing that always caught his eye when he left home for school, to play out, go on an errand or to meet his Dad after work. Even abroad he could bring that picture of the church steeple into his dreams of going home.

He turned and looked back towards the Graig. Along the bottom of the cliff stood a row of stone-built, slate-roofed houses standing like white granite-faced sentries, overlooking and guarding the town below.

As they walked up the hill towards his old home, Jenkins remembered how, when he left the house on early spring mornings, with the mist coming off of the River Tawe and spreading across the valley and on towards

Ystradguinlais, he would see the steeple of St Matthew's in Pontardawe, rising through the white cold blanket of mist, until the church's stained glass windows reflected the morning sun, like red, blue and golden diamonds.

He noticed that the old quarry behind the houses on the Graig seemed to have been abandoned, because the usual clamour and movement as he remembered wasn't there. He could see the afternoon sun shining on the white-scarred cliff workings. A silent reminder of the past.

Taff Jenkins and Dai Jones came to the row of snow white terraced cottages on Graig Road. When they arrived at number five, Jenkins was about to knock on the door but stopped. Other memories came flooding back.

This time of day his father would be leaving home for the two till ten day shift in the steel works across the Tawe, opposite the station. His father, dressed in his overalls, heavy boots and brown leather cap, would lift Dick up to his own head height and shake him gently, saying loudly, "See you tonight, boyo!" Then he would clump off down the steep steps.

But that was nearly thirty years ago.

"Tell you what!" Dai said, "why don't we go to one of the other houses first and see what the people there know, perhaps they'll be able to tell you what happened to your family or where they have moved to. You don't want to upset anyone do you, mate?

Come on let's go next door, OK?"

"It'll be all right, Dai. Might as well start at the beginning, hadn't we? If we start in the middle, we'll only have to go back and start all over and we don't have time for that, do we?"

Jenkins knocked on the door of number five and waited in anticipation, not knowing what to expect. Nothing happened. He knocked a second time, a little louder.

He was still expecting to see his mother open the door and stand in the doorway, in her usual enquiring way, dressed in her green and black checked dress, white cap tied under her chin and white pinafore.

When he heard the clatter of wooden clogs on the slate kitchen floor he almost froze, fearing he had made a mistake and it was his mother's clogs he heard approaching the door. The thought went through his mind, it might be a ghost. "Don't be so bloody stupid!" he said to himself, at the same time glancing at Dai Jones, hoping he hadn't seen the fear in his eyes.

He took a deep breath as the door opened slowly and quietly, not creaking or squeaking as he remembered.

The face of a little girl peered at them around the edge of the door.

"'ello," she said "Pnawn Da."

The girl was about ten years old, much the same age as his sister when he left home. He thought for a minute he was dreaming, then he realised his sister had had blonde hair and was quite a lot taller. This little girl was tiny, with raven black hair and she was carrying a baby: brother or sister? He couldn't tell.

"Pnawn Da," he replied, "Is your Mammy or Daddy home? We'd like to talk with them."

"Mam!" she yelled out, over her shoulder. "There's two men out the back, they want to talk with you."

A woman shouted back, "All right, all right, I'm coming. Don't shout so loud, you'll wake the bloody baby. Wake him now and we'll never get him back to sleep, you know what the bloody boys are like!"

At that, a tired looking woman of about thirty-five years old appeared. "'ello, you from the Steel?" she said referring to the steel works across the river.

"No we're not, my name is Richard Jenkins and this Dai Jones from Glais. We're here to see if you know what happened to my parents. Before I left the village to join the army about twenty years ago, I lived here with them." Then he added, "I am sorry I don't recognize you, have you lived here long?"

The woman replied, "Look! Mr Jenkins, is it?" He nodded. "We've been here just over five years. There was another family living here before us but it wasn't anyone called Jenkins. They were the Evans's I think, moved to Cardiff or somewhere in that direction, before we took over the house. Sorry I can't help you any more than that." She looked down at her daughter, "Go on Rosie, get back inside before the school mitcher man comes looking for you! Sorry mister!" and the woman shut the door without giving her name.

"No use being downhearted." Dai realised what Jenkins was going through. "Let's go to the house next door, number three ain't it?"

"Alright Dai, no need to be so pushy, lets try and get things straight before we knock on any more doors. Perhaps they're new people too."

"Tell you what Taff, we'll toss a coin, 'eads for number three, tails for number one. What do you fink?"

"OK, OK," Jenkins replied, beginning to feel a bit peevish at Dai for thinking for him.

Dai dug into his coat pocket and found a halfpenny coin. "Shall I toss?" he asked.

"Go ahead," Jenkins replied. "Go on, get it over, will you?"

Dai tossed the coin, caught it and placed it on the back of his left hand, covering the coin with his right.

"Yessie Christ! Let's have a look, Dai! Stop messing about, will you?" By this time Jenkins was beginning to get frustrated and angry with Dai and himself. But when Dai took his hand away from the coin and revealed the coin had come down heads, he realised how stupid and paranoid he was becoming. "Relax, relax," he told himself. "We're getting there."

He led the way to the back door of number three. If he remembered correctly, it was Evans the mine that lived there, not to be confused with Evans the coal. John Evans the mine used to work in the private coal mine near Rhos, on the road to Neath. Both of Evans' sons would probable have gone to work in the mines. It was usually a family tradition that if possible, boys would follow into their father's trade or occupation. For a variety of reasons it didn't always happen: ill health, moving home, marriage, etc. Jenkins remembered both boys well enough, because they were all about the same age. They went to school and played rugby for the school team together.

He knocked on the door. The man that answered the door was barely recognizable as the big fifteen stone Evans the mine he used to know. Evans was past his fifties, with ingrained coal dust in the creases around his eyes and ears, which had become impossible to remove. No matter how many baths and scrubbings he took, it was a coal miner's trade mark. Now Mr Evans, who seemed to have shrivelled up, he was so small and bent with arthritis, looked up at them. Then, looking more closely at Dai Jones, said, "Pnawn Da lads, are you looking for the boys? They ain't back yet. Jack's at work and Robert is down the station in Clydach. They won't be back till six, so if you want to see them, you'll have to come back when they've had their dinner."

His voice was weak and shaky, he held on to the door as if supporting himself. Before either of the visitors could speak, a woman's voice called from inside the house, "Who is it John? Who are you talking to? Ask them to come, whoever it is."

John Evans was watching Dai and Taff as Mrs Evans called out her questions and invitation. Suddenly he realised who Jenkins was. "By God," he said his voice seeming to get stronger but higher pitched. "Anne! It's Dick Jenkins, come and see, come and see."

"Who?"

"Dick Jenkins from next door, number five, you remember, don't you?" At the same instant he grabbed hold of Jenkins' hand and tried to pull him into the kitchen. The kitchen door to the parlour burst open and a large plump, round-faced woman rushed through the door. She saw Jenkins ducking under the lintel of the back door.

"Richard Jenkins, Richard? It is you, it is, isn't it?" She rushed at him grabbing his hand and then around his arm, asking a barrage of questions, lasting for almost a minute before she took a deep breath. Just enough to give Jenkins the time to make any sort of reply.

"Hello Missis Evans, Pnawn Da, how are you all? Yes it's me and it's great to be home." He answered her questions as they came flooding out.

"And who is this?" she asked giving Dai a fierce but not unfriendly look.

"This a mate of mine, Dai Jones from Glais; he's been helping me out since I left the army. I've come back to find my family, because I haven't heard from them for years, perhaps you might know what happened to my Mam and Da." He had always referred to them in that way. It was the first time he had said 'Da' when talking about his father, since he had left home.

Annie Evans hugged him again, "Well first of all we'll go into the parlour and have a cup of tea; you like tea don't you, Richard? Or would you rather have a beer?"

John Evans looked at her in protest, as if to say, "That's my beer, and those are the only two bottles I've got left." Annie ignored him.

"What is it then Richard? Dai? Don't worry about him, he can go to the pub later on if he wants a pint."

Jenkins and Dai looked at John Evans; they put him out of his misery.

"Tea will be fine Mrs Evans, honestly, neither of us drinks a lot, so tea will be very nice, thanks."

She went back to the kitchen, leaving the parlour door open while she made and poured the tea, firing questions at Jenkins and Dai, mostly, of course, at Jenkins. He answered her questions as quickly and honestly as he could, mostly about his leaving home for a career in the army. His travels in the Far East and Africa, the times he had been wounded and, more importantly, the number of times he had seen Queen Victoria.

"What was it like to guard her in Buckingham Palace, and what happened at the Tower of London?" Annie was still asking questions and he was still talking when the first of her two sons came home from work.

Jack had finished his shift at the private mine near Rhos, the same mine that his father had toiled in before ill health had caused his premature retirement at fifty years old.

When Jenkins stood up as Jack entered the room, he almost fell over in amazement.

"Where the hell did you come from?" he shouted gleefully. "For crying out loud Dick, this is wonderful. How long are you staying then? Are you still in the army?"

They gripped each others' hand, trying to out-shake the other.

"Are you stopping long enough to go for a pint? Bob'll get home soon. He'll be back from the station in about half an hour."

"Which station's that then?" Dai said, saying something for the first and it seemed only time that afternoon.

Jack said, "Well, who's the boyo then, Dick?"

"Sorry Jack, this is Dai Jones, my one and only mate since I left the army; if it wasn't for him I'd still be moping around Bristol and it's the quietest he's been since we left Swansea this morning."

Jack suddenly realised he hadn't bathed yet and said to Mrs Evans, "What are we having for supper tonight, Ma? Will there be enough for these two?"

"Of course there is, even if you have to go without. Don't worry, I'll find something," she replied. "You go and get your bath, the water's on the stove and you can have the bath in the scullery, 'cause I'll be in the kitchen getting supper ready. Now boys, while we're waiting for Bobby to come home, you can tell us what has happened to your sister and your Mam since she moved to Swansea. We know your Dad passed away and your sister married, but after your Mam moved away we haven't heard from her, or your sister."

He told them it was his fault for not writing home regularly, and that he'd only written a couple of letters while he was abroad. He hadn't received many either, not that he was blaming anyone. His Mam probably had written, but her letters hadn't got to him; it had been known for ex-soldiers to receive letters years after they'd left the army. So it wasn't to say that he would never ever receive any of the letters that his mother had sent him. He didn't like to tell them that his Mam had died. He wanted to pick the right moment.

Then the parlour door opened and a figure almost as tall as Jenkins stood in the doorway. He to had to duck into the room.

"Remember my Bobby?" Mrs Evans said, pushing him towards Jenkins.

"Bloody hell," Robert, as he preferred to be called, exclaimed.

"There's no need for that language," his mother chided him, "You're still not too big to put across my knee, you know!"

They all laughed as Dai and Jenkins eyed up the man in the black uniform. He was massive, six feet three, very wide at the shoulders and weighing about eighteen stones. In the uniform of the Glamorgan Police.

Jenkins held out his hand to his old friend; the uniform put him off a little and he was unsure what to say or do, but Robert wasn't. He grabbed Jenkins around the shoulders in a huge bear hug.

"Richard, old son, what the hell are you doing here? Where have you come from? Where have you been? The last time I saw you, you were getting on the train at Ponty Station and then I heard you'd joined the army, but that was over twenty years ago, eh?"

So, after he disengaged himself from Robert's grip, they all sat down and waited for Mrs Evans to cook the evening meal. While they waited they exchanged stories and tales of their lives and travels over the last twenty or so years and why Jenkins had finally come home.

After supper, except for Mrs Evans, they all went to the pub across the river from the railway station and continued to discuss their lives and families up until that time. There was a great deal of joviality and the noise of their cheerful banter went on until Dai suddenly realised they had to catch a train back to Glais or walk, and neither he nor Jenkins fancied being late back to Dai's home.

On the way to the station, Robert asked Jenkins if he knew when his mother moved to Swansea and who she moved in with. Did she have any relations or friends there? When told it was perhaps at her sister's house that his mother had gone to live and her name was Sadie Williams, Robert said he would get his friends at the Swansea station to make inquires.

"What part of Swansea did your aunt live in, Dick?"

"The last time I went to visit Auntie Sadie, she was living in St Thomas, that's all I remember, but it was near the Norwegian Church, opposite the docks. Even then she was getting on a bit. I hope your boys can find something out, it'll be a real help."

Robert replied, "Don't worry mate, if she's there we'll find her, probably by tomorrow evening, OK?"

"OK then, see you tomorrow night. Got to go now or we'll miss the train; we'll see you then. Cheers now!"

With that Jenkins and Dai took-off at a run to get the train to Glais.

The next day they mooched about the villages, looking up a few friends and one or two of Dai's relations. Then Jenkins went on his own to visit his old school in Alltwen and then watched the rugby team play a team from Ross School.

He hadn't watched or played much rugby during his service, but was, he knew, a pretty good player himself. He had derived so much enjoyment from the game, and he suddenly realised how much of his family and the valley life he had missed. He said to himself, "I don't intend to miss any more."

But that evening bad news and a terrible shock was waiting for him.

At five o'clock with Jenkins' patience on the decline, he and Dai went to the Evans' home on the Graig.

Robert hadn't arrived home from work at that time, so they spent the next hour chatting with the Evans' mostly about Jenkins' time spent in Bristol, looking for his sister, and the work he was doing. He also realised the he had been talking about May Andrews and how he missed her company.

Dai raised his eyebrows as he said to Jenkins, "Taff, boyo, you're a deep one, ain't you? You never said anything about May before."

"Mrs Andrews to you, Dai. Don't you dare say a word to her or anyone else when we get back, or I'll chuck you in the bloody docks whether the tide's in or out. So keep your trap shut, OK?"

Dai nodded, feeling he'd gone a bit too far and looked innocently up to the ceiling, not daring to say another word.

Just then the back door to the kitchen banged open and Robert's huge bulk blocked out what was left of the evening sunlight. Without any preamble he said "Good! You're here, but it's not good news, I'm afraid. There isn't any point trying to dress up bad news, Richard, I'm sorry to say."

Jenkins was sat at the kitchen table and started to stand up. Robert said, "No mate, you stay there, 'cause what I have to tell you isn't nice. Mam! Have you got any whisky or gin that Richard can have? I think he might need it, if you wouldn't mind getting him a drink, please."

Mrs Evans went into the parlour to get the drink. Robert shut the door gently behind her.

"Listen Richard, it's not going to be easy for any of us, but I'm just going to tell you the facts as a detective inspector from Swansea told me on the telephone this afternoon. It seems that your mother was attacked and robbed at her home in Myers Street, St Thomas, last September."

Jenkins sat in the chair stone-faced, just watching Robert, who went on:

"As a result of her injuries, she died where they found her, in her bedroom. It seems a considerable amount of money may have been taken, but the exact amount isn't known because she was probably the only person who knew it was there, except the man who robbed her. The man who has been charged with her assault and robbery at this time is on trial at Swansea Crown Court."

Robert watched Jenkins face but there was no sign of any change in his stone-faced friend's demeanour; his eyes like sky blue crystals stared into the flames of the coal fire.

"The trial's been going on for nearly two weeks now and is due to end in the next two or three days."

Dai said, "Do you think this bloke's going to get his come uppance? How's the trial going? Have you been to the court Robert?"

"Look Dai, stop a minute, will you? I don't know what is happening in court, I haven't been, so I don't know the bloke who is being tried, except that his name is Gifford and he's a slimy, horrible git. It seems he came off of a ship and couldn't get back to his home port. Some vicar or other asked Mrs Jenkins to put him up for a couple of nights." Robert stopped then continued.

"When she hadn't been seen for a day or two, someone started to ask questions. Then the police found her in the house and from a description from the vicar traced this bloke Gifford down to a ship at the docks. That's where he was caught and arrested. It's taken all this time to get him to Crown Court and by what the inspector said, it's likely he'll be found guilty with all the evidence presented against him.

"Richard! Are you all right?" Robert asked, concern showing on his normally amiable features.

"Yes, I will be, don't worry. Can I have that drink now?"

"Mam, you can come in now, please."

Mrs Evans, who'd been listening at the slightly opened door, came in with a tray of glasses and a small bottle of whisky, put the tray on the table and said: "I'm sorry Richard, please accept our sincerest condolences. If there's anything at all we can do for you, please don't hesitate to ask. Please!"

Mrs Evans was in tears as she left the room.

Jenkins stood up and went to the window and gazed out across the valley as he had seen his mother do. He drank the whisky in one swallow. Now a pale stone-faced man, who refused to give in to his personal thoughts and feelings.

In a wooden voice he said, "Thanks Robert, thanks for finding out, and thank you everyone for your kindness. I'll have to go now. Dai, I think I'll walk back to Glais, all right?" Dai tried to interrupt. "By myself!"

Then as an afterthought he said to Robert, "Do you think it'll be OK for me to go to the trial tomorrow?"

"Yes, I imagine so. Shall I meet you at the Crown Court at about ten o'clock, you and Dai? Do you know where the courts are?"

" No, but we'll find them. We'll be there, eh Dai?"

With that last remark he left the house and started his last walk to Glais.

Chapter 3

Hannah Jenkins

Seven years before Dai Jones brought Jenkins back to Swansea, Mrs Hannah Jenkins had moved into her sister's terraced house on the corner of Myers and Pindey Streets junction, in the St Thomas area of Swansea. When she looked out of the front room window she could see the Norwegian Church next to the King's Dock Road on the edge of the docklands.

The church was visited by numerous seafarers, who were looked after and found a bed and food whenever and whatever the length of time of their visit to Swansea. The sailors' religious convictions were looked after by monks and priests of varying faiths who visited the church regularly.

Hannah Jenkins had, on occasions, with her older sister Ellen, gone to the church to help prepare food and clean the sailors' sleeping accommodation. She felt it was her duty to help anyone who might need it: race, religion, age, wealth or otherwise had never come into it. If she could help in some small way, she would. Three months after moving into her sister's house, Ellen died very suddenly, leaving Hannah in the house and alone.

She hadn't another relative close by that she could contact. Her daughter Martha had married an English soldier, then moved to Bristol the day after they married. That was five years before Hannah moved house to be with her sister in St Thomas.

Martha hadn't written home since moving away, so there was no known address for Hannah to send a letter. Another thing was she couldn't remember her daughter's married name anyway. Hannah knew that her son Richard had joined the army when he was seventeen years old. She had written to him several times but he had only replied twice, once when he was sent to Africa and the other time whilst he was in South Africa, telling her of his wounds. She often wondered what had become of them both. Most of the time she felt so lonely, even when her friends came to call, trying to cheer her up.

Mrs Jenkins had been widowed at a fairly early point in her married life and had lived in the old terraced house overlooking Pontardawe in the Swansea Valley for nearly sixty years from the time she was born until her move to join her sister. The house had once belonged to the private mine owner her father David and mother Mary had worked for, almost all of their lives. Whilst they were alive, her grandparents had lived in the same house and worked for the same people, mother and grandmother as cooks in Mr Jeffries' house, Johnno and her grandfather in Mr Jeffries' coal mine. Then the council took over the ownership of the miners' terraced houses. The people living there didn't mind too much because they stayed as a community with their closest friends and neighbours.

Nothing seemed to change and all the residents knew that unless some catastrophe happened, they and their families of the future would always have a home. The private mine owners had a habit of evicting retired or sick miners and their families, then replacing them with fit and healthy workers. Now that the local council had taken on the ownership and responsibility for keeping the properties in good order and repair, the residents, including Hannah and her husband Owain, were very happy. Her mother and father had inherited the rent book, house and jobs ten years before Hannah was born. In the same way rent book, house and jobs were passed on to her and Owain.

She had only been married to her husband, a big strong rugby-playing miner, for two months, when her father was killed in a terrible mining accident in the local private coal mine, where he worked with his son-in-law. A build-up of methane gas had been accidentally ignited in some way. Her father and another miner died in the ensuing explosion. Owain was extremely lucky that day. He had been in the first tram up to the surface that morning and was on his way home when the explosion occurred. Her father Johnno, who had been on the same night shift as Owain, being the foreman, sent Owain and most of the other miners home. Johnno and one other miner, Cliff Bishop, Johnno's best mate, had stayed down the pit checking some props that might have needed replacing by the day shift. The explosion was so great it caused severe damage to the mine, which was never repaired. The mine was reopened a year later, a new shaft being sunk and new roads from it built.

Johnno's and his partner's bodies were never recovered. Their families never being properly able to say goodbye was the thing that upset them them most. Hannah's mother Mary died of shock a couple of weeks later, although the general consensus of opinion amongst her friends was that she died of a broken heart. Fearing for her husband Owain's life, Hannah insisted that he change his job and after a couple of months and a lucky break, Owain landed himself a   job on Neath's river docks loading and unloading sand and coal barges. Finally more tragedy blighted her life. Her married bliss came to a tragic end.

Owain enjoyed fishing in the tidal river at Neath. He often took his pet terrier with him for company, because it was a five mile walk from the village of Alltwen to the riverside at Neath. Since he no longer played rugby, walking and cycling became his exercise and fishing his sport. On one of his Sunday fishing trips, his dog Pee Wee, a triple-cross breed, bad tempered, terrier, tried to chase a swan across the mud skirting the river banks. Pee Wee's little legs couldn't cope with the water-soaked mud and he became bogged down. Although the tide was coming in, Owain, who couldn't swim and weighed almost eighteen stone, waded into the mud to get his dog. No one heard his shouts for help as the mud and water became deeper with the tide racing up the river towards them.

The ebb tide showed where Owain and Pee Wee met their demise.

Being so lonely, and fearful that the house in the Graig Terrace had become unlucky, Hannah took up her sister's offer and moved in with her. She was happy enough until her sister passed away six months later. Hannah realised that even though she had only been there a short time, it had made Ellen a little less worried and to feel more loved and cared for as she passed into oblivion. Hannah was the sort of person who could make friends easily wherever she was and that was where the Norwegian Church came in. Her old seamen friends returned at regular intervals and she made new acquaintants almost every day. She was happy in her new home, in her street and with her life. But she still hoped for her son and daughter's return. She wouldn't admit it but she missed them both terribly and at times became a little frightened and worried that when her time came neither would be home to comfort and help her. Hannah Jenkins hadn't seen, and only twice heard, from her son Richard since he had joined the army almost twenty years before. The last time was from somewhere in South Africa and saying that he had been wounded, not too badly. He had tried to consol her by asking her not to worry. Hannah had never heard another word since then.

Hannah, as she was known to her few best friends in St Thomas, was a diminutive, five foot, still sprightly, careful, and as was said before, a kind, helpful old lady, who didn't have a bad word for anyone. One afternoon in September 1913 she was humming happily to herself working on a patchwork quilt that she had spent many hours on. It was almost finished. It would be one of a display that the Ladies Circle planned to enter in an Arts and Crafts exhibition at the Town Hall in a week's time. The exhibition was to be in aid of the various charities that would be sponsored by many different groups such as the Ladies Circles from all parts of Swansea and the surrounding villages. The many and varied colours and patterns of the quilt seemed to be at their best, as the sun streamed through the parlour window on to the artistry of her nimble fingers. Those nimble fingers had been her lifeline, enabling her to live a little more comfortably with the extra money she earned making clothing for her neighbours and friends. Until she had to turn work away, her skills had become to widely known. The little money she had saved from her work and her husband's insurance, which she had refused to spend, was kept in a large tin box, under a pile of old 'Daily Post' newspapers in the built-in wardrobe of her bedroom. There was a lock on the box but only for show. It had been broken years before. In all, the money amounted to a little over a hundred pounds. To some, it would be a fortune, enough to buy a house. When Hannah went to the box to make her 'deposit' as she often called it, she would say to herself, "I must bank my savings. There might be a fire in the house one day, then where would I be?" The tin box was also getting almost too heavy for her to move, with the weight of various denominations of bank notes and coins dating back to the eighteen-eighties and nineties. All the copper coins – farthings, halfpennies and pennies – were packed into three large earthenware jars, as were the silver coins, threepencies and sixpences, shillings, two shillings and half crowns. There were also three gold sovereigns mixed in amongst the silver, 'for luck' Hannah said as she pushed the box back under the newspapers. It was the last occasion that she put the box away. Hannah had often thought about buying the house from the owner, but then thought perhaps it would be better to share the money between her son and daughter, when they came home. If they came home.

That day in September 1913 a local parish priest asked her if she had a spare room. If so, would she rent it out for a few days because the Norwegian Church accommodation was full and there were several seamen from the ships in port needing a bed because the ships' captains were not being allowed to take on any cargoes.

The Reverend Ivor Thomas said, "Mrs Jenkins, there have been problems with the miners in Clydach Vale and the usual coal reserves at the docks are diminishing faster than they can be restocked. Therefore the men from the ships are unable to get back to Bristol, the West Country and other parts of the British Isles. They won't be leaving until their ships have had their holds loaded with the best Welsh, deep mined, coal, which the rest of Britain needs to keep its fires and furnaces burning." He continued: "Can you see it in your heart to helping these unfortunate men of the sea, by accommodating one or two in your spare room over the coming three or four weeks, at least until this coal miners situation is resolved?"

The Norwegian Church administration clerk would come and pay for the visitors' lodgings.

Hannah thought it over carefully, "All right," she decided; a little more money would be very welcome. "I won't need to touch my savings now, will I?" she said to herself. Then to the Reverend Thomas, "I do hope the men they send will be well behaved and not drunkards, otherwise I'll have to send them packing."

Thomas smiled, "I'm sure you will, Mrs Jenkins, of course."

Her little house was kept in an immaculate condition. The dark brown leather three-piece suite was always polished, as though it was new and had just been delivered. There were several hand-made leather patchwork cushions decorating the furniture and the wall brasses, glasses, clocks and ornaments that decorated the parlour were all shining and dust free. A white linen tablecloth, with raised white silk flower petals embroidered into it, covered a highly polished antique oak round table, with a set of matching chairs arranged neatly around it. A glass vase of fresh-cut carnation flowers stood exactly in the middle of the table. The colourful carnations gave the tiny room a glow of warm light in the middle of what was, in fact, a tiny living museum. Whatever the time of year or whatever the weather, flowers, usually carnations, were displayed on the table. Sometimes, if she could afford it, she also placed a vase on the window-sill facing the street. It was her way of making visitors welcome.

A few days after the parish priest's initial visit, he knocked on her door again. When Hannah opened the door she saw the weather was very stormy. She hadn't noticed the rain and wind before, as she had been having a little nap.

"Hello, Mrs Jenkins." He didn't give her time to reply. "After our little talk the other day, as a last resort I've brought this young man along to see if you can put him up for a night or two. Young Roger here is going to be at the docks for a few days because he missed the train going back to Liverpool and his ship won't be sailing for some time." He looked at her expecting a reply, but there wasn't one. "We haven't any accommodation at the Norwegian Church, so as you are one of the few ladies who volunteered your home and services, perhaps you will take Roger in, is that all right, Mrs Jenkins?" It seemed to Hannah as if the priest was begging and about to cry. "Please Mrs Jenkins, the weather is atrocious, it'll be dark in half an hour and there isn't anyone else that I can ask: please will you take him in?"

"Of course, vicar, of course!" She said, looking at the ginger-haired visitor, her guest. She motioned to him, inviting him in. The man had been standing there gaping in amazement at the conversation taking place between the old lady and the vicar. He didn't understood one word of the Welsh language they spoke and was almost surprised when she said in South Wales accented English:

"Please come in, Mr?"

"Williams," he replied. "Roger Williams. Thank you very much Missis, thank you." He squeezed past her into the tiny parlour. "What a nice house you've got Missis: I hope I won't take up much of your time."

He took off his seaman's cap, revealing a crop of auburn hair, tied at the back in a short pigtail. He had long sideburns the same colour as his hair, pink-rimmed eyes and very pale skin, almost albino. He wore a seaman's thick knitted jersey, grey sealskin trousers and seamen's boots. He wasn't particularly tall, about five foot seven inches, but to Hannah he looked like a giant. He looked down at Hannah and grinned. It was meant to be a friendly smile; he was trying not to intimidate her, but it didn't quite come out the way it should.

Hannah was a little surprised at his appearance, but tried to return his smile with a meek little smile of her own and a nod of acknowledgement.

The priest continued, thanking her in Welsh, and finally said, "The Norwegian Church will pay for his food and room: will two shillings and six pence be enough for each day? You must say if it isn't going to be enough; you will, won't you Mrs Jenkins?" With that he took her tiny hand and pressed half a crown into it. "'Bye now, see you both tomorrow, all right?" With that he turned and walked off quickly towards the docks clutching his hat to his head to prevent it blowing away in the gusts of wind. As he walked his huge black cloak billowed out around him, as if the wind and rain was trying to drag it from his hunched-up scrawny shoulders. He had to grasp it to his body with his free hand to prevent it being torn away.

Williams watched Hannah as she closed the front door.

"Cup of tea, Mr Williams?" she asked.

He nodded, "Very kind of you, Missis; no sugar, just a touch of milk, please!"

"I can make you something to eat as well; it's almost my supper time anyway. Would a boiled ham sandwich be all right tonight? I don't have too much else in at the moment, because I wasn't expecting visitors this week." She was so happy to speak to someone, she didn't give him a chance to answer. "Is that all right, Mr Williams? Good."

It was years since she had spoken to someone other than in her natural language. She found it difficult to translate what she needed to say into English. There were very few occasions when she needed to speak anything but her own language, Welsh. Sometimes a foreigner would come to the Norwegian Church and he would only know a few words of English and that would make it difficult for her to converse with the stranger as well. But she said to herself, "We always managed, didn't we?"

Then to Williams: "That's right, make your self comfortable, I won't be long with the tea!" With that she disappeared into her little kitchen.

He nodded and took a seat on the leather sofa, pulling one of the patchwork cushions in behind his back. He hadn't felt as relaxed and comfortable in years. "So I might as well make the most of it, 'cause I won't get another chance like this for a long time."

The Reverend Thomas didn't go back to Hannah's house for two days. When he did on the third day, there was no answer to his knocking on the door, front or back. The curtains were drawn and as he had arrived early at about eight-thirty in the morning, he assumed that Hannah had either gone shopping or perhaps was still in bed, which he doubted, because he knew that she was an early riser and was often over at the Norwegian Church at six or seven o'clock in the morning, when she helped out. She would serve breakfast to those sailors who had stopped overnight, because most of them would have to get back to their ships, to sail on an early tide. No one had seen her at the church and when Reverend Thomas went back to her house and asked her neighbours they all replied that they hadn't seen her for a couple of days either. The Reverend Thomas started to worry. There was no sign of a disturbance, even when he looked through the front room window between a gap in the curtains which hadn't been quite fully drawn. What actually did arouse his suspicions and worry him a little were the flowers scattered on the floor and table. The vase which had held them was still upright on the centre of the table, but not in the centre of the table-cloth.

Thomas said to the woman standing near him, "You know, Mrs Phillips, Hannah Jenkins would never have left those flowers lying around like that! Have a look will you?"

Mrs Phillips did as she was asked then turned and nodded, saying, "I think you're right, Mr Thomas, something is wrong!"   "You had best try and get in there, hadn't you. Tell you what, old Elsie over the road usually looks after a spare key for some of us, she might have one for Hannah. Shall I go and ask?"

"Yes please," Thomas replied. "Quick as you can, eh?"

Mrs Phillips was back in less than two minutes, a big brass key dangling from a short piece of cord. With a sharp "Thanks", Thomas snatched the key from her hand and pushed it into the keyhole of the solid oak door. He pushed it open slowly, apprehension beginning to creep in, hoping against hope that he wouldn't find what he was expecting to find. As he moved forward into the front room he could see no signs of movement anywhere, neither was there a sound coming from anywhere in the house. He heard a rasping sound which seemed to come from just in front of him. He stopped as the hair at the back of his head seemed to curl and a cold shiver ran from the top of his head right down his back. Fear almost stopped him in his tracks.

Then he realised, it was his own heavy breathing that caused the rasping sound. He cursed himself quietly for being so stupid, hoping that Mrs Phillips, who was directly behind him, hadn't heard him. He asked Mrs Phillips to stay by the front door as he went from room to room looking for some sign of Hannah.

The parlour, kitchen and both bedrooms were empty. He went into the back yard, the privy toilet and coal shed; nothing! She must have gone to town or was visiting a friend although no one had noticed her during the last couple of days. It was unusual, but she didn't have to tell anyone everything. He and Mrs Phillips left the house, the door was locked and the key handed back to old Elsie.

"If anyone sees her please inform me at the church, or any of the clergy there, and if she isn't seen by tomorrow evening I would be most grateful if someone would leave a message for me at the Norwegian Church, please."

He nodded to the people who had come to see what the disturbance was about, pulled his cloak around him and walked down the road towards the docks. Then the Reverend Thomas realised he hadn't done that which he had meant to do when he went to the house in the first place. He hadn't informed Williams that his ship would be sailing on the early morning tide the next day. He began to wonder what had happened to Williams. He looked the sort that could find his own way around; perhaps he'd gone back to his ship anyway so there shouldn't be any need to worry about him. "Mrs Jenkins should be my main concern," he said to himself, as he entered the King's Dock Road.

During all of that day and the next, the Reverend Thomas and Hannah's neighbours made enquires about her, asking whether anyone at all had seen her in the district or knew if she had gone to visit friends or relations. Some of her many friends began to search the back yards of the rows of terraced houses and the disused buildings that dotted the area. A few thought of going to the Docks Management, to ask if a search could be organized in and around the area of the Norwegian Church. They were eventually dissuaded after the vicar told them that the police had been informed of her disappearance.

The police inspector assigned to the case told the Reverend Thomas that he would put as many men as he could spare for the next day or two to search the immediate area and the docks.

After the first two hours the search was brought to a halt. Hannah had been found. She had been in her house all the time, killed by an unknown intruder it was first thought. Her tiny body had been stuffed into the built-in wardrobe in her bedroom and covered with the old copies of the Daily Post. It was somewhere the Reverend Thomas had failed to look.

The local policeman who had actually found her and knew her quite well told her friends later it looked as if she'd just gone to sleep. But he of course knew she hadn't. There were no signs of violence or any injury at all. It didn't look as though she had suffered much pain, if any. But who had covered her with the newspapers? Those were his first thoughts.

Near her, also covered by the newspapers, were a large empty black tin box and three large pottery jars, the type used for bottling fruit, etcetera. There were no signs of disturbance at all. The detectives and the newly formed forensic science section were called in. There wasn't a great deal of evidence at the scene but these new experts found it: two sets of fingerprints on the tin box and jars, the same on the door handles throughout the house and a folded leather belt in the spare bedroom, which had been left by the bed. There were prints all over the house in fact, on almost all the cupboard door handles and on the vase on the table in the parlour. Other fingerprints were found, but they belonged to the vicar, Mrs Phillips and the policeman who had been first on the scene. Because of the dust-free and highly polished furniture, all the fingerprints were highly visible, most on the furniture could be seen quite clearly with the naked eye.

When Hannah was examined by a pathologist with the detective in charge of the case, Inspector Peter Marshall, looking on, it was found that the old lady had been struck a blow with some hard object to the base of the cranium – the skull – which had broken the medulla – that portion of the spinal cord which is contained inside the cranium. (In the medulla are the nerve centres which govern respiration and the action of the heart.) The pathologist said that the shape and the weight of the object used when striking Hannah could quite easily have been a hard knuckled fist or the side of the hand striking a blow to the back of the neck. There was some bruising with a small cross-like mark showing on the bruise, but nothing to show Hannah had been hit with anything like a club, although a very solid hard object had been used to hit her.

The pathologist Dr Martin Atherton's report read:

After examining the body and after making a diligent study of the cranium and the vertebrae at the base of the cranium, I suspect Hannah Jenkins was hit in the back of the neck, at the base of the skull, with an object something similar to the side of a hand or a fist. The blow fractured her skull, at her age being thinner than the norm, damaged the medulla, causing shock, unconsciousness and then heart failure. If the lady hadn't died almost immediately, she most certainly would have been suffocated by the weight of the newspapers covering her head and body. The cross-like mark on the bruise looked as though it was caused by a small object, perhaps a ring, with a raised cross at its centre, probably worn by her assailant. There were no other signs of assault on her person. In my opinion she was killed by a blow to the back of the cranium, which in turn caused heart failure.

The time of death was between 11pm on the 8th September and 2am on the 9th September 1913.

Signed: Martin Atherton, Pathologist, Swansea Pathology Department, 13th September 1913.

"Thank you, doctor!" Inspector Marshall, who had been watching the examination closely and read the final report, turned to his assistant, Detective Constable Carpenter, "Come on, let's go and find the miserable bastard who did this." Marshall wasn't known for letting his feelings be known. But this murder was a bit too vicious, even for his stony temperament. When they got back to Myers Street in St Thomas, a forensic team member approached Marshall.

"I think we may have something for you to go on, Inspector." He showed the Inspector three or four strands of hair. "These were found on her dressing gown sleeve and there are some on a pillow on that bed; they look the same, a reddish colour, but we'll be able to tell you more when we get them under a microscope, all right, Inspector?"

"Yes, fine. Be as quick as you can will you? I've got a feeling we haven't got much time."

"OK, Peter, as soon as possible."

"Anything else?" Marshall glared at the technician, as if to say, "Don't get too familiar with me laddie!"

But the man continued, not seeming to notice Marshall's anger, "We've found a few coins in the cupboard where the old lady was hidden." He hesitated for a second.

"Come on, what's so important, Alan? Get on with it. I'm guessing I don't have a lot of time, the evil bastard has had too long a start on us, OK?"

Alan ignored Marshall's impatience. "Listen, there are eleven coins, nearly all silver, there are a couple of copper ones as well, and three brand new, never been in circulation, gold sovereigns, only minted this year. And there are two distinct fingerprints on one of them as well. One I can see already, is the lady's, the other looks like a thumb print, much larger than hers; it almost covers the face of the coin."

Marshall became very calm, and to Alan, ice cool, the simmering anger melting away. "Thanks Alan, thanks! Show me exactly where they were, will you?"

Alan showed him the jar where the sovereigns had been found and the places under the newspapers where the remainder of the coins had been discovered. "Can I give you my assessment at this time?" Marshall nodded his consent.

Alan's theory was that Hannah Jenkins had let the killer or killers into the house because she knew the visitor and invited the person or persons into the parlour. Perhaps she had been asked about money and having refused to answer her assailant, turned away towards the dining table. At that point she had been attacked and fallen forward on to the table, knocking the vase of flowers over. Her hand prints could be seen starting at the edge of the table and sliding forward under the edge of the table cloth. The killer's reaction was to pick up the empty vase and put it back in its original central position on the table leaving his fingerprints on the vase and table as he righted it and at the same time trying to prevent Hannah's unexpected weight tipping the table right over. Realising the predicament he or she was in and that Hannah might be dead, the assailant decided to hide the body in case someone called. Without thinking he left the flowers where they had fallen. There was no place in the kitchen or parlour to hide the body, so her assailant took her upstairs, found the cupboard half full of the newspapers and decided to hide Hannah's body there. It was unlikely that a woman would have been strong enough to carry the body up the stairs, even if she could hit hard enough to knock Hannah unconscious. Whilst the assailant was hiding Hannah in the spare room cupboard he found what Alan suspected were her life savings, but he may have been in a hurry and left some of the coins. If there had been more gold sovereigns, the robber-killer, whoever he was, would have to be very careful where he was going to spend the money. The people in this area aren't very wealthy.

"And that goes for the likes of us as well, Inspector," Alan smiled.

"Anyone who has spent a gold sovereign or sovereigns in the last two or three days is suspect," Inspector Marshall said to his waiting team of detectives. "You know who and what we're looking for, so let's get on with it."

It had to be a man, thought the inspector; this was too callous for a woman to do.

After Alan had finished his theory, Marshall thanked him and then went downstairs to the parlour and found Constable Carpenter. Marshall thought that too much of a mouthful – Constable Carpenter this, Constable Carpenter that – so Marshall called his favourite skivvy 'CC'.

"CC, what've we got?" he said. "Any witnesses?"

CC nodded, "Yes sir, half a dozen but no one seems to have much to say; a couple of them have made statements, saying they saw her in the street and spoke to her. That was a couple of days ago but no one since. There is one that sounds much more interesting and it's possible he may have introduced the killer to Mrs Jenkins; the Reverend Thomas, a local parish priest. He knows, I mean knew, Mrs Jenkins very well, he says!"

"You've taken statements from everyone, haven't you?" Marshall said.

"Yes sir, all except the Reverend Thomas. I thought perhaps you should hear him out first, sir."

"Well done, CC: all right, show him in. If he's got a lead we'll have to get it out of him as soon as possible." When the priest came into the parlour and sat at the table as he had been with Hannah just that few days ago, his nerves got the better of him and he started to shake visibly.

Marshall put his hand on the vicar's arm. "Relax sir, take it easy, you'll be all right; would you like a drink of water? CC, would you get the Reverend Thomas a glass of water – or a cup of tea?" he nodded at the priest.

Reverend Thomas shook his head and said sadly, "No thank you. I'm sorry, Inspector, I am mortified. I think this is maybe all my doing; perhaps it's my fault that this tragedy has happened. I may well have introduced Hannah to her killer. I'm so sorry!"

"Look, sir, whatever you did or whoever you introduced to the deceased, I am sure what followed wasn't your fault. Could you please tell me what happened at the time you introduced this person to Mrs Jenkins. To start with, was it someone you knew? Was it a man or woman? Could you describe the person fully? You know, facial features, hair, eyes, the person's height and weight – roughly – please! Give us as much detail as possible." The inspector was very careful not to indicate whether the person was a man or woman. He wanted to hear the description from the priest's own mouth, so that a defence lawyer couldn't try to tip the balance in favour of the killer, by upsetting the evidence of any prosecution witness.

Slowly Reverend Thomas described the day he took a man he knew as Roger Williams, who he thought to be a seaman stranded at the docks, to Mrs Jenkins' home. He went on to say how he had persuaded Mrs Jenkins to take Williams in as a lodger for one or two nights. The priest then described Williams as about five feet seven inches tall, pale skinned with pink-rimmed eyes, reddish hair tied at the back in a short pigtail and long sideburns He wore a leather seaman's cap and black seaman's jersey. He didn't wear any sort of coat even though it was quite cold and raining. He carried a green duffle bag for whatever belongings he owned or needed. The only sort of jewellery he wore was a thick silver or gold ring, with some sort of cross stamped or printed on it. Then he added he had left the man in Mrs Jenkins' capable hands and went home. No! He hadn't thought there would be any danger to Mrs Jenkins. No! He never could imagine this horror happening in this community. Then he broke down sobbing and went on to his knees and started to pray for forgiveness and Hannah's soul.

The inspector nodded to CC and to the priest, "Take him out of here, get him home, we'll visit him when he feels a bit better." He turned to a uniformed police sergeant who had been standing nearby. "Did you hear all of that?"

The sergeant replied, "Yes sir, every word. I've taken note of it."

"Good. Get your men and any others you can scrounge and find the bastard before he does get away. Start with any ship that is docked at this time; find out if any ship has sailed on this morning's tide and which ship sailed yesterday, if any. Then we'll search from the sea area back to this place. If we do it the other way round he'll probable slip the net. Mind you, he may have made a run for it already on those early ships. There's a lot to get on with so please get going. Oh! and ask someone to get hold of CC and send him to me at the Norwegian Church as soon as possible."

Within two hours Williams was identified by other seamen and stevedores, and the police searchers were directed towards a small cargo ship that was just slipping her moorings. A police launch blocked the ship's exit from King's Dock and a search party boarded her. After an hour a uniformed policeman found Williams hiding in a paint locker. The ship's captain said the man had offered to work his passage back to Liverpool. As the captain needed a deckhand he signed Williams on just before the ship was due to sail. Williams, when he was asked about his lodgings at Myers Street, was all bluster and denial, claiming he'd never been to that street.

"I never 'eard of it, mate!" he said to CC, who by that time had met up with the arresting constable on King's Dock.

"I went an' stayed at that Norwegian Church in the rest rooms. I 'ad a bed there for two nights an' I've got people 'oo can prove it, too."

He was then asked why he was hiding in the ship's paint locker. "I fought the rozzers was after me, after that fight I 'ad last night."

"What fight?"

"I don't 'ave to tell you if'n you don't know. Anyways, I ain't telling any you coppers nofing."

He was taken back to Myers Street and into Hannah's house, where Inspector Marshall was there, holding out his hand as if to greet him. He took Williams into the kitchen and shut the parlour door. Turning towards Williams he punched him so hard in the stomach that Williams went down clutching his middle as though he'd been shot.

"Hello, Mr Williams, how do you do? I'm Detective Inspector Marshall and I don't shake hands with murdering bastards, especially with lying, murdering bastards like you! Now, why did you kill poor old Mrs Jenkins?" He paused waiting for an answer. "Was it because she didn't feed you properly or was it because she caught you stealing something?"

"I didn't kill no one, I dosn't know what you be talkin' about, guv."

"Don't you guv me, it's Mr Marshall to you. Now, where's the stuff you pinched from her? Tell me now before I beat the hell out of you and then have you searched, or I can make things easier for you if you tell me, then you won't have any more pain. Understand? Otherwise, everything will be very hard and nasty. Nor will you like what my men can do to you and get away with. Now, are going to talk?"

Still clutching his stomach, Williams gasped out, "No chance, I ain't done anyfink wrong, guv!"

Marshall slapped Williams hard across the face. "Guv me again and it'll be the last time you call me it, understand?"

"Sure boss, I get it, OK, OK!" He raised his hand to protect his head from further blows. None came. There was a tap on the parlour door; CC stepped into the room.

"Everything OK, sir?" he asked.

"Fine, fine. Has his duffle been found? Yes? Good! While you're here, strip search him before we take him to the station, it'll save time and I don't want him getting rid of anything before we get him there."

Williams said "Eh! You're not supposed to do that: I 'aven't done nofing, I told you."

"And I'm supposed to do what I need to, to find a killer of old ladies, that's what I'm doing, all right? Get on with it, CC. I'll send in another man in case this bastard gives you any trouble."

After the search, Williams was taken to the police station and booked in, along with the contents of his duffle bag and clothes. He was put in a cell and told by the station sergeant to strip.

"Wha' for? I already done that once; I ain't goin' to, OK?"

"Joe!" the sergeant called to another officer. "This little man is being obnoxious and bloody awkward, come and give me a hand, I can't hang around waiting for him to do as he's told."

When Williams saw the size of the constable who had entered the cell, he rapidly undressed and threw each article at the sergeant, swearing and cursing at the bloody English police. Joe stepped forward again clenching a huge fist.

"English! English is it boyo? What's the matter with you, are you really as stupid as you look? You're in Wales, boyo! God's own country, and this is Swansea nick."

When his clothes had been taken away, Williams complained bitterly, "Eh! what you doin'?" He picked up the boiler suit that had been thrown to him. "I ain't wearin' this rubbish. Give us back me cloaves: you can't do this, it tain't right, boss."

A week later an inquest took place at Swansea Coroner's Court, but despite all the witnesses and the weight of evidence presented by the inspector and his team, the verdict was an open one.

The verdict by the coroner was that Mrs Hannah Jenkins died of a blow to the cranium, and thence the medulla, the trauma causing shock and heart failure.

The coroner continued: "The blow or a fall, neither of which can be absolutely verified as being attributed to an assailant, probably happened between twenty-four and forty-eight hours before her body was found. Therefore I believe an open verdict is a verdict that will allow the police to continue with their investigations as there is sufficient reason to believe that the late Mrs Hannah Jenkins may have been assaulted before she died. Until the facts can be ascertained, an open verdict will remain for the foreseeable future."

As Inspector Marshall and Constable Carpenter left the court, Marshall said, "Well at least we've got the bugger for robbing her, even if we can't find the rest of the money, of which, in my opinion, there most definitely was a lot more. He," referring to Williams, "had been found to have a gold sovereign hidden in the base of his duffle bag. He must have stashed it away to pick up later, in case he got caught with the rest of the money. Maybe even given it to one of his no-good mates to look after. On second thoughts, I doubt very much if he'd do that, as the old saying goes: 'Don't trust a thieving liar or a mate!'. So I wonder where he's got his hidy hole? It must be on or near the docks somewhere, because his sort would never wander far away from his stash."

"Do you think it's still in the house, sir?" CC asked, trying hard to be helpful.

"Shouldn't reckon so, CC. How would he get back to it? Besides the house has been pretty well taken apart; there wouldn't be many places they haven't searched."

"It's still a possibility though, sir?"

"By the way, CC, how long have you been in this detective game? A year or two perhaps?"

"Oh no, sir, just four months. I'm still waiting for my exam results."

"For crying out loud, what the hell are you doing out here?" Marshall's vicious streak reared its ugly head. "You should be in the office. I was told it was your detective sergeant's exam results you were waiting for. Go on, get back to the station and send out someone with a few years' experience and hopefully three stripes on his arm."

CC left at a run. The only thing that saved him from complete humiliation was that no one else was close enough to hear what Marshall had said. As he walked back to the police station he realised that Marshall's patience was just about to come to an end, especially as William's refused to confess or even speak, no matter what threats were made against him by Marshall.

It was 7th May 1914, the fifth day of the trial of one, Roger Gifford, for the Assault and Robbery of Hannah Jenkins.

Courtroom 3 at Swansea Crown Court was extremely large, very well lit and airy. Bright sunlight shone through the windows set high up near the ceiling all along one side of the room. The walls of the room below the windows were in deep shadow. The shafts of sunlight streaming across the room showed millions of particles of dust disturbed by the people milling about in the well of the courtroom.

Gradually the people involved in the duties of the court took their places in the seats of the court allocated to them, prosecution and defence barristers in the front rows, their solicitors directly behind them with their clerks and helpers. All were in their courtroom finery, which showed their position and status in court. The barristers were in black gowns and white bow ties or cravats and chalked wigs. Ushers in their black gowns trying to use what little authority they thought they had by demanding of the spectators, reporters, and even prosecution and defence teams, "Silence in court".

The solitary defendant, sitting in the dock flanked by two prison warders from Swansea Prison, both of whom seemed more concerned at the amount of verbal abuse being directed at the prisoner from the gallery behind them, than he himself was. He completely ignored the hostile, derisory, threatening and abusive remarks directed at him. The spectators, some of whom had been witnesses and had given evidence against him, sat or stood in the spectators' gallery which wasn't much more than fifteen feet behind and above the dock that he was sitting in. He just sat there staring straight at the judge's rostrum, trying to ignore the jibes and threats coming from the people behind him. There was a ghost of a smile on his thin lips, as if everything was a huge joke. It seemed to everyone who watched him that he wasn't the slightest bit interested in what was happening around him.

As ten o'clock on the morning of the fifth day of the trial approached, the noise in the court settled to a hum of quiet voices, the barristers straightened their wigs and capes and coughed loudly trying to clear their throats. The senior usher moved to a door situated behind a large, decorative, antique looking, leather chair, which was set exactly in the centre of the rostrum, in front of the now completely attentive crowded courtroom.

The door opened and a tall figure entered the room.

"All rise," the senior usher called loudly.

Complete silence swept through Number 3 Court.

The judge, an imposing figure, was dressed in long red robes, black sash and a cummerbund. He also wore a long white wig and pince-nez, perched on his bulbous red-tinged nose. He stood in front of his chair, made a slight bow to the legal representatives and sat down. They in turn bowed to the judge and took their places on the familiar hard wooden benches that were a feature of the old style courtrooms.

Mr Evan James-Roberts QC, the judge, then nodded to the Clerk of the Court who was standing facing him.

"Please ask the jury to come in."

The clerk, giving a slight bow, turned and nodded to an usher standing close to a door at the side of the room, the jury room. The usher tapped on the door and opened it, beckoning to someone just inside the entrance. A nervous looking young man entered the court and walked quickly to a seat on the front bench of the two allocated to the jury. He sat down facing the judge but looking at the floor. He was followed in quickly by eleven other men, nearly all quite young and looking shame-faced, none looking towards the judge or the defendant who was looking defiantly at them, all except one older man, in his late fifties, who had entered the courtroom last and sat on the end of the front bench. He sat upright staring across the courtroom at the assembled reporters, as if trying to dissociate himself from the rest of the jury.

The judge again nodded to the clerk of the court, who turned to the jury and said, "Have you elected a foreman to represent you?"

The young man who had been first to enter the court stood up and replied: "Yes, your honour, I am the foreman!" He looked like a frightened child, who was about to receive a hiding. He was shaking visibly and he was dreading the thought of delivering the jury's verdict.

The clerk of the court turned towards the defendant, who had been watching the foreman with great interest, seeing him shaking and hearing the slight panic in his voice. "Will the accused please stand?" It was more of an order than a request. It didn't matter either way, because one of the prison warders sitting next to the prisoner stood up and gave the man a hard nudge in the ribs.

"Come on, boyo, on your feet!" he hissed.

The prisoner stood up slowly, gave the warder a dirty look and whispered back at him, "Don't have to dig me so hard, Mr Evans. I'll have a bruise there for weeks now!"

"There'll be more of them when I get you back to the nick, so keep quiet and pay attention. All right?"

Turning back to the jury and addressing the foreman, the clerk said. "Have you reached a verdict on the first charge, breaking and entering into the house at 21 Myers Street, St. Thomas, Swansea, on which you are all agreed?"

The foreman facing the judge replied, "No, your honour, we are not all agreed," hoping it was the best way to address the judge.

At that point the judge intervened, "I will accept a majority verdict; have you reached a verdict on which the majority of the jury agree?"

"Yes, your honour."

"How many of you agree?"

"Eleven, your honour."

"All right, Mr Foreman, what is the verdict on the first charge?"

"Not guilty, your honour!"

"That is a majority verdict of the jury?"

"Yes, sir."

The watching crowd in the gallery were too stunned with disbelief to make any protest. But there were many angry faces turned towards the jury, waiting for the next verdict.

The change of tone in Judge James-Roberts' voice registered surprise and disapproval, if not disbelief, even though the he tried hard to maintain his usual equilibrium. The foreman was by now trying desperately hard not to look at the judge, who was looking with some distaste at the jury. The clerk, also looking surprised, was not his usual competent self.

Roberts nodded to the clerk of the court. "Continue with the remainder of the charges, please."

"On the second charge of stealing property and money from that address, guilty or not guilty?"

"Not guilty, sir!"

"Is that the verdict of you all?"

"No, sir, the same majority decision."

"On the charge of assaulting the occupant of that address?"

"Not guilty, sir!"

"A majority decision?"

"Yes, sir."

The jury foreman looked defiantly along the row of jurors, at the older man sitting at the end of the bench. The man gazed at the window across the courtroom, watching the white clouds drift past across blue skies.

The defendant turned towards the gallery, his back towards the judge and gave the thumbs-up to his watching supporters. He could feel the simmering anger from those who had reason to think him guilty of the crimes he had been charged with. He was smiling and started to laugh, thinking it was a huge joke.

A woman in the gallery shouted at the judge, "You can't allow this, he's as guilty as sin!"

Another shouted, "We'll get you for this, you scum, you're finished Gifford, you'll see!"

The judge banged his gavel to silence the growing sound of angry voices and dissent. "Mr Gifford, this is a court of law, my court! There is a law of Contempt of Court, a charge which I shall bring against you or your supporters or for that matter anyone else who continues to disrupt the proceedings of this court. This is not a theatre for you to use for your self-gratification."

The murmurs of protest continued and the ushers went across to those in the gallery calling out "Quiet!" several times before the judge used his gavel again. The ushers' contempt showed as they turned their backs on the people in the gallery who had showed utter disregard for the old lady, whose life had been devastated by the brute standing in the dock.

The judge looked directly at the now smirking, defiant, defendant and said: "Mr Gifford, it seems as though the jury did not believe the evidence as presented by the prosecution counsel, but I and many other observers may have different views." Then the judge went on. "The counsel for the prosecution cannot appeal against this jury's decision but there is no doubt that in the future you will be appearing before other juries of our legal system and it is more than likely the verdicts on the charges that will be brought will be different to those verdicts brought in today, much to the cost of our innocent population. Mr Gifford, you are free to go!"

Judge James-Roberts finally turned to the jury. "I congratulate the person who did make the correct analysis of the evidence and stuck by his decision. To the remainder of you, you will not be required for jury service ever again. A report of this trial will be sent to the police and an investigation may take place. You are formally discharged."

Turning to the Clerk of the Court, he said, "Go and pay them their pieces of silver, it seems to me they deserve it."

With that he stood up and bowed to the court, with an usher's voice echoing in his ears: "All rise!"

Dai Jones and Jenkins stood and watched the crowd of spectators leave the gallery. Some were cheering Gifford, others were threatening to tear him limb from limb if they ever got the chance. Then Gifford was ushered by the prison warders down to the cells to collect his belongings and property, before being formally discharged from the authority of the prison service.

Jenkins was devastated. Neither he nor Dai Jones knew anything of the robbery and murder of Hannah Jenkins. They had only been told of it the day before by Robert Evans, Jenkins' police constable friend. As Evans didn't usually work in Swansea, he only heard of the trial through the police grapevine. He was just as shocked and upset by the crime against someone he had known all those years before, even more so that it had been committed against the mother of one of his old friends.

"What the hell were those blokes thinking of? Even without hearing and seeing all the evidence, it was pretty obvious Gifford was guilty as sin. You can tell almost by the reaction of the people in the gallery that the verdict was absolutely wrong," he whispered to Dai as they watched the jury file out of court.

Jenkins and Dai Jones had only arrived at Swansea Crown Court in the morning two days before. It was then they heard the prosecution and defence counsellors making their final submissions and Judge James-Roberts giving his summing up of the evidence and the case as a whole.

It was a cut and dried case, a police sergeant had told them, as they went into court to watch the case the day before.

They had heard enough from the Reverend Ivor Thomas, Police Inspector Marshall and one or two of Hannah's neighbours to convince them that the man in the dock, who had been charged with the offences against Jenkins' mother, was as guilty as sin.

"But why hadn't he been charged with murder?" Jenkins asked.

The inspector said that at the time of the assault and the death of Mrs Jenkins and during the months after his arrest Williams insisted his name was Roger Gifford and had refused to confess to anything. Although there were fingerprints on the coins found in the house and hair on the sleeve of his coat, and his fingerprints all over the rest of the house, there was nothing at all to prove he had actually assaulted her or robbed her. He didn't wear any rings when he was arrested or any other jewellery. His defending barrister even had the audacity to say Hannah Jenkins had given Gifford the gold sovereign and he had only helped her count the coppers when she asked him because she had dropped some just before going shopping one morning. He had no idea where she kept her savings. Except for the sovereign in his bag, which he admitted Hannah Jenkins had lent him for the train fare back to Liverpool, and the fact he refused to admit anything, the jury thought the evidence was fairly weak. As he had stayed in the house for a day or two, his fingerprints were bound to be there. There was nothing of any value in his property or clothing, except the sovereign.

Gifford had more of a smirk than a smile on his face when he arrived at the office below the court. The senior warder gave Gifford his personal documents, a bus warrant and some cash he had earned whilst working as a cleaner on the Swansea prison remand wing.

"How'my goin' to git back to the nick then, boss?" The warder stared back at him. "I got to pick my cloves an stuff up from there, an' it won't be safe fer me to walk the streets by meself, will it? An' I never expectid to be out so quick, did I?"

Smirking inwardly to himself at the jury's decision, he thought, "What a result! Fought I was goin' to git twenty years at least ."

The warder glared at him and said, "Sign here, if you can write, and get the bloody hell out of here. You're nothing to do with us anymore. It's only a fifteen minute walk to the nick. If that's too much for you, your solicitor said if you wait at the back entrance to the cells he'll give you a lift there, OK? I've just had a message from the nick as well; someone will pick you up from the there when you've collected your gear. Or you can walk to the bus station and use the bus warrant: your choice."

"Fanks, boss." Gifford held out his hand, as if he wanted to shake hands with the warder.

"Get stuffed. Let the shit out, John, get him out of my sight." He turned his back to Gifford and continued playing cards, Beenie, with the other warders.

Gifford stepped through the door into the vehicle unloading area, which was below ground level at the back of the court building. His solicitor was standing next to an expensive looking car. There was no one else around. He walked to the car and sat in the back seat, the solicitor closing the door after him.

"So this is where all the gazzoma goes, eh? Keepin' you well off, eh, an' in the pink. Bloody 'ell I could do wive a bit of this, mate!"

The solicitor ignored Gifford's sarcasm and drove to the prison, watched Gifford knock on the wicket gate, and drove off. Hoping he would never have the misfortune of seeing the lucky, evil cretin again.

A few minutes later the wicket gate in the main door of the prison opened and Gifford reappeared, carrying a large brown paper bag, which contained some articles of clothing and a few personal possessions.

He turned to the prison warder who was standing by the wicket gate. "I 'ope I won't be seein' you agin then, boss. Fanks for the room; I'd recommen' it to my mates but it stinks, OK?"

"Not as much as you, you evil sod," the officer replied. "You'll be back quicker than you can blink and I'll be here to see you through reception." With that the warder shut the door, blocking any more stupid comments from the now ex-prisoner.

Gifford turned and saw about a dozen people waiting a few yards away from the prison entrance. Some he knew and some he didn't recognise. They were nearly all smiling, laughing and clapping as they came forward to welcome him out of prison, some slapping him on the back and shaking his hand, and a couple of women, although they thought him the ugliest bloke on earth, came forward and kissed him on the lips.

What they were all so pleased about was that he had beaten the system and the police. The police at the time, because of their reputation with the miners' strikes and incidents during the last few years, were thought of as bullies and government lackeys who would never be trusted again. So no matter how evil the crime committed, as long as it was outside the people's own local parish, it didn't matter. If the accused person or even known criminal beat the police at their own game, that was OK. It didn't matter that someone had been robbed and assaulted; none of his friends or supporters cared about the victim. It was the criminal code. No grassing on your mates, no confessions, just beat the system and the police as often as possible, because that way the cowards and crooks thought they would have the upper hand over 'bent' police.

As the crowd walked away from the prison gates, one of Gifford's friends, Jacko, said, "It's OK mate, we'll get a taxi to take you to the docks, it'll be waiting around the corner next to the Paxton Pub. We can all have a good drink there and then we'll take you to the docks; there's a couple of tramp steamers leaving tonight on the late tide. We've got a chance of getting you a berth. All right?"

Gifford just nodded. He was a bit overwhelmed by the greeting he'd received. "I'll be glad to git the first pint down me," he replied. "I'm gaspin' mate, been lookin' forward to this for a long time."

They were walking towards the pub on the corner of Paxton Street, when without warning, two men in smart suits and bowler hats came out of the pub and stopped directly in front of Gifford. Each man was at least six feet three inches tall and at the same time as they stopped in front of Gifford, produced police warrant cards.

"Mr Roger Williams?" the senior policeman asked. He continued without giving Gifford a chance to reply, "Known as Alan Robert Williams?" Gifford shook his head. "Known as Roger Alan Gifford, you are under arrest for the murder of Hannah Jenkins. Anything you say will be used in evidence against you!" He took out a set of handcuffs.

Most of the small crowd hadn't heard what the policeman had been saying but when they saw the handcuffs they started to push and crowd forward shouting and cursing, pushing the policemen back against the pub wall.

Seizing his chance, Gifford, now Williams, ran back the way he had come, back past the prison gates and along Oystermouth Road, the sea front road, towards the Glamorgan Arms.

Several men including prison guards and policemen came out of that pub after a lunch time drink, preparing to go back to work.

Police Constable Robert Evans from Glais was amongst them. Jenkins and Dai Jones had asked Robert to have a drink with them after the trial, to thank him for all the help he had given Jenkins by getting Police Inspector Marshall to explain the case against Gifford.

Robert had also introduced him to the Reverend Thomas and a few of Jenkins' mother's neighbours.

As they left the pub they took their leave of Robert, and told him that they would see him when he got home, because Robert was about to go back on duty with his colleagues. They heard a shout from the direction of the Swansea Jack pub, "Stop him, Stop him!"

Williams had a fifty yard start on the two policemen who were chasing him. He was running close to the prison wall towards the Glamorgan Arms. Williams swerved towards the edge of the pavement as several policemen and prison staff tried to block his way. Robert Evans immediately recognized him as the man who had got away with the assault and robbery of Hannah Jenkins: he had been at Swansea Crown Court on another case and heard the emotional protests. He made a dive at Gifford, missed, but forced him further towards the road. Gifford who, whilst running, was watching the men and especially Robert Evans, whose clutching hands slid down his legs and slapped on to the road. He didn't notice the long leg of Jenkins shoot out, until he tripped over it. Stumbling forward and trying to regain his balance, he looked around at his pursuers. He didn't notice the traffic. Only one man was heard to shout a warning, "Look Out!", but it was too late. A local bus travelling along that road smashed into Williams before the bus driver realised the man was there. The five-ton bus wheels crushed the life out of Williams before the bus had come to a stop.

The driver sat behind the wheel shaking with fear. Luckily there were no passengers or there may have been a bigger problem, screaming, crying women perhaps! One of the policemen got to him quickly.

"Don't worry mate, it wasn't your fault. The stupid bastard was trying to run away from policemen who were trying to arrest him."

He tried hard to calm the driver who had began to sob, after realising what had happened. The policeman hailed a taxi and took the driver off to hospital, realising the shock of Gifford's death could kill the driver as well. A number of policemen and prison staff called to the driver words of encouragement as he was being driven away. Then most of them went back to work, not in the least bothered by the man's death.

There wasn't one word of sympathy for Williams or Gifford, only cruel jibes, such as, "Hey Taff! He should have worked on his side-step. Mind you, being English, he wouldn't ever have had a decent one, would he?"

One of Robert's police colleagues said vindictively, "You tackle like that against the screws on Saturday, Bob, and we might as well give them a three point start." His friends and the prison staff laughed at the thought of his missed tackle. Most of them were looking forward to the annual 'friendly' rugby match, Police versus Prison Staff.

Williams's friends, seeing what had happened and who the witnesses were, began to walk quietly away, except one woman who was stupid enough to be heard to say, "Look, the bastards have shot him, he's dead. We're going to have to report them, ain't we?"

Jacko said to a few of his mates, "No they didn't, don't be so stupid, even rozzers ain't that stupid, just leave it, aye. 'Is own daft fault for runnin' that way, ain't it. Let's go, eh? I'm off anyway. See you agin sometime, OK?"

The crowd began disperse with a little extra cajoling from those police that had come from the pub, until all that remained was an ambulance and a couple of policemen and the bus which would have to be lifted by crane off Gifford's remains, when it arrived.

One or two prison guards thought it might be worth another drink, to calm their nerves, so to speak.

"It was a terrible sight," the prison warders told the prison governor.

"I think we must all be in shock!" their spokesman, Will, said.

"Do you all want to go home?" the governor asked.

"No thank you, sir, we'll manage."

The governor continued, "An extra half an hour in the cells won't hurt the prisoners; we'll put it down to staff shortages, all right?"

As the governor left to go to his office, one warder said to the spokesman, "Will! What the hell was that all about, shock and nerves, for Christ sake! I didn't see anything, did you?"

"Listen, George. After this late lunch break it'll be half-past three. Then it's normal tea break. Then at four o'clock it'll be early tea for us, 'cause we're on evening duty, remember. Which means we won't have to start work until five o'clock. So in half an hour when we've finished this cuppa we can go back to the pub until five o'clock. Afterwards, while I'm in the pub, the terrible memories of the accident will come flooding back and I shall have to go sick."

"But Will! What about us?"

"Look George, go sick in turn. Take a week each, the governor won't notice or even know."

"Someone will want the overtime, won't they?"

"Now put a sock in it, I need half an hour's kip before tea break, all thanks to that stupid bugger Gifford or Williams, whatever his name is. The governor is so worried about the rest of the cons kicking off, he's keeping them in their cells, pretending he's doin' it for our health. I *do* believe!"

"Yeh, well then, we'll make the most of it while we can."

"Shall I ask the governor if some of us ought to go to his funeral? It could mean another day off, couldn't it, George?"

"Christ Will, you're an evil, conniving bastard yourself. One day, mate, you'll be behind those bars, not here with us. You ought to stop trying to con everyone, because when you do get found out, the chief warder and the governor will have your guts for garters! I'm off!"

"George, what's the matter with you, can't you take a joke? The bastard's dead, serves him right for murdering that old lady!"

"Maybe, Will, but sometimes you go too far, and it's my job and my family that I worry about, so I ain't going along with you this time, all right? I'm going back to the pub; you coming?"

* * *

Jenkins and Dai Jones had decided to leave Robert Evans to deal with the aftermath of the accident. He knew as much as they did about the incident and who the victim was. So there wasn't any need for them to make a statement; there were plenty of coppers and screws to do that.

But no one knew about the tripping over Jenkins's outstretched leg.

Dai noticed the little smile on Jenkins' face, "What have you been up to, you crafty sod?" he asked.

Jenkins smile got bigger, "Well I did have a hand or a 'leg' in flattening the bugger. I mean, he went for his 'last trip' over my leg. When Robert missed his tackle, I stuck out my leg. I know it wasn't much, but I am pleased we got the murdering bastard. It'll save the police money and time chasing the horrible shite. It's also a bit of revenge for me and my Mum, eh?" Jenkins looked hard at Dai. Something was in the look that his friend had never seen before.

"OK by me, mate!" Dai replied, realising he shouldn't take the matter any further.

When Robert got home to Alltwen that evening, he told his family about the result of the trial and the incident that followed. It was suggested by Mrs Evans that Robert visit Jenkins and Dai Jones at Dai's mother's house, give them the information about the resting place of Hannah and then show Jenkins the house in Myers Street. Perhaps he could collect what items he might like from her possessions, which were all still there. It might help him put his mother's memory to rest, before he returned to Bristol. He could then try to find out what exactly had happened to his sister and her family.

Mrs Evans said to her husband and sons, "Richard must be absolutely devastated at the decision of the jury and by the loss of what must be all of his family. Perhaps showing him our sorrow won't mean anything to him, but to show him our friendship and support and that we are always going to be here for him will help him through these next few months. Robert, you will tell him that, won't you?"

"Of course I will mother, you know I will."

That same evening Robert went back to Glais and met with Dai and Taff Jenkins in the Bridge Pub. He told them that he had arranged with Inspector Marshall for Jenkins to visit Myers Street and see if there were any of his mother's possessions that he would like to keep. If any items were to be left, arrangements could be made for the furniture and Hannah's belongings to be sold or auctioned off and the money be sent on to Jenkins, no matter where he was living at the time. This time, Jenkins was almost overcome by people's kindness and willingness to help, even though he didn't know most of those who were coming forward to give it.

Jenkins accepted the assistance that was offered and decided, after visiting his mother's resting place, he would leave for Bristol as soon as possible.

The next day, after a good breakfast, Jenkins, Dai Jones and Mrs Jones left on an early train for Swansea.

Robert told them that he would meet them at Myers Street, at about ten o'clock, and that he would bring the key, which had been held at Swansea police station since Inspector Marshall took charge of the investigation.

No one had entered the house since the first week of the incident, but the police and neighbours had kept a close watch until a decision was made about who would take possession of it if there were any of Hannah's family who might still be alive and would come forward, otherwise possession of the property, would be returned to the landlord.

Most people, including those involved in investigating the robbery and murder, were pleased to have Jenkins come forward, because until he had, the house and Hannah's belongings would be left in limbo until a judge decided what should happen to everything and that could take many months.

The train stopped at St Thomas and it was only a short walk to Myers Street, which Mrs Jones was very pleased about, as she found great difficulty in keeping up with Dai's quick stride and Jenkins' long one. When they arrived, Robert was waiting for them, looking very smart in his silver buttoned black uniform, with a large silver Glamorgan police crest on his helmet.

He handed Jenkins the front door key and gestured with a small wave of his hand for Jenkins to go first. As Jenkins inserted the key into the keyhole, he felt as though a freezing hand was passing down his spine. The hairs on the nape of his neck seemed to stand up as he turned it slowly in the lock. The lock felt a little stiff at first, but gradually eased as the key was fully turned, until Jenkins heard the click of the lock. He took hold of the door handle and turned it slowly, his anticipation and excitement rising until he thought the top of his head would blow off.

At the moment he pushed the door open, again, he expected to see his mother standing with open arms, welcoming him to her house. When all he saw was a darkened room, he instantly reverted back to his usual stony, pretending, indifferent, self.

He began wondering what the hell had got him into that state, especially as he knew his mother had died six or seven months ago. He walked to the table and pulled out a chair and sat down quickly, knowing that if he didn't, his legs might turn to jelly. Slowly he began to look around the parlour, noticing that his three companions had followed him into the house. Mrs Jones, noticing his normally healthy complexion had gone almost white, laid a comforting hand on his arm. She realised although Jenkins was worried, he would never admit it

"It's all right, Taff, don't fret; things will sort themselves out, you've just had a bit of a shock. Can I get you a drink of water or something, lovely boy?"

"No thanks, Mrs Jones, I'll be fine in a minute, don't worry your head. I've had to put up with worse than this. Just give me a minute while I get my bearings, OK?"

Together they wandered around the house, making a list of everything. Taff Jenkins asked each of his three friends if there was anything they would like to have. He said he would take the mantle clock and a few ornamental pots plus two silver broaches that Mrs Jones found in a box in the sideboard.

After a little encouragement, his friends chose one or two items for themselves. Everything else could be sold or auctioned and the money given to charities. Jenkins said he would go to the Norwegian Church and speak with the pastor and ask him to make the arrangements. It seemed his mother, Hannah, worked for that Church, so therefore perhaps any monies made might be better used for its good causes.

He hadn't been to the spare bedroom where Hannah had been found, but did pay a visit to her bedroom and tried to imagine what she was like in her little house. He had heard from her neighbours, one or two of whom had come to enquire of the visitors, how sprightly and quick she was to grasp a situation and help out or see the best, but not the worst, in people. It was her kindness and willingness to help which had turned out to be her downfall.

Everyone who had known her told him how proud he should be of her, and one lady gave him a small photograph from a newspaper story about the Norwegian Church. His mother was standing arm in arm with her sister at the door of the church. It had been taken by a newspaper photographer just weeks before her sister passed away.

He went into the back yard to use the privy toilet. His mother, he remembered, loved growing her own flowers and there were a few still growing in pots in the back yard. Growing along the walls and roof of the privy and the coal shed were the trailing stars of a blue flowering periwinkle plant. The vine-like trails emitted from three large pots on top but at the back of the privy roof. They ran down the walls and between a two foot space between the privy and the coal shed, making a green and blue blanket on the walls.

Jenkins noticed one of the pots had turned almost on its side. Standing on a large wooden log he reached up with one hand and turned it back up on its base, but it fell back towards him slightly, as if it was unbalanced. He managed to catch it in time to prevent it falling to the ground. In trying to replace it in its original position, he realised that the earth inside the pot needed refilling and packing in properly, so he pulled the pot towards him and as he did so it tipped. The root of the plant came free and what earth there was covering the roots fell out, almost emptying the pot. He took the flower pot down from its position on the roof and laid it on the ground. At that moment Robert and Dai came into the yard.

"What you doing, Taff?" Robert asked.

"Just fixing this pot: it looked as though it was going to fall over and it would probably break if it hit the ground, I reckoned."

Dai, who had walked towards Jenkins, said, "Do you want a hand? Looks a bit heavy to me, mate!"

"No, you're all right, I can manage," Jenkins said.

Dai, who could now see directly into the pot, said enquiringly, "What's that in there then, Taff?"

"Dirt! Earth, you soft sod, what do you think they put in flower pots these days, you daft bugger, Dai?"

"Well, it don't look like dirt to me, Taff, see for yourself, mate: looks like a cloth pack or something!"

"All right, Dai, lets have a look then!"

Jenkins looked into the flower pot and there to his surprise was a mouldy looking cloth pack, more like a small bag. He reached into the pot and took hold of the bag, feeling slightly squeamish. It felt soggy but contained hard lumps of some sort. As he lifted it out of the pot he saw another pack, flat, about an inch thick and about four inches long. Robert had come across the yard to see what was going on so Jenkins handed him the first 'parcel' and Dai the second.

"Who's going to open his first?" Robert asked. "Go bloody careful, won't you?" he said to Dai, nodding to him to open the smaller packet first. Carefully Dai tore at the thin rubber cover on the packet; as he did so he showed the two men watching his every action. When he had torn off almost half the rubber cover, they all realised what was in the package, white five pound notes, about twenty of them. Dai's hands were shaking; he'd never seen that much money all at once in his life.

Jenkins nodded to Robert, "Go on, open the other packet," he said.

Robert took out his pocket knife and cut the binding that held the bag- top together. "Hold out you hands," he said to Jenkins.

Jenkins did so as Robert tipped the bag and out dropped silver and copper coins, fifty or sixty of them, and amongst them was a flash of yellow. Most of the coins began to fall on to the ground.

"Careful mate, you don't want to loose this lot do you." Dai was almost dancing around the yard.

Robert said, "I'm not sure, mate, but I think this lot must have belonged to your mother. I hear there were a few silver and copper coins found in the wardrobe in the spare room, we can check with the inspector but I think this little lots will be yours. The thieving bastard must have hidden it here with the intention of collecting it later when all the commotion had died down. Who'd have thought of looking in those sort of plant pots? This little lot might have been miles away, if Gifford hadn't been stopped.

"Look, Taff, I'm your friend but I'm afraid this money will have to go to the police station to hopefully be identified as your mother's." Robert held up his hand to stop Jenkins's protest. "Even if it cannot be proved outright that it was hers, then it is almost certain that a judge will confirm that as it has been found on her property and as the last occupant of the property there is a good case for it to be declared as hers, especially if her fingerprints are on any of the coins or paper money. Perhaps it was Gifford who hid the money, even if, to some people, it was a strange hiding place. Mind you, Gifford seems to have been a crafty sod."

Dai Jones said, "How is anyone going to prove it is her money or the thieving bugger that's got his come uppance under that bus? How is anyone going to prove it one way or the other, eh?"

Robert went on, a little exasperated, "I just told you, Dai! There's a thing called fingerprints!" he looked at Jenkins and Dai. "You know about those, don't you?" They both nodded.

"Yes! A sergeant at Bristol explained them to us a couple of months ago."

"Well then, I'll bet you both a quid that, besides all of our fingerprints and perhaps Gifford's, Taff's mother's fingerprints are almost certain to be on every one of the coins and the paper money in that packet and bag. So, thinking about it, we shouldn't handle the money anymore, all right?"

With that he took a handkerchief from his pocket and carefully scooped some of the coins into it. The remainder he shoved back into the rough bag. He laid the white five pound notes on the top of the coins and took the whole bunch into the kitchen, where he found an empty bread bin. Placing all the money in the bin, he tied the lid down with string taken from a kitchen drawer. Then he found some white plaster tape, used for first aid to cuts and grazes, etcetera. He taped the lid of the bin down on four sides. Next he took an indelible pencil from his coat pocket and signed two of the plasters. He gave the pencil to Jenkins and indicated he should sign the other two sides of the lid. Then he asked Dai to sign the top of the lid.

"What's this all in aid of then, Robert?" Dai asked.

"Well, when we get this to the station and give it to Inspector Marshall, he will realise that it cannot be tampered with until the lab boys have checked the money out for fingerprints and counted it, putting a totally correct figure on the money. If Gifford and your mother's prints are on the cash, it is evidence that 'A', the money was your mother's, and 'B', Gifford stole it, intending to retrieve it later.

"Mind you, I have to say this Taff; this is what I feel has happened and hopefully I'll be proved right, then everything will be yours. Really though, it'll be up to the boys in the laboratory and then the detective inspector and probably the chief constable, but it shouldn't be long before you'll have an answer."

"How long do you reckon that answer might be in coming, Robert?" Jenkins asked.

"Could be a week, could be tomorrow," came the reply.

"I suppose that'll have to be OK; there's no rush is there?" He looked at Dai who nodded in agreement. "If it's going to be longer, I'll leave you my Bristol address and my boss's telephone number at the docks, will that be OK?"

"Sure. Now let's get this lot handed in at the station and then we'll get hold of that vicar and ask him to sort out an auction for the rest of your mother's property. All right, Taff?"

Jenkins nodded. "Right then we'd best be getting along then hadn't we? The sooner we get things started, the sooner I can hand back the keys to the landlord, although it will be many a year before anyone will want to come and live here, don't you think Dai?"

Dai nodded his agreement again. He had hardly said a word the whole time they'd been at the house. He wasn't his usual cheery self.

As Jenkins turned the key in the lock for the last time, he felt the awful feeling of a great loss and the sadness that he'd never felt before, realising hadn't seen his mother before she passed away and so wasn't able to say goodbye. He tried to imagine her feelings and thoughts over the years and in the last minutes of her life, hoping that her demise was quick and painless without suffering.

Then he thought of Gifford and hoped that the last few seconds of his life had been terrifying and excruciatingly painful as the bus hit him and the wheels ran over his frightened screaming head and body.

"OK Robert, Dai, I'm ready, let's go, eh? Mrs Jones!" Jenkins called. Dai's Mam hadn't said one word; the men had almost forgotten she was in the house with them.

"Richard," she was almost crying, "I'm so sorry that things have turned out so badly for you, but I am pleased that horrible man didn't get away with his crimes and that hopefully you have something worthy to remember your mother by.

Later, Mrs Jones having left earlier, Jenkins and Dai were on the train back to Glais when Jenkins came out with a request that shook Dai Jones to the core. "I would never have expected it in a million years" he said later.

"Dai, mate, since I left the army, you have turned out to be one of the best friends a man could ever have asked for. There is something I want to tell you, but for the time being I need you to keep quiet about what I'm going to ask you to do."

"Aw, for crying out loud Taff, get on with it can't you? What? Do you want me to knock somebody off or something? 'Course I will if the price is right, who is this bad bastard then? Come on out with it, mate!"

"No, it ain't like that at all, you daft sod, if it was I would do it myself. I've had enough practise over the years, that's what they teach you to do in the army, you know." He laughed at the expression on Dai's face.

"Well, what the 'ell is it then, Taff?" Dai could hardly contain himself. "If you don't tell me soon, we'll be at my Mam's 'ouse and then it'll be all over Glamorgan. You know what all old women are like for gossiping, don't you? Come on, tell me, for Christ sake man!"

"You won't laugh will you Dai? Because if you do I'll have to kill you, all right?"

"OK, I won't laugh. Now what do you want to tell me that's such a big secret, eh boyo?"

Jenkins hesitated, then took a deep breath, "I'm going to get married!" he blurted out.

"Don't be so daft, Taff. Who'd 'ave you? Since when 'ave you been going out with the ladies?"

"Well, I'm going to ask May Andrews"

"What? Why? When?"

"Because I think I must be falling for her; I can't stop thinking about her. She's a lovely woman and I miss her company and friendship. I've felt like it since we left Bristol. I know she likes me a lot and I know she is a very religious person, but I'm sure she needs more than just the Salvation Army."

Dai retorted quickly, "Better not let 'er 'ear you say 'just' the Salvation Army like that, owerwise there won't be no marriage or a friendship even. You know May. Best be careful 'ow you say things, eh?"

Jenkins ignored him, "I need a family, like you do, and I need someone to go home to at night, someone to talk to. I'm a bit fed up talking to a load of blokes all of the time. With all my family gone, I have to make a new start; that's right, ain't it, Dai?"

Dai Jones looked up at Jenkins. "You poor old sod, now who would 'ave thought you were getting soft in your old age. Now what 'xactly do you want me to do? Go and ask May if she'll marry you?" Dai ducked, as Jenkins raised his hand as if to slap him.

"No, you silly sod, can't you see? I'm asking you to be my best man."

"Now ain't that a bit premature, mate? You 'aven't even asked the lady yet. What 'appens when, if you ask 'er to marry you, she turns you down? You'll feel a right Charlie, won't you, boyo?   Listen mate, when she says 'yes!' ask me again and I'll probably say OK. Will that do for now, Taff?"

"Yes, thanks. But don't breath a word of what we've said until the time comes!"

Jenkins felt sure in himself that the time would come soon when he would ask May to marry him. He couldn't remember another time when he had this same feeling for anyone. He hoped it would last and hoped that one day she might feel the same way about him. She might already, he thought to himself.

Mrs Jones had caught an earlier train home and by the time they got to the house, a meal was waiting for them both.

Dai kept winking at him and smiling and Jenkins thought he might be stupid and let the cat out of the bag. But Dai was just trying to unnerve him, laughing at him.

"What's going on, boys?" Mrs Jones asked.

"Nothing, Mrs Jones. Dai's playing the fool and he'll get a thump for it afterwards if he doesn't stop."

"Come on boys," Mrs Jones chided. "Come on, eat your dinners before the others come home; anyway the food is getting cold."

Jenkins didn't know how he was going to thank her for giving him lodgings and her kindness in going to Myers Street with him and Dai. Although she hadn't done anything, her being there had helped him face entering the house, not knowing what he might find. It was different facing enemy soldiers and seeing his comrades dead or wounded beside and around him.

Entering his mother's house had been an eerie, saddening experience. He hoped he would never have to go through anything like that again with anyone, or perhaps a future family for that matter. If it wasn't for the friends who had been with him at the house, he may never have understood the horror that had befallen his mother.

He knew that his mother couldn't have been a vengeful woman, but he knew that revenge wasn't wrong, especially when it was directed vicious evil people such as Gifford. It was all over now, except that one day, hopefully, the church authorities would allow him to have his mother's remains removed to lie alongside his father in the chapel graveyard at Alltwen. They would then be looking over the valley that stretched to Swansea in the distance. They'd also be together in the village they knew, with the years of happiness and sorrow everyone experienced during a lifetime. He could then have some comfort knowing that his parents were lying together where they couldn't be parted again.

He also thought perhaps that if he was able, he might be able to bring his sister and her daughter home to Alltwen. Eventually they might all be lying together.

Jenkins had, after taking one last look at what had been his mother's home, locked the front door and handed Robert the key. In that instant he knew he had lost all ties with his family in Wales. He gave Robert his address in Bristol and watched as it was written in the policeman's notebook. Then they all walked slowly to St Thomas railway station to get a train for the last time back to Mrs Jones's home in Glais.

That afternoon he told Dai Jones that he had decided to go back to Bristol as soon as possible.

Dai replied immediately, "I was expecting something like this, mate, and I know my missis would be expecting me back soon, so she will be pleased. I asked Robert to telephone the harbour master at Swansea Docks, to find out when Captain Redone is taking the *Welsh Lass* to Bristol again."

"A bit ahead of yourself, Dai; you'll be reading my mind soon, you bugger."

But Jenkins was pleased that Dai realised how he was feeling. Although he didn't want to leave his mother again, he felt that the lady in Bristol might be waiting for him as well. But he was hopeful he hadn't got his wires crossed, even though the next few months might become difficult after he proposed to her.

"OK, Dai, when's the skipper thinking of sailing, then?"

"Tomorrow night's high tide: that do you Taff?"

"Of course it will you, silly sod. Thank you! Will we be docking at Bristol Sunday night or early Monday morning?"

"Probably Monday, if everything goes OK!" Dai replied.

Robert and Mrs Jones had been watching the two friends talking and heard the gist of their conversation. So when Jenkins told them of his decision they nodded their approval.

At least he would still have a couple of contacts in his home village.

Chapter 4

Knife Attack

It was four o'clock Friday afternoon when Jenkins and Dai Jones arrived on the dock alongside the *Welsh Lass*. Captain Redone was waiting for them.

"Come aboard, Captain?" Dai called.

"Aye, what are you waiting for Dai, the bloody boiler needs stoking and this bloody oaf Danny here, is bloody useless. So come on and start doing the job you want to be paid for. How's it going, Taff? Everything go all right? I heard about your Mum and the trial. I'm sorry, mate, I wish there's more I could do or say. I feel pretty hopeless about these sort of things. Do you want to help out with the cooking again? Taff, I'll understand if you don't; we'll still get by though, eh Dai? But I've bought some decent grub in this time, just in case! I know you won't ruin it, so we should be pretty well fed on the way home."

"Fine, Captain, fine! I just can't scrounge off of you can I? Besides I've got to do something for my passage, haven't I?" Jenkins replied as he climbed the gangplank after Dai.

The passage to Bristol was quite uneventful, just a reversal of the Bristol to Swansea trip, and arriving at two o'clock on Monday morning.

Dai had already told Jenkins the ship would dock at about that time, so he asked Captain Redone if they could stay aboard until about eight o'clock in the morning.

Redone said, "I would have to leave someone on board anyway; there are too many thieves wandering around the dock at night and the dock patrols are pretty useless so I'd be happy for you to stay until at least my new deck hand gets on board. He can see to things until I finish my business on shore."

Jenkins replied, "Thanks Skipper. It will save me a long walk home and I'll be able to start work straight away, as soon as I leave the ship." The ship was moored about half a mile away from the Dock's Office. "So I'll be right on time and ready for work when the Harbour Master arrives. What about you Dai? You going straight home?"

"I'd better do, or the old lady will be after my hide if I don't. Besides I've got to get some sleep in: we're back out on the evening tide, ain't we Skipper?"

"Aye, we are," replied Redone, "and we'll have to be loaded by seven at the latest, so I'll be expecting to see you around three this afternoon, OK, Dai?"

"Aye aye, Skipper. I'll be seeing you later in the week then Taff. Keep your head down for the time being and I'll see you next weekend, all being well. Don't do anything I wouldn't do, either!"

Jenkins held out his hand to Redone, "Thanks, Captain, your help was very welcome."

"Any time, Taff, and by the way, I'm always looking for a good galley hand, don't forget will you? If you need another trip just look me up or let Dai know, all right?"

"Will do skipper, thanks again. Dai, before you take off, thanks for your help and your time: I really do appreciate the help you've given me. Anytime you need a favour or some sort of help you know you only have to give me the nod, all right?"

He stood at the top of the gangplank and watched the little crew disappear into the darkness of the docks that were devoid of any shipping. The lights of Bristol, which could be seen twinkling in the distance, were dwarfed by the huge flood lights of the ships in dock that were having their holds emptied or filled with various cargo.

After a last check around the little steamer, making sure the hatches were battened down and doors shut, he went down to the warmth of the ship's galley, made up his bed and settled down for the night.

The noise of ships' hooters and sirens woke him earlier than he had anticipated. Luckily the galley stove fire had stayed in all night; it was still hot enough to blaze up within five minutes and get a half-filled kettle to boil in a further five minutes.

A breakfast of tea, toasted stale bread and beef dripping was his start to the day and after a hot wash and shave he felt good enough to present himself to Mr Roberts and get settled back into his work. It was only a ten minute walk to the Harbour Office so he took his time, trying to identify the new ships docked along the harbour. Most he hadn't seen before but one or two of the local tramp steamers he recognized and as he walked on he acknowledged the friendly wave of one or two of the crewmen he knew by sight. He thought about stopping for a quick chat, but realised he would probable make himself late for work.

He noticed that the docks were teaming with stevedores loading and unloading the many ships. Shouts to and from the ships' crews, the stevedores and the crane drivers added to the noise of the clanging crash of shunted railway wagons.

He had to keep his wits about him, as he could quite easily be run over by the railway wagons, or hit by a swinging cargo net. He walked quickly and carefully, for there were also other dangers such as slippery cobble stones, cables, ropes, and large metal rings which were used to moor the visiting ships alongside the allotted mooring space on the harbour wall.

Fifty yards or so from the office he heard a commotion coming from the side of the building furthest away from him. Three or four men were shouting, it seemed at each other, or perhaps at one man. Suddenly a figure ran from behind the office building, being pursued by two men.

Jenkins recognized the first figure as old Mudhog Jack. He didn't know the men chasing after Jack, but felt immediately that those two weren't just chasing him just to get a light for their pipes which is what Jenkins thought they were holding in their hands. So he started to jog towards the men. After thirty yards Jack slipped on the damp cobblestones and then tripped over a mooring ring. In seconds the two men were on him, grabbing him with their free hands and raising what Jenkins thought were their fists, preparing to strike the old man.

At the start of the chase Jenkins had jogged forward trying to get into a position to see what was happening. He was about twenty yards away when he realised it was knives the attackers were holding.

His shout was so loud that one of the attackers stumbled and almost fell on to Jack. The other, a smaller more agile man, stepped back and glared at Jenkins; a vicious, malevolent look on his face. Then Jack took his chance, clambering away over the edge of the dock wall and falling into the mud: the tide was on the ebb and he knew it.

Meanwhile the smaller man darted towards Jenkins, the knife held in the palm-up position.

Two or three yards from Jenkins he stopped in a crouched position, turned his head and growled, "Come on Bill, let's do this nosy bastard first; teach him to mind his own business, eh?"

Bill, a pale, pockmarked, pudding-faced, stocky man, glared at Jenkins and replied, "Bugger me, he's a big bastard, ain't he Jimmy boy? It's going to take some cutting to put him down, ain't it?"

Jenkins watched the one called Jimmy, as he turned to face Bill. "Well you best get on with it then 'adn't you? You pair of yellow shits. Tell you what, I'll take Bill first, 'cause he's the biggest yellow lump of shit I've seen in years. Fancy letting a little shite like Jimmy boy fight your battles for you, eh? Or does he have to wait to get the easy pickin's?"

As he was trying to goad them, Jenkins was moving round like a boxer, trying to find space so that he wouldn't trip when an attack came. He took off his jacket but didn't wrap it around his arm as knife fighters often did; he wrapped one sleeve around his right hand and left the remainder of the jacket dragging on the floor, at the same time turning his right shoulder and side towards Bill.

"Thinks he's really funny, don't he?" Bill said as he rushed at Jenkins from five yards, his arm raised and the knife held in his right hand. He swung the knife in a downwards motion towards Jenkins's head. Without moving his feet, Jenkins swayed back in line with the attacker's left shoulder. Bill was about a yard away when something slashed into his left eye with such speed and force, it stopped him dead. The pain that came with the blow was so severe, he screamed in agony and he collapsed on to the dock cobblestones.

Jimmy stopped. He had seen the strike and didn't know exactly what had happened not realizing that it was the weighted cuff of the loosely hanging sleeve that had been flicked like a wet towel at and into Bill's left eye.

The cuff had a piece of old bicycle chain sewn into it. Jenkins had seen this crude weapon used in many a bar fight, sometimes just as he had used it, and at other times as a knuckle duster. Usually the cuff of the sleeve with the chain was wrapped around the hand, to give extra weight to a punch, especially when it was literally hand to hand fighting.

The way he had used the cuff was firstly to keep his attacker at a distance, next to cause maximum surprise and shock, and finally to cause as much pain and injury to his opponent, with as little exertion to himself as possible. This would allow him to concentrate on the second of his attackers and if necessary on any other opponents who may try to join in the fight.

If he had allowed his opponent, Bill, to get in close and perhaps grab hold of any part of his clothing or body, it would have given Jimmy a chance to get in behind his back, almost certainly with dire consequences. The way Jimmy held his knife showed that he was something of a knife fighter.

Jimmy looked at Jenkins and then at his moaning, crying, mate. "You bastard!" he screeched at Jenkins. "What've you done to 'im? You kilt him." He was circling Jenkins looking for an opening.

"If I had killed him he wouldn't be bawling now, would he? Come on you little shit, let's see if you're as good as you think you are, eh?"

Jimmy gripped his knife tighter and rushed at Jenkins, the twelve inch stiletto knife held with a bent arm, in a palm-up manner. As Jimmy closed to arm's length, he suddenly straightened his arm and stabbed at and up towards his adversary's belly. Jenkins, seeing the attack was being delivered with a left hand, took one pace back and to the side, allowing the man to drive past his stomach.

Jimmy thought he had him. But instead Jenkins had dropped his jacket and opened his own right hand and palmed off Jimmy's knife arm, grabbing the knife wielding hand as it passed his belly, holding it and the knife in a vice-like grip. Jimmy was completely off-balance as he was swung slightly away from the line of his knife attack. At almost the same instant Jenkins kicked his attacker with his steel tipped boot, into the side of the left knee. The crack of the shattered bone could be heard fifty feet away. Jimmy screamed in agony and went into shock almost immediately, fainted and was sent crashing to the ground.

Bill was trying to get to his knees, blood pouring down his face.

"Jimmy, Jimmy where are you? 'Ave you done the bastard yet?"

"Billy, boyo!" Jenkins grabbed him by his coat lapels and put his face right up to the blood and tear stained blubbering features of the injured man. "When you two are capable of doing a man's job, I'll be waiting for you, with a gun next time, not my coat and shoes, do you hear me? Listen you bag of garbage, the next time I see you anywhere near the docks, I'll have police on you quicker than you can blink your one eye and Jimmy can hobble away on his one good leg." Jenkins leaned even closer to Billy, pressing his forehead against the eyebrow of Billy's good eye and in a growling whisper said, "If the police don't get you, I will and I'll finish the job I've just started." Then he continued, "I'd better take these knives, 'cause you really don't know how to use them and I would hate to see you cut yourselves. Now! you get on your feet and find someone to give you and your mate a hand to get to the hospital. If I'm any judge, they'll have to take that eye out now, because it won't be any use to you any more."

With that he picked up his coat and swung it over his shoulder, the weights in the end of the sleeves giving him a warm comfortable feeling. He turned his back towards the two injured attackers and went to the edge of the dock wall, where he'd last seen Mudhog Jack disappearing over the edge. Although Jenkins took his time searching the area, there was no sign of the old man. He hoped Jack had got away safely, and if he had he would probable make an appearance later in the day or maybe the next.

When he walked into the office five minutes later, Mr Roberts and his two deputies were there. They had been watching every move of the 'incident', as Mr Roberts referred to it when they discussed it later.

"Good morning, Taff. Good start to the day, eh?" Roberts said as he winked at Jenkins. "Everything go all right in Swansea?"

"I'll have to tell you about that later, Mr Roberts. Do you know who those two blokes were?"

"No, but they weren't much good at scrapping were they?" Roberts smiled.

"Cup of tea, sir? Jenkins asked. "Before we start what looks like a very busy day."

Peters, one of Mr Roberts' two deputies, looked ashen faced and for some reason, quite shocked, at what he had just witnessed. His first comment was, "Did you have to be so vicious, Jenkins? What you did there was utterly uncalled for, it made me feel sick to my stomach; it looked as though that man Billy's eye was hanging out."

Jenkins looked at Roberts: they were both thinking, "How did he know the man's name?" Roberts and Jenkins had never seen the men before, at least not in the docks area.

Worrell, the other deputy, looked on in amusement.

Roberts stepped in quickly: he could see Jenkins was still hyped up and didn't fancy Peters' chances in any sort of argument.

"Mr Jenkins, would you please go and put the kettle on?" This was more of an instruction than a request and Jenkins picked up the kettle and left the room.

Roberts turned to Peters, a look of fury on his normally sublime features. "Mr Peters! It looked to me as if Taff, *Mr* Jenkins, almost certainly saved old Jack from being killed or severely injured. By taking on those two men, who were prepared to use a knife on both himself and Jack, I believe *Mr*," again

Roberts emphasized the 'Mr', "Mr Jenkins, needs to be commended for his actions. I will ensure that a report on the incident be sent to the proper authorities and hopefully he will be rewarded for his efforts."

He looked at both of his deputies, "You both witnessed what went on, didn't you? So both of you should add your comments as witnesses to my report. Is that understood?"

Worrell nodded his agreement but Peters replied:

"I'm sorry sir, Mr Roberts, I'm afraid I can't really agree with your view or assessment of the incident." He paused, then went on, "I think Jenkins could have handled the situation in a less violent fashion. What he did was absolutely evil. Surely as an ex-soldier he could have stopped at blinding or crippling those men. Especially when neither of them had touched that dirty old pig."

"Mr Peters, I am not going to argue with you but I am going ahead with my recommendation to those in authority. If you wish to write a report of your version of events, fine, but please ensure it is an honest, blow by blow, account of the incident. All right?"

"Yes sir!"

At that the conversation came to an abrupt halt as Jenkins re-appeared in the office doorway after filling the kettle from the outside water tap.

Jenkins went on, "OK, where do you want me to start, Mr Roberts?"

"Have your tea first, Taff, then we'll talk about it. Don't you worry, there'll be plenty of work for you to get on with; we've been saving it up for you," he smiled, "for when you got back, boyo! Don't forget lunch–time; we'll have that chat, all right?"

"Certainly, Mr Roberts. I'll come to the office. I need to find out about certain things first, don't I?"

He had a busy morning, checking the different ships at their moorings, seeing some of the captains and following up their requests. He had so much to occupy him, thinking about his personal life or what Mr Roberts wanted to talk about.

As he was walking back to the office, a thought came to him about the two men that had attacked Mudhog Jack. Although most of the clothing each man wore was completely different from the other, both men wore dark green waistcoats and light green neckerchiefs. They and the remainder of their clothes were disgustingly filthy. "So I wonder which gang they belong or belonged to?" he said to himself.

Jenkins met Mr Roberts during lunch break. They talked about the week of his Swansea visit, his home and family which no longer existed there.

"Will you be going back again and make a start in Wales then, Taff, my boy? You must still have some roots there somewhere."

"Not that I know of, Mr Roberts. All my family seem to have passed away, except perhaps the Johnson's who used to live up near Builth Wells." Then after a minute's thought said. "It's almost thirty years since I last saw my cousin Alwyn. His family used to own a farm near the market, just across the river from the old town hall. They've well over a hundred acres of arable land I reckon. My Mam and Dad used to take me and my sister over to visit them every Whitsun. We would go over on the train to Brecon and then get a bus to Builth. It was a great weekend out, just like a holiday, 'cause we stayed all the weekend.

"Me and Alwyn used to be allowed to sleep in the barn, in the loft above the cattle stalls. It was great. Then we were allowed to feed the animals, you know, the pigs, chickens, geese and turkeys and a bloody great cart-horse that my uncle used to call Tiny. It was daft, do you know the horse was that big, my uncle who was six feet tall had to climb on the rails of the stable stalls to get on his back, and when he was on, he looked like a pimple on some one's bum.

"Do you know, Mr Roberts, I never for one minute thought about them during the last week, or for some years before, either. Terrible ain't I? Next time I'm over that way, I shall definitely look them up. Yes! I hope they'll still be there. I'll feel a lot better if I can find them all still alive and kicking."

Roberts, who had been sitting behind his desk, nodded in agreement and said, "Taff, it happens to lots of people these days; everyone seems to be moving about the country looking for better jobs and such like. They have to, because the way things are going, anyone who does have a job had better work hard to hang on to it. Otherwise they'll be like the other poor sods who are being laid off, not finding another one and broke."

Changing the subject, Jenkins asked, "OK Mr Roberts, what's been happening here, then? I haven't heard any rumours this morning. Anything that I should know about? Is the coach house still standing? How are the gardens?"

"Hang about, Taff, you've only been gone a week and there are still plenty of weeds for you to get your hands on. Yes! There are a couple of things you need to know… Hold your horses! Give me a chance, will you?" He saw Jenkins was trying to butt in. "There were a couple of phone calls during the last week, one was from an inspector asking that when you got back, to go and see him as soon as possible, but there's no rush, OK? No! He didn't tell me what it was all about, just to go and see him: he's got some information he'd like to tell you about, all right?"

"Right, sir. Mr Roberts, sir, now what was the other call about? Important, was it sir?"

"Taff! Will you stop asking questions and listen? What I am about to tell you is very important, all right?" Roberts was smiling at Jenkins impatience. "I had a phone call from the Sally Bash in Bristol, the captain there said, as soon as you arrived back from Swansea, would you please telephone the Citadel. The captain said to phone after lunch, if it's convenient for you."

"Where can I phone from then, sir? I'm not allowed to use this phone, am I? Only if it's an emergency, aye sir?" Jenkins noticed the two deputies watching him. Peter's gave Jenkins such a malevolent stare it made Jenkins smile.

"There ain't no emergencies 'ere that I can see," Peters objected before Jenkins had asked to use the phone.

"Nor that I can see," Jenkins replied, trying to goad Peters into saying what he wanted to but didn't really have the nerve to in front of the Harbour Master.

Noticing Peters' animosity towards Jenkins, Roberts decided to add a little spice to the confrontation, to see just how far Peters would go in antagonizing Jenkins.

"All right, Mr Peters! At this moment I am the only person to know whether this call is an emergency or not. No Mister. It isn't an emergency but it is very important. So I am going to say he can use the phone when it is free and there isn't anyone in this office who needs to use it. Not *wishes* to use it, *needs* to use it. Do you understand Mr Peters?"

"Yes Mr Roberts, of course I do, but me and him," he said gesturing to the other deputy, "aren't allowed to make private calls and you are now letting a junior man use it!" Peters started to whine.

"When you speak to me and lecture me in that tone, Mr Peters, you will address me as 'sir'! If I need a lackey to tell me the rules of running this harbour, I shall resign at the first sign. But I can assure you, Mr Peters, you shall not be the one to take up the position of Harbour Master. I have already made that clear to my superiors, as you will find out later in the Annual Floating Harbour Master's Report."

Peters glared at the Harbour Master, pushed back his chair, stood up and rushed out of the office. His usually pale sickly face turned to a beetroot red.

As he went past, he saw the smile on Jenkins face, his enemy's face. Roberts didn't. Jenkins knew that Peters was now the enemy. The whole office building shuddered as Peters slammed the door.

"My, he does have a temper," Roberts said.

Worrell, the other deputy, who rarely interfered or voiced an opinion on anyone's politics or personal matters, had noticed the smile and said to Jenkins, "Taff, that was a brave thing you did for old Mughog. Where on earth did you learn to fight like that? It wasn't regulation army training was it?"

Jenkins was somewhat taken aback, 'Good morning' or 'Good night', were the only words Worrell had ever uttered to him during the couple of months they had been working at the Harbour Office.

"Well, no, it wasn't regulation stuff, but I was in the army when I learned to fight like a back street brawler in the back streets and pubs in North and South African townships and the Middle East bazaars. Most of the tricks I learned by just watching, but I have been in one or two scraps in barracks and learned to fight the hard way, taking an occasional battering for my pains."

"Well, Taff, – it's OK for me to call you Taff ain't it? – in my view what you did out there was the right and proper thing to do. If it wasn't for you, old Mudhog would be dead meat; he ought to be thanking you, he did!"

"And I expect he will," Mr Roberts interjected. "Now come on both of you, the back slapping is over, let's get some work done, eh?"

Worrell always did a good job and was painstaking in his approach to his work, or any task that might be his to complete. It had been Worrell's idea to give Jenkins the out tray on the office counter, basically to save time, and Roberts had agreed to the idea.

If for any reason someone wanted Jenkins for an errand or task, he would write Jenkins a message and leave it on the counter, in the out tray. It just meant Jenkins was to take the message and get on with the job. It was used by the three men in the office and saved Jenkins having to run back to the office each time he finished a job and ask someone what he was supposed to do next. He would often pick up a sheaf of papers, leave the office, go from task to task and sometimes wouldn't return to the office until all the work he'd been given was done, or it was lunch time. Then, if there were any more papers in the tray, he would pick up a new sheaf of instructions and carry on with the job.

Mr Roberts was very pleased with his protégé's progress, very rarely interfering with Jenkins's work. Once or twice Peters had tried to muck up Jenkins' little system, but found that with Mr Roberts' backing Jenkins was virtually his own man and was allowed to do the jobs in his own way.

Now Jenkins had another ally.

Roberts picked up the pile of papers from the out tray and handing them to Jenkins, said, "Best get on with it then, Taff, before old misery guts comes back in sulking and looking for a row. Oh, by the way, best make that call at lunch time, perhaps it'll be more important than you think. Eh!"

Jenkins left the office and on his way out literally bumped into Peters.

"Good morning, Mr Peters," he said sarcastically.

"Yeh!" came Peters' reply. "It will be when I've had my way. Your time will come, Jenkins, just wait and see. You won't have old Roberts to back you up either, just you wait, you sarcastic jumped up shit."

Jenkins realised then how vicious, vindictive and volatile the man was. He wasn't a man anyone wanted or needed as an enemy but it looked as though Jenkins had just gained a fully-fledged, foul-mouthed one.

"Now, now, Mr Peters, there's no need to swear, all that does is prove you aren't a gentleman!"

Peters almost choked with rage but deciding retreat was the best form of defence, he slunk back into the office, slamming the door behind him.

During most of the morning Jenkins was on tenterhooks: he hadn't felt so excited since he had received his first pair of rugger boots, as the English toffs would call them. He felt his stomach turning with anticipation and wondered if there was anything wrong with May. Perhaps the Citadel Captain, who was

May's commanding officer, wanted to give him bad news. Otherwise he couldn't think of a reason for the Salvation Army Captain to leave a message for him.

By the time he got back to the office, he was worried to the point of being sick. It can't be bad news, he told himself as he picked up the phone and asked the operator for the Bristol Citadel's number.

"Hello, Salvation Army Citadel, what can I do for you?"

"I've been asked to ring this number because the Captain there has a message for me."

"What is your name sir and I shall go and ask."

"I'm Richard Jenkins!"

"Hello Richard, this is the Captain!" A lady's voice answered. There was a hint of laughter in the voice. "Come on Richard, don't you recognise me?"

"Bloody Hell! Sorry. Blinking Heck! Is that you May? You're not really a captain, are you? You were a lieutenant last week: blinking quick promotion you people get, ain't it?"

"Yes it is me, May! And I'm now in charge of the Citadel. Aren't you going to congratulate me, Jenks?"

"Of course I am, Captain May Andrews. It's great news for you and the Citadel, congratulations. A big responsibility, ain't it? You must be up to it though, or they wouldn't have promoted you, would they? He went on hurriedly, "May! Sorry, Captain! I do hope this isn't going to upset our friendship and little walks. Because I really have appreciated your company over the last few months and it's something I've missed lately."

He stopped abruptly, thinking he might be going too far.

She laughed: he tried to imagine her at the other end of the phone line, in her smart navy blue uniform and red-edged bonnet which she wore when she was out working for the Salvation Army. When she laughed it seemed a whole new world opened up for him but he didn't dare say anything about his feelings for her.

"Slow down," he told himself. "You don't want to drive her away, do you? You idiot."

"May, what was the message I was supposed to get when I rang the Citadel? Are you going to tell me now or do I have to come all the way there to get it?"

"Jenks, don't worry, I'm the message. I just wanted to talk to you because I've missed seeing and talking to you, my friend. I wanted to tell you about my promotion and perhaps meet and maybe have a little celebration. If you would come to the Citadel at the weekend for a little get together, it would be marvellous. A few of my friends will be here and I wouldn't mind if you brought one or two of your own; they would be very welcome."

"May!" Jenkins almost stumbled over his words, "I'll come and bring my friends, but I wish I could come and visit you sooner in the week, if that's possible. I've got lots to tell you about my trip to my home and I really do need to talk to you. Do you think we could come to some arrangement? I'd appreciate it if you could ring this office and leave a message with Mr Roberts or Mr Worrell. I wouldn't leave it with Mr Peters, because we don't trust him. He's up to something nasty and none of us know exactly what it is at the moment. But if anyone answers the phone, when you ring, ask their name strait away. If it's Peters, say 'Sorry, wrong number'. I shouldn't have to ask you to do this, but it is important because of his underhand, nasty, nature and I'd rather you didn't get involved in the situation that is beginning to develop here. If you phone after lunch it would be better. Mr Roberts will always answer."

"Jenks, love, don't worry. I'll make sure the right person gets the message. I am looking forward to seeing you and hearing your news; bye now, see you soon I hope! Oh, and be careful, won't you, love? Bye."

Jenkins was a little shaken – 'Jenks, love' – 'love', not once but twice. "Does it mean what I hope it means?" he said to himself, hardly believing what he had just heard.

He found it difficult not to smile as he approached Worrell, who was just returning to the office after his usual lunch-time walk.

"What's the matter, Mr Jenkins?" Worrell said with his usual formality. "You look like the cat that's just had the cream."

"I feel like it too, Mr Worrell," Jenkins said breaking into a huge grin. "But I hope it won't turn out to be sour. Sorry, but I can't stay and tell you about it 'cause I've got too much work to get on with." At that Jenkins picked up a sheaf of papers from his out tray and rushed though the door.

An hour later he returned to the office and was confronted by two police constables, Mr Roberts and his two deputies. One of the policemen spoke to him in a matter of fact, demanding way.

"Are you Richard Jenkins? Were you involved in an incident concerning a man known as Mudhog Jack and two men who attempted to assault him this morning?"

Not having any reason to deny anything that had occurred Jenkins admitted that he was.

"We would like you to accompany us to the Docks police station to answer some questions." It wasn't a request really, the tone was 'if you refuse we'll take you there anyway'.

Jenkins looked at Mr Roberts who nodded his head as if to say, "Go on, you'll be OK, don't worry."

"OK, let's get it over with," he said to the constable, and started towards the office door.

As Jenkins did so he glanced towards Peters who was standing just in front of his desk. He saw that the deputy had a malicious, smirking grin directed at him as he went past. Jenkins made as if to dart at Peters, who took a couple of quick steps back towards his desk, lifting his hands and arms as if to protect himself from any blows that Jenkins might direct at him.

"Constable, constable!" Peters shouted, alarm in his voice at Jenkins sudden feint towards him: both policemen by this time had passed through the office door.

"Yes, sir?" one replied, turning towards Peters and seeing Jenkins standing almost alongside him. "What is it, sir?"

"Nothing, just wondering how long Jenkins will be in custody, constable."

"Custody, sir? Who said anything about custody? No, sir, he'll not be with us for very long, just a few questions and such like. Not to worry."

Peters replied, "That's a relief then, I was thinking it might be someone else," he said looking at Worrell. "Will we have to do his work whilst he is under arrest?"

The policeman, with a look of exasperation, said, "Sir, Mr Jenkins is not under arrest or in custody, neither will he be, so don't worry over this little episode. He'll be back in a very short space of time, in fact before you know it. Come on Mr Jenkins, he'll have you hung, drawn and quartered before you know it."

As the policemen and Jenkins were beginning their walk towards the police station one of the constables remarked, "He's got it in for you, Mr Jenkins, what've you done to him? He seemed to get quite upset when we first went to the office and said we wanted to speak to you."

Jenkins replied casually, "Nothing I can think of. I haven't said or done anything to the man; he's been like that ever since the day I arrived here. I'm employed as Mr Roberts' assistant and not Mr Peters' helper, or skivvy I think the word would be. We've just not seen eye to eye since the morning I arrived. It's OK though: I don't like him or his attitude either. Sometimes it happens in work situations, I suppose, so I'll have to put up with him until one or the other of us gives in or moves on. Nothing to worry about though, constable."

Nothing else was said until they arrived at the police station, where he was met by Inspector Hazelton. They shook hands and Hazelton led him to the detectives' office and offered him a chair. Jenkins sat down opposite Hazelton's desk and waited.

Hazelton looked at Jenkins for some thirty seconds, as if he was waiting for Jenkins to make an opening remark. As it seemed Jenkins wasn't going to say anything, so Hazelton opened the conversation by asking Jenkins how the trip to Swansea went. He seemed genuinely sorry to hear of the cruel way of Jenkins' mother's death and the miscarriage of justice at Gifford's trial, as reported to him by his colleagues in the Glamorgan Police.

But there was some good coming out of the whole affair. The money Jenkins, Dai Jones and Robert Evans had found in his mother's back yard, had been declared legally hers. Therefore, as the only known surviving relative, since his sister had also been pronounced legally dead, the money - £154. 15s – was his by right.

Jenkins just didn't know what to say in reply, except, "Thanks, inspector."

"Don't thank me, Taff. I had nothing to do with it, I'm just passing on a message. By the way, I've been told to ask you, would you like the money as it was found or in a cheque, so that it can be paid it into a bank of your choosing? No rush, when you're ready, let me know, all right?"

"Right, Taff, what I really brought you here for was that we, the police, hear you had a little run in with a couple of scallywags on the dock near your office this morning. As you know, the miscreants, who are both now in hospital, attacked an old fellow known as Mudhog Jack. For what reason? We can only surmise. We know there was an argument between his assailants and another man whose name we haven't yet ascertained, but we will when we find old Jack."

"Why do you want me then, inspector?"

"To see whether or not you can help us confirm our suspicions of who is the leader and organizer of the local dockland gangs. If there's anything at all you have seen or suspect, let me know or give a message to any of the docks policemen and ask them to pass it on to me. I'll make arrangements to see you at a safer place, other than your office. OK?"

"Fine, inspector, fine. I'll try to be a bit more observant in future."

"Yes, but don't make it to obvious and don't go asking too many questions. They will answer themselves, by what you see and take note of. Right, let's talk about those two this morning. What exactly happened? I need to know in case they try to make a complaint against you and I want the full facts from both sides including all the witnesses. Ah yes! We have some good observant witnesses, who I'm sure will back your version of events."

"But I haven't told you anything yet. OK!" said Jenkins with a sigh of resignation, and went on to tell Hazelton his view of the attack on Mudhog Jack and the resulting fracas, leaving out about the piece of bicycle chain. Which at that moment was still sewn into the end of the sleeve of the coat he was wearing.

"Bit lucky, weren't you?" said Hazelton.

"Yes, I suppose I was, lucky to be there to stop them killing old Jack. I still wonder why they wanted to kill him; that old fellow doesn't harm anyone. He keeps to himself and scrounges things out of the dock: that's all that keeps him alive, poor old sod. OK, inspector, if that's all for the time being I'll be on my way; is that all right?"

"Sure, but before you go, I would like you to make a written statement about the incident with Mudhog. We have opened a file and anything that refers to the incident has to go into that file, all right?"

"OK, but who actually reported the fight then, Mr Roberts?"

"No, no, nor Mr Worrell, neither of them wanted to say anything until they heard that a Mr Peters had reported the incident to the police. Then they both made statements, which has backed up your version. Although, strangely, Peters didn't mention that those two evil cretins had attacked old Mudhog,"

Hazelton went on, "only that there was a fight outside the office and two unarmed men had been badly injured by a vicious bully."

"Yes, they were unarmed, after I took the knives from them. As it stands at present, I didn't intend to report this to the police but after that statement by Peters, I think perhaps I shall bring charges against those thugs and see him stand up in court and make his statement again. If Mr Roberts and Mr Worrell will back me up in court, even if we can't get Mudhog there, we should perhaps get them both sent down for trying to kill me. That'd be OK, wouldn't it, inspector?"

"Yes, Taff, it would but I think this Peters has a ulterior motive, I think he's trying to muddy the water for one reason or another, maybe to blame you. He may want to get you away from the office and that part of the dock; perhaps he's got some little fiddle going on. Everyone working on the docks usually has, present company excepted, of course. I don't suppose you've been there long enough though, have you?"

"Well I haven't thought of a fiddle yet," said Jenkins.

"Before I get someone to take your statement, I'd like you to look at some of these photographs. I'll tell you why afterwards, all right Taff?"

He brought out a photograph album from his desk drawer, passed it across to Jenkins and asked him to see if he knew any of the 'faces' as Hazelton called them.

Jenkins looked at each page of eight photographs carefully, eventually picking out four. Two were easily recognizable as Billy and Jimmy, the two men who had attacked Mudhog. The third he recognized was Jaccob Purkinji. Although easily recognized, the man in the picture was twenty-odd years younger than the day Dai Jones and himself had seen Jaccob in the shop. The fourth picture shocked him; it was Peters, or someone very much like him. Then he turned another page and there was another photograph of someone bearing an uncanny resemblance to Peters. He looked at both pictures again trying to compare them. There were several differences which in the end caused Jenkins to become confused. Was it Peters or a different man?

Hazelton had watched him turning the pages and noted the ones he had stopped to look at, realising that Jenkins had become confused over the last two pictures.

"Haven't you realised it yet? Those photographs of the two men you thought were Peters could be him or maybe they are twins from another family. We've never been able to decide if it's Peters or if there is any connection between the two people in the photographs. One is definitely a man called Tony Anson and he's in prison at the moment. We've only one set of fingerprints and they belong to him, the man in prison. So until Peters breaks his good, clean living mode and does something that we can arrest him for, we'll never find out if the men in those photographs are related or not."

"What's this Anson in prison for, how long is he doing time for, then?"

"He put his wife and kids in hospital, gave them a terrible beating he did, but he denies it, as these bastards do. Claims he was miles away, doing a job in Bath at the time. He got five years for it. His wife, in her statement, says it was him and she hasn't changed a word of it since. She wasn't well at the time. It was pitch black in the house, except one small light on the landing. Mrs Anson was in bed and said, 'I saw a dark figure of a man, I thought it was my husband.'

"Mrs Anson said that she had seen the man as he passed in front of the bedroom window. It was dark outside but she saw his shape quite clearly. Then she went on to say, 'The man I thought was my husband was stinking of beer and very drunk. I couldn't give him what he wanted, because he made me feel sick. I knew it was him because of the shape of his head and his rough skin and stubble on his face. He didn't speak except to say, "Lie back and enjoy it!" His voice was a bit horse; I thought it was the beer making him sound like that or maybe he had a sore throat.'

"Then without any warning he started to beat her, because she wouldn't respond to his demands. She screamed, so he beat her more and harder. Her kids said they thought they heard their father come into the house and watched him go into their mother's room. They could only see his dark shape and thought it was their father. When they cried he gave them all a hiding as well, telling them all to shut their mouths or he'd kill them. Then he left the house saying he was going to the pub.

"A couple of witnesses in the pub recognised him as Anson. Some thought it odd as he usually had short hair. When they saw him, his hair was almost down to the back of his neck. As he hadn't been to the pub in the last couple of weeks, no one actually commented on it. He usually drank alone, so no one spoke to him that evening. He only drank one glass of ale, said goodnight, and left.

"One of the kids saw a local bobby and told him what had happened. When the policeman heard the tale, he waited for Anson until he came back from the pub, or so he thought. Gave him a terrible battering and arrested him.

"Anson claimed that he left Bath at ten pm, pinched a lift on a goods train back to Bristol, arriving at ten thirty: then he took a late tram to the end of his street. Enquires were made but no witnesses were found or came forward.

"No one really believed him anyway, especially after his wife insisted he was the man who'd beaten her and the kids. We could hardly recognize him when he was interviewed and photographed. When he was arrested, no one gave a thought to the length of his hair or that Anson was completely clean shaven.

"'It looked,' the arresting constable said, 'as if he had shaved that morning.'

"Someone thought that Anson looked a lot like Peters but as Peters lived across the other side of the town, it was decided that it was unlikely that either knew of each other or where they both lived. Anson claimed he had never heard of Gordon Peters or of anyone by that name. Neither had Peters heard of Anson.

"Some of the neighbours, claimed they'd seen Anson's wife around the centre of Bristol and the docks as well, with different blokes, although she hadn't been seen taking any of them home.

"Anson admitted he tried to keep her on a tight rein, by not giving her very much money. It looked like that when he was away doing some job, legal or not, she was out earning money for her and the kids.

"Anyway, Taff, look-alike or not, Anson's doing five years, but I reckon he might be due out in the next six months if he's been behaving himself."

"Here's a question for you, inspector. Where did you get the photos of Anson and the other bloke from? The ones in the book, I mean."

"Taff, the one on the right is definitely Anson. I was in the office when my then sergeant stuck the photograph into the album. The one on the left was already in the book and he mentioned the likeness then. But I haven't seen this Peters you've mentioned so I can't really make any comparison between him and Anson. One thing though, Taff, try not to let him know that you are watching him. Otherwise he'll either stop any activities he may be involved in or have you stopped, one way or another. Remember he knows what you can do, but you don't know what his intentions are towards you, or how, and who with, he'll carry out those intentions. So, Taff boy, watch your back."

"I already do, inspector, especially after my first welcome to Bristol. I've got to go now, thanks for your time, but hopefully someone will be waiting for me to call. Please let me know what progress there is with my sister's enquiries, won't you? I know you're pretty busy and I appreciate what you've already done, but I feel a bit anxious in case you never find the vicious bastards that did this terrible thing to my sister and her family. I won't hold you up any longer, inspector: I can see you've got plenty to do, so I'll be on my way. Cheers now!"

"Phone me any time," Hazelton replied. "Anytime!"

When Jenkins got back to the office, Mr Roberts, who was alone at the time, said, "Before you start running round the docks, Taff, I've got a message for you. Mrs Andrews phoned and said she would be able to meet you tomorrow evening at the Citadel, about seven thirty. By then they, Mrs Andrews and her Salvationist friends, will have finished their meeting. She finished off by saying don't be late because she has been missing you."

"May didn't say that did she, that she had been missing me? I don't believe it."

"You had better believe it, boyo, and don't be late, especially as it seems she's in charge there and gives the orders," Roberts replied with a big grin. "I see you like taking orders, Taff, no matter who gives them."

Jenkins started to go red with embarrassment, realising that Roberts had guessed how he felt about May Andrews.

"No, Mr Roberts, I'm used to taking orders but I don't 'like' taking them, not since I left the army. Neither can I imagine Mrs Andrews giving me any!"

Roberts began to laugh, "Don't take me so seriously, Taff, I'm only joking, because my missus and me realised from the day you started talking about Mrs Andrews, just how you feel. Don't worry, we won't say anything to another living soul, all right?"

"I'd best get going with these jobs then, Mr Roberts, or I'll be finishing late and I thought I'd better get up to the coach house and sort things out. There must be a right old mess, 'cause I didn't have time to tidy up properly before I left for Swansea."

"OK, Taff. See you when you finish or when you get home. Tell you what, I've got one of the van drivers to take me home tonight, so if you're finished by the time I go, you can get a lift with me, all right?"

"OK, Mr Roberts, thanks; I'll try and be here before you go, so I'll see you then."

With that he ducked under the door lintel and disappeared at the run.

At the end of the working day, he was alone in the Harbour Office as he was waited for Mr Roberts. He began to sweep the floor and tidy the room. It had always been his last task of the day, since his arrival to work at the docks.

Both of the deputies' desks were pushed up against the outer wall of the building. The desks had never been moved from their positions, so Jenkins usually swept around them, picked up any fallen scraps of paper and, if the occupiers of the desks were absent, dust and sometimes polish the tops. In some ways his army training had made him fastidious when it came to cleaning anything. If he couldn't see his face in a polished top, it wasn't clean.

As he swept, he noticed Peters' desk had been moved: it was about an inch away from its normal position. At that time he didn't attempt to move it but knelt on one knee and peered through the gap between the back of the desk and the wall. There wasn't much light at the back of the desk, but he thought he could make out a dark square patch on the wall. He couldn't see anything at or on the back of the desk so he began to lift it back into place. As he did so Peters came into the office.

"What do you think your doing?" he snarled.

"Cleaning the office and pushing your desk back against the wall, Mr Peters. Somehow it had been moved away from its usual position. It was like that when I came in."

Peters' attitude changed immediately, a grudging word of thanks was uttered. Jenkins couldn't believe his ears. 'Thanks!' coming from Peters meant there was definitely something secretive and crooked going on. Jenkins was sure that one day soon he would find out what Peters was up to, and when he did Peters would be finding another job or answering questions at the police station.

No matter how long and what it took, Jenkins decided to make it his aim to find out exactly what sort of secret life Peters was leading. He knew there wasn't any evidence, but what with Inspector Hazelton's information and the man's nature and attitude Jenkins was guessing that Peters was definitely hiding some sort of crooked past and perhaps was leading a double life style. No one knew anything about Peters, his family or previous work history, except that his previous employer had closed the boatyard at Weston super Mare because of the number of break-ins and thefts that had occurred, mostly after the arrival of Peters. It was never actually suggested that Peters was involved. The references supplied by the boatyard employer, though not of an exemplary nature, said that as a clerk it would be difficult to find a better one.

His personal and family life were never examined. The Docks Board and Mr Roberts were only interested in the standard of work a clerk could provide. Peters' previous work record proved to be of the standard that was required at that time.

Roberts gave Jenkins a lift home as promised, so in return for the favour Jenkins spent an hour or two in Mr Roberts' garden. He cleared weeds and pruned some of the fruit trees. Dusk was beginning to fall and dark shadows slowly appeared in and around the orchard where he was working. He was about to put his tools away and go to the coach house, as he preferred to call it, when he heard a cry and then screams from the Roberts' house. It seemed to be coming from the kitchen or the back hallway of the main house.

As he ran towards the sound of the screams, then shouting, swearing and crashing of furniture, he saw through a window that had been broken three men struggling on the kitchen floor. Mrs Roberts and the children were huddled in a corner of the kitchen, Mrs Roberts screaming like a banshee.

"Help!" she screamed over and over. She was absolutely terrified as she watched her husband struggling and being beaten by two attackers. One of them had a knife and was trying to press it against Roberts's throat. Roberts, lying on his back, was holding on to the attacker's wrist with all of his gradually-waning strength. He watched with fearful bulging eyes, unable to breath, as the knife was forced downwards towards his throat. The second attacker was lying half across Roberts' legs, preventing him from kicking out in his own defence. He was half-turned towards Mrs Roberts and the children, ensuring they made no move towards escaping or interfering with the assault on Roberts.

This second man was first to see the arrival of Jenkins and he struggled to get to his feet. He was too slow getting up or in shouting a warning to the man with the knife. He had just got into the kneeling position when Jenkins hit him with the fist holding the concealed bicycle chain knuckle duster. The man, Joseph Woods, was hit in the right temple with such force, that when he eventually recovered consciousness he was in the Bristol Royal Infirmary with a policeman at his bedside. He didn't know why he was in hospital or what had happened.

Jenkins' ruthless attack on Woods startled both Roberts and the knife-wielding assailant. Roberts released the man's wrist, but as he did so Jameson, for that was his name, turned slightly to look over his own shoulder. In that brief second Jenkins grabbed him around the neck from the back with one arm and taking hold of the knife hand's coat sleeve, twisted the sleeve at the cuff, gripping with such ferocity that Jameson lost all feeling and strength. The circulation seemed to have disappeared from his arm and the knife slipped from his grasp falling harmlessly across Mr Roberts' chest.

Dragging Jameson off Mr Roberts' body, Jenkins kept hold of the sleeve and his neck. He put the man on to one of the dining room chairs and held him there.

Mrs Roberts had stopped crying. She went with her children to help Roberts, first to his feet, and then to a comfortable armchair. They were all shaking with fear and fright: until that time not a word had been spoken.

Everyone, including Jenkins, was trying to catch their breath.

Jenkins was the first to speak, "Mrs Roberts, please take your children up to the bedrooms, all of you! I'll call you down when we've sorted this out. It won't take long, I can assure you."

"Thank you Mr Jenkins, I can't think of any way to thank you for your kindness and help at the moment, but I will."

"It's all right, Mrs Roberts. I'll look after your husband; don't you worry, everything is under control. We'll get the police and an ambulance here soon, then hopefully everything will be back to normal. I'll make sure that everything is all right, so please don't worry any more."

She looked at him, "I'm sure it will, Mr Jenkins, I'm sure it will, thank you," as she followed her children to their bedrooms.

Jenkins turned to Mr Roberts. "How you doing, sir?"

"Much better, thanks."

"Do you think you're all right to phone the police? You had best phone for an ambulance for this scum too, sir." He pointed to Woods with his foot. "If the police don't arrive soon I'll have to knock this evil cretin out as well because I don't know how long I can hold my temper, or hold on to him, so if you don't mind Mr Roberts, the telephone, please!"

Forcing his forearm tighter into Jameson's throat, Jenkins released the man's wrist and made what is known as a single wing lock. Standing behind Jameson's chair, Jenkins's left forearm was placed across Jameson's throat. Jenkins then put his own right arm under Jameson's right armpit and with his right hand reached up and around the back of Jameson's neck. With his own left forearm already across Jameson's throat, Jenkins, using his left hand, grasped the bicep of his own right arm making a bar across the man's throat, that he could tighten to choke the man or release at will. Jameson's right arm hung helplessly in an out of the way position above his own head. His left arm, though not exactly useless, couldn't be moved to do anything untoward, because as Jenkins was standing behind him, at any sudden movement renewed pressure could be applied to his throat, choking him into complete submission or unconsciousness.

When Mr Roberts returned from the hall way where the telephone was situated, Jenkins asked him to take four silk sashes from the curtains. Then directed by Jenkins, Roberts formed a loop in one rope and passed it over Jameson's right wrist. The prisoner was then told to raise his left arm above his head: at first the man refused but when further pressure was applied to his throat, he soon obeyed Jenkins' order. Releasing the strangle-hold on Jameson, Jenkins with the help of Roberts tied the helpless man's arms behind his back and then to the chair back. They then tied his ankles to the legs of the chair. He was eventually trussed up so tightly, that even if the chair had been smashed to smithereens, some part of it would still be attached to Jameson.

"What about this man?" asked Roberts, indicating the unconscious Woods.

"Well, just in case he regains consciousness before the police arrive, we had better tie him up as well. I should keep him on his belly if I were you, then if he does come to and tries to stand up, he'll find it very difficult without the use of his arms, won't he? Not enough rope, Mr Roberts? Pull both their belts from their trousers and use them for his legs and arms, OK Mr Roberts? Can you manage, do you need a hand?"

Jenkins noticed that Roberts looked very pale and was sweating profusely.

"Come on, sir, have a sit down and watch this thug, just watch that he doesn't try anything silly, although I can't imagine him getting out of those ropes, can you?" After he'd dealt with the prone captive, he asked, "Did the police say how long they would be, Mr Roberts?"

There was no answer. He looked towards Roberts who was reclining in an armchair. It looked as though his boss had fainted. Jenkins began to feel a little worried, two unconscious men and a cursing, moaning, thug. What would the police say?

Mrs Roberts came into the room and started fussing around her husband, bathing his head and face in cold water. After a couple of minutes Roberts came to.

"How are you and the children?" were his first words to his wife.

"Don't worry dear, we're all fine," she replied. "The children will be down in a minute or two, when I give them a call."

"Mrs Roberts, it might be a good time for us all to have a drink, a cup of tea perhaps? Then you can tell me what happened, what started all of this. How do you both feel? Do you think you're up to it?" Jenkins asked the couple, who he could see were still trembling from the effects of the assault.

He wanted to find out what had happened before the police arrived. Perhaps the Roberts family could tell him, whilst the details were still fresh in their minds.

It turned out that after arriving home, Mr Roberts had taken his family to the village, half a mile down the country road. It was a pleasant evening for the walk and they all seemed to enjoy it. They went to the village shop and bought a few items for their evening meal, afterwards visiting a family friend's house next door to the shop. They were there for almost half an hour, chatting and drinking a glass of wine, whilst the children played on a garden swing with their friends' child. They weren't out of the house for more than an hour.

When they entered their home, everything seemed quiet and quite normal. Mrs Roberts went upstairs to change her dress, leaving the children playing a game of cards at the kitchen table, and Mr Roberts went into the scullery to put on his slippers. He put them on and straightened up: as he did so a figure that had been crouching in a dark corner of the room leapt at him and knocked him to the floor. He scrambled to his feet but as he did so a second man appeared from behind the scullery door. He pushed Roberts back into kitchen. The first assailant, Jameson, had a knife and rushed at Mr Roberts causing him to trip and fall to the floor. As he did so Mrs Roberts came into the kitchen, saw what was happening, grabbed the children to her and started screaming, thinking her husband was about to be killed.

The only thing that was said by either thug was, "Where's the key you old bastard? Tell us or I'll cut you to pieces."

Roberts, who by that time was fighting for his life, never had time to answer, besides which he could hardly breath. Jameson had gripped him by the throat with his left hand and was trying to use the knife with his right.

In fact Roberts didn't have any idea which key the man was talking about. It was about that time that Jenkins had come crashing into the room.

"Mrs Roberts, will you take your husband and the children into the parlour. Just for a couple of minutes. I think this chap," he said, indicating the bound-up Jameson, "wants to tell me something. Don't you, mister?" The vicious threat in his voice would have frightened anyone, even if that person wasn't bound and tied to a chair.

By now beads of sweat started to break out on Jameson's forehead. The temperature in the room seemed to have risen and it wasn't just the kitchen stove. After the family had left the kitchen, Jenkins picked up Jameson's knife. He went behind his captive and without any warning dug the point into the slight indentation at the base of Jameson's right ear.

The thug started to whimper, "Mister, mister, don't, don't do it, I never meant to 'urt the old sod, honest. I'll tell you what you want to know, anyfing you like!"

"All right, you yellow lump of trash. Who sent you here and what were you after, aye?"

"Nobody sent us mister, 'onest!"

He flinched and tried to pull away from the knife point as it pressed further into his ear. The pain was excruciating. Jameson's face was contorted with the pain of this evil sort of torture. Again the pressure of the knife point was increased until the thug could no longer put up with the fear of dying and the pain that was increasing by the second.

"All right, all right!" Jameson cried out, trying to turn his head away from the knife point and look over his shoulder towards Jenkins. "It was our boss, our gang boss. I can't tell you his name 'cause none of us 'cept one or two of his best mates knows him. We gets told what to do an' when to do the job. That's all, see! We just gets a message an' we goes an' does it."

"No, it ain't all, see? What gang are you in? You shites. Where do you work from? What key are you after? Aye, Aye?"

As Jameson and Jenkins were the only two people in the kitchen, no one else was able to hear what was being said.

Jameson whispered, "We're called Commodores; I don't know what it means, but that's what they calls us."

"Who calls you that, you bastard?"

"Everybody on the docks, the other gangs and bodies."

"How many gangs are there then? On the docks?"

"'Bout five I reckons."

"How many in your gang, then?" Jenkins asked.

"Honest I don't know, we never works togever, 'cause then we won't know who the other geezers be, will us?"

"What key were you supposed to get, then?"

"I dunno, it was supposed to be a big brass 'un wi've a silver number 10 on it. I fink it was supposed to be in the kitchen pantry or the scullery cold room. Under a blue an' white cheese dish cover. But we couldn't find one anywhere. But then the old bloke came in an' caught us, so we didn't 'ave it any 'ow.

Jenkins, realising there wasn't a great deal more information he would be able to get out of Jameson, gave the man a bang on the temple with the handle of the knife, causing more than enough pain to keep him subdued. Then leaving the door between the parlour and the kitchen open he went and sat with the Roberts family waiting for the police to arrive.

Twenty minutes later a police van and car with half a dozen policemen arrived, followed closely by an ambulance. One of the police officers, Haxton, was known to Jenkins, as he had taken him to the police station earlier that day to see Inspector Hazelton.

"Bloody hell, Taff, you do get around don't you? What's been going on here, then?"

Jenkins explained his part in what turned out to be a failed robbery by the two thugs he'd caught and about the assault, the knife attack on Mr Roberts and the fear that been caused to Mrs Roberts and her children.

"Well, Taff, I'll have to ask you and Mr Roberts, when he's well enough, to come to the station and make a statement, OK?

Will you come tomorrow morning? The quicker you make your statement and the Roberts' make theirs, the quicker we can get these evil bastards put away. I'll come to the house for Mrs Roberts' statement some time tomorrow afternoon, OK?"

By this time both prisoners had been taken out of the house, Woods under escort to the hospital and Jameson to the police station where he was to be charged with attempted murder and assault. Woods, when he regained consciousness, would be charged with the same two offences to begin with. Other charges such as breaking and entering and robbery with violence would also be considered.

When Roberts was sufficiently recovered and the whole family was having a cup of tea, he said to Jenkins, "Did you notice, Taff, they were both wearing dirty brown waistcoats and neckerchiefs? Didn't those other two who attacked old Mudhog Jack have the same colour waistcoats and neckerchiefs? Do you think it's some sort of gang uniform?"

"Well, Mr Roberts, those two at the docks had green waistcoats and scarves, didn't they?" Roberts nodded in agreement. "I think you're on to something there though, Mr Roberts. Perhaps the police would like to know about that in the morning. It's a small clue for them to go on don't you think, sir?"

Just then Mrs Roberts interrupted them. "Do you fancy staying for supper, Taff? I've had this stew on all day and I'm damned if those horrible men are going to stop us eating it. I expect everyone is starving."

The men both nodded their thanks; the children, both over their fear and the excitement, began to lay the table.

Whilst they waited for their dinner, Jenkins asked Roberts about the key the two thugs had come to find.

"What was so important about it that someone was almost prepared to kill for it?"

Roberts stood up and closed the parlour door. "First of all, Taff, when you're in my house, you are to call me Cyril. All right, at work it's Mr Roberts, of course. I'll not have a friend of mine, especially one that's just saved my life, Mr Roberts-ing me in my own house."

"OK, Mr Roberts, sir; I mean Cyril, OK!"

"Now then," Cyril Roberts continued, "I think the reason they want that key is someone intends to try and rob the Floating Harbour strong box. The box is kept in the Dock's strong room, in the Dock Administration Building. The key to the box isn't in fact kept here at all: why anyone thinks it is, I cannot imagine. Yes, I do keep keys to the office and the office safe key on a ring; they're in my trouser pocket now, but as they're all of the same make and shape, you need to know the number of each key to fit each lock, otherwise it'll take ages to unlock anything. The key they were looking for is in a safe, in the Docks General Manager's office, along with several others that all look very similar. There is a watchman on the building day and night and also regular patrols by the Docks Patrol. So I cannot imagine who gave them the information. Whoever it was overheard me or someone else talking about keys and strongboxes and jumped to the wrong conclusion. I can't remember ever saying anything about sculleries and cheese dishes. They must be barmy," Roberts concluded.

At that Mrs Roberts put her head round the door and called "Dinner's ready, call the children down please, Cyril!"

It was nearer supper time by the time dinner was finished, the table cleared and washing-up done. The children helped their mother to dry the dishes and put the crockery and utensils away.

David, the youngest, put two or three plates into a kitchen cupboard then turned to his father and said excitedly, "Is this what they were looking for, Dad?" as he pointed at something in the cupboard.

Roberts, who was still sitting at the table smoking his pipe, stood up and went to the cupboard to see what the boy was pointing at. Jenkins, curious to see what the boy's excitement was about, turned in his seat and watched Roberts go to the cupboard.

Roberts bent down and reached into the cupboard. "Well I'll be damned!" he exclaimed.

Mabel Roberts, also curious about the contents of the cupboard, heard his surprised remark. "There's no need for language like that, Cyril, especially in front of the children. Now what has David found?"

"Would you believe it? It's a blue and white cheese dish. Who on earth put that in there? I've never seen it before."

"Yes, dear, I put it there yesterday. I bought it at a jumble sale at the local school on Saturday; it only cost a penny and I couldn't resist it. Considering the one your mother gave us is cracked right across the lid, I thought it was a good replacement. I was quite pleased with it."

"Didn't you hear that evil cretin say that he was looking for a blue and white cheese dish, m'dear?"

"No! I'm sorry Cyril, I was too frightened to hear or see anything properly. I thought those men would be coming after me and the children, once they had finished with you. I was so frightened."

"You don't have to worry about that any more my love, you did the right thing by screaming and looking after the children. Taff here heard you: it was a good thing he was in the garden, wasn't it? He saved the day!"

Jenkins smiled an acknowledgement. "Pleased to be able to help, Mrs Roberts, any time! Come on, Mr Roberts, sorry, Cyril, let's see this dish, eh?"

Roberts picked up the cheese dish and took it to the table. Jenkins and the rest of the family gathered round, gazing at the piece of china that had caused so much trouble. It was blue and white all right. Nothing special about that. It had a royal blue Japanese floral pattern on the cover, which rested on a plain white base. A perfect fit.

Roberts lifted the lid, there was nothing inside it, on the dish that is. He turned the cover up so that he could see the inside. Barely visible was what looked like a piece of white sticky tape, about two inches long. He pulled the tape off revealing a key with a gold number ten.

Roberts said with some exasperation in his voice, "What on earth is it doing there? This is ridiculous." He took the key from the dish cover and put it in his pocket. "I'll sort this out tomorrow morning," he said. "Now then, thanks David, but its off to bed for you and Jenny; we've all had a hard day. Oh! By the way, you mustn't say anything to anyone when you go to school tomorrow, because we don't want anyone to find out about this key. It might be important to someone who shouldn't have it, so it's only our secret, remember. If anyone else finds out that I've got it, then it could only be one of us who has told someone else, couldn't it?"

Both children nodded their agreement, and Jenkins, to encourage them, said, "OK, Mr Roberts!"

Mrs Roberts, happy and all smiles, said, "Right, Cyril, I'll take them up and be off to my bed as well. I've had enough excitement and worry today to last me a year. Goodnight Taff. Many thanks; I cannot tell you how grateful I am."

"You really don't have to be, Mrs Roberts. Any decent man would have tried to do the same, I'm sure. Goodnight now, I'll have to be off to my own bed, because I don't want my boss telling me off for being late in the morning, do I?" He grinned at Roberts and said, "OK Cyril, thanks for the supper, see you in the morning. Are you walking down or going by van?"

"Van!" came the reply. "OK. See you about seven then. Goodnight!"

With that Jenkins went to the coach house and prepared the things he would need in the morning, then went to bed.

Sleep wouldn't come though until the early hours. By that time he had thought about and mulled over everything that had happened over the last day. Clues were beginning to appear, but clues to what and who, he had no idea at all. He had his suspicions but that didn't mean any clues that arose fitted those suspicions, or in fact were really clues to anything.

When they met in the morning, he and Roberts set out for the docks. Jenkins carried the cheese dish carefully wrapped in an old towel and newspapers, in his old army knapsack. They had decided that the police should have it as evidence. So there it was, tucked tightly alongside his lunch of packed sandwiches and tea bottle. Roberts had the key they'd discovered in the cheese dish connected safely to his office key ring.

The van arrived promptly at seven am. Thanking the driver, they climbed into their transport, Roberts in the front passenger seat, Jenkins crammed in the back with a load of empty flour bags.

Except for the morning pleasantries, little was said during their drive to the docks. They kept their thoughts to themselves until they arrived at the Harbour Office. When the van arrived at the dock, Roberts and the driver, who had both alighted from the van, began to roar with laughter.

"What's up, what's up?" Jenkins shouted, as they both pointed at him and the driver almost went into hysterics.

"Look in the window," Roberts said, almost crying with laughter and going weak at the knees.

Jenkins turned to the window, which reflected his image like a mirror. He almost fell over with shock; he was like an alabaster statue, covered from head to foot with flour. At first he was furious, then saw the funny side of his appearance and laughed at himself along with the others. It was the first time since he had arrived in Bristol he was able to see the funny side of anything. His friends had noticed before that he didn't seem to have a sense of humour, but now Roberts could see that he had. At least it might help Jenkins to get over the last few terrible months that he had suffered. Jenkins had never once openly complained about anything that had happened to him. His friends often asked each other if the others knew about his health and well-being. Was he well and OK? How was he taking the dreadful tragedies that had happened to him since he arrived in Bristol? No one actually knew and no one wanted to be the one to ask. So everyone just stood back and waited until he was ready to say how he felt and what his thoughts were.

When the three men stopped laughing, the driver and Roberts tried to brush the flour off Jenkins' clothes, making one awful dust cloud as they did so. He went to the outside water tap, took his jacket and shirt off and turned the tap on full blast. Although it was very cold, he put his head under the water to clear the flour dust from his head and body. After giving his shirt a good shaking, he used it to towel himself dry. By this time the driver had driven off to the rest of his duties. Both Roberts and Jenkins continued to giggle like school girls, until they arrived back at the office door.

They were the first to arrive and as they entered the office, Roberts said, changing the subject, "Taff! I do believe there is something in that idea about the waistcoats and neckerchiefs. Did you notice the other stevedores and dock workers, they all had a similar sort of paraphernalia in the different styles of dress. A lot of them looked as though they were wearing a sort of uniform." He paused for a second and then went on: "There was nothing smart or really noticeable about anyone, except that each group of five or six men working on different ships or jobs wore something almost identical to the other men in that group."

"Such as?" Jenkins asked.

"Such as similar seamen's caps with a certain type of badge or buttons: others had coloured waistcoats or scarves, or rings or patches sewn on to their jacket sleeves or pockets," Roberts explained. "They're organized gangs, aren't they?"

Jenkins said, "Mr Roberts, they're organised like a bloody army, one big regiment divided into sections, platoons and companies."

Roberts replied, "Taff, I'm sure the Docks Company managers must have organized the men in such a way, so when they work together it ensures the maximum efficiency of the gangs, especially when they're loading and unloading boats and barges."

Jenkins asked, "But were they issued with some sort of uniform?"

"I doubt it very much," Roberts replied. "Cost too much, won't it? Perhaps the additions to the men's clothing was their own idea, so they'd recognize each other in the noise and depth of the ships' holds. Perhaps there's nothing sinister about nine-tenths of the gangs working on the docks and on our part of the harbour."

"I agree," replied Jenkins, "except that the other tenth of the working gangs are up to something and I'll bet it isn't just this lot called the Commodores. What's that supposed to mean, I ask you? The gang must be organized by someone who has some semblance of an education and authority and who knows the ins and outs of the dock and harbour authorities. And the comings and goings of the shipping in and out of the harbour. I've got a nasty feeling we haven't seen the last of them yet!"

Roberts interrupted Jenkins just as the office door opened and Joe Worrell entered the room, closely followed by Peters.

Roberts went on, pretending not to notice Peters' arrival, "Yes!" he turned to Worrell. "Yes, Mr Worrell, I was just telling Jenkins here what a close shave I and my family had last night when two men broke into our house and tried to rob me, but I don't keep any money or valuables in the house."

"My goodness, Mr Roberts, are you all right? Are your family safe?" It was Peters who interrupted, his voice fawning in his attempt to show genuine concern.

Roberts, who had turned slightly towards Jenkins and Worrell, winked at them before turning back to Peters.

"Oh yes, thank you, Mr Peters, everything is fine now, no one was hurt except one of the robbers. My next door neighbour came in unexpectedly, just to get some oil for his lamps. He had been out shooting rabbits in the back fields and still had his shotgun. Well, you should have seen those crooks faces, they nearly died with fright."

Jenkins was watching Peters, whose next question was surprising.

"Did he kill them?"

Roberts replied, "Kill who, Mr Peters?"

"You know, I mean the robbers." Peters stuttered trying to cover up his curiosity.

"Well, almost," Roberts answered quietly, "that is if he lived through the night: he took a terrible smack to his head. Mind you the bloke who was trying to knife me didn't come off much better. He had to be taken to the hospital before the police took him to the station. I think they both were going to be charged with attempted murder and robbery with violence. Mind you, Mr Peters, the one who wasn't hurt, was singing like a canary even before the police arrived."

Jenkins had to suppress a smile as Roberts said, "That neighbour of mine knew what he was doing, he almost strangled the bloke who had the knife with the cretin's own arms. It was unbelievable. He started blurting out names and places before the police had even been called."

Peters couldn't hold back any longer. "What names were they Mr Roberts? Do you remember them?"

Jenkins leaned forward a little, trying to gauge a reaction from Peter's face as Roberts replied, pretending to think hard before he answered: "Oh yes, I remember. I don't think I shall ever forget. The one that was unconscious and taken to hospital was called Woods. The other bloke who had the knife was called Jameson."

Peters glanced quickly at the floor as Jenkins realised there had been a flutter of recognition in the man's eyes. When Mr Roberts mentioned that Jameson had said that both of the assailants belonged to a gang called the Commodores, Peters' face blanched a whitish-grey colour.

At the same time he said, "You'll have to excuse me for a few minutes, sorry, but I need the toilet."

As Peters left the room, Jenkins and Roberts smiled at each other, trying to restrain themselves from laughing out loud.

Worrell watched both men, wondering what the joke was and hoping it wasn't at his expense.

"Don't worry, Joe," said Roberts. "Everything is fine now so let's get on with our work, aye? Otherwise I'll be paying you all for nothing. Right now I'm off to the Docks Administration Offices: I've got a little parcel to return. So I'll see you in an hour."

Jenkins went on his rounds carrying out the tasks that were noted on his 'dockets' as he often called to them.

It was a good day for getting his work done. The sun had come out and he whistled tunelessly as he walked to and from the various boats' offices and the one tanker ship that needed to be directed to her mooring. After speaking to the ship's captain and giving him the directions to the Floating Harbour Master's Office, Jenkins went to the Docks Administrative Offices where he found the Floating Harbour Master, Mr Roberts.

As they walked back to the Floating Harbour Master's Office, they discussed their suspicions about Peters' unusual behaviour, attitude and undeniably secretive actions, and possible association with some of the dock workers, especially those who were known to be on the fringes of, or members of, the lawless gangs that roamed the docklands. But apart from being noticeable because he had been seen on a couple of occasions near to or talking to suspicious looking men, there didn't seem to be any proof of wrong-doing by Peters.

By the time they returned to the office, it was almost time for work to finish for that day.

Peters and Worrell had just about finished putting their various documents and ledgers away as Jenkins and Roberts entered the office.

"I'll be off now then, sir. I have to be at the Citadel by seven tonight and with having to change into a decent shirt, I won't have much time to get there after going home. So I'll see you in the morning. Good-night, sir."

He had deliberately been formal, so as not to give Peters too many ideas about his familiarity with Mr Roberts and their discussions.

He turned to Worrell, "'Night, Joe." Then to Peters "Good-night Mr Peters, see you tomorrow, eh?"

Worrell and Roberts both nodded and said, "Good-night, Taff, have a nice evening; see you in the morning, God willing."

Peters just stacked the documents he was holding, and placed them in an opened drawer in his desk, slammed the drawer shut and left the office, ignoring Jenkins completely but mumbling to Roberts "'Night, Mr Roberts!"

Jenkins shrugged his shoulders and followed him out on to the dock, deciding not to follow him to the main gates but made his own way along the edge of the harbour wall, noting the names of the ships and boats moored there.

Welsh Lass was moored nearest to the dock gates. Seeing her Jenkins walked close to the little ship, hoping to catch a sight of Dai Jones or Captain Redone. But all her hatches and holds were closed and there was no sign of life aboard.

"Perhaps I'll see Dai tomorrow, if the *Welsh Lass* is still in dock," he said to himself.

By the time he had arrived at the dock gates, Peters had disappeared from sight and Jenkins began his long walk home.

He hadn't walked more than half a mile when a dock's van pulled up alongside him.

"You Jenkins?" the driver asked.

Jenkins replied, "Aye, I am, who wants to know?"

"Well I've been sent by your boss, Mr Roberts, and told to take you 'ome, 'cause you've got a very important meetin' tonight. I've got to wait for you to get changed, then take you back to the Docks road for you to get a tram into Bristol. It's OK, mate, 'cause I got to make a delivery up this way, an' I know Mr Roberts very well, a good bloke 'e is, ain't 'e?"

"Yes he is, thanks for the lift too. Who are you then?"

"Bob Weller. I've been drivin' this van fer nigh on five years now, so there ain't much I don't know about this place. So anyfing I can 'elp wiv, jus' let me know, OK? 'Specially as you're a friend of old Roberts."

"Well I ain't exactly a friend of Mr Roberts!" Jenkins protested.

"That ain't how I sees it mate, nor 'im, I'm thinkin'."

As the van rattled along, Jenkins wondered what was happening to him. During his service in the Guards, all his thinking had been done for him; where to go, when to go, what to do, how to do it. There was no what, where, when, who or why: just get on with it. But now, everything that needed to be done, when and where it was to be done, or even why it needed to be done, was up to him.

In the Guards, even his friends were often made for him and put around him. His enemies were usually put in front of him or looked for him. Here in civvy street he made his own friends and enemies, looked out for them both and if necessary fought with and against them both. It looked as though it would always be like this from now on.

When the van arrived at the coach house he was sweating, as if he had just run all the way home, but he was washed, shaved, changed and back in the van in record time. By the time he was dropped off at the Docks tram stop, he felt much better. As he waited for the tram he began to feel excited in a way that he had never felt before. Then he started to worry that the feelings he began to experience would fade and by the time he arrived at the Citadel there'd be nothing left.

The tram was on time and fifteen minutes later he was standing outside the Citadel main door. He began to pace up and down, wondering if he was too early or too late. Then he realised he was frightened to go in. He couldn't believe it.

"I've never been this frightened in my life, even when I was being shot at, even when I was wounded," he began berating himself. "You stupid sod, get a grip of yourself, what will she think if she sees you like this?"

He took a deep breath, took a pace towards the door and reached for the handle.

At that moment a voice from behind him said quietly, "Excuse me mister, are you going in?"

He turned towards the voice and saw a group of five or six youngsters, all about fifteen or sixteen years old. There was one a lot younger, about nine, a red haired, tiny, girl.

"Come on mister," she piped up in a shrill soprano voice. "Let us in, will you? We'll be late; whasamatter, scared?"

"Shush! Shush!" Her companions told her off.

He stepped away from the door. He *was* scared he told himself, and it took a little girl to notice. With that, he followed them as they rushed into the Citadel.

May Andrews held out her arms as the youngsters rushed towards her, the little red-headed girl winning the race to get into her arms, hugging May as though she was the last person on earth. Looking over the heads of the children, May was already smiling, but when she saw Jenkins her smile became huge. She carefully untangled the little girl's arms from her own and very gently made her way through the crowd of happy youngsters. They all realised then that there was something happening in the hall that they'd never seen before.

Mrs Andrews was walking towards and holding out her hands and smiling at a complete stranger. They couldn't believe it. There were also four or five adult members of the Salvation Army in the hall. They realised, and understood that they would have to take the meeting that evening, because the Captain wouldn't be capable. Not with the look and presence of the man who had entered the room.

No one knew if he was a close relation or whether he was someone beyond the usual church life. Everyone in the hall just stared in amazement. Jenkins and the Captain didn't even notice them, as she guided him to a chair at the back of the congregations seats.

"Hello Jenks, love," were her first words. He just looked at her happy radiant face.

"Hello May!" After that he was dumb struck.

It was her deputy that took prayers that evening.

Even though May took part, her heart wasn't in it. Usually nothing ever took her away from her duties or her prayers, although she had felt that over the last few weeks something else was beginning to take over her life besides God. Whatever it was that might be next to God, it would never overtake her feelings, the love of her religion and her duty to God.

She knew that Jenks, as she called him, had come into her life. Even though she knew he might never become wholly involved in it because their views about God differed so widely. Jenkins had told her when they first met that when he lived in the valleys he had believed in the version of God that he'd been taught in the Baptist Chapels of the Welsh valleys.

Having been abroad for so long and been marched to the British Army's version of church services, then seeing different religions and ceremonies performed in Europe, Africa, the Near and Far East, Jenkins had come to the conclusion that although all people needed to believe in something or someone, it wasn't necessarily the Welsh, English, Scottish or Irish religious beliefs, or for that matter, any other country's religion in the world, that were right.

The only people that he knew of or could understand were the people of the world, that believed in their families, from birth to death. If they had to fight, it was usually because they were attacked because of their beliefs. They defended themselves and their families or home, because it was their form of religion. Their family was their god, although it was never referred to as that. If they wanted to pray for themselves or their families, they did. Who they prayed to was for them to decide and not because someone told them they had to believe in a god.

Jenkins didn't, or wouldn't, criticise any person or race for believing in any kind of religion until something came along that wasn't the cause or partly the cause of so many wars. So he would wait until something or someone, without lecturing or browbeating, convinced him that what he believed was wrong.

May decided that she wouldn't try to convert Jenkins to anything. So when they met, religion was never spoken about, even when she was in her Salvation Army uniform. During the prayer meeting that evening, Jenkins sat next to her as she prayed and sang one or two hymns. She didn't seem embarrassed at all as she sang in her beautiful mezzo-soprano voice and went on her knees to pray.

Later the meeting turned into a band practice night, so Jenkins and May left the building and went for a walk along the gaslit streets, past the local terraced houses listening to the sounds of singing or families arguing and babies crying.

Mothers were smacking their children, then yelling at their screaming babies to be quiet! Or shouting at them, "If you don't stop crying and screaming, I'll give you another slap. Now wait 'till you father gets home, there'll be another hiding for you when he gets back from the pub. You'll see! 'Specially, if you don't get to bed now."

"Sorry, Mum, honest, I didn't mean it, Johnny started it, why don't you tan his arse?"

"Get to bed you little bugger, go on. Quick or I'll tan yours."

Jenkins and May listened to all of this mayhem coming from the rows of two-up and two-down, run down, overcrowded houses. As they walked they sometimes cringed, smiled, even laughed at what they heard coming from the half-opened windows and doors.

It was a close-knit community all right. Everyone living there knew exactly what was happening in every house and to every man, women and child in the street. There was always someone watching from the open windows of different terraced houses, as if they were designated sentries, taking their turn to keep watch. As the police weren't welcome in these streets, it was natural for a watch to be set up because the amount of criminal activity that occurred in the streets of Bristol at that time was beginning to rise, mainly due to the poverty of the area.

If strangers were in the vicinity, people would come out of their houses and if they were thought to be undesirable in that area, one or two of the men might challenge them. It wasn't always safe to walk in these terraced streets after dark either, whether a person lived there or not.

Luckily May Andrews was well known throughout the district. She and her companions had worked with the people there for years, every since the Citadel had been set up. She knew most of the children and their parents, because she had in emergencies helped deliver many of the babies born in the area around the Salvation Army church.

Wearing her uniform and the new insignia of her recent Captaincy, she put her arm through Jenkins', showing anyone who wished, their friendship and perhaps their future companionship.

Over two hours later they arrived back at the Citadel, during which time Jenkins related almost all that had happened to him, about Dai, Captain Redone and all the old and new friends he had found. He told her of his sadness at the death of his mother, about the robbery of her house and the demise of the man who had committed the murder, although he didn't actually mention his part in the man's 'accident'. He knew that May wouldn't or couldn't approve of violence, no matter what the reasons.

When they arrived back at the Citadel, they realised he might miss his tram home if stayed any longer. Plucking up a different sort of courage, he took hold of May's hand, leaned forward and kissed her on the cheek. As he did so he murmured, "Good-night May, love." She in turn kissed him on his cheek.

"'Night Jenks. I'll phone the office lunch time tomorrow; try and be there, because it'll be important."

"Why's that, then?"

"Because I'll want to speak to you. Come on love, I'll walk you to the tram stop."

"It's all right," he replied. "I'll need to have a little time to think and it won't be right, you having to walk back here by yourself again. I'll be waiting by the phone tomorrow, love. Good-night May, I have to go."

He released himself from her grasp on his arm turned and walked away. He didn't look back, but he knew she was watching as he rounded a corner out of her sight.

For the next few weeks they were often seen together, either at the Citadel prayer meetings, although Jenkins couldn't actually get on his bended knees to pray, or in the centre of Bristol at different Salvation Army street meetings with the Salvation Army band.

May was always at the front, rattling a collection box or leading the singing of hymns or Salvation Army songs. She was never embarrassed or worried about what other people thought or said about her or the Salvation Army. May, as the Captain of the Citadel, led the way. That was her style although she had never been taught to lead or manage anyone or thing. She was a natural leader and everyone, whether they knew her personally or not, respected her for her work in the community and her religious principles.

Jenkins went with her: not followed her, accompanied her, not wanting to lose sight of her or her companionship.

She took him on a number of occasions to her home near the Citadel, cooked him a meal and they talked about everything: his army life and her army life were usually the main topics but occasionally he would ask about her life with her family and the baker.

Gradually as the weeks passed they began to understand fully their own and each other's future aspirations and feelings for each other.

It gradually dawned on him that May might want him as her companion for life, although marriage had never been mentioned. He on his part knew without doubt that his whole aim of what was left of his life was to marry her. He knew that it was too early to ask her for that privilege, he also felt what love actually meant when he was with her or away from her. To him she was a lovely woman, not plain and not beautiful in appearance, but her beauty radiated from her inner self.

A number of her friends often commented on the glow that seemed to surround her, as she went around performing her duties, visiting the sick in hospitals or at their homes, delivering some of their babies and accompanying relatives to the funerals of the deceased.

May Andrews was always available to anyone who needed her help, comfort or prayers. Richard Jenkins decided then that he loved her.

One July morning as he was doing his rounds with the dockets, he almost bumped into Mudhog Jack. They hadn't seen or spoken to each other since the assault on Jack. Jenkins held out his hand and when Jack took it, they shook hands like long lost pals.

At the time they were standing under the bows of a tramp steamer that was moored near the dock gates. Large crates and sacks shielded them from the prying eyes of those intent on committing any sort of misdemeanour.

Firstly, Jack thanked Jenkins profusely for "saving my skin!" Then he went on to say it was the nearest he had ever come to being found out.

"Found out about what?" Jenkins asked.

"Found out about doing my job!" replied Jack.

"What job?"

"Keeping my eye on the gangs of thugs that operate here in the docklands."

"Why are you telling me this? That's bloody dangerous knowledge ain't it?" Jenkins said angrily.

"Look, don't worry, Taff, somebody has to do it, don't they? There's only me, you and my boss that knows. See, I had to tell him about you, because sometimes I need some backing and as no one else knows what I'm doing here he told me to tell you what I've been doing, all right? Then perhaps if anything was to happen to me, then you could, if you would, let him know."

"Who is he, then?"

"His name's Mike Shuker: he works in the Admin Office by the dock gates, OK?" Jenkins started to protest but Jack went on, "Look, mate, you don't have to follow me around, just do as you've been doing before: sit on the bench outside the office and have a chat. That way you'll know I'm OK. If you want, I can give you bits of knowledge that might help you with the problems you've had in the past. I know you been trying to find out about the dock gangs. Maybe, later perhaps, I can help you out there as well. You'd be surprised at the bits of gossip that I hear about everyone and everything," he paused and shook his head.

"Not many people take much notice of me nowadays. I've been hanging around here so long, that most of the time they don't even see me, except that bastard Peters! Yeh, you watch him, evil swine he is, though it looks like butter wouldn't melt in his gob. You just be there for me, will you? And please don't mention this to anyone. Too many mouths can get too many split lips, can't they?"

They shook hands and prepared to go their separate ways.

"All right." As Jenkins agreed he shook his head in disbelief at what was happening. "Just don't take any chances, will you?"

As they left the cover of the ship and stores, Jenkins breathed a huge sigh of relief, hoping that they hadn't been seen.

Over the next week there was no sign of the gangs or any sort of incident around or in the docks area. The atmosphere at work had changed; it was almost sociable but not friendly between Peters and the others but he did manage to say the niceties each morning and evening and although it was never directed at Jenkins, he was at least polite to Mr Roberts and Worrell. Everyone thought his attitude had changed for the better and up to a point it had.

Then one morning at the beginning of July, Inspector Hazelton visited the office and what he told them was a surprise to all.

Jenkins was the first to greet him. "Well now there's a sight for sore eyes," as they shook hands. "It's a long time no see, Inspector. To what do we owe this honour, eh?"

He guided the inspector into the office where Roberts and Worrell stood up, surprise and consternation on their faces. Worrell began to twirl the ends of his moustache nervously; he had never been one to be comfortable in the presence of any member of the constabulary, not that he was anything but a law abiding citizen, but such was his upbringing and family background that policemen were the last people to have any contact with.

"Morning Inspector, what can we do for you?" Mr Roberts gestured their unexpected visitor to a seat, Peters' chair, because he hadn't arrived for work at that time. "Cup of tea? It's a bit of an early start for you isn't it?" Roberts went on, giving Jenkins a nod towards the kettle. "I expect we could all do with one, don't you?"

Worrell, anxious to be out of the policeman's sight, signalled to Jenkins that he would make the tea and disappeared through the office door to fill the kettle from the tap outside.

Inspector Hazelton took his notebook from his jacket pocket, opened it and asked, "Do either of you know a Mr Gordon Peters?"

Roberts replied, "Aye, of course we do, he works here and you're sitting at his desk. Is there something wrong? Has something happened?"

"You could say that. He was arrested last night for giving his wife and kids a battering at their home. He's a wife and child beater. His wife is in hospital, as are two of their five children. They've all taken a terrible battering. If it wasn't for his oldest daughter, she's just twelve, no one would have reported it. Luckily, there was a policeman patrolling that street at the time and the little girl ran to him and asked that he stop her Dad from hitting her Mum."

"He was just in time Reynolds, the policeman, said. If he hadn't got there when he did, Mrs Peters would have been on a slab in the morgue. Two of the youngest girls were also taken to hospital, one with head injuries and one with a broken wrist."

He stopped, letting what he had said sink in, then he continued, "It seems that the two little girls aged five and six had found a box of jewellery and trinkets under the floor boards of a built-in cupboard in the parent's bedroom. Mr Peters found them playing with them, like toys. He went berserk and started to kick and punch the poor little mites. His wife, slattern she might be, tried to stop him but it seems she had no chance. He went at her with his boots and a wooden knob-headed walking stick. When Reynolds got to them, Mrs Peters was on the floor unconscious and he was about to hit the poor woman again. Reynolds told us that when Peters saw him enter the bedroom he attacked him with the stick, so Reynolds had to use his truncheon to defend himself and control Peters."

He paused, "Now Peters says that he was attacked by his wife and was defending himself, because she was wielding a knife. We looked all over the house and the only thing resembling a weapon was a small knitting needle, which was found under the bed, and it is believed that from the filth and rubbish there, it hadn't been moved for years. So it doesn't seem likely that it was used during the incident."

Jenkins asked, "How is his wife and the children? I know he has five kids; what has happened to the other three?"

"They'll be all right, Mrs Peters' sister has taken them in. The two in hospital will stay there until their mother has recovered and they can eventually all leave together. That's the best anyone can do at the moment – unless it's to hang this evil bastard we've got on our hands."

He raised his hand signalling that he hadn't finished. "He will be charged with attempted murder, assault with intent to kill, child molesting and assault on a police officer. We also intend to charge him with being in possession of stolen property, because the jewellery we found couldn't possible have belonged to him."

He shook his head and went on. "There must have been several hundred pounds worth there, perhaps more. We also found this filthy bottle-green waistcoat on the bedroom floor." He went on, "We know that a gang of villains from dockland wear similar clothes. I wonder have any of you've seen Peters wearing anything like it at any time?"

They all remained silent, wondering exactly what sort of man they'd been working with.

Worrell, who'd been watching and listening, stepped forward. He'd never been one for gossip, or listening in on other people's conversations. In the case of his dealings with Peters it was always about docks' business.

"I've got something to say about the waistcoat," he blurted out. "I saw him wearing it on the day those two villains attacked the old man. He has worn it three or four times before, during the last year or two, usually when he went for a walk around the harbour during lunch times or when he was on his way home. He used to unbutton his jacket on the way out of the office, but when he came into work, he would always button his jacket over it. Usually it couldn't be seen. I didn't take much notice of it or him, otherwise he would always make some nasty remark, like 'What the hell are you looking at?' and then swear at me. I notice he never swore at me in front of Mr Roberts, though."

"All right, thanks Mr Worrell."

Worrell stopped for breath, he'd never been so forward in his life and he wondered for a moment if what he was saying would be believed, or would his bemused audience actually realise that he had spoken up for the first time in his life, against someone he thought would never be a friend. "In for a penny," he thought to himself and went on:

"I saw that, when he did that, opened his jacket I mean, stevedores or dock workers often stopped him and had a chat, or handed him an envelope or small package. I really didn't take a lot of notice because we all talk to the people on the harbour or in the docks area, it's often part of the job."

Inspector Hazelton looked at him closely, "Are you sure Mr Worrell? About the packages I mean."

"Oh yes, sir, absolutely: I am as sure as I see you standing there."

"Right then, Mr Roberts, do you have a spare key to Mr Peters' desk drawer? I presume that they do lock, don't they?"

"That's right, Inspector, we all keep our own desk keys, except Mr Jenkins, he doesn't have a desk, do you Taff?"

"OK then, sir, to make everything legal and be seen to be fair I'd like every drawer and cupboard in the office to be opened, so that the constable and I can examine each one. That way I shan't have to get a warrant to search Mr Peters' desk, because you have all volunteered to allow me to search this office of your own free will. As Mr Peters is in custody and suspected of being in possession of stolen property, then I have the authority to search any and all of his property and possessions, but none of your good people's personal things, only if you were to give me your permission. Is that all right, sir?"

Roberts replied, "Certainly, Inspector, in my own case, be my guest. I'm sure you'll find nothing to interest you in my desk, or the remainder of the office for that matter. Perhaps Mr Worrell will give his own consent, then I'm sure everything will be in order."

Worrell nervously assented to the request by nodding his head, and mumbling, "All right", though he wasn't sure whether or not he could remember if there was anything incriminating in the desk. He didn't think there was, but wasn't absolutely certain.

"All right then, Mr Roberts; Mr Worrell, will you please unlock any drawer or cupboard with any of the keys that are in your possession. Before that will you please give me any spare keys that you hold for Mr Peters' desk. Thank you!"

The next few minutes went by as Inspector Hazelton and his constable watched as his requests were carried out by Roberts and Worrell. Jenkins stood by the office counter, a bemused smile on his face and wondering just what the policemen were going to find.

It turned out there was absolutely nothing that interested the searchers, except a list of names that didn't seem to have any bearing

on the administration of the office or the Floating Harbour. The list revealed that the men named on the paper were in groups of five or six under other names such as Spikers, Dock Rats, Stowaways and, among them, the Commodores. There were seven or eight other named groups on the paper that went into the policeman's notebook.

Asked if anyone recognised the groups of names, Roberts, Jenkins and Worrell all shook their heads. Jenkins did, in fact, notice one of the groups to be familiar, the Commodores, but he didn't mention it to the detective inspector because he thought to himself that he might need to know who they were later, after he had spoken to Mudhog Jack.

After completing his search, Sergeant Hazelton thanked them for their co-operation and went on his way.

Before leaving he turned to Jenkins. "We are still continuing to make progress with your sister's case. Don't you worry, Taff, I won't give it up until I've got an answer, all right?"

"Thanks, Mr Hazelton. If I get anything else on these gangs I'll let you know, OK!"

"Just take it easy," Hazelton replied. "They really are a lot of dangerous bastards; well you already have had experience of that haven't you, so go bloody careful, won't you? I don't want to have to go digging you out of the harbour mud. See you, sometime soon, OK? Oh! I very nearly forgot, Taff. Will you come to the station as soon as you can? The money has arrived from Swansea and I'm sure you'll have some good use for it, eh? I'll see you there, then. Bye now, watch your back, won't you?"

Roberts had a perplexed frown on his face when he heard the inspector's parting remark.

"What's he mean by that then, Taff?" he asked.

"Nothing much, Mr Roberts. You know what its like around here, always someone trying to nick things or come the hard man. When one man goes down, if he is the hard one, it won't be long until someone else tries to take over. Could be mayhem around here for the next couple of weeks, I imagine. Not us though, we don't have anything the gangs want, do we?"

Roberts spoke up, "Hang on, Taff, jumping to conclusions don't you think? Peters might be vicious to his family, but that's perhaps because he's just an evil bully. The things his children found just might be his family heirlooms, eh?"

"And perhaps I'm the bloody King, Mr Roberts. There isn't a lot of point making suppositions is there, but if Peters is a gang boss then he has to be a right evil, vicious, bugger to stay on top of the pile of mire that those men are in. We'll just have to wait and see what crawls out of the next cesspit, before we say anything that might bring the muck down on our heads, if you both get my meaning?"

"Mr Worrell, my turn to make the tea, I think," continued Jenkins. "I expect we can do with a fresh cup after all the dust that's been disturbed, eh Mr Roberts? Then I'd best get on with my job hadn't I, considering Mr Peters won't be in, eh?" I hope you won't be expecting me to do his work, Mr Roberts, 'cause you know I don't have a clue what you all do here. It looks too complicated for me and I ain't much of a writer, honest, Mr Roberts."

"Well now, Mr Jenkins, there's a thought! That is an excellent idea. Mr Worrell and I will teach you to do our work, so that if the circumstances arise, for instance if I have to go away for some time on a course or a long business meeting, or perhaps Mr Worrell is ill, heaven forbid, then you will be able to take over our work. Then Harbour's business won't grind to a halt. What do you think, Mr Worrell? Good idea, eh?"

For the first time Worrell smiled, "A grand idea, Mr Roberts, a grand idea."

Jenkins, a worried look on his face, said quickly, "I won't stop for another cup then, Mr Roberts. I'd best get on out with these dockets." He moved towards the office door.

"Otherwise, as you say, the Harbour business will grind to a stop, won't it?"

With that parting shot he disappeared through the door.

Roberts grinned at Worrell, "What a very good idea, eh?"

Later that day Jenkins telephoned the Citadel and arranged to meet May. He needed to tell her about the money and what he wanted to use some of it for. He knew that May was in a position to find out about the documents required and how to arrange for the caskets of his sister's family to be exhumed and transferred to Swansea, then on to the Gwyn Baptist Chapel, the cemetery nearest his and their original home. If there was enough money and time he would arrange for his mother to be buried with them, next to his father who was there already. Their names could be added to his headstone after they had all been re-interred.

When they met that evening and were taking their usual walk he explained what he wanted to do. She took hold of his face in both hands, pulling his head down, so that she could look into his eyes.

"Do you know Jenks, my love, that's the nicest thing I have ever heard anyone offering to do for anyone. It's a wonderful gesture from a wonderful man; I'll do every thing that I can to help you take them home."

Jenkins blushed bright red with embarrassment. He continued nervously trying to explain himself.

"What I want to do, is to make sure that the money isn't wasted. My parents worked like slaves for it, especially my mother during her last few years, and I'm blowed if I'm going to spend it all on beer and a good time. She alone deserves more than that. They need to be buried together, facing along the Swansea Valley looking towards the sea. It has a beautiful view across the village and along the hills, following the river Tawe to the coast. That's what I think, May, I hope we can make it happen."

May stared at him, "Listen Jenks, love, we can make anything happen with His help. I shall pray for you." It was the first time she had mentioned God and prayer since they had been walking out together.

"Besides, Jenks, we both have friends and know people who can help and have the knowledge to make things happen, so don't worry, we'll work it out together"

By that time they had reached her little terraced house and she invited him in for supper.

He always felt comfortable being with her and never felt he had anything to prove. He was warm and happy, as he sat watching her cooking supper and pondered over what he had told her.

He thought about the people in Swansea who were of so much help when he needed it, of Dai Jones and Captain Redone and the policeman Inspector Hazelton, who seemed always ready to help. Also Mr Roberts and his wife: if it hadn't been for them he would never have been in the position that he was in at this time. He would probably have been in prison breaking rocks, or slogging it out on some labouring job, that is if he could get a job, with the way things were turning out. Mind you, plenty of people had warned him about leaving the army and just how hard it would be to settle into civilian life.

Now he had found May it was easier, although he still couldn't understand what and why everything had happened to him since leaving the battalion. Not one of his old mates would have believed him if he ever went back and told them. Perhaps one day he might, because every so often there was a battalion reunion and one day he might attend one.

He tried to convince himself that it was time to tell May just how much he loved her and would she marry him. It felt like the right time but when he opened his mouth to tell her and ask her, nothing came out.

They spent another pleasant evening together, discussing his ideas and her suggestions and the future. As he left to go home and was on the tram, he cursed himself all the way, for not telling her exactly how he felt and what he would like them to become. He could say man and wife to himself, but not to May. He hardly slept that night, thinking of the chance that he'd let slip by.

"The time will come soon, I hope," he said to himself. "I don't fancy winding up as a lonely old man."

Chapter 5

A Misunderstanding

The next morning, whilst helping Joe Worrell and having decided it just might be all right to learn about the other work in the office, Jenkins was sitting at Peters' desk, copying information on to dockyard forms.

"What the hell are you doing there, Jenkins?" a familiar voice snarled. "That's my bloody desk. Jump into my grave as quick would you? Get out of my chair. What? Am I expected to work standing up?"

Jenkins stood up and pushed the chair back. "Well there's a nice surprise, Mr Roberts. Doesn't look as though I'll get that training after all, does it?" He looked at Peters, "Do you think you can work today then, Mr Peters? It looks as though someone took a disliking to your face. Does it hurt? I hope!"

"Don't be funny with me, Jenkins, I'm not here to be sneered at by the likes of you."

Roberts stepped forward and peered at Peters' bruised face. "We were told that you'd been arrested," he said without any malice.

Jenkins interrupted grinning as he said, "We were told you attacked a policeman's truncheon with your face: looks like it was true as well, don't it."

"Now that's enough of that, Mr Jenkins, no need to make fun of a man's injuries. Come on, Mr Peters, what's happened?"

"There was a complete misunderstanding. Me and the wife had a row, she pushed me, I pushed her and she fell over one of the girls, Annie, who banged her head on the edge of the chest of drawers. I went to pick my wife up, but because she is a big woman she was too heavy for me to lift and I fell on top of her at the same time knocking the other little girl over. I'm afraid she hurt her wrist quite badly but it really was an accident.

"Anyway, neither my wife or the police are pressing charges, because it was and still is a family matter. I've made a complaint against that stupid policeman who attacked me with his truncheon. Do you know? I had to go to hospital for treatment."

"No charges then?" Joe Worrell asked.

"Course not! 'T'ain't what you hoped for is it? You little nark!"

"As I said just now, Mr Peters, there isn't any need for that sort of rudeness, so please let's get on with the job, if you're able, that is. Are you?"

"Course I am, Mr Roberts," Peters replied still angry and glaring at both Jenkins and Worrell as if daring them to make any further remarks.

"Right boys, we're a bit behind with the work today, so let's get on with it, eh?"

Jenkins took a handful of dockets from the out tray and went on his rounds. He'd just finished his first circuit of the docks, when he heard a piercing whistle and looking around saw Dai Jones and Captain Redone standing on the bridge of the *Welsh Lass*. They were just finishing off mooring the ship. When they'd finished, the skipper signalled to Jenkins to 'come aboard'. Jenkins, pleased to see a friendly face, did as he was bid.

"Long time, no see," said Captain Redone. "How are things, eh?"

"Not so bad, Skipper, not today anyway!" He went on to tell them about his ideas about moving his family back to his home village and the help that had been offered him by May and her friends. Then about Peters and the attack on the Roberts family.

Dai, changing the subject, said, "What else then, Taff, you've not asked her yet, have you?"

"Asked what?" Redone said inquisitively.

"If she'll marry him, that's what!" Dai said peevishly. "Do you know what," Dai pointed at Jenkins, "he wants to make his bloody mind up, otherwise they'll both leave each other on the shelf and that'll be a real pity. They're made for each other." He laughed, "Besides that'll be the only time I can get a new suit and her at home a new hat. Now come on Skip, Taff, got time for a drink?" They both nodded.

"Yes but remember I've got to go back to work," Jenkins said. "And I don't want a bollocking or the sack."

Dai went on, "OK lets go. I've got a bottle in the galley; we can have a drink up here or in the Skipper's cabin. What do you say, Skipper?"

"The cabin would be best Dai, we don't want to drop Jenks in it do we?"

It was over half an hour before he could get on with his job and by that time he began to feel a little the worse for wear, though no one noticed it.

That same evening, Jenkins went straight to the police station from work. He had arranged to meet May at the station at six pm.

Inspector Hazelton was waiting for them, with him was the station Chief Inspector, a large red-faced man, who seemed to be bursting out of his tight-fitting uniform jacket.

After the formalities of introducing the couple, the Chief Inspector offered Jenkins his own heart-felt condolences and as much official and personal help as he was able.

Hazelton produced a pad of official looking documents. They were the application forms for removing and transferring his sister and her family from the Bristol cemetery, to be re-interred in the Gwyn cemetery in the Swansea Valley. Inspector Hazelton had already filled them in on Jenkins' behalf and the Chief Inspector had recommended to the Bristol magistrates that his sister and her family's remains be taken to Wales.

The forms were already signed by a magistrate to that effect, with the City of Bristol to bear the cost of the journey. An undertaker was also recommended to accompany the bodies to Wales, but Jenkins would have to pay his fees. It would be better to arrange the journey by train, the inspector suggested and the police would provide an escort to Temple Meads railway station.

Papers were also provided for the transference of his mother's remains to the same chapel cemetery: it didn't seem as if anything had been left to chance.

Everything had been approved, signed and sealed by a magistrate at Bristol Magistrates Court, although the papers would also have to be approved and signed by a magistrate in a Swansea Court on behalf of Swansea Council. He could only recommend to the Welsh police and Swansea Council authorities that Jenkins' mother be moved to the Swansea Valley cemetery. Jenkins would have to wait for their approval before his mother's casket could be exhumed, but Inspector Hazelton said he couldn't see any objection being made, due to the extenuating circumstances of his family's demise.

May suggested that all the relevant details be left to the undertaker in Bristol, as his experience would be invaluable. She said that she would telephone her counterpart in the Swansea Citadel to make similar arrangements, when permission was received from the Swansea Council.

Finally the Chief Inspector said he would get in touch with the senior officer at Swansea police, to try and arrange for his mother's exhumation and transport to the Gwyn cemetery on the same day that the event would happen at Bristol, therefore having the family funeral on the same day which would allow Jenkins to greave for his lost loved ones at the same time and in the same place, allowing them to be together always.

Having thanked the policemen for their help once again, Jenkins and May turned to leave Hazelton's office.

"Wait a sec' Mr Jenkins, please sit down. I almost forgot another reason I asked you to come to the office." He pulled open a desk drawer and took out a white cloth bag and placed it on the desk.

"Open it please, Mr Jenkins," the Chief Inspector said quietly.

"If you would please be as quick as you can and count the money then sign this receipt, I can get back to my other duties because even in such a short time that I've been out of my office people are demanding my attention. So I shall have to ask that we don't have to do a recount. The inspector and I will witness the transaction and your lady friend can witness the count is correct"

"Yes, sir, fine, thank you," Jenkins replied as he began stacking the coins and notes into piles and columns. When he had finished, the total came to £135. 3s. 11d.

"Enough to pay for the funerals and everything else twice over," he told May.

She smiled and nodded, "I'm so pleased for you, Jenks," she whispered as he replaced the money in the bag.

It was almost two weeks before the arrangements were finalised. Two days later, the caskets containing his sister and her family were exhumed from the Bristol cemetery. During these procedures, May said a prayer as each of Jenkins family were removed from the graves. The local priest who had been invited to witness the exhumations prayed with her. Jenkins could only stand

and watch, his face set like stone. Under the watchful eye of Inspector Hazelton the caskets were transported under police escort to Temple Meads station. There a luggage van had been specially connected to the morning ten o'clock Bristol, Cardiff and Swansea commuter train.

Jenkins, with May, were pleasantly surprised to see Dai Jones and his wife, and Mr Roberts and his wife, waiting at the station, all insisting that they accompany Jenkins and his family to Swansea, then to the funeral at the Gwyn cemetery.

Jenkins had been told by Hazelton, just before the train left Temple Meads, that his mother's casket would be at the Gwyn Chapel waiting to be re-interred with the others.

The funeral would take place at two o'clock in the afternoon, so there would be quite enough time to travel to Swansea, where the cars would be waiting to take everyone on to the Gwyn Chapel.

The Chief Superintendent at the Swansea Central Police Station, having heard the details of the crimes committed against this one family, had made all the necessary transport and escort arrangements for the funeral cortège to arrive safely and on time at the cemetery. He told his deputy it was probably the worst tragedy he had ever had the misfortune to hear about. Every assistance must be made available to the stricken ex-soldier.

Everything went like clockwork. Before Jenkins realised it, he was standing next to May and his friends from Bristol at the Gwyn Chapel graveyard, watching his mother being buried for the second time, now next to his father's grave. His sister and her daughter were buried together, alongside her husband, Andrew, a few yards from her parents.

It wasn't until the vicar the Reverend Ivor Thomas, who had accompanied his mother from Swansea, had said his final prayer, that Jenkins realised just how many people had come to say goodbye to the family: his mother's friends from the Norwegian Church and Myers Street, Robert Evans and his family, Dai Jones's mother and father and, surprisingly, Inspector Marshall, who told him later that he had to come to the funeral to see Hannah Jenkins and her family laid properly to rest.

A buffet had been arranged in the Chapel Hall and as Jenkins and May were about to enter the building, someone put their hand on his shoulder. He turned to look at the bulky tanned man, holding out his hand in greeting.

"Hello Dick, we had to come, my wife and me. Couldn't believe what had happened to Aunt Hannah and your sister."

Jenkins stared at the man, "Sorry, I don't know who you are, I'm afraid."

"You sure, you old bugger?" The reply was in Welsh, "Or is it Richard bach!" Jenkins stared harder into the man's face.

"Bloody hell!" he shouted in delight. "It's you, Alwyn, ain't it? Where did you spring from?" Then he remembered May and switched back to English. "How did you get know about this funeral, then?"

Alwyn looked puzzled, then realising that the lady in the Salvation Army uniform didn't speak Welsh, said, "We do have papers in Builth you know, and this has been in the paper for weeks, you know, the murder and the court case. It's usually me that reads in our house, as we don't listen to the radio very much because its mostly English programmes. So everything is in the paper, that's how I got to know about this. I like to keep up with the news."

After introductions had been made with May and the rest of Jenkins' many old and new friends, Jenkins and Alwyn Johnson talked about their lives and families, Alwyn's farm at Builth and Jenkins' army service, his new found friends and life in Bristol and his job at the floating harbour.

That part of his new life he was happy about, but there was still some unsettled business concerning the death of his sister and her family. After explaining the way his sister and her daughter and husband had died, he said quietly, "There's a score to settle," glancing at May, making sure she hadn't overheard him. Along with his feelings for May, that was the real reason he wanted to stay in Bristol. Until that was settled he wouldn't be going anywhere.

It wasn't until everyone had left the chapel hall that Jenkins realised that he and the Johnsons were they only members of the family left. It came as a complete shock, now that he knew there wouldn't be any close family that he might be able to turn to. For the first time in his life, he felt the reality of being alone and lonely. He knew that he could for the time being rely on May, but for how long, he wondered? Would she consent to a marriage proposal? He didn't want to ask in case she refused, wanting to be just 'Good Friends'. He decided to bide his time and get on with life. "Just as it comes," he said to himself.

He turned to May, standing at the door alongside her, shaking hands with and thanking the departing mourners for their condolences and sympathy.

Finally Dai Jones and his wife came to the door to leave and as he did so Dai said, "We'll be seeing you both for dinner next Sunday, is that all right, May?"

May looked at Jenkins who just nodded, "Yes, thank you Dai and you Mrs Jones."

"Please, my name is Agnes!"

"Agnes, we would be pleased to come, wouldn't we Jenks?" May said. "What time? Seven o'clock?"

"Oh no! We have dinner at one o'clock in our house on Sundays."

May went on as diplomatically as she could, "Of course, lunch- time dinner, I completely forgot, dinner at lunch-time. I have to have my dinner at about seven pm, because I often work late. I get confused as well. Sometimes," she added lamely.

"Don't forget then, Taff, roast shoulder of pork and all the trimmings and if you can manage that, a nice plum pudding for afters. Bye both." Agnes who hadn't said a word all day, was positively trilling.

Jenkins shook Dai Jones's hand. "I haven't got enough left in me Dai to properly thank you for your help and friendship through these last few weeks. Any time you or your family need me to help in any way, for any reason, just tell me! You don't ever have to ask."

"What are you going to do now, Taff ?" Dai asked.

"We've been offered a lift back to Swansea with Police Inspector Marshall: there's a train leaving for Bristol at six o'clock and we told him we would like to be on it, if possible. We should be back home by half-past eight at the latest. What are you doing Dai? Getting the same train?"

"No, we're staying with my Mam for the night. As the *Welsh Lass* is docking tonight, we'll get a berth on her for tomorrow night's tide. Agnes and me have done it once or twice before. Anyway she's a better cook than you, matey!"

They shook hands and Agnes pecked Jenkins and May on the cheek.

"See you Sunday," Agnes called back, as they disappeared out of the Chapel Hall gates.

That Sunday was one of the most pleasant days that Jenkins could remember since he left the hospital bed. Firstly he met May at the Citadel after the morning service, then walked her to Dai and Agnes's home. The three children were sent into the small tidy garden to play, after the visitors had been introduced. Then the Jones's and their guests had a drink before the meal and spoke about the journey to Wales, the funeral service, the meeting of Jenkins' relations and what a sad, long, exhausting day it had been.

"But some good has come out of it," Jenkins told his hosts. "At least my family are together, I've made and met some fine friends and found one or two relations that I didn't realise still existed. I'm really unhappy at losing my family but pleased I was able to bring some sense of order to my life. I will go back and visit them as often as I can. It's thanks to you all and Mr Roberts with his family, that I've been able to get on with my life."

He raised his glass of beer in a silent toast to them.

The children were called in and everyone sat down to Agnes's 'Sunday Dinner' as Agnes called it, although May insisted in a whisper to Jenkins, "It is still lunch."

It was almost the best meal he had tasted for months, even at May's house, although he didn't dare say that to May.

Dai and Agnes hovered around their guests until their every request was satisfied.

Both Jenkins and May had to admit and congratulate Agnes on the best Sunday dinner that they had been fortunate enough to be invited to in years. That's how May expressed herself for them both.

It was an hour later that the couple said their goodbyes and thanks for the dinner, May half-heartedly offering an invitation for Sunday lunch to the Jones's at a later date knowing perfectly well that she couldn't possible turn out a meal with the same succulent meat and vegetables that Agnes had produced; not unless she could cook something that the Jones family had never seen or tasted before.

She told Jenkins of her thoughts, ideas and fears but he brushed them aside saying, "Not to worry love, it's not likely that we'll invite them to lunch or dinner next week, is it? So we'll both give it some thought and maybe we'll ask them round in a couple of months time, all right May, love?"

Her next meeting at the Citadel meant they couldn't dawdle, and May said that she would go on ahead, as she never liked to be late in welcoming the congregation.

He didn't go to her prayer meeting, but went for a walk around docklands. He had become a familiar figure around the docks in the short space of time he had been working on the floating harbour, so no one took a lot of notice of the tall, slightly stooped figure walking slowly past the silent ships at their moorings on the dock walls. A man with such a nondescript look very rarely attracted much attention in that area of the docks.

His route took him past the Administrative Offices, which were just beyond the high wall. Almost next to the office buildings a wicker gate had been set into the wall. It wasn't very noticeable from the road, although three or four large stones had been removed from one side of the locked gate, making a small tunnel-like hole through the four foot thick wall, into a dark short corridor, along the side the administrative building.

He peered into the darkness of the passageway but couldn't see anything at its end, which seemed to be about twenty yards away. He did think that he could hear voices raised in an argument from somewhere but couldn't make out just how far away the owners of the voices were.

Jenkins didn't investigate any further, as it didn't seem to be his business anyway. Later after meeting May he told her about the tunnel.

"Ah yes!" she replied. "That leads into an old sailing ship's hulk. It's quite big and it's upside down; its been there for years, they tell me. The dockers and the stevedores use it as a rest room but mainly as a shelter from bad weather. There is an illegal bar there that everyone knows about, including the docks Management Committee. As there has never been any trouble since the bar started up, about two years ago, the managers haven't bothered to try and close it down. Mind you, I wouldn't like to see you coming out of the Hulk, as it's called, because it's a filthy place; the stench is overpowering. They call it a hiding place for the rats. Which rats I can't say."

Jenkins looked at May in surprise. "You've actually been in there, honestly?"

"Yes, I used to take a collection box around this area, especially on a Saturday or Sunday afternoon. One of my Salvationist ladies who accompanied me that day, dared me to go in and see if I could collect any donations from the men who were there that afternoon. I remember it very well. This time though it was a Saturday afternoon, pouring with rain and it wasn't so very long ago. In fact it was while you were still in hospital. I hadn't met you then. At the time our collection activities hadn't produced much at all. The people's generosity has begun to wane over the last few months, perhaps it's because of the slow-down in the work here, or the so-called depression.

"Anyway, my friend dared me, so I had decided to go in and try and make a collection, so I did. It really is a disgustingly filthy place and the men who go there were, and still are, too. They were mostly too drunk to see or stand.

"I stood just inside the door: it was very dark and dingy and very difficult to see. There was one group of men in the corner at the back of the room, rather 'place'," May corrected herself, "sitting around an old crate, drinking beer and it looked as though they were playing cards. A man who I think looked like Mr Peters, the one who works in the same office as you, called me over. Then without another word or asking his card playing compatriots, he took all the money from the table and put it into my hands.

"There were five men around that table and although one or two made as if to protest, no one did. I think it was that man Peters, Jenks."

She went on as if still shocked by the incident, "All he did was glare at the other four men in turn and put his hand towards the inside pocket of his coat. They all glowered back but didn't seem capable of saying or doing anything. He had some sort of power or threat hanging over them, so that they were unable to move or say a word. Then he said to me, 'Lady, don't ever come here again, it could be very dangerous for you. Goodbye! George!' he said to a tall half-blind man, 'See her out!' I almost ran out of the place.

"I asked the man George, who'd been looking at me in a queer way, had he lost his sight? He said, 'No! I'm just blind in one eye.' He was wearing an old army jacket with stripes on the sleeves. The whole jacket was filthy as were the rest of his clothes and it seemed so were the rest of the men's clothing. I could still see those stripes on the arms of the jacket that he was wearing. I asked him how long he had been out of the army. He said he'd never been in the army and didn't have any intentions of joining either."

"How may stripes were there, May?"

"There were two or three on each arm, I think! Really ragged and dirty they were."

"Were there any brass buttons on the jacket?" Jenkins asked. His eyes lit up, he was becoming more than interested, excited perhaps. "Were there any badges on the collar, did you notice? Not cloth ones like the ones you wear on your uniform, May. Small brass ones, like miniatures of a soldier's cap badge; you've seen those things before, haven't you, May?"

"Well you know, Jenks, I've already told you, it was almost dark in the Hulk, but come to think of it, we were outside when I saw his jacket. Yes, there were a few buttons on the coat, although I don't know how many and the jacket wasn't buttoned up. I think there was a little collar badge on the right side but there wasn't one on the side nearest me, the left side."

"Do you by any chance remember what the little badge looked like, May love? If you can remember, we'll be one step nearer to the man or men that attacked me and old Limpy."

"I'm sorry, Jenks love, it was just a little badge to me. I could hardly see it in the light by the door, even though I was just outside. After leaving the Hulk, my friend and I ran almost the whole way back to the Citadel, in case someone came and tried to take the money back. Do you know, that afternoon we collected almost four pounds; three pounds two shillings from the man in the Hulk. If it was Mr Peters at that card table, I think I should go and thank him properly. I'll come to see you at the office and I could do it then, couldn't I?"

"Yes love, that would be fine and very good of you. Though it might embarrass him: men are easily embarrassed you know, especially when they don't want other people, and especially their work mates and friends, to find out how generous and kind they can be. Another thing, what if it isn't our Mr Peters? He would be really embarrassed, wouldn't he?"

After seeing May home that evening, he went to the coach house feeling a lot happier, now that some sort of evidence was beginning to appear. He went to bed, mulling over what new and old facts there were, and if they could be built into a case when the perpetrators of the attack and murder were brought to book.

That night, he slept as soundly as a day-old baby: nothing disturbed him until he woke with the sound of Mrs Roberts' cockerels crowing, welcoming a new day.

* * *

It was on the Tuesday following his discovery of the Hulk, that Jenkins decided to do something about May's visit to the place. When Peters was out of the office, Jenkins telephoned the Docks police station and arranged to meet Inspector Hazelton, explaining that he had one or two possible clues to the identity of his assailants, on the afternoon of his arrival at Bristol.

The inspector's interest was aroused when Jenkins told him of the conversation with May, about the Hulk and the administration offices. He didn't mention the people that May had spoken about: he and May would tell the inspector about the card players and George when they met. They arranged to meet at the Citadel, so as to catch May before her usual Tuesday evening meeting. The inspector said that he wanted to hear first hand what she had to say about the Hulk.

At their meeting May told Inspector Hazelton of her visit to the place, why she had gone and who was there.

Her friend and colleague, Salvation Army Lieutenant Jenny Porter, was a witness, as she was standing in the doorway and observed the generosity of the man playing cards.

The inspector enquired, "If the Lieutenant was asked, would she confirm the details of what you saw and heard, Mrs Andrews?"

"Of course she would, Inspector, she saw and heard everything that occurred, and in fact spoke to that fellow George, who was told to see us away from the Hulk. Jenny told me that he was a bit backward and dull. When he spoke to her, he wasn't very clear or forthcoming in answering the few questions she put to him. He kept looking at the man that looked a bit like Mr Peters, as if waiting for instructions. Mind you, Inspector, there didn't seem to be any sort of criminal activity going on there, just men drinking and playing cards.

"As I told Jenks, I didn't actually feel threatened until that man who gave me the money said, 'Don't come back, because it could be very dangerous.' It wasn't what he said, it was the evil and venomous way in which he said those words. After his generosity I couldn't understand that last remark and the tone he used; it sent shivers down my spine."

"Perhaps he didn't like you paying the Hulk too many visits, just in case you were lucky or unlucky enough to observe something that you weren't meant to." The inspector answered the question for her.

Then he went on, "Could you tell me about the army jacket this fellow George was wearing? I'd like to know in case it has any bearing on the case. There is one other thing, Mrs Andrews, would you be able to identify those two men, Peters and this fellow George, if I were to ask you at a later date? Please believe me, I don't wish you to go against your beliefs but perhaps if I asked you to identify the jacket, it wouldn't go against your Church's teachings, would it?"

May shook her head. "That should be all right," she replied, "but I shall have to ask my superiors about identifying those men. It may be against the Salvation Army rules and principles, I don't know."

"Unless anything some thing more serious comes about, then I wouldn't have to ask you or your friend to do anything other than to write a statement. Would that be all right, Captain, mam?"

It was the first time Inspector Hazelton had deliberately acknowledged her rank and position. May felt so proud; he was treating her as a professional, equal at last. She had to grab Jenkins arm and squeeze it.

Jenkins looked at her and smiled. "There's nothing at all to worry about, love; we'll be here to look after you and your friends. Besides, even the thugs and bullies around here dare not let you and your friends at the Citadel come to any harm. If they ever did, then I'm sure that between us, Inspector Hazelton, his men and some of your friends here, we would soon resolve any incident that might worry you."

"Thanks Jenks, and you Inspector. I'll check with my superiors about identifying someone: at the very least I'll be able to give you a straight forward honest answer. I'll telephone you as soon as I get a decision from headquarters.

"Come on Jenks, I've got a meeting to go to and you've a tram to catch," she went on quickly, almost in the same breath, "and you promised to make me supper, or was it to buy me supper?"

During the wait for the answer to her questions, May and Jenkins met almost every evening after work and between her various Salvationist meetings.

Jenkins felt that his waiting for some sort of sign in their relationship wasn't to be to long in coming. He tried to relax, be calm, but knew that one day very soon he would have to ask her how she felt about him and perhaps marriage.

He hated the thought of losing her and her friendship, especially as the thoughts that had begun to enter his head were that he knew he was in love. "Soft sod," he told himself. He had only once before encountered those sort of feelings. That was with a girl he had walked out with, when he was seventeen. The girl had turned him down, very gently, but he'd felt a right fool. That was a turning point in his young life; he had to get away from her, because she lived in the same row of houses as he and his family. So not bearing to see her every day and feeling ashamed that he and she would know that she had rejected him, he joined the army. There were no thoughts of other girls from the valleys; he couldn't bear the idea of being rejected again.

It was almost a week before May received her answer from Salvation Army headquarters in London. She told Jenkins and then Inspector Hazelton at the police station that she, as a private citizen, was at liberty to identify any person who committed a criminal act that she may have witnessed, although it was stressed that she was bound by the Salvation Army code, that if the act being committed was to help another poor or helpless person, the decision to proceed with making a statement or identification would be entirely at her own discretion, and with God's help, the correct one.

The inspector thanked May and told her that if and when he or his men found the man 'George', the man with the jacket, he would ask her, her friend Jennie and Jenkins, to come to the police station, to see if they could identify him and perhaps make statements about the afternoon at the Hulk. He also hoped that Jenkins would be able to identify the jacket if 'George' was still wearing it or had it in his possession.

They didn't have long to wait, in fact that same evening a man named as George Vickers was arrested attempting to sell stolen watches to Jaccob Purkinji.

Purkinji had decided to turn over a new leaf, as business had gone downhill since Dai Jones and Taff Jenkins had visited his shop. Everyone seemed to know that the police were keeping a close eye on the shop, so all visitors were closely scrutinised as they entered and left the building.

When Vickers had presented the watches to Purkinji for valuation and sale, he did not know, or could not have known, all the customers entering the pawn shop were being observed and noted in a log book by a police detective.

The pawn shop owner put an eyeglass to his eye and pulled the window curtains together, such as they were, as if to shut out the sun's bright glare from the filthy window. It was a signal to the police. Vickers thought it was to keep out prying eyes. He was unlucky, too; usually the shop was only under observation for a couple of days a month, because of a police manpower shortage. But he wasn't to know that, anyway.

A detective constable was watching the shop as part of an ongoing investigation about street crime, especially about the increased number of pick-pocket gangs in the central shopping area of the city. He remembered that it was only that morning that an Inspector Hazelton from the Docks Division had requested help from all the city's police forces to trace and report anyone wearing old army jackets, no matter who gave the wearer the jacket or what condition it was in.

He immediately telephoned the City Centre police station, informing the duty detective sergeant of his observations and what in fact was a signal by Purkinji that suspicious items, perhaps stolen, were being offered to him to evaluate or buy.

Two constables were immediately sent by bicycle to the scene, which was only three streets away, to assist the detective in arresting Vickers.

George Vickers had no idea that Jaccob Purkinji had given him away to the police after first declining to purchase the stolen goods. Or that the jacket he was wearing was to be the first reason for his arrest. Also he, like the others who had attempted to sell or pawn stolen items at the pawn shop, were a couple of streets away before they were arrested, with the stolen items still in their possession. None ever realised what part Purkinji had played in their arrest and eventual conviction.

It turned out that Purkinji made a more lucrative business of selling information to the police than he ever had with pawning items from the poor and less well-off citizens of Bristol Central and Docks areas.

George Vickers had the intelligence of a two day old rat. Of every question asked of him the answer was always in the same vein.

"Ask da boss, 'e tells I what I gotta do, copper!"

The sergeant questioning him said "What does he tell you to do, George?"

"Ev'ry fing, copper!"

"What's his name, George?"

"Boss! wat you fink, copper?"

"Where is he now, George?"

"Were'u fink, copper! down da docks, das where 'e is, das were 'e always is, ain't it, copper!"

"Where did you get the watches, George?"

"Din't you know, copper? Off da Boss, 'e allus gives me stuff, see."

"Why does he give you things like watches and jewellery, George?"

"Why'u fink, copper? To git money."

"Why, George?"

"Well, cause 'e can't, can 'e? 'E's da boss, 'e 'as to stay an' look after da goods, don't 'e, copper?"

"What goods, George?"

"'U know, all dat stuff da boys git wen de go owt in da nite. Boss 'as ta look a'ter it, don' 'e. Case some fievin rat 'as a go at nickin' it. If'n dey nicked it off'n 'im, 'e wouldn't be boss anymore would 'e an 'e'd be a bit nasty wiv it I reckons, eh, copper?"

"George! Were you ever in the army? Because your wearing an army jacket: is it yours?"

"Naw, course not. Boss give it me, din't 'e? 'E 'ad free of dem, an one nite it was rainin' wa'nt it. I never 'ad one so boss give me one cause I was freezin', see." George stopped for a second. "An' 'e sess I looks tidy. Don't I, copper?" Detective Sergeant Whitman smiled, "Course you do George," he agreed, but winked at the constable sitting next to him, who in turn grimaced at the smell and state of the man sitting at the opposite side of the table.

Vickers was a slovenly looking object, about six feet tall, but when standing slouched forward as if trying hard not to be noticed. Even whilst he was sat at the table being questioned, he slouched forward on to the table, staring at the policemen with pale blue almost vacant eyes. His long, greasy, grey-streaked black hair grew down past his coat collar and looked as though it had been cut off ragged with a pair of shears. His cheek was badly scarred from his right eyebrow to the point of his chin, as if he had been slashed with a knife, the scar showing up almost white under the sallow, almost olive skin. The colour ended at his shirt collar, which was unbuttoned, showing a pale, dirt-covered, scarred, chest.

Apart from the army jacket, he wore a dirty grey and blue striped shirt, navy blue trousers which were ripped at one of the knees and the backside, and a pair of old boots, with the soles hanging off.

The most interesting thing about Vickers' clothes was his waistcoat. It was a bottle green colour, not very old and surprisingly quite clean, the colour standing out within the remainder of his dirty, unkempt appearance. George noticed the sergeant looking at his waistcoat and pulled his jacket together.

"Nice ain't Copper? It's mine, so don't fink nofink else; awright, 'an you!" he said to the constable. "Wat you lookin' at, eh? Boss give me it, see, he 'ad some for us boys in the gang."

"The gang, George?" the sergeant asked quietly and in the most friendly tone he could muster. "Which gang's that, then?"

George Vickers, sensing this copper was only asking friendly questions, almost before he realised what he was saying, blurted out, "You knows don't ee, da Comodos."

"Oh! you mean the Commodores, don't you?"

"Aye, dats right copper, da Commoders."

Vickers felt really pleased with himself, thinking he hadn't said anything he shouldn't have and not having given his boss or anyone else away.

"Right George, fancy a cup of tea?" the sergeant asked. "It's almost dinner time anyway so we might as well have a break. They make a good thick soup and bread in the canteen for prisoners. It's a long time until we'll be able to get you some supper, if you're wanting to stay with us tonight, eh?"

George knew it wasn't really an invitation and his cursing almost turned the air blue. "Bloody 'ell copper, wat's goin' on, eh? I ain't done nuffink wrong, I jus' took da stuff to da pawn man, to git some money for da boss. I never got no money for da stuff, so wat did I do wrong, eh?"

"It's OK, George, we'll have another little chat this afternoon, all right? We will tell you then what's going to happen."

For a second or two it looked as if the prisoner was going to try and stay where he was. The policemen looked at each other, the constable waiting for the nod from the sergeant to move the prisoner to the cells physically. Suddenly Vickers pushed his chair back and stood up.

"OK, copper OK. See you s'afternoon, OK?"

The dullness and tone of his voice hadn't changed during the whole of the interview. Except for his use of the word 'copper' there didn't seem to be any animosity or anger in the man. He seemed to be lost without being instructed to do or say something by the 'Boss' of the Commodores. The sergeant hoped that if they kept at Vickers long enough, then the boss's name would crop up sooner or later.

"Hopefully sooner than later," he told himself.

Later that afternoon the interview with Vickers was resumed. Inspector Hazelton was invited to sit in, although technically it was not his case. When Vickers was picked up with the suspected stolen property, he was in fact on the Bristol City Division patch and therefore Hazelton had no jurisdiction over the case. He had been at a meeting with his opposite number from the City Division. The name George Vickers cropped up in conversation, who was being questioned about to an attempt to sell stolen property at a pawn shop owned by Jaccob Purkinji. Vickers had admitted in a roundabout way that he was a member of a gang called the Commodores operating in the Docks area. The name Commodores and a pawn shop owner called Purkinji had suddenly increased Hazelton's curiosity. He asked if the investigating officer would mind if he sat in on the next part of the questioning of Vickers.

For almost five hours after resuming the interview, the detective sergeant and constable were frustrated to the point of exhaustion in trying to get George Vickers to give a straight forward coherent answer to their repeated questions: about the valuables found on him at the time of his arrest, who the boss was and what were the names of other members of the Commodores.

His stock answer that afternoon was, "Dunno, boss, honest."

He spoke quietly, staring at his hands or the floor, never at the officers. With all their combined experience and guile, neither of the detectives could get him to give 'boss' another name.

Inspector Hazelton asked if he could try another approach.

The Sergeant nodded his approval, "Certainly, Guv, anything to try and break this deadlock. We'll be here all night otherwise: ask away, Guv, ask away."

As Hazelton sat down opposite Vickers, the prisoner looked up at him without any emotion in his pale ice blue eyes. But Hazelton's opening remark surprised Vickers and the two policemen in the room.

"Hello, Mister Vickers, my name is Hazelton, Charlie to my friends. What do your friends call you, then, Mister Vickers?" Although it may have surprised Vickers to be called Mister, there was no reaction in his demeanour or the expression on his face.

He looked at Hazelton and in a very quiet voice, hardly opening his mouth said, "What's da game den, copper? I ain't got noffin t'say t'you, 'ave I?"

"Course not, Mr Vickers, all I want to say is I need your help to find a friend of mine; he works on the docks, a stevedore I think, a big fellow, broad, a bit like you but not so tall. Oh, and he's got ginger hair. Have you seen him around, eh?"

"Watsa stevedore, den, copper?"

"He's a chap that loads and unloads ships, you know there's hundreds of them on the docks, aren't there?"

"Oh yeh!" replied Vickers. "I knows what you means now, don' I?"

"Is it OK to call you George? Because I need some friends too, you know; I've only got a couple. You don't get many being a copper, do you?" Hazelton turned to the other detectives and winked.

"OK, den. Don try an' be funny, aye. I ain't daft, so don try noffink, OK."

"Sure, George, sure. I only need to know about my friend Ginger; he's not in your gang is he?"

"No 'e ain't but 'e might be in t'other lot, 'e might, I expect."

"Who's the other lot then, George?"

"One lot wears brown waistcoats, don't they?" Vickers, realising that he and the boss weren't being spoken about, relaxed. "Aye!" he replied. "Dat lots da Sailors Mates."

"Sailors Mates? That's a good name for a gang; what do you reckon, George?"

"Yeh, s'pose it's OK, as long as de stay out ov 'r' way!"

Hazelton was warming to the task now, "What are your boys called then, George? So I don't get mixed up with who is who. You know, don't want any trouble do I, when I'm trying to find Ginger, my mate?"

"Da boys are called da Commerders, don' know why, don' know wat it means eiver, just da Commerders, an we wears green waiskits, so we knows 'r' gang in da street or on da docks."

"So are there any other gangs you have to know about? Don't they come into your territory?" Vickers looked puzzled. "The Commodores' territory, George, where no other gangs go, you know what I mean?"

"Course I does, un we cassunt go into ders, cause we 'as to fight if'n we do."

"Who else can stop you going into their territory, George?"

"Ders da City Boys, de 'as blue colours an buttons on der 'ats. Den da Brisol Lads, them 'as black bolin 'ats an weskits an den them overs, you called dem da Steeveders, din't 'e?

"What colours do the Stevedores have then, George? Do they have colours as well, mate?" There was a slight change in George's attitude, at least someone was trying to be friendly and not trying to catch him out or get him to say things he didn't want to.

"Aw! Dey doesn't 'ave coulers, jus dem big hooks de uses for lodin' an' unlodin' da ships. Das all." Like the boss said, he wasn't to answer questions about the docks. He didn't say anything about talking about the different gangs, because if people didn't know, they could get hurt going into the wrong place, couldn't they?

He had been hurt once for doing just that. They scarred his face for just going into the Bristol Boys patch when he was trying to get home because it was late and getting dark. He made sure he never went into another gang's patch again. He began to try and explain all this to Charlie, who sat and listened without interruption to everything George said.

When he had finished, Hazelton said quite casually, "This boss of yours seems to be a decent bloke?"

"Looks after you, don't he?

"Does he work on the docks too?"

"Aye 'e do dat, in da 'arber office."

Hazelton pretended to ignore Vickers last sentence. He turned to the detectives sitting behind him.

"Anyone got a fag?" He winked, trying to convey to them to act as casually as possible. There might be a possible breakthrough on the way.

The sergeant offered Hazelton a cigarette, who gestured him to offer Vickers one as well. The sergeant sighed. "Bloody hell," he said to himself. "These are my last two, I'll have to send out for more and it'll come out of petty cash if I've got anything to say about it."

He offered the almost empty Woodbine packet to Vickers and for the first time that day, his face changed into a broad grin.

Hazelton wished Vickers hadn't, because as the prisoner leaned forward and removed the cigarette from the packet, the most disgusting set of vile rotting teeth were revealed and the filthy stench of Vickers' bad breath wafted across the table making Hazelton's stomach heave. Vickers looked at Hazelton, the grin had changed into a smirk.

"Fanks, copper, never 'ad a fag off'n a copper afore, first time, eh!"

Hazelton tried to smile as he lit Vickers' cigarette; he then lit the one he had taken for himself. He very rarely smoked and gagged as the smoke seemed to find it's way into his lungs without him actually drawing heavily on the cigarette. He tried one more time to get Vickers give up the name of his boss.

"Look George, I'd like to meet your boss. You say he's goes to the Harbour Office. Which office? Does he work there? Do you know if he works there?"

"Naw, I dunno if'n e works der. I seen 'im go der, dats all."

"But you don't know his name?"

"Naw, I tol' you aw'ready, I dunno 'is bloody name. 'Ow many more times, eh? An' even if'n I did, I ain't gonna say it, not now. If'n I did an' 'e foun' out, I be a dead 'un, aw'right?"

"OK George, thanks for your help. Take him back to the cells, Sergeant. He can be charged with being in possession of stolen property in the morning. Best give him a decent meal, he deserves it. Something soft, we don't want him getting toothache in the cells tonight, do we?"

Vickers stood up to almost his full height, a scowl spreading over his face.

"Wat'u mean, aye? Fanks fer yer 'elp. I don't 'elp coppers, see. boss says I ain't gotta 'elp coppers an' I never 'elped you, see?" Vickers became angrier as he tried to figure out how he had helped the police. He couldn't understand it.

"I never said nofink!" he shouted at Hazelton and the detectives and made a lunge towards the inspector, but before he could make any sort of contact, two brawny police constables who had been waiting just outside the interview room, rushed in, grabbed him by each arm and frog marched him back to the cells.

The detective sergeant held out his hand to the inspector, "Great work, Inspector; how many Harbour Offices are there, sir?"

"Only three, shouldn't take long to turn them over should it? See you again sometime, OK?" said Hazelton, as he shook the sergeant's hand.

Before he left Bristol Central police station, Hazelton asked for a copy of Vickers' fingerprints to be sent to his office, and that he be informed if and when an identity parade was to be held connection with the attempt by Vickers to sell the stolen property to Purkinji in the pawn shop.

The desk sergeant, Harry Walters, promised to pass on his request about the fingerprints and informed him, after making enquiries, that an identity parade was to be held the very next day. A constable had been sent to Jaccob Purkinji's shop that very afternoon, requesting him to attend the police station the next morning, at ten o'clock.

"Harry! Would you inform the investigating officer that I shall hopefully be able to bring three more witnesses to try and identify Vickers in a case that I am investigating, which has many similarities to his own. If it's possible to do this, then it may bring my case to a conclusion sooner, with more and stronger evidence. It is Sergeant Whitman's case we're talking about, isn't it?"

"Yes it is, sir. I'll ask Whitman and phone you at your office at about five pm."

"Great, Harry, that'll give me time to get in touch with my witnesses because I don't want to miss out on any chance or piece of evidence to get a conviction on the evil bastard I'm after, who controls one of the gangs that are operating the docks area. Right, I'm off. See you tomorrow. Bye now."

Hazelton left in a rush. He had a car waiting in the police courtyard and was back in his own office in fifteen minutes. He telephoned Mr Roberts in the Floating Harbour Office and asked him to inform Jenkins that he might be required to attend an identification parade at Bristol Central police station.

"No, it doesn't matter that Mr Peters knows where Jenkins is going. If he knows it might stir him up a bit and get him to do something unusual or out of habit. You could even say to Jenkins that he was going to be asked to identify one of the docks' gang members. Say you haven't been told the gang's name or the name of the suspect prisoner. Tell him the gang has been identified by the colour of the waistcoat that gang members wear. That should get the gang boss wondering and worrying, shouldn't it?

"I hope Mr Jenkins will make a good witness for something I have in mind. I don't want him jumping to conclusions, so I cannot say what I would like him to identify. It would be wrong of me to tell you as well. I'm afraid we have to look at every option and possible suspect, because things seem to be getting out of hand and the more vicious, hard cases, are attempting to take over the gangs these days. So we have to use all our resources and try and take these leaders out of circulation as soon as possible. Anyway, please pass on the message to Mr Jenkins as soon as you can. Good afternoon, sir. Oh, by the way, sir, I shall inform Captain Andrews this evening, so there won't be any need for you or Mr Jenkins to trouble yourselves saying anything to her, unless, of course, Mr Jenkins is visiting her later."

Roberts thanked the inspector and replaced the telephone in its cradle. He then turned to Joe Worrell and at the same time looking towards Peters said:

"Looks as though things are progressing well, Joe; seems as though something serious has happened down at the station. No one has said what it is, but the inspector seemed happy about his enquiries. Will you tell Mr Jenkins to come and see me later, preferably before he goes home. I've something important to tell him."

"What's the secret then Mr Roberts?" Peters said. "Ain't we supposed to know what's goin on round here? Can't tell what's comin' or goin' since that Jenkins arrived. He always seems to be up to something, don't he?"

"Now, now Mr Peters, I don't think Mr Jenkins is up to anything, he has just been asked to go to the station, maybe it's in connection with his sister's demise or the attack on him, you know, the day he arrived at Bristol. It could be anything. It might even be that the inspector has some idea that he can identify a gang or member of a gang. Really, though, it shouldn't be any business or concern of ours," going on before Peters could reply, "should it?"

Worrell smiled at Peters and said condescendingly, "Fancy a cup of tea then, Gordon?"

Peters banged the book he was holding down on to the desk, his permanent scowl deepening and his face going crimson, his anger flaring up. "I'll give you tea, you snidy little swine: you know what you can do with your bloody tea?" His voice rose to a shriek, "Get out of my bloody way, you dirty little rat. Get back to the hole you crawled out of. Go on get out."

Roberts said loudly, "That's enough of that Mr Peters. Go outside and calm down, don't come back in until you can. Then come and apologise to Mr Worrell: you had no reason to take that tone or attitude, the man was trying to be helpful."

"Helpful my ass!" By this time Peters was almost screaming. He stood directly in front of Worrell who was more than a little anxious. Turning his back to Roberts, Peters put his face up close to Worrell's and whispered quietly and quickly, "Listen carefully you crawling little shit, remember this: there are some very nasty pieces of work hanging around these docks and you work here. You have to walk along these docks every morning and night, so if you don't watch out a little accident could very easily happen. So don't ever try and be clever or funny with me again, all right!"

He walked out of the office and slamming the door so hard behind him that it shook the building.

"What did he just say then, Joe?" Roberts enquired. "Did he threaten you? You seem a bit worried, are you all right?"

"Nothin', Mr Roberts he didn't say nothin', only that I ought to be more careful, 'cause accidents can happen."

"Don't you fret, Joe, accidents only happen if you let them, OK? Tell you what, for the next few weeks you walk to and from the dock gates with me or Mr Jenkins. You usually arrive before us in the mornings, so you can wait at the police post until either Jenkins or myself arrives. We'll walk in with you, then we'll see if any accidents happen, eh? Your tram stops just outside the dock gates, so we'll see you all right, Joe, don't worry yourself. Go on, make that cup of tea, I'm gagging for a drink."

Joe went outside to fill the kettle. There was no sign of Peters but Jenkins was just arriving from his docks circuit.

"I'll have one of those, Joe, my throat's as dry as a camel's foot and I feel nearly as smelly."

Joe grinned, "Never smelt a camel's foot or even seen a camel, so I wouldn't know, would I? Have you?"

"Course I have but it's a long story so we'll have to go into it later. So what's with the long face, somebody have a go at you, then?" Jenkins held up his hand. "It's OK, I can guess. Don't worry Joe, he'll get his just reward soon," Jenkins punched his own hand, "and I hope it's me that presents it to him."

Jenkins met May that evening in her little house where they discussed how they would go about the identity parade.

May said, "Inspector Hazelton told me it would be quite simple and straight forward. If we can, Jenny and I should pick out the man we saw in the Hulk and nothing else. I don't know why he's asking you to attend, perhaps you've seen something or maybe you'll know someone on the same identity parade." Then she asked, "Jenks, did he say why you had been called?"

"No not a word, perhaps he wants me on the parade: maybe it's me he wants to identify."

"Don't be so daft; what have you been up to? You're making me worried now. If that was supposed to be a joke, it wasn't funny at all." She tapped him lightly on the arm and said, "Next time it'll be a lot harder, OK?"

Jenkins was smiling. "Its all right my love, the inspector told me he has something to show me that might have been mine but he wouldn't say exactly what it was. Perhaps it may help with his enquiries on another case he's investigating. So please don't worry love, I'll never let you down."

He leaned over and kissed her cheek; he was still too frightened to tell her how he really felt about her. What he didn't know though, was that May was aching for him to tell her how he felt and what their future might be.

May knew his feelings for her were more than platonic, but didn't know what his reaction might be if she was to ask him outright.

"It's getting late, Jenks, so we'd better call it a day, don't you think? We have to be up early as usual and if you don't watch the time, it'll be an awfully long walk home."

Jenkins was reluctant to leave her cosy little home but seeing the sense in her remarks, took her gently by the shoulders and kissed her cheek again.

"Good-night love," he mumbled. "See you tomorrow, eh?"

May almost offered her mouth to be kissed but turned away in the last instant. Afraid to take their affair any further.

"Night Jenks, love; careful on the way home. Don't be late at the police station will you? I'm bringing Jenny with me but I'd rather you arrived with me as well, because I've never liked places like that. They always seem so cold and threatening. Go on Jenks, go home before I go on with my rambling and you'll miss that tram. Good-night, love."

As he stepped through her front door, she closed it quickly behind him, in case she surrendered to her thoughts of asking him to stay.

They met at the Bristol Central police station the next morning, Jenny and May both arriving before Jenkins.

May smiled, "Hello Jenks," as she greeted him with a peck on the cheek. Jenny her friend smiled nervously and shook him by the hand.

Jenkins said, "Morning ladies." He could see the tension in their faces. "I'm a bit anxious too, but everything will be OK, so don't worry. Let's go and find the inspector shall we?"

They didn't have far to look. Hazelton and a constable were waiting for them in the entrance hall of the police station.

Hazelton greeted them cheerfully, "Morning ladies, morning Mr Jenkins; everything is about ready. I'm pleased to see you're not wearing your uniforms ladies, because some of these rascals may recognise you when you're out in the town, doing your work. It's better that the Salvation Army isn't compromised and we shall do our utmost to keep it that way, although we are very pleased that you are able to attend. We, that is the Chief Inspector and I, along with other policemen involved in the investigation, are most grateful for any assistance that you may be able to give.

"Will you please follow Constable Greaves, he will show you to the waiting-room, where we will come and fetch you when we are ready."

They didn't have long to wait, it was only a matter of minutes before the constable appeared and beckoned to May to follow him. As she stood up to go with the policeman, she turned and smiled at Jenkins although the look on her face showed her to be a little worried. Her usual confidence and poise seemed to wane, as she realised the responsibility she had taken on, or what the results of her future actions might bring.

Jenkins stood up and took her hand. "There's no need to worry, love, no harm can come to you, the constable and his mates will make sure of that." He kissed her cheek, but when he realised the constable and Jenny were watching, he flushed a deep crimson with embarrassment. His tanned skin couldn't hide the redness.

May followed the constable out of the room.

Jenny said without looking at Jenkins, "I know I shouldn't be saying this and you could say it isn't any of my business, but don't you realise, Jenks, that you could make that woman the happiest person in the world. You would then probably be the happiest man, if you only had the nerve to say how you feel about her."

Jenkins looked at Jenny in surprise. "You're probably right about everything you've just said, but I honestly don't know what I should say. I told someone before how I felt about them then found out she didn't really want to know and went around telling our families and friends. I felt so scared and embarrassed that I took off and joined the army. That was over twenty years ago and I'm going to be very careful in what I say in the future. I want the person I have the feelings for to know what I'm saying is true and I'll only say it to the right person if I really mean it."

Jenny replied, "You don't believe in taking any chances, do you?"

"How can I allow anyone to take a chance with me? No one knows what I'll be doing next or if I'll ever stay here or feel the way I do now. No, no, don't worry, I'll not be going anywhere just yet, we'll have to wait and see how things turn out, won't we?"

The constable stuck his head around the waiting-room door. "Your turn, Miss," he said.

Jenny looked at Jenkins, "You will talk to her, won't you? Tell her, I mean, how you feel and about the future. You will, won't you?"

Jenkins just nodded. "I'll see," he mumbled. "I'll try."

It was almost ten minutes before Constable Greaves came to the room to collect Jenkins. By that time all sorts of thoughts and ideas were tumbling around and through Jenkins' mind. He did understand Jenny's concern for her friend and she wasn't the only person to see how he felt about May and how she felt about him. Dai Jones kept reminding him as well.

Greaves led Jenkins along a brightly lit corridor to a partly open large solid-looking brown door. Jenkins could see beyond the entrance into a room with extra bright lighting.

It seemed to be full of people most of them standing against a long wall of the room. A sergeant, who Jenkins recognised as the desk sergeant of the Bristol Central police station, approached him and asked, "Have you ever been asked or done an Identity Parade before sir?"

Jenkins shook his head.

"Nothing to worry about, sir. I shall ask you to walk along this line of men and see if you recognise any of them. I shall accompany you. If you do recognise anyone or something, just tell me and touch the person on the right shoulder. Do nothing else. Don't speak to me or the suspect, all right, sir?"

Jenkins nodded.

"Do you understand, sir? Shall I repeat my instructions?"

"No thanks sergeant, it's OK."

As he walked along the line of twelve men, even though they were tall, short fat or thin, smart or scruffy, he realised that they all wore army uniform jackets, with a variety of buttons, badges, stripes, colours and emblems. Some looked as if they had just been issued from army stores, some looked as if they had just been pressed for a military parade. The remainder were the worse for wear, dirty, muddy, torn and with one or two stripes still on the sleeves, although in one case hardly recognisable, they were so dirty.

After looking at each face his eyes were drawn to the jacket each man was wearing. He didn't recognise anything until he was almost three-quarters the way along the line when he looked into the eighth man's face. Shock stopped him in his tracks. He almost said to the man standing in front of him, "What the hell are you doing here?"

The sergeant stepped close to Jenkins, "Are you OK, sir, something wrong?"

Jenkins looked closely at the man who stared defiantly back at him and replied, "Yes, I think there must be, Sergeant," as he placed his hand on the shoulder of the man he thought he knew and recognised.

"OK, sir, continue along the line, please."

Jenkins followed the sergeant's final instruction as he was directed along the remainder of the line. He tried to look closely at the remaining three men and their uniform jackets but couldn't see anything recognisable about any of them, or their jackets.

As he was shown out of the room, he looked back and could hardly believe his eyes. "What the hell is Peters doing here?" he asked himself.

He was then taken to an interview room; Inspector Hazelton, May and Jenny were waiting.

Before he could open his mouth, May asked excitedly, "What do you think, Jenks, love? Did you recognise anyone there? Perhaps the same man that Jenny and I did?"

Jenkins looked at Hazelton, who raised his eyebrows as if to say, "Well did you?" Then said very formally "Did you recognise the man you touched on the shoulder, Mr Jenkins?"

"Yes I did Inspector, was it who I thought it was? Because he didn't seem to recognise me."

"Who was it then, Mr Jenkins?"

"Gordon Peters, of course, the Deputy Floating Harbour Master. He works in the FHM Office with Mr Roberts, Joe Worrell the other deputy, and me. I see him every day."

The inspector held up his hand to stop him. "Well Mr Jenkins, the ladies recognised him as well, as the man who was playing cards in the 'Hulk' one Saturday afternoon and gave them all the money that was on the table at the time. Very generous of him wasn't it? They also identified one of his men, a man named George Vickers. Vickers was told by a man, who we think was the boss of a gang called the Commodores, to see the ladies out of the docks safely. Which thankfully he did. I personally think the man who gave Vickers that order was Peters although I cannot actually prove it.

"Now," the inspector began, "this is something that no one else knows, except three officers here at Bristol Central Station. The man you all identified as Peters, isn't Gordon Peters! He is known to the police and prison authorities as Rob, short for Robert Smith." He looked at the two Salvationists, "The man you saw in the Hulk!" then at Jenkins, "We are almost sure that man is Peters, the one you know and work with !

"The man you all recognised in the line up was in fact a recently released prisoner who has just finished serving a long sentence. He is not the Peters we all know. He was released from prison on Monday, and has come to us to ask us to reopen his case and to help us with our enquires. Prison officers thought they recognised him as the brother of an ex-prisoner, whose name they knew and checked out, and who was a George Peters."

He stopped for a moment to get his thoughts in order, then continued, "Don't forget, everyone, everything I'm going to talk about at this time is all supposition. There are very few actual facts to go on, so anything I say mustn't leave this room under any circumstances. The reasons I'm going to tell you about all this confidential information is perhaps other things may have come to your notice, that you haven't thought about or recognised as being important enough to be spoken about or reported. So if by any chance you do think of anything that might be of any importance to this case, please don't be afraid to contact me or one of my officers. I will then make arrangements to meet you. Is that all right for you all?"

May and Jenny both nodded in agreement. Jenkins muttered "Aye, that'll be fine!"

"Ladies, I know I can count on your discretion, it is unlikely that you will come into contact with either of the main parties again, so you shouldn't have any worries on that score! But if either of you do, don't be afraid to contact me or the duty sergeant at the docks station anytime. Someone will come to see you as soon as possible.

"Mr Jenkins, I'm sure I can count on your co-operation, although it will be under very trying circumstances. I know your good sense will prevail; any help you can give will be greatly appreciated. Thank you all."

He went on, "We, I think are dealing with one of the most vicious and evil men that I have had the misfortune to have heard about for many a year."

"Why don't you arrest him or something?" Jenkins asked.

"Later we might, we believe, and so does this new man, who we shall call Rob Smith. They, Peters and Smith, are in fact half brothers. Different mothers, same father. We also now believe that Peters raped and beat Smith's wife and children. Smith was blamed for the attack and rape, but although Smith vehemently denied the crime, he was convicted on his wife's evidence. Smith's wife thought that it was Rob, her husband, who had come in drunk. It was a dark and cold night, there were no lights. Peters knew Rob Smith's wife usually worked late in a local pub, except for that night. She was not working in the pub on the night of the crime and Peters knowing this, but not knowing who she and Smith were, went to their house. He knew where she lived, because he had followed her home on several occasions, perhaps to attack or take a chance and rob her of the little money and valuables she had." The Inspector paused again.

"Not seeing or hearing of any sign of her husband, Peters took a chance, possibly to commit a robbery. But, seeing Smith's wife alone, attacked her and her family." Hazelton paused then went on.

"As the house was in darkness all she could see was a familiar looking man, who suddenly attacked her. I think Rob Smith arrived home almost dead drunk, seconds after Peters had left the house and just before the arrival of a policeman, who had been alerted by the screams of the wife and children.

"Peters didn't know Rob Smith, he'd never seen him before and didn't know that he had a half brother. In fact neither of them knew of the existence of the other. Their father had died many years before either of them left home and married. Peters' mother passed away recently, about a year ago in fact, so as we shan't be able to talk to her. We'll have to try to find someone else in the family, brother or sister, aunt or uncle. It'll probably take some time, so progress will be slow, everyone will have to be patient. My view on cases like this is, if there is any truth at all hidden somewhere in the past, it deserves to be dug out and revealed, even if it's not what we expect or want to hear or see." He stopped and waited for a reaction. Each one nodded in agreement but said nothing.

"Although Peter's mother knew his father's name, she refused to reveal it to him. Gordon was registered in his mother's maiden name, Peters. Smith's mother admitted she had no knowledge of Rob's father's name. After the baby's delivery she never gave it another thought. Later in life, Rob Smith never bothered to try and find out. The nearest he came to looking was reading his birth certificate and not seeing his father's name, threw it back in the drawer where he'd found it then promptly forgot all about it until he got married. Even then no one asked any awkward questions, no one seemed to be in the slightest bit worried that his father wasn't named on the certificate."

The inspector's final statement surprised Jenkins. "Mr Jenkins, would you please stay for a few minutes longer, we have found something that might interest you a great deal.

"Ladies, thank you for your time and excellent information. I'm positive we can use it well enough to secure a conviction later."

"Ah, but we identified the wrong man and George hasn't done anything wrong, has he?" May protested. "I wish we could have done more." She looked at her lieutenant.

Jenny replied, "Didn't the Inspector say that he was in possession of stolen property or something? Surely that will have some bearing on the matter."

The inspector looked at her, "That's true. It's unlikely he will be charged with any offence if he is prepared to identify the 'boss' of the gang that he runs around with, the Commodores. If he refuses and continues to be loyal to the boss he'll have to be charged with at least 'being in possession of stolen property'. If that happens he'll go to prison for a very long time. His criminal record is atrocious. It's 'as long as my arm' as they say.

"Well, ladies, thank you for your time and help, it has been much appreciated. I've arranged for transport to take you to the Citadel, if that's where you wish to go. Goodbye, ladies." He shook hands with each in turn. "Perhaps I may wish to call on you again, but in all seriousness, I do hope I don't have to. Except," he looked at Jenny, "socially."

Jenny blushed almost scarlet; she could hardly get the word "Cheerio" out as she rushed from the room. May followed her out, smiling at Jenkins and the inspector. She stopped at the door.

"What have you done to my friend, Inspector? Do you know, she will be expecting you to visit her soon, she's so naïve you know, about men, I mean. You're not married are you? Jenny would be so disappointed if you are, because if a man says he'd like to visit socially, it means to ladies like her that he wants to visit and walk out with lady he has asked."

Inspector Hazelton was shaken to the core. "I'm very sorry; I gave the wrong impression, madam." He was very formal.

Jenkins laughed: he'd never seen a man in Hazelton's position squirm so much.

May said, "Don't worry, Inspector, I'm only teasing. I'll tell Jenny not to read too much into your last remark, all right?" Turning to Jenkins, "I'll see you later Mr Jenkins, about supper time, is that all right?" She came back into the room and kissed him on the cheek. "Don't be late love, will you?" Then she was gone, hurrying to catch up with Jenny.

Hazelton turned to Jenkins, "Come with me, will you, Mr Jenkins? I've something to show you that might interest you, it won't take long. You do have the time don't you?"

"OK, Inspector, not to worry. Mr Roberts gave me the morning off to come and see you, so it's not a problem. Besides, you've made me bloody curious now so I've got to have a look, haven't I?"

Jenkins followed the inspector to an office. There was very little light in the room owing to the very small window being set high in the outer wall. The glass was grey with dirt, not having been cleaned in years.

When Jenkins entered the office, he saw a figure standing in the corner. As Hazelton turned the light on, Jenkins said, "Who's this, then?" Then as his eyes became accustomed to the brightness of the electric light, he exclaimed, "Bugger me!"

The shock and surprise in Jenkins' remark convinced Hazelton he had at last made progress in finding the ex-soldier's attackers and old Limpy's killers.

The army jacket, now draped over a tailor's dummy, had been found and recovered during a search of the Hulk. It had been hidden inside a large wooden beer barrel used to support a makeshift card table.

The search had been carried out in secret with the backing of a court order and had taken place at three o'clock in the morning when the Hulk was deserted. Anything that had been moved was replaced exactly where it was found except the jacket; another similar to it had been left in its place. Unless someone from the search team had blabbed, no one knew that the jacket had been found.

Hazelton said, "Mr Jenkins, I have to ask you formally to identify this jacket. Do you recognise this army uniform jacket?"

"Barely!" Jenkins replied quickly. What's left of it, yes it is mine and it was taken from me when I was attacked on my first day here in Bristol. Yes it is mine. The buttons left on are Coldstream, so is the collar star. Whoever took it at least left the stripes on, or nearly on." Someone had tried to remove the stripes but had ripped the sleeves, so left them where they were, although covered in grease and dirt.

He turned the jacket inside out, "Well, there's my number, look inside the right sleeve. It's also on the back of the collar, here: someone tried to blot it out but black Indian ink is almost impossible to remove. The only way is to cut it out. I always put my army number in two places, so if anyone nicked any of my gear, they probably would cover up or cut out the number in the collar or the obvious places where we had been ordered to sew or print the number, but not always in the less noticeable places, which only I or the other owners would know."

Hazelton smiled, "Thanks very much, Mr Jenkins; now we can make some progress. Here's something else you might like to know. We have found some lovely fingerprints on the buttons of the jacket, thanks to the work you put in when you burnished and polished them, even though they're not as nice and shiny as they were when you last wore your uniform.

"One thing, though, before you go. I'm going to need your fingerprints in case we find any other than yours, which I'm sure we will. I know for a fact, there are at least two sets on the large buttons and just one or two prints on the small buttons on the cuffs."

The inspector pressed a buzzer on his desk: ten seconds later a constable entered the office. "Go with Greaves, Mr Jenkins, he will do the honours. Thanks for your help; be seeing you again soon, hopefully in court, helping us to put some evil sod away."

They shook hands and Jenkins followed the constable from the room.

What Hazelton didn't tell Jenkins was that he hoped to identify Jenkins' attacker, the killer, and the leader of the gang known as the Commodores, by the end of the day.

Whilst Jenkins was being interviewed with the two Salvation Army officers, police had been sent to the Floating Harbour Office to arrest Peters. Purkinji was arrested at his shop and brought to the Docks police station. The two thugs, Billy and Jimmy, were already in the cells, as was Jameson.

After Jenkins and the ladies had left the police station, another identity line-up was held. This time, the man who was known as Rob Smith was placed in the line-up. Deliberately, but unofficially, each of the prisoners was walked past the open door of the room where the line-up was being held, then taken to other cells at the end of the building. On seeing Smith, every prisoner made some sort of remark or slight acknowledgement to say that they recognised him, not as Smith but as the 'boss' of the Commodores.

Billy said as he limped past the door, "How's it going, boss?" Smith looked at him without any kind of recognition. As Jameson passed, he winked at Smith but didn't say anything.

George Vickers said to his escorting policeman, "Wat's da boss doin 'er den copper? Bin arrestid 'as 'e den?"

"No! Don't worry about him, Vickers, he's just in telling us things about some of the questions we need answers to."

"Wat? 'e's tellin' yu coppers abat fings, yu say?"

"That's right, spilling his guts," the constable smiled. "Telling us all about you and the rest of your gang and what you've all been up to in the last couple of years."

Vickers tried to break away, back towards the room with the identity line-up. The constable, who was too quick and strong for Vickers, gripped the prisoner's arm tighter and dragged him off to the cells. With the aid of another constable, he shoved him into a cell already occupied by Billy and Jameson.

Vickers immediately went into a violent rage, kicking and head-butting the walls and door, shouting almost incoherently. "'E's tellin' da coppers, 'e's tellin da coppers!"

Jameson and Billy grabbed hold of Vickers and held him, face against the cell wall.

"Who's tellin' the coppers? What's he tellin' them, George?" Vickers face was so contorted with rage, he was spitting and dribbling, unable to get the words he wanted to use out.

"'E sed not t' tell coppers nuffink, but 'e is, 'e's grassin' us up, 'e's grassin up da boys of da Commerdors."

Jameson turned Vickers to face him and took him by the throat. "'Ow do you know, George? 'Ow do you know, eh?"

"I seen 'im in da line-up and dat copper tol' me dat da boss is squeelin' on us all, see."

Billy and Jameson looked at each other. Billy patted George on the cheek. "Not to worry, George. If'n 'e 'as, we'll do 'im real good, won't we, Jamie boy?"

Jameson nodded, "Aye, real good, George, if 'e does grass on us." The evil threat in his voice made George shudder.

Outside the cell door Inspector Hazelton and recently promoted Detective Sergeant Cowley grinned hugely at each other as they walked quietly away, Cowley motioning to the constable sitting outside the cell door to be quiet and take notes of everything said in the cell.

"Well, we've had a good start, Cowley; let's hope the rest of the day goes just as well, eh?"

But it didn't!

A Docks policeman went to the Floating Harbour Office that morning to report large amounts of flotsam in the harbour. It would require clearing before ships could be moved from or to their moorings.

Peters was late that day: it was almost ten-thirty when he turned up for work. He had scrounged a lift across the harbour on a small boat. No one except the boatman knew he had come that way. Neither of them knew each other, and, putting two shillings into the boatman's hand, Peters reminded the man that they never would. Seeing the money the boatman agreed and disappeared, deciding an hour or two in the pub would be better than rowing for a living.

No one saw Peters arrive, as everyone was out of the office that morning. That suited him as he had one or two items he needed to put away, before anyone came back and saw what he was doing.

Later, as the office door opened, Peters rose up from the back of his desk in some surprise at seeing a policeman there.

"Good morning, sir. I've come to report flotsam in the harbour; can I give you a hand?"

Peters, who was trying to lift the heavy desk back in position, shook his head. "No thanks Fred!" At that minute the telephone rang.

"Shall I get that for you, sir?"

"Yes please, shan't be a minute," Peters replied.

The constable picked up the phone, nodded and said, "Yes sir, right sir." As he put the phone down he looked at Peters, surprise on the constable's face.

"Was that for me, Fred?"

"No sir, for me, I'm afraid."

"What's the matter, Fred?"

"I'm sorry sir. I have to ask, are you Gordon Peters?"

"You know I am, don't be so bloody daft!"

"Well, Mr Peters, I would like you to come to the station with me."

"Why? What for Fred? Who wants to see me then, eh?"

"Inspector Hazelton. I think he wants to ask you if you know anything about a robbery that took place a few days ago. Did you see anything or anyone, for example?"

As the constable said "Robbery", Peters realised that the policeman had said more than he should have and guessed it wasn't just an invitation to answer questions. The coppers could quite as easily ask him any questions they wanted to here in the office. Peters made a move towards the office door.

The door opened at that same instant and Joe Worrell stepped through into the office. The constable, slightly alarmed, made to block Peters' exit but was a split second too slow. Peters grabbed Worrell by the jacket lapels and swung him around in front of the policeman.

"There's no need for this, Mr Peters, let the man go."

"I'll let 'im go when you get back be'ind that desk, other wise…" A thin, six inch bladed knife appeared in his hand as if by magic.

Peters turned Worrell back to face the policeman, pressing the point of the knife into the frightened clerk's throat. "Now you skinny little shit, we'll see if you bleed yellow or red, eh?"

Peters looked at the constable who seemed to be working up the nerve to charge across the room.

"I wouldn't if I were you, Fred; he'll be dying before you get half-way and I'll stick you before you can lay a finger on me. Get it? Now you, Fred, turn around and face the wall. Get down on your knees you big oaf and put your hands at the back of your 'ead. Do it!"

Fred, realising the situation was completely out of his hands, did as he was ordered.

"Now you, you little git, on your knees, now lie down and put your sticky maulers behind your head, quick, before I start cutting your balls off. I'd just love to do that, you little twerp. What's the matter now, eh? You dirty little bastard! You've shit yourself." Peters' voice rose to a scream, "You've shit yourself!" Peters kicked the prostrate man in the ribs. Worrell moaned in agony and started to sob.

"Don't start that you little bastard, I ain't started anything yet." He kicked him again. "Stop your blubbering, now! Or I'll cut your tongue out."

Worrell's crying became worse, tears pouring down his face. Without another word, Peters leaned down, grabbed Worrell by the hair and pulled his head back, exposing the petrified young man's throat. The upward thrust of the knife into the victim's throat stifled the scream into a gurgling, choking, sound causing the police constable to half turn and witness the terrifying demise of the quiet hard-working family man and father, a man who had never been a threat to anyone in his life, except to Peters' promotion chances. Now neither would have that.

The policeman, Fred, let out a roar of rage and pushed himself awkwardly to his feet. Anger overwhelming him; he pulled out his truncheon and, putting all caution aside, rushed across the office at smirking, mincing Peters.

Peters was beside himself with elation. He felt the blood rushing around his head and body. "I've done it, I've done it! Bloody easy it was."

He didn't know why, he couldn't care less. He was laughing to himself, even as Fred swung his truncheon towards his head. Peters ducked under the constable's head-high swing and instantly switching hands slammed the knife up and under the centre of Fred's exposed rib cage, directly into his heart. Peters twisted the blade, ensuring it went into its maximum penetration, and then withdrew it slowly, watching the agony and shock on Fred's face.

The dismay and contortions of pain on the policeman's face made Peters laugh hysterically. Slowly Fred Edwards' life ebbed away on the office floor, the bright red blood seeping into the old carpet and turning black as it started to mix with the blood of Joe Worrell.

Realising the situation he was in, but not understanding exactly what had made him kill the two men, neither of whom in fact had ever physically harmed him, he stood over their recumbent bodies surveying the results of his fury, his anger and rage slowly subsiding.

He had been in a similar situation some years before, but then, as now, he'd become sufficiently aware of his surroundings and the likely outcome of any investigation. If he hung around and was found in the vicinity of the Floating Harbour Masters' Office, he would almost certainly be caught, suspected, then blamed for the killings. Peters knew he would be suspected, as would Jenkins and many other dock workers: now he was about to make sure there would be no blame attached to himself. If it turned out otherwise, he'd have to be ready to make a run for it.

Blame anybody but himself was the thought flashing through his mind as he dragged the two bodies close in behind the reception desk. He knew they wouldn't be seen at first glance, either from the doorway or through a window.

Taking some old rags from the store cupboard he cleaned what blood he could see from his hands, and, after checking in the mirror, a couple of spots from his face. Satisfied with his appearance, he went to his desk and pushed it back against the wall, checking through the window at the same time that no one was approaching the building.

He had a bit of luck on his side that morning as he had come to the office late. Mr Roberts and Jenkins were out and the only person who knew he had come to work was Joe Worrell, "who wouldn't be saying a word, would he?"

He pulled out the bottom one of three drawers and turned it over emptying the contents on to his desk. Nothing had been noticed or said when the drawer had been briefly examined by Inspector Hazelton during a search of the office that had taken place a few days before. No one would have noticed the false panels in the front and the bottom of that drawer. It looked and weighed exactly the same as the other drawers in the desk. The skill and craftsmanship of the work that went into making the hiding place was unlikely ever to be repeated because the desks and remaining furniture in the office were made to plans designed for the wealthy owners of large country or town houses. The craftsmen who produced this sort of furniture had long since past away, taking most of their secrets with them.

Placing the drawer in its usual position but on top of his desk, Peters took hold of the handle and slid it across to the right, revealing half an inch wide slot. Poking two fingers into the slot, Peters found a tiny catch and pulled it upwards. The whole of the drawer front came free, showing an internal false wall. A small space about an inch deep, covering the fifteen inch length and twelve inch width of the front of the drawer was revealed. Under the bottom floor of the drawer was another space of about an inch in thickness and the width and length of the drawer.

Inside the bottom space at the back of the drawer, on a cardboard tray and packed tightly with thin cotton cloth, was a collection of gold and silver jewellery, a few diamonds and rubies and half a dozen gold sovereigns. The front part of the drawer held another cardboard tray containing several gold and silver chains, a couple of fob watches and one gold watch, inscribed with its owner's name. Plus a soldier's silver South African campaign medals and a Long Service and Good Conduct medal.

The joints cut into the wood were so delicately and cleverly sawn, the weight of the drawer so exact, it was virtually impossible to see how the secret compartments were constructed. Peters had found the secret compartments by accident. During his first couple of days in the office, he'd been cleaning the old desk up. It hadn't been done in years. Whilst empting the desk drawer, it had fallen from his grasp. He caught it by the handle, as he did so he pulled slightly on the handle revealing the space behind it. With infinite patience Peters had worked at the drawer until it revealed its secrets. It had contained papers and two old gold coins, property of some long time dead wealthy business man.

Now all the stolen property, which he had made his business to acquire from his nefarious dockland associates, had to be taken to a place where they would be safe but could easily be retrieved if he needed to go on the run. He thought to himself it wasn't likely, because, although the police wanted to arrest him, there wasn't any evidence that could link him with any crime, because he didn't believe he had ever committed any. At least not that anyone could prove. Not until now.

Members of the Commodores would never give evidence against him. They all knew that he would cut out their tongues if there was even a suggestion his name was mentioned to the authorities. He was known to be the most vicious, evil, 'boss' of all the dockland gangs. Most knew where he worked but few even thought about finding out his real name. 'Boss' was good enough for them.

Peters parcelled the jewellery into two strong, large envelopes, taped them together and addressed them to one of his oldest friends, a man who worked in the lost property office at Bristol Temple Meads railway station. He placed the parcel in the box used for Harbour Master's daily outgoing official mail, knowing that later in the day Jenkins would collect and take the mail to the Docks post office.

After putting the drawer back together and replacing it in his desk, he checked around the office for any tell-tale signs of his having ever been there.

Making sure that the office door was properly locked from the inside, Peters climbed out of the open window at the back of the building, and went to the outside toilet and washed his hands and face in the cold water tap situated there. Then made his way calmly and quietly to the dock gate police post. Although it was almost eleven o'clock he was barely noticeable as he walked the few hundred yards to the police post, so much was going on around the ships moored along the docks.

When he reached the police post he checked no one was outside the building, walked quickly past the half-opened door and ducked under the window towards the main dock gate. When he'd passed the window, Peters straitened up to his full height, turned around and walked back past the open post window.

As he did, he looked into the room saying, "Morning Jerry, how are you?"

A surprised docks policeman looked up from a form he was completing and with some testiness at being disturbed, replied "Morning, Mr Peters? Blimey, it's gone eleven o'clock. What's the matter, have a heavy night?"

"No. No, Jerry. Nothing like that, just a little family problem. Got to rush though. You know what Mr Roberts is like for punctuality. Bye!"

Peters had barely taken ten steps when Constable Jerry White called out, "Hang on, Mr Peters, wait there a minute will you?"

Peters knew immediately that it was very unlikely that the killings had been discovered and he shouldn't draw any suspicion to himself. So he stopped, turning to face Constable White, normally an affable big, broad shouldered man, without an ounce of malice in his character. He was usually found at the dock gates, greeting most of the dock workers with daily pleasantries and little jokes. He had a smile and kind word for everyone he spoke to.

Without any alteration in his demeanour, Peters replied, "What can I do for you, Jerry; something for the Police Charity Ball is it?"

There was no humour in White's answer though. "No thanks, Mr Peters, it's not that. I've been told to inform you that you're wanted at the station to answer some questions, to be put to you by Inspector Hazelton." He saw there was a question in Peters face and answered, "No, Mr Peters, I don't know why! I've just been told to inform you that the inspector wishes to ask you about certain incidents that you may know about, over the last few months."

"Are you arresting me, Jerry?"

"Oh no, sir, not at all; I'm just asking you to accompany me to the dock police station."

"If I say no, I haven't the time?"

"Then I suppose I shall have to ask whether or not I should arrest you: I suppose I should ring the station."

"No, don't do that, Jerry. I'll tell you what, I have to go to the office and tell Mr Roberts what's happening and give him a couple of forms." He patted his jacket, over the inside pocket. "If you walk with me to the FHMO, we can cut across the mole to the Administration Buildings and then back to the dock station. You'd best bring your bike, Jerry, then when you have delivered me to the inspector you can ride back along the Dock road, can't you?"

"All right, Mr Peters, as long as you stay close. It's a good idea but why don't I telephone your boss, easier and quicker that way, ain't it?"

Jerry was always looking out for the easier option and always shied away from taking too much exercise, as could be told by his girth and weight.

Peters replied, "I know Mr Roberts was going to a meeting this morning, though I don't know exactly where, because I've only just got here, haven't I? Perhaps there's someone else there, Worrell or Jenkins maybe? Mr Roberts will need these papers urgently. The writer needs a quick reply, so if you don't mind, Jerry?"

Constable White may have been a little slow but no one could call him stupid and he always did as his superiors told him, no matter how laborious or what the cost. He went back into the office, beckoning Peters to follow. White picked up the phone and dialled the switchboard to speak to the operator. When she answered he asked to be put through to the FHMO. He waited a minute or two, waiting for the familiar "You're through, sir!" but the operator said in her stilted operator's voice, "I am sorry sir, the number you required is not answering." That made him smile briefly: the number was not answering – ridiculous.

With a grimace, PC White said, "OK, Mr Peters, let's start walking."

As Peters walked, the plan he had begun whilst in the FHMO with the bodies of the constable and the clerk, began to take shape, making an alibi that would be difficult to break.

When they arrived at the FHMO, Peters walked in front of the policeman and went as if to open the door knowing already that it was locked. The key was in his pocket when he suddenly realised that if it was found on him, the police would definitely suspect him, even if he had been innocent. He knocked on the door. No answer.

PC White went to the window nearest to the door to peer into the office. Although it was daylight, very little light shone into the room. He knocked on the door. There was no answer. White went back to the window and took another look.

"I think I can see something in the middle of the floor, a carpet, it looks like it's got a very large stain or it's a very strange pattern." PC White suddenly became very alert. "What's that there?" he asked Peters, pointing to what looked very much like a boot or shoe, peeking out from behind the reception desk. Peters didn't answer.

The constable's face went grey, almost white. He looked at Peters, who asked, "What's the matter, Jerry?"

"What's the bloody matter, that's somebody's bloody foot, that is. Come on, we'll have to get in." Anxiety showed on his usually placid, benevolent features.

"Look!" Peters pointed. "That back window looks as though it's open!"

"All right, you stay here Mr Peters, don't move. I'll go and see if I can get in at the back. If any of your mates come, get them to stay here. No one's to move." With that he started off towards the back of the Floating Harbour Master's Office.

As the constable disappeared around the corner of the building, Peters took the office key with its small blue tag from his pocket and threw it as far as he could, about thirty yards across the cobbles. It bounced once and slid over the edge of the harbour wall into the water. The last he saw of it was the identification tag flapping in the breeze.

He took a quick look around the area and was pleased to see no one was in the vicinity close enough to have noticed what he'd just done. He smiled to himself, knowing now that he couldn't possibly connected with the murders that had taken place in the office. He had a witness and alibi that couldn't be broken.

Just then White came rushing back to the office door. "We've got to get in. I'll have to break the door down: I couldn't get in through that window."

"What's happened, Jerry, what's going on?" Peters, pretending to look alarmed, asked the constable.

"It looks as though there are two bodies in there, and I think one of them is a policeman. I can't see who it is because most of the body is hidden by a desk or something. Come on, give me a hand, I've got to get in and see who they are. Mr Peters, will you go and get something heavy to break this damned door down. Anything. And get a couple of men, I might need a lot of help. By the way where's the nearest telephone?"

White was clearly becoming very angry with frustration and inability to think clearly and quickly. This Peters seemed most unhelpful, but seeing he was required for questioning at the station, he was probably thinking the police should help themselves.

At that instant Mr Roberts and Jenkins approached the office.

"Morning Mr White, can I help? What's up, Mr Peters? Bit late aren't you? Trouble with the family?" Roberts held up his hand as he saw the consternation on the constable's usually unconcerned face.

"Mr Roberts, Mr Jenkins, do either of you have a key? Ah, good!" as both men pulled their office key from their pockets. Will you please open the door? Quickly, if you don't mind, Mr Roberts?"

Jenkins, realising that a serious situation had arisen, moving swiftly unlocked the office door and stepped back allowing Constable White to push past him into the gloomy interior of the office. He moved slowly around the reception counter, almost tripping over Worrell's body. Placing his hand on each body in turn and then recognising his work mate, Constable Fred Edwards, he shouted to the three men just outside the office entrance.

"Everyone is to stay outside until I tell you to come in, if I tell you to come in. Just stay where you are until I've used the phone to ask for more police assistance. People have died in here."

The three men looked at each other, Jenkins and Roberts with disbelief, Peters with apparent shock. He slumped on to the bench outside the door looking as though he might pass out any second.

Roberts, with concern in his voice, said, "Are you going to be all right, Mr Peters? My goodness, you don't look so well; would you like a drink or something? Mind you, this is such a shock for us all, isn't it?"

Peters was looking at the ground, a ghost of a smile appeared and just as quickly vanished when he noticed out of the corner of his eye Jenkins watching him.

There was a shout from inside the office. Constable White called, "Do you think one of you men could come in here and tell me who this person is?"

Roberts said to the other two, "I'm sorry, I couldn't, I've never seen a dead person before, so if you don't mind I'd rather not."

Peters looked at Jenkins, "Not me thanks, I can't stand the sight of blood, you go Jenkins, you're used to murder and mayhem, you'll have seen more of it than the likes of us."

Jenkins reply wasn't what Peters expected. "As usual, always get someone else to do your dirty work, eh, Peters? You haven't got the guts to do it yourself, have you? By the way, where is your key? You could have unlocked the door, couldn't you?"

"No! I've left mine at home or lost it!" Peters replied. He turned away, not wanting to get involved in an argument or he might say something to cast suspicion on himself.

Jenkins went to the office door, a thoughtful look on his face. He called, "It's me, Mr White, Jenkins. I'm coming in, OK?"

White called back, "Come on then, Mr Jenkins, tread very carefully, I don't want you to disturb anything, just step to the end of the counter, you should be able to see the bodies from there. Have you ever had to deal with the dead before Mr Jenkins? If not don't worry, you'll be OK; it's not a nice sight though, so take your time, won't you."

"It's all right, constable, I was in the army for twenty years and saw enough bodies in North Africa and the Middle East. I don't scare easily."

"No, I don't believe you do, Mr Jenkins. I've already heard about your exploits in the short space of time you've been here."

By this time Jenkins had already noticed the policeman Fred Edwards. He glanced at Jerry White who was staring at the bodies almost unable to contain himself.

Jenkins whispered, "Sorry, Jerry. Fred was a good bloke, sorry to see him like this."

He turned towards the second body which was lying face down on the floor. Jenkins didn't even bother to turn the body over, he knew from the clothing that it was his work mate, Worrell, blood still surrounding the throat wound. He knew immediately the wound had been made with a knife, causing the death of young Worrell.

Turning to Constable White, he said sadly, "It's Joe, Joe Worrell, the other deputy. Christ! They didn't kill each other did they? But looks like they've both been knifed, don't it?"

"Don't be daft, Mr Jenkins. Yes, they've both been killed with a knife. Someone's killed them and took the weapon with them.   OK, Mr Jenkins, thank you. Will you wait outside with the others? We'll have to wait now for Inspector Hazelton and his murder squad to arrive. I'm sorry about your friend Worrell. Someone will talk to you later; we'll have to have statements, you see, from all of you, so will you please ask the others to wait until you're told you can go. Thanks."

White shut the office door and Jenkins went to tell Roberts and Peters about the constable's instructions.

The first question from Mr Roberts was, "Who are they Jenks? Do you know them?"

"Yes Cyril, I know them. One poor sod is a policeman; you both know him, Fred Edwards. The other, of all people, is Joe Worrell. I couldn't believe it. I don't know about Fred but Joe has never harmed a soul that I've ever heard of. He's, I mean he was, a good family man without a grudge against anyone, almost! Not like some I know around here!" He looked directly at Peters, the loathing in his eyes enough for everyone to see.

"There ain't no need to look like that, Jenkins." Peters retorted. "I ain't done noffin', nor would I, see. You shouldn't say things either, 'cause crap sticks, don't it? Anyway, what do you think I be, some sort of criminal or somethin'? You'd best keep them sort of remarks to theeself, mister!"

Roberts butted in, he could see the argument developing into something nasty. Calm down both of you. Mr Jenkins, there wasn't any need for that, will you apologise to Mr Peters, before things go too far."

"Sorry Mr Roberts, can't do that, the man knows what I think and how I feel. Though I'll say no more – for the time being."

He gave Peters a ferocious look and went to the edge of the dock and stared out across the harbour, his white face showing his anger.

Just then two police vehicles pulled up outside the FHM Office and a dozen detectives and policemen, led by Inspector Hazelton, stepped out of them.

Constable Jerry White met them and explained the grim situation to Hazelton. Within a minute the building was surrounded and a couple of the men were sent on patrol to keep inquisitive dockers and harbour workers away from the area. The unusual arrival on the docks of car loads of policemen sent most of the workers either leaving the jobs they were engaged in to see what was happening, or scurrying for cover, in case it was a police raid. "Like rats leaving a sinking ship" one manager described the exodus from a cargo hold.

Roberts, Jenkins and Peters were taken in turn to a police van and questioned as to their whereabouts that morning, also what they were they doing and who were they with at the approximate time of the murders which had been timed between eleven-fifteen am, when Constable Edwards had taken a call from the switchboard operator, Janice Longstaff, until Constable White had first seen the bodies at eleven-forty am. They all were able to account for their movements that morning; Roberts and Jenkins of course at the Docks police station until five minutes to eleven.

They then walked back to the office, where they saw Constable White and Peters at the office. Peters was with PC White from approximately eleven o'clock onwards, although White couldn't state exactly what time Gordon Peters had arrived at the police post and spoken to him.

White and Peters at the time hadn't realised that Mr Roberts and Jenkins were at the police station, helping the police with their enquiries and taking part in an identification parade. They had been there since ten am.

Mr Roberts had been the last person working in the office to see Joe Worrell alive. Roberts told the police that at nine-thirty am he had given Worrell instructions to complete some shipping forms and take them to the administration offices. That task would have taken about half an hour. A clerk at the administration offices confirmed Joe had arrived there at about ten-fifteen am. After handing over the shipping forms, Joe had a cup of tea and a chat with the clerk, visited the toilet and left at about ten-thirty am. He seemed quite cheerful, because he was whistling as he left the building. Several other workers at the offices confirmed the clerk's statement.

Since he first spoke to Peters, Jerry White admitted, the man had barely been out of his sight from the time of his arrival at the police post, until the discovery of the bodies.

A number of dock workers were asked about Constable Fred Edwards' movements. It was part of his daily routine to patrol the harbour and if anything caught his eye or was reported to him, he would invariable pass the information on to the manager or department clerks responsible for that area. Two stevedores said they had watched PC Edwards enter the FHMO at about twenty to eleven. They knew the time because they were told to have a break and be back by quarter-past eleven. No, they hadn't gone near the office because they had seen a policeman go there and besides they wanted a "mug of char", "'cause they'd been at work, grafting!" one of the stevedores sneered at the officer taking their statements.

They were asked if they had seen anyone else go into the office, "No!" said the more vocal of the two stevedores, "But when that first copper went in, as we was goin' for our tea, 'e said somfink to somebody who was in there. An' I saw somebody move past the winders. I never saw who it was properly though, so I can't tell you who it were. Say mister, is somebody kilt in there or what? Seems like too many rozzers in there for just a robbin', don't it?"

The policeman taking their statement, grunted, "Sorry, mate, can't say what's happened, I don't know meself yet. I expect we'll all find out soon enough, eh! Anyway thanks for the information, it might be very useful. If the inspector needs to talk to you, we'll find you on the vessel there, will we?"

"Yeh, be there all day I expect, maybe see you after." The stevedores wandered off, back to the ship they'd been working on. One was cursing the other for telling the police too much.

"What if the boy's 'ad seen you, they'd 'ave our guts for garters, wouldn't they?"

"Aw shut up, if'n you don't tell 'um, they won't know, will they?"

Inspector Hazelton and his team of detectives became more frustrated and angry as the day passed. There didn't seem to be any sort of forensic clue that could be used in the tracking down and apprehending of the killer.

Hazelton tried desperately to analyse what little evidence was left by the man who had so cold bloodedly killed the two men. His forensic team had found fingerprints of several people in the building and after taking samples of the men that worked there and the two constables involved, the conclusion was reached that the murderer must have worn gloves. Either that or the crime was committed by one of the three remaining men who worked in the FHMO which at the time seemed highly unlikely as they all had unshakeable alibis, or so it seemed. What he needed was a witness and it didn't look as though one would appear. He told his detectives to take the office apart and find something, anything, to trap the killer.

Hazelton was distracted for a minute or two, when PC Jerry White asked him what the inspector wanted him to do about Gordon Peters.

"Well, what about him?" Hazelton asked. "For Christ sake, constable, can't you see I'm busy?"

"Sorry sir, but you wanted to have him in for questioning about theft and robbery. I was told to bring him in but not to arrest him. If it wasn't for him we might not have been at the scene until much later, because he asked to come here to give some papers to his boss, Mr Roberts."

"I don't think we'll worry about him for now, PC White. He's still here and he hasn't run off, has he? OK, we'll pull him in later, when this mess has been sorted out, all right? I'll let you know when I want him brought in. Let Mr Peters know that he's not to leave town, because if we have to chase after him I'll throw the book at him and it'll be the heaviest and biggest I can find. Let him know, constable, that I won't have forgotten him and we, the police, have long arms: he won't get very far, OK?"

It was later in the afternoon that Mr Roberts asked Hazelton if it was possible for either Jenkins or himself to enter the office to collect some files and the mail that required posting.

"I really don't like having to ask you this but there are a few important files to be collected and some letters to post. I'll be able to work from the administration building or home if I can collect some of the files I need and this morning's mail. It'll probable be requests from shipping companies who will require moorings over the next few weeks or months. I have to answer their requests quickly."

He hesitated. "I know this sounds extremely callous, but we may lose a lot of business. Joe would know that and agree if he was still here, I'm sure."

Jenkins, who was never too sure about Peters, had been standing close by when PC White told Hazelton why he had brought Peters to the office. When Mr Roberts returned from his conversation with the inspector, Jenkins said quietly, "Did Peters happen to give you anything today, Cyril?"

"No, Jenks, why are you asking?"

Jenkins told Mr Roberts what he'd overheard in the conversation between the inspector and Constable White.

"Strange that, Taff, isn't it? He hasn't said a word to me, or given me anything. Jerry White must be mistaken, eh? If Gordon Peters has got something, he'll let me have it I'm sure. Not to worry Jenks. There'll be enough to do, sorting out the mess when the police leave. I'm going into the office to collect the mail and some files: Hazelton said it's all right. Is there anything you need? I'll pick it up if there is. No? Right I'll be back in a few minutes. OK!"

When he walked nervously into the office, he was appalled at the mess the police had made; everything seemed to be overturned or damaged. It looked as though a tornado had ripped through the room.

He made his way gingerly through the mayhem of the once well organized, clean and well laid-out office. He was pleased to see the bodies had been taken out, but the huge bloodstains on the carpet and other parts of the floor turned his stomach. Not being used to such sites, he felt his stomach churning as he realised just what had happened to poor Worrell and the constable. He couldn't imagine, nor did he want to, what had been done to both men. Just the thought of what might have been done to them made him want to get out of building as fast as possible, before he was sick.

Just as he was leaving, a member of the forensic team called him back. "Do you want to take this mail with you, Mr Roberts? Looks as though it needs to be posted. We'll be locking up this office before we go and putting a police guard on it for a few days at least, until we finish our investigation, so you had better take it with you now."

Roberts took the envelopes handed to him, noticing the ones he had intended to post, also one with two envelopes taped together, the address having been written in Peters' handwriting: 'To the Lost Property Department at Temple Meads Railway Station'. The address wasn't unusual, he had noticed that several times in the last year or two letters had been sent there from the Harbour Master's Office. At the time he assumed it was to do with lost property found in and around the harbour that may have come from railway transport or people. Peters often took that task on himself. But it was one of Jenkins' jobs to post and collect the mail from the administration offices post room. Peters would never do it for him.

When Roberts got outside, he took a couple of deep breaths then told Peters and Jenkins what he had seen.

"It is unbelievable that someone could do such a monstrous thing, it makes me ashamed to be a human being. I'll never understand what makes someone so vicious and callous." He turned away from the two men, trying to hide the tears that welled up.

Jenkins took Roberts by the arm, "I think you would be better off at home Cyril. Come on I'll walk you to the police post, you'll be able to get a lift from there, OK?"

He turned towards Peters, "What are you going to do now, Mr Peters? You know the police have said you're not to leave town, so what have you been up to, I wonder?"

Peters was furious. "What the 'ell has it got to do with you Jenkins? Go about your own business and keep out of mine, right!"

"Leave him alone!" Roberts demanded. "Haven't we had enough trouble for one day, without you two shouting and arguing?" "Come on Jenks, let's go. Here, you'd better post this mail this afternoon, otherwise most of it will arrive too late to be of any use, then we'll be losing a lot of business." Roberts handed the letters over. "Come on, I have to get away from here. I really don't feel well."

As Roberts and Jenkins walked away, Jenkins half turned to look at Peters; the look on the man's face was enough to convince him that the man he was looking at had something to do with what had happened in the office that day. But there would never be any proof.

Peters, who had begun to talk to a small group of stevedores, had a grin on his face and mouthed the words, "Crawling bastard!" at Jenkins.

Jenkins continued on with Mr Roberts until they arrived at the police post. Roberts went inside to arrange a car for himself, while Jenkins walked on to the administration building.

He was used to the office staff who worked in the building and a few stopped and offered him their sympathy and condolences, asking what had happened and were the police close to catching the killer.

His stock answer was, "Thanks, but I don't know how the police are getting on. It doesn't seem that they have enough information at the minute to say if they have any idea who killed the men. Sorry I can't say any more."

It was the same when he arrived at the post room. He replied to the clerk's questions in the same way as he placed the mail on the office counter.

"Am I too late for today's collection?" he asked the young female clerk, Annie.

"No, there's another ten minutes before the postman arrives to empty the boxes."

"Damn!" Jenkins cursed. "The letters haven't had postage stamps put on them, can you do it for me? I don't have any money, at least not enough to put stamps on all of these."

"That's all right," the girl replied. "I can book the stamps to the FHMO, if you'll sign for them? We can recover the cost from that account later when things get back to normal. Sorry, Mr Jenkins, I didn't mean it like that. I know they won't ever be back to normal for anyone. I'm awfully sorry for their wives and children: what a thing to happen. I really can't imagine it." She blurted it out in anger and sorrow. "They were such nice blokes, who could have done such a thing?"

As the girl was speaking, she was sticking penny and two penny stamps on the dozen or so letters. She was about to place a stamp on the thick doubled-up envelope packet, when she said, "I think I had better weigh this one because it does seem rather heavy. It may need a three or four pence stamp."

Placing the packet on the postal scales, Annie announced it needed a four pence stamp as it was three times the weight of the other letters. Jenkins wasn't taking too much notice; he was looking out of the window as Annie was about to stick the stamp on to the envelope.

Annie uttered, "Ugh! What's that?"

Jenkins turned back from the window. "What's the matter love, seen a rat or something?"

"No not a rat, something on this packet; it looks like a stain. Look, there in the corner, where we're supposed to put the stamp, can you see it? Is it dried blood? It's nearly black."

"Yes, yes I can. Well, how did that get there? Can you get some more light in here? There's something else in that stain as well."

Annie opened the office curtains as far as they would go and turned on the recently installed electric light. Holding the packet up to the light, Jenkins could see the familiar blurred outline of what looked like a fingerprint.

His thoughts turned to whose handwriting was on the envelope. "There's only one person whose hand-writing is as neat as that, Gordon Peters." Mind you, that didn't mean that it was Peters' fingerprint in the bloodstain, even if they were on the envelope. He had definitely written the address, so if his prints were not on the paper, it would mean there was something peculiar going on.

"Stop playing detective," he told himself. "Just because you can't stand the evil bastard, doesn't mean he killed anyone!"

As the print was completely dry, it couldn't be either his own or Mr Roberts; mind you, a policeman had handled the letters when they were handed to Mr Roberts.

He looked at Annie, "There's only one thing for it love, the police will have to see this, best give the Docks station a ring and ask for Inspector Hazelton. He'll know what to do. Tell you what, Annie, I'll make sure he knows who to thank for spotting the stain, if it is a bloodstain! I hope it *is* a clue to finding the killer: it's a good job you spotted it. If you'd stuck a stamp over it, no one would ever know about it, would they?"

Annie nodded in agreement, a faint smile coming to her worried face.

"If it really is a fingerprint, let's hope it's a good clue, eh? The police are going to need some luck as well as witnesses and good police work. Look, Annie, I have to go now. There's someone special I have to see tonight and I don't want to be late. I don't expect the police will be long in coming to collect that packet and I've got a good contact in the police station, so next time I come in with the mail I'll let you know if it is a good piece of evidence or not. I think everyone who works on the docks should help in trying to find the murderer or murderers otherwise no one will ever feel safe, will they? 'Bye now Annie. Oh! You'd best not tell anyone else except the police about the packet; better to keep it between ourselves, eh?"

With that parting remark Jenkins headed for the dock gates and home. If he was quick he might be lucky and catch the early tram. Then he could have a quick bath and shave and put on some clean clothes before getting the returning tram back to the Citadel, where he had arranged to meet May. When May had finished her prayer meeting and work they were going on to her home for supper.

This time he intended to tell her how he really felt about her and try to find out about her true feelings for him. He was hoping she wouldn't be shocked if he found the courage to propose marriage to her. If she refused, he could only hope that it was because it might be too sudden for her and that she needed more time to consider his proposal.

He began to realise whilst he was sitting in the old tin bath in front of the fire, washing in lukewarm water, that if May had heard about the murders, she might not want to give him an answer today, if at all.

"There you go!" he said to himself. "Backing out again, you'll find any reason not to ask her to marry you, you gutless sod."

By the time he got on the tram to the Citadel, he was raging at himself. It wasn't until he alighted at the Salvation Army building that he had settled down enough to greet May in his normal light-hearted fashion. It seemed to him that just seeing her and feeling her air of quiet calm helped him make up his mind at last. "I will ask her, I will ask her," he whispered to himself under his breath.

"What did you say, love?" May asked.

"It's OK, May, I'll tell you later when we are having supper. It is at your house isn't it, love?"

"Don't worry Jenks; yes, I've already made supper, some thick leak and potato soup and fresh bread. All I have to do is warm the soup, and I've made some apple dumplings for pudding. I thought you might like them."

She went on excitedly, Jenkins couldn't understand why: "The apples are from Mr Roberts' garden, they are lovely. They're the ones you brought last week. I couldn't eat them all, so I made some into dumplings. I think you'll like them, Jenks."

She put her arm through his, pulling him towards her, settling in comfortably as they walked the sun-lit streets towards her home.

"When we've had supper we can talk about your day, can't we love? Been busy have you?" She spoke, it seemed, without a care in the world.

Jenkins mumbled, "Yes, fairly, love." He couldn't say anything until he knew if she had heard about the murders. He tried to think how he was to tell her about the killing of Joe and the policeman. He knew that she knew Joe, having visited him in the office a week or two after he himself had started work there. May had received a message saying that Joe's wife had gone into labour whilst Joe was at work and could he leave and visit her in the hospital.

When Joe came to work the next day, he couldn't stop talking about the baby girl who'd been born the night before. May had offered to go to his home and look after their other child, a little blond-haired boy, until the mother Hanna was allowed out of hospital. May stayed and looked after the little boy for almost a week before the mother went back home. A minor complication had occurred with the new baby's breathing. A few days later the baby's breathing had improved and was well enough for the obstetrician to decide it was safe enough to take the baby girl home.

To May's delight, the couple had named the baby after her: she was called Josephine May Worrell. May did admit to Jenkins that Josephine May was about the sixth baby girl named after her. "I'm truly very honoured that the parents trust me so much that they give their children my name," she told him proudly. It proved to Jenkins at the time what and how the local people thought of her, a trusted friend to them all.

He felt proud to be seen walking out with her. He still didn't know that May actually felt the same way about him. That's what she wanted to talk to him about after they had finished their supper. May wasn't too sure how she should go about telling him about her feelings for him. She said to herself often enough that she was sure that she loved him.

It was not the same sort of love she had for her God, which was quiet and gentle and fulfilling. She knew God was there to answer her prayers, but it wasn't the same as the physical love she had known of her long-departed husband.

She knew that Jenks was the man who could give her the companionship and physical relationship that she missed so much. But she still wasn't sure if Jenkins felt the same way about her: if she told him of her thoughts and feelings about him, he might run a mile.

"I'll have to be very careful how I go about this," she told herself. "You don't want to frighten him away for good. There you go, making excuses: tell him, or he'll never know. Say a little prayer before you tell him. You'll need all the help you can get, silly!"

Later that evening they were sitting next to each other outside May's comfortable kitchen, watching the sun go down behind the ships in the dock, its waning light reflected on the river as it wound its way around the headland and into the Bristol Channel.

May said to Jenkins, "I've had enough, I can't stand this any more!"

"What's the matter love? Have I said or done some thing wrong?" Jenkins was flabbergasted.

"Of course not, silly! It's just that if you're going to ask me to marry you, you're taking an awfully long time about it. So I've decided to ask you. Will you marry me, Jenks love?"

"You mean you wanted me to ask you, May? I didn't know, honestly. I'm sorry, I was so scared that you would turn me down. I love you very much but as I'm not a religious bloke and don't believe in the things that you do, although we could be good friends, I couldn't imagine you accepting me as your husband. The way we have both lived must seem to you as if we have been living in different worlds. I really have been trying to get the nerve to ask you for weeks. He took a deep breath. "But every time I try to tell you how I feel about you my legs turn to jelly and I just cannot get the words out."

"What were you going to ask me then, Jenks?"

"To be my wife, of course!"

"Now, see how easy that was, you old silly? Of course I will, yes, of course I'll marry you and be your wife forever. I love you very, very much and I need you to be my husband and friend for the rest of our lives. I promise

I won't try to change the way you think about God and my love for Him, as long as you can accept that's how it will always be. I shall always be your loving wife and you will come first in my life, no matter what." She looked at him, almost out of breath with her outburst of love and acceptance.

Jenkins had stood up, watching her face as she accepted his proposal. He almost fell, his legs actually felt as if they *were* turning to jelly. He sat down with a bump.

"I think I love you as much if not more than you love me. I cannot say how it feels, but if something or someone was to take you from me now, it would destroy me. I cannot imagine a day going by without having you in my thoughts and in our lives."

He took her calm, gentle, face in both of his hands and kissed her for the first time on the lips. She wasn't shocked nor did she pull away, but after a few seconds returned his kiss.

They both knew then they were right for each other.

Not knowing that May already knew about the murders, Jenkins decided not to tell her. Today wasn't the time. May guessed that Jenkins knew what had happened in the FHMO but decided not to press him about it. They could talk about it another time soon.

She had been told whilst the prayer meeting was being held. May then said prayers for the two men. Although she knew Joe Worrell, May decided not to visit his wife Hanna and the children until they could come to terms with his demise in their own way, perhaps in two or three days. May had been told by a policeman that Hanna's and Joe's parents had been informed and they were expected to take the family to their own homes in the morning.

Jenkins missed his tram home that evening, but it didn't worry him. He almost danced all the five miles to the Coach House. Even though it was gone midnight when he finally arrived he still felt so good that he decided to wake the Roberts household and tell them the good news.

He only knocked loudly on the kitchen door once. A bedroom window above the kitchen was immediately opened.

"What's going on? Who's that?" a frightened squeaky child's voice called out. "Go away or I'll tell my Dad!"

Jenkins called back. "All right it's only me, Mr Jenkins. Tell your Dad I'm going to get married, will you?"

Roberts voice came from behind the bedroom window. "I heard that, Mr Jenkins. Congratulations! Now go to bed and I'll see you in the morning. Goodnight!"

Jenkins whistled all the way back to the Coach House and was still whistling as he fell asleep.

The next morning, at six am, Mrs Roberts was knocking on the Coach House door, waking Jenkins from the most fitful sleep he could remember in the last few months. He was still in bed when she burst into the room.

She wanted to know if it was true that he had proposed marriage to May and his proposal had been accepted.

Mabel Roberts was so excited that tears glinted in her eyes as she grasped Jenkins' hands, then dragged him to her in a hug that took the breath from both of them.

"Mabel," Jenkins gasped. "What will Cyril say if he sees us like this? You in your nightdress and me? Well I'm still in bed. He won't believe either of us, no matter what story we cook up."

"Don't be so daft, you silly man. I woke him up before I told him where I was going. Mind you, Jenks, I doubt very much if he actually heard me because he was still half asleep. I told him you were coming for breakfast, so he was to get up and put the kettle on. We, you and me, would need a strong cup of tea by the time I'd finished talking to you. So come on, kettle will be boiling and it's bacon and eggs to celebrate."

"By the way," Mabel went on, "we, that is Cyril, me and the children, want to be first on your guest list, no matter what May wants. All right love?"

It was the first time she had shown her affection for him. It seemed as if in her eyes he and May would be at the foremost of her thoughts right up until the wedding day.

Mabel just wouldn't stop talking about the forthcoming wedding. Even Roberts couldn't quieten her when she became so excited.

They would all have to wait until May decided when the date would be and Jenkins had a feeling that it could be a long engagement. There wasn't any hurry; they had only really started to get to know each other in the last few weeks. That didn't matter to him, it would give them both time to save and prepare for their future together.

He told himself that he had to find May and thank her for reminding him just how much they felt about each other. He had been stupid in not realising just how much they thought of and about each other. It must be love, he kept saying to himself. What else could make him feel so much for a woman, who he didn't really understand or know of her thoughts and beliefs? Perhaps he would in the future, when they settled down to a calming, happy married life.

Chapter 6

You're Under Arrest

For the rest of that week, Jenkins tried to concentrate on plans for his future wedding. The couple talked about nothing else, even putting the tragic demise of the two murdered men at the back of their thoughts, though of course neither May or Jenkins forgot what and where the evil event had taken place.

Mr Roberts had arranged for a small room in the administration building to be made available as a temporary Floating Harbour Master's Office.

Other managers and office staff all made their feelings known to Mr Roberts, Jenkins and Peters, saying how sad it was that such a terrible crime had taken place right in their work place, a real shame. Many of them asked after the victims' families and what was happening about the funerals.

Some knowing that Jenkins had seen the horrific aftermath of the murders, extended their sympathies to him, asking how he felt and whether he could go back into that office to work again. Because of the sort of person he was, Jenkins said he wouldn't be worried about working there again, not in the slightest, although he said, when the police had caught those who had committed the crime and had finished their investigation, the authorities should clear every thing out then destroy the building and rebuild it. That way, although there would be memories, a new start could be made to get on with their own lives.

Roberts in some ways agreed, but was still grieving, unable to think clearly about the future. He thought it better to give a lot more time and thought to the situation, before making any suggestions or a decision.

Peters went out of his way to vent his feelings on the killer or killers of his friend and the constable.

"If I ever get my hands on the murdering bastards…" he would leave the question unanswered and if there wasn't a reply would continue: "I'd help the hangman string them up myself," he told all the office staff and friends when he had any reason to speak with them.

The staff's thoughts were mainly to do with the fact that the police seemed to be no nearer finding the killers than they were at the time of discovering the murders.

"What a pity that the young mother and her children have been left without a husband and father," was the general comment. "How is she bearing up?" – the usual question.

A collection for her was taken. Everyone who worked in the docks and yard was asked to make a donation, no matter how small.

It was discovered that the insurance policy that covered accidental injury and death in the docks wouldn't cover young Joe Worrell's murder, but a police service insurance policy covered the death of policemen whilst on duty.

Even though most of the dock workers didn't know Joe Worrell, the seeming unfairness of the situation caused angry murmurs throughout the various factions of the labour force. Strike action was one of the suggestions being bandied about. A committee of stevedores and dock workers approached the Dock and Floating Harbour management to discuss various suggestions for making some sort of payment to Joe's wife Hanna in the form of a welfare grant and widow's pension.

It was firstly confirmed that the little family had no income. Joe had taken out a life insurance policy of sixpence a week just three weeks before he was murdered, therefore the insurance company wasn't legally obliged to pay his estate anything, although a ten pound contribution was made to the collection for Joe's family.

After actual threats of strike action were made and diverted, the management stated: "Owing to the unusually tragic circumstances surrounding the death of Joe Worrell, the Management Committee will match the amount of the dockyard collection and make an award of one pound per week as a permanent pension to Mrs Worrell during her lifetime." The pension was then to be passed to her children, if her demise happened before the school leaving age of the youngest child.

The management made it clear to the representative committee that this would be a one-off award. Their stipulation was that this type of pension and payment would never be paid by the Floating Harbour and Dock funds again.

There was a lot of moaning and grumbling from the workers' representatives but an agreement was made for the sake of the Worrell family. At the end of the discussions a second suggestion was made to the workforce: if any worker wanted to receive a pension, or be insured against any injury or death whilst going to or at work in the confines of the Floating Harbour or Dockyard they would find an insurance representative in the administration offices ready to do business. An arrangement would be made for those who wished it to have three pence per week stopped from their pay and put into a pensions fund. At the end of their employment with the authority after at least ten years, workers would receive pensions according to the number of completed years they had worked for the company. If they wished, after leaving the company's employ, they could continue to pay the insurance in the form of a death benefit for their families. The management received the authority to set up and run the fund for the workers, stipulating that for every penny that each worker paid in, the Harbour Authority would donate a like amount.

After putting the suggestion to the work force and having received a mandate, the workers' representatives signed a document of agreement.

One of those representatives was Gordon Peters. He made his name by being the first worker to sign the document. Later he would be the first worker not to pay his promised dues. He wouldn't be available.

Many of the dock workers took up the authority's offer in those first few months after the murders. Later the dock management made it mandatory for each individual to be insured whilst working anywhere in the docks.

Reward notices were placed in many of the dock building windows and on prominent sites such as doors and dock walls offering a reward of one hundred pounds for information leading to the arrest of the killer or killers of the clerk and the constable.

The problem that came later was about the information offered. Most of it tended to be misleading, if not sometimes ownright lies.

Gordon Peters, for the first day or two, spoke to what was left of the Commodore gang and a few other of his acquaintances, suggesting that a certain person or gang may have been in the vicinity of the office and why didn't the police know about it. Rumours abounded around the dock and harbour area: eventually the names of men and gangs, who had never ever been near or associated with the docks, were being named as the killers. In the three days after the crime more than fifty names had been put forward to the police, each informant saying he or she deserved the reward because he or she saw a man or two men or even three men leaving the office.

The police threatened to summon the miscreants for wasting police time, but that didn't stop many more trying to claim the reward.

All except for one informant.

He had left work early on the day of the murders, about eleven fifteen, because he had to make a report to his supervisor, after which he took the three days holiday which he had promised himself for months. His destination was Pembrokeshire. A friend's cottage was waiting for him and he hoped for good weather, he use of a boat and some fishing. On the train rumours abounded amongst his fellow passengers about the murders at Bristol Docks, continuing until the train reached Carmarthen.

The man stepped off the train at Carmarthen and went straight to the station office, where he showed his identity card to the station master, stating that he had urgent information for the police at Bristol Docks police station. The station master, hearing the urgency in the man's voice, straight away showed him to the telephone and left the office.

On receiving the call and listening to the man's tale and request, the desk sergeant passed him through to Inspector Hazelton. The sergeant, who wasn't easily surprised or shocked, would have been, had he heard Hazelton's, "Bloody hell, Jim! Is that you?"

"Aye, 'tis that," the customs officer, Mudhog Jack, replied.

"You old bastard, where've you been? Haven't heard from you for months. How are you?" He paused for a second. "Christ it must be important or you wouldn't have got in touch, at least not over the phone. Is there something wrong, mate?" He listened to Jim's story as certain events were described and who was the main individual concerned in those events.

At the end of Jim's concise narrative he said gravely, "Thank you Jim, thank you! Come and see me when you get back, there's no rush, not now I know where to find the evil conniving bastard. Thanks again."

He put the phone down and shouted, "Sergeant! We've got the bastard, come into my office and bring a few of the lads with you."

Mr Roberts, Jenkins and Peters were working quietly at their desks in their temporary office, when Hazelton knocked on the door and walked in.

"Afternoon Mr Roberts, Mr Jenkins. Nice afternoon for it, ain't it Mr Peters?"

"Yes, 'tis a nice afternoon, Inspector. Bit stuffy in here though, wish I could get outside for a few minutes. Can't get that bloody window open, it's stuck," Peters replied with what he thought was a friendly grin.

There was no grin on Hazelton's grim features as he said, "Yes, Mr Peters, we'd best go outside because there's not a lot of room in here, it makes me claustrophobic. I have something to say to you, *sir*! In private."

The disdain of his look and the tone in his voice made Peters sit upright. No one ever spoke to him in that tone of voice before. No one ever would again.

"What do you mean? Officer, what do you want?" He pushed his chair back and stood up. Although three inches taller than the policeman, he felt threatened and didn't like it.

Hazelton was standing directly in front of him, blocking his exit through the door. Jenkins was sitting to his left side facing his desk and a large window. Mr Roberts sat at his desk directly behind Peters.

Peters shook his left arm slightly and something dropped into his hand. He thought it had gone unnoticed. Although Jenkins couldn't see exactly what had happened, he saw the look of the fear of being trapped in Peters' face and his bearing. It looked as though he had tensed up and was ready to run or fight. He realised Peters was a threat; he could also see Peters was becoming increasingly desperate and angry. He laughed, "What's up, Peters? Caught up with you at last have they?"

"Shut your stupid mouth you daft bastard, or I'll…"

"Or you'll what?" Hazelton interrupted. "Do the same as you did to Joe Worrell and Constable Edwards?"

"What the 'ell you on about? Like all coppers, eh? Talkin' frough your pointed 'at agin." He hadn't realised it but he had dropped into his usual semi-educated speech he used when talking with his gangland cronies.

"Whatchyoumeen aye? watchyoumeen?" he was almost screeching. "I ain't done noffing see, I ain't done anyfink."

Roberts and Jenkins by this time had moved slightly away to the left of the room.

Hazelton's voice took a more formal tone, "Gordon Peters you are under arrest for the murders of Joseph Worrell and Constable Robert Edwards on Wednesday 20th August 1914. Anything you say…"

Hazelton was unable to finish the sentence, because a long pointed stiletto appeared in Peters' left hand. At the same time Peters grabbed Hazelton's coat lapel with his right hand.

Hazelton had been prepared for some sort of retaliation, but not the appearance of a knife. He attempted to step back, tripped on a door mat and went down, partially blocking the doorway. The fall had ripped his coat from Peters' grasp. A detective who had been waiting just outside the door, made a move as if to tackle Peters.

Hazelton shouted, "No! He's not going anywhere! Leave him to sweat it out." His colleague dragged him back into the hallway.

"Come on, boss! I'll get the lads; we'll drag the bastard out."

"Not now you won't, he's got a very dangerous-looking knife with which I think he's already killed two men. I don't want any of you copping it, do I?"

"Sergeant Rogers has brought a revolver, boss: shall I fetch him? You know we may have to down him especially as he's got those two blokes in there with him."

"Look, Davies, if I'm right, there's a bloke in there just itching to take that knife away from him, and if he gets the slightest, I mean the slightest, chance, Peters will be disarmed and in hospital in the next half an hour."

Hazelton was wrong, it took Jenkins a total of five minutes to lull Peters off-guard, disarm him, beat him and have him ready to put in an ambulance, which arrived almost ten minutes later.

Hazelton looked at Davies and said, "I was wrong, it took him less than half the time."

Davies replied, "Bloody hell, boss, I'm glad we don't have to go up against him; how did he do it? What did he do?"

"Ask him," Hazelton said pointing to Mr Roberts.

Roberts was approaching them, visibly shaken, but he smiled when Davies ask what had happened in the office.

"Well, it was like this. Mr Peters shouted at us to get back across the room, away from the window. At the same time he slammed the door shut and barricaded the door with his desk and a chair.

"Jenks, the crafty sod, said, 'Can we sit down, Mr Peters? Where do you want us?' Peters replied 'In the corner there, not on the floor. I won't be able to see you both there, use your chairs.'

"I was already in the corner; Jenks picked up my chair as if to hand it to me – it's a very heavy one – but he threw it across the floor at Peters, who was only ten feet away. Smashed into his legs it did.

"Peters went down in a heap but managed to keep hold of his knife, which made it all the worse for him. He half sat up and tried to stick Jenks in the leg, but he was a bit too slow. Jenks already had his chair in his hands: he slammed it on to Peters' legs first; it sounded as if a bone was broken in one of them. Next he jammed the chair legs either side of Peters' chest trapping him on the floor. The stretchers between the chair legs were almost crushing Peters' chest but not quite. The chair legs were a little too long, so that stopped the chair going all the way on to Peters' rib cage." Roberts caught his breath before going on:

"Peters was still slashing around with the knife, so Jenks wrapped one sleeve of his jacket around his hand. I thought it was to prevent Peters cutting his arm but he didn't use it like that, he used the other sleeve like a whip, down on to Peters head. It was that fast I don't think Peters even saw it coming. He was unconscious in a split second. I've seen Jenks in action before and he was quick and hard. Not like this though, he was really vicious and violent with the speed. Something to do with the sleeve, I think.

"Peters still had the knife, so, not being sure if he was out cold, Jenks stamped on his hand: I think he must have broken some fingers; then he prised it loose. The knife is still on the office floor."

"Thank you Mr Roberts, are you all right now? Not hurt, eh? Good, go and find yourself a nice cup of tea. I'll send Mr Jenkins to find you afterwards, OK?"

Roberts nodded his thanks and went off with a policeman to find some tea.

As Jenkins approached them, Detective Constable Davies eyed the nondescript-looking figure, noting his slightly hunched shoulders, his uncut straggly blond hair and recently grown moustache. It was the eyes the held the attention of Davies longest. Ice blue, with hardly a flicker, in a stone-like tanned face that didn't seem to be the slightest bit troubled about the damage and injuries he had caused to Peters.

Davies held out his hand to Jenkins. "Congratulations, sir!" was his opening remark. "A good job you did there, Mr Jenkins; you stopped us having to shoot him. What ever you did stopped him good. Thanks."

He looked at Hazelton. "We won't require a statement will we, sir?"

"Not this time, Davies, not this time. I think Mr Roberts can do that. We don't need too much fuss, although we must congratulate Mr Jenkins officially for helping us in the arrest of a most dangerous killer, at a later date, of course. Mr Roberts will be waiting in the staff tea room, Mr Jenkins. I imagine you could do with a cup after that. Perhaps something stronger, eh?"

"Thanks, Inspector, tea'll be just fine for now."

He left them discussing the next procedure to be done in connection with the capture and arrest of Peters after his discharge from hospital. Although they had their man, charging and convicting Peters was going to take a lot of evidence, questioning and work.

Davies said vindictively, "Boss, when Peters is hanging from the end of a rope, I'd like to be there to see it."

Hazelton snapped at him, "You wouldn't, you know, it'll live with you for the rest of your life. You'll wake up in the night, having a bad dream about it.

I know, because I've been present at a hanging. It's not our job to take part in executions, just to get the convicted evil bastards there. OK, Davis, I'm going back to the station. You and the lads sort this place out and then you and Sergeant Rogers can get up to the hospital and start questioning Peters when he comes round."

Hazelton continued, "I've just thought of something. I've only just realised that since Mr Jenkins was discharged from the army and arrived here in Bristol docklands six or seven months ago, he was attacked, almost killed and put in hospital for three or four months. After leaving hospital at the end of March or beginning of April he has put three or four members of one gang, the Commodores, in hospital and they are now in the nick awaiting trial. And he's hospitalised one or two from other gangs we know about."

Hazelton went on, "I can't understand what has attracted all this trouble to him but if he stays here in Bristol much longer, there won't be any gangs left operating in the docks. Christ, we'll be out of work!"

Davies replied, "Can't be a bad thing, can it boss?"

"You hope!" The sarcasm in the inspector's answer sent Davies on his way.

The police had enough evidence to charge Peters with murder on two counts and being in possession of stolen property. The fingerprints of his left hand were also found on the office window, on the outside, left there when he pulled himself up to climb out of the window.

What was even more damning, after his clothing and footwear were examined, was the matching indelible imprint of his left boot, found in the blood-soaked office carpet. It could only have got there after the murders. His boot still had a minuscule amount of blood on the sole, which hadn't been properly scrubbed.

The packet taken to be posted by Jenkins was found to have Peters' thumb print on the blood stained corner of the envelope. The newly-recruited forensic team concluded that it was made when the blood was still wet and must have been put there before the blood congealed. As blood congeals very soon after exposure to air, the thumb print must have been made by Peters within minutes of the murders. The jewellery, gold coins and notes found in the envelopes were all identified as being stolen and were reported to the police since and during the months that Peters had arrived and begun working in the Floating Harbour Master's Office.

Later, Inspector Hazelton was able to identify something else for Jenkins, but it would be weeks before he could surprise him with what they had found. The charges began to mount up and Inspector Hazelton, after being able to match Peters' fingerprints to those on the silver photograph frame which held a picture of Jenkins' family, began to suspect that Peters was responsible for the death of Jenkins' sister, husband and their daughter, but wasn't sure how. Because his prints were found on the picture frame, it did not mean he was in the house at the time of the killings. Hazelton was convinced that in some way Peters was connected with that crime.

It seemed that it wouldn't be too difficult to prove that he was responsible in some way for almost all of the many robberies, assaults, burglaries and murders that had happened in the Bristol docks area since his arrival. One or two of the weaker members of his gang, unconnected with many of the more serious crimes, had, on a promise that they would be dealt with more leniently, and in the hope of saving themselves, implicated Peters and the more prominent gang members of the Commodores in every crime they themselves knew about. When added together, these totalled over one hundred and thirty robberies and thefts and three murders that hadn't yet been solved. Hazelton and his team interviewed and questioned them many times, to ensure that the information was as near to the truth as possible.

Now Peters was held in custody and almost certain to be convicted of two murders. Perhaps he would open up and confess to the killing of the three people in number 21 Guinea Street or identify those that did the murders. Hazelton knew that he needed more evidence to back up those charges.

It wouldn't be too long in coming.

The day after being arrested for resisting arrest, Peters was charged with the murders of Worrell and Edwards, then remanded in custody in Bristol Horfield Prison.

Amongst those already on remand were most of the senior members of the Commodores gang, none of them very happy that Peters wasn't there with them, especially as they thought he had been 'grassing them up'. All sorts of threats were being made against him by the men he had used to commit crimes for him. He'd 'grassed' on them, why shouldn't they 'grass' on him? He'd be very lucky if he didn't get whacked, one of the prison warders told his colleagues.

Through his connections with the prison authorities, Hazelton arranged for Peters to be accommodated with his gang members on the same remand wing of the prison. Peters on his arrival on the allocated remand wing, couldn't understand why the members of his gang, the Commodores, tried to ignore him. Even George Vickers.

He decided that perhaps too many of the other cons and screws would be watching them. Maybe he could go to have a word or two in the morning while they were on exercise in the yard. Best to talk then, specially if he could get in between one or two of them. Peters knew they would have to walk in single file around the yard, and weren't supposed to talk. The prisoners could always get around that rule, because notes would be passed around, or whispered conversations would take place when the were out of the hearing of the prison guards. Often there would only be half a dozen warders for every hundred prisoners.

Although Peters had been charged with two murders and shown the evidence, he still didn't believe that the jury, any jury, when he went to court, would ever find him guilty because no one actually saw him do the murders.

The next morning the exercise yard was over-crowded, so the prisoners were ordered to walk the circuit in pairs and allowed to talk to their partners, but not to those in front or behind. He noticed that George Vickers moved to the other side of the yard as he approached, so seeing one of the other Commodores gang members, Jameson, he fell in beside him to walk the Circuit, as it was known by the cons and staff alike.

They had walked a full circuit before either said a word. "How's the boys doin'?" were Peters first words.

Jameson stared at him, "Doin'? Watchyamean, doin'? Yu fink yer goin' ta grass dboys up again? Eh boss?" he sneered.

"Grass? Me grass? Watchew talkinbout, Jamie? I ain't grassed nobody up. Ever, see?"

"Yous a bleedin' liar, mister, you was sin by us all. The coppers, de tole us you was tellin' dem about de boys and de Commoders. An we sees you dere in de line-up, an yous was talkin' to der coppers. We sees yous." It was final.

Suddenly whistles were being blown, and orders were being shouted by the warders at prisoners across the other side of the circle who were crowding about three or four men wrestling on the ground. One of them was George Vickers.

Four prison warders moved to the inside of the circle, drew their truncheons and faced fifty or sixty men on their part of the circle, barking orders for the men to close up, sit on the ground and stay where they were. Closed up, so that when they sat on the ground, the pairs of men were no more than two feet apart, the prisoners waited for further orders.

"What 'appens now?" Peters asked Jameson.

"Dis boss!

Peters never saw the broken half of a razor blade or even felt it. He thought it was a slap. He put his hand to his face; when he took it away he saw the blood, then he felt it streaming down his neck.   He pulled his shirt from his trousers and tried to reach his face with the bottom half of it. He stood up, glaring down at Jameson, who smiled up at him.

"Twasn't me boss. Twasn't me." He nodded to the two men behind him, Billy and Jimmy. They both grinned at him.

Jimmy said, "All da grasses git dat, boss. Den we can tell who dey is, cassn't we, boss, eh?"

A prison warder, seeing Peters standing, shouted, "Hey you, sit down, afore I nick thee!"

Jimmy whispered, "Next time it's your bleedin' froat, see."

Seeing the blood on Peters' face, the warder said, "Oh, got a little problem as ee, Peters? Yeh, I see by your face you will 'ave, won't thee? Let's have a look at you. Bugger me, you be that murdering bastard, ain't ee? Couldn't have 'appened to a better bloke. I expect you'll 'ave a few more problems like that while you're 'ere, won't ee?" He didn't even attempt to find out who had slashed Peters' face.

The warder turned and shouted to a colleague standing at an entrance gate to the main prison. "Get a scab lifter to sort this horrible bugger out, will ee John?"

When Peters entered the remand wing a prison hospital warder met him and took him to the prison hospital treatment room. On examining the injury, the medic said, "Tain't a bad cut; happens a lot in 'ere 'specially to you grasses."

"I ain't no bloody grass!" Peters almost screamed. "I never grassed nobody in my life."

"Tell you what, Peters, I believe you: lots as won't, so calm down and let me put a few stitches in that cut. You'll be as right as rain when I've finished."

Peters started cursing. "You ain't gonna stick no needles in me. You ain't a bloody doctor, so you'd better leave it till he comes in. Awright?"

"'Sir', you call me 'sir', you smarmy evil bastard."

Peters was livid. He stood up and rushed across the treatment room at the medic trying to kick him but slipped on the polished floor, falling on to his back. Cursing and struggling, he tried to get to his feet. The medic, who had been in the same situation many times before, calmly pressed the alarm bell on the wall near his desk at the same time pulling out his police whistle and giving several blasts.

The treatment room door flew open and half a dozen prison warders burst in, one shouting, "You OK, Charlie? How many more times this week, eh?"

Charlie, the medic, retorted, "Well, looks like you all need the practice, seeing how you all get out of breath so quick, don't it, Terry? Take this bastard downstairs, he tried to whack me. I'll do the nicking sheet later. By the way, the doctor won't be in for another four or five days, will he? This toad wouldn't believe me, the bastard. Callin' me a liar and he thinks he's a hard man, don't 'e?"

Dawson, the warder, said, looking at Peters, "You're in jail now, Peters, you 'ave to do as you're told and it's best to believe what we say, 'cause, if you don't, you might get a battering. He cuffed Peters around the head with a massive opened hand just as the prisoner was getting to his feet, knocking him back to the floor.

"I didn't say you could get up, did I?"

"No, mister."

"It's 'sir' to you shite bag. 'Sir' to all staff, an we ain't your bloody skivvies, awright Peters?" Peters nodded. "Get him up, get him out. Right lads, show him the ropes, eh!"

Three warders grabbed him by the arms and hair and with Dawson shoving his truncheon into the prisoner's back, they marched Peters to the punishment cells.

"Bring him back after tea," Charlie shouted. "I'll put some stitches in then!"

The next few weeks were a nightmare for Peters. First he was put on the Governor's report for attempting to strike the Medic. Then had to be restrained when he swore and spat at the Governor when he was told he would be in solitary confinement for three days on a diet of bread and water.

The punishment did subdue him, at least the warders and Governor thought it had.

He was kept in the punishment cells for a couple of days longer to check that he had actually brought his temper and attitude towards staff and other inmates under control. A week after the attack in the exercise yard, when it seemed that he intended to accept the prison rules and warders' orders, he was taken back to the remand wing.

The facial wound had begun to heal, but without sutures and proper treatment the scar began to look septic, sore and red. The wound would eventually heal properly but a livid scar would adorn his already morose features. He never spoke to or was spoken to by any of the gang members and very few of the other staff and prisoners.

Meanwhile the evidence was growing in the Docks Murders, as the newspapers called it. Several of the Commodores gang members had been invited to turn King's evidence. Four of them, George Vickers, Jameson, Billy Hoskins and Jimmy Butcher, realising what the weight of the evidence could be against the gang, but not knowing which of them would be accused for the various crimes committed, laid the blame for everything on to Peters, their 'boss', thinking they would receive lighter sentences when convicted.

After their initial appearances in the magistrates court, all the members of the gang were committed for trial at Bristol Assizes, later in the year.

Hazelton and Sergeant Whitman visited the jail on many occasions to question each member of the Commodores gang in turn, ensuring that their visit and the identity of the gang member that they were visiting was seen and noted by other members, and most especially Peters.

During the interview between Inspector Hazelton and George Vickers, George started by saying that he and Jameson had been the men who "Done dat solger on da 'ill, yous knows, wen dat 'ouse blewed up, same time. 'Member copper?"

"Yes, George, I remember; you put the soldier in hospital for months didn't you? Old Limpy, who was with him, died, didn't he?"

"Dat wasn't me, honest, boss Dat was ole Jamie. He pushed ole Limpy out of da way to git at di solger. I fink Limpy fell down and bashed is 'ead. Poor ole sod, I seys. Sorry 'bout dat, copper. Limpy was one of us, 'e was."

"Well then, George, who blew the house up and killed all those people?"

"I dunno, copper. Da Boss was der an' so was Billy an' Jimmy. I dunno wat de was doin' der, tho', 'onest. Me an' Jamie was sent to git der solger boy. Not Limpy, 'e was in de gang wive us, 'e shewed da solger da way, so's we could git to 'im. Is was an accinden not dilberite, 'onest.

Peters, having been told by Inspector Hazelton about the mountain of evidence being built up against him and the information being given by the Commodores gang members, decided to tell the policeman almost everything. Everything, that is, that he could blame on the members of his gang, crimes he knew and had no part in, realising if he was going to hang he might as well take the others with him, even if he had to make up more lies to get even with the rest of the gang.

Peters told the detectives in his statement: "Yes! on the night old Limpie died, we were in 31 Guinea Street." He then admitted going to the house to talk to a man and two of his mates. They belonged to another gang. Peters said he wanted to work out a deal with them. After a while, just as the man's wife, her daughter and a friend came into the house, an argument and a fight started.

Peters with Billie Hoskins and Jimmy Butcher beat two of the men to the floor, but the husband of one of the women, he said he didn't know which woman, got into the kitchen with the women and girl. Butcher and Hoskins went after the man. One of them, Peters didn't know which, stuck a knife in him. He grabbed hold of the kitchen stove to stop himself falling but they dragged him off it. As they did it came away from the wall. Again, he didn't know which one did it – but one of them, Butcher or Hoskins, smashed his head with a club. They all had one – a club. Then Billie locked the kitchen door to keep them in.

The women were screaming their heads off and they could all smell the gas and decided to get out. Billie Hoskins, after the fight, lit his cigarette from the gas fire, which was burning. They grabbed one or two things, silver frames and a silver cup and a few other things, then got out of the house quick. They left and walked up the hill to the street where the soldier was attacked. Just as they got to the alley there was an explosion, number 31 blew itself to bits.

"It wasn't anything to do with me, honest, Mr Hazelton, honest," whined Peters.

"We'll see how honest you are, mister, when we get statements from the rest of your lads, eh?"

"Come on, inspector," Peters said indignantly. "You know they ain't my lads, they ain't nothin to do with me and never have been, all right?"

The trouble for Peters was that Hoskins and Butcher told a different story. Both said after the fight in number 31 Guinea Street, they could all smell gas coming from the kitchen, maybe because the gas cooker had come away from the wall. Peters shoved the women and child into the kitchen, locking all of them in. Then he, Peters, lit the living-room gas fire himself. When Butcher went to turn it off, Peters pulled a knife and threatened them both saying, "If you don't want to get it as well, you'd best get out quick!"

"What did he mean?" Hazelton asked Butcher.

"'E would kill us'n too." Butcher shook his head. "An' 'e would 'ave too, inspecter. An' 'e would 'ave, I can tell 'e.

Then the three of them ran for it leaving the occupants of number 31 trapped.

They swore it was Peters who killed Jenkins' sister, her husband, his niece and two other men. Knowing the men were unconscious and the women and little girl were trapped, he deliberately locked and barred the door from the kitchen to the living room with a key and jammed a chair under the door handle.

After Hoskins and Butcher and other gang members had made their statements they swore to the police their statements were true.

A week after their arrest, a magistrate from Bristol Magistrates Court, seeing the overwhelming amount of evidence already presented against the all of the defendants, sent their cases to Bristol Crown Court assizes.

It was thought that it would be weeks before a date could be set for Peters and the Commodores to appear in the Crown Court. During those weeks of waiting Peters became almost a model prisoner, keeping himself to himself and following all the prison rules and instructions given him by the warders. He knew that the evidence was so heavily weighted against him, he hadn't a chance in hell of escaping the rope, so he intended to give the authorities a run for their money – by escaping from Horfield prison.

He still had one or two 'pals' who could be implicated in some of his dealings over the years: they wouldn't escape jail if he were to inform on them. He couldn't care less whether they went to prison or not, as long as they were prepared to do his bidding and get him what he needed.

First he began to cultivate George Vickers' friendship. Previously Peters had only *told* George what he had to do. He never *asked*.

He began by catching George alone during the time the inmates were sent to 'slop out' (do their ablutions) after being unlocked from their cells first thing in the morning. Both were in adjoining lavatory cubicles, none of which had doors but were separated by wooden partitions. No one else was using any of the other cubicles at the time.

Peters started by saying, "I see yer a bit short on the baccy, George. Do you want a bit, I got some in me cell if you want it, mate."

George went red in the face. "Yer cassent talk ta me, boss, yer a grass ain't 'e? Somebody sees me an 'e talkin', an' we'll both git done over, won't we, eh?"

Peters went on carefully making sure that they weren't being overheard or seen, "Listen, George mate, you're OK! I ain't grassed up nobody, see." Then Peters said casually, "There was this bloke you saw in the line-up at the nick, everybody says was me. Well it wasn't me, see. I wasn't in the nick that time, 'cause I was at work in the 'Arbour Office. I can prove it, see. Ask the bloke in charge of the Floatin' 'Arbour. Go on, ask 'im!"

"'Ow am I gonna do dat den, boss? I'm in 'ere, an' wassis name is out der. 'Ow am I gonna do it den, eh?"

"Tell you what, George, I can write a letter for you to 'im, if you wants, askin' 'im to say where I was on that day and askin' 'im to come an' see you an' tell you himself. Whatdyou say to that, then, George? See, you gotta help me 'cause I ain't no grass, not on you any'ow. So do you want me to do that, eh? Com'on George, I always thought us was mates, wasn't we? When you sees old Roberts, you'll know I'm tellin' the truff, won't you? Anyway, come to my cell later, I'll get you the baccy, all right?"

George, although he had seen someone looking the spitting image of Peters at the police station, feeling that perhaps Peters might be telling the truth, decided to take up Peters' offer of writing to the Floating Harbour Master and asking Roberts to visit and tell him where the boss was, at the police station or in the FHM Office.

The promised letter never did arrive at Mr Roberts' office, although one left the prison to the Temple Meads station lost property office. Addressed to one, D Haxton.

George Vickers began telling the other members of the Commodores being held on remand that there was another man at the police station line-up who looked almost exactly like Peters. It was a trick by the police to get the gang to turn on Peters. At first none of the gang members believed Vickers. So he asked them to talk to Peters themselves. Several of them did, including Jameson and Billy Evans.

Peters convinced them that at the time of the line-up he was working in the FHMO with Mr Roberts and he had a letter to prove it. Whilst he was talking he waived an envelope in front of them. Jameson, who was slightly more intelligent than the others, said, "Come on, we ain't all stupid, you know's we can't read, don't thee."

Peters was waiting for that. "It's OK, you can get one of them screws to read it for you then you'll know its true what I've said."

Jameson looked doubtful, "Yous must be jestin', we never talk to coppers or screws, yous knows dat, doesn't thee?"

"Tell you what," Peters replied, "I'll get the vicar to read it to you if you like; ow's that suit you eh, Jamie?"

"I doesn't trust no do-gooder, cloud punchers eiver. Anyways 'e ain't in till Sunday, so what we gonna do then? Boss," he added sarcastically. "What we gonna do, eh?"

Billy Evans, who had been standing by watching the argument, butted in. "I knows 'oo can read, dat fella in the cobblers shop, da one dat shows us what ta do, watcha fink, Jamie boy? Watcha fink?"

"Yeh, 'ee's a con too, whasis name, Burt, ain't it? An 'ee's doin' ten years, ain't 'e? 'E'll do fine. Give us the letter den, an' we'll get it to 'im. Jimmy's started workin' in dat shop, learnin' to mend boots, so 'e can take da letter can't 'e, OK?"

Peters said, "Don't forget, that's my letter, I want it back soon 'cause I'll need it in court, won't I? One question, do you blokes know what this Burt is doin' time for?"

Billy piped up, "Yeh, 'es doin' ten years for forgery, that's what they call it, ain't it? When de copy o'ver peoples writin'."

Peters smiled to himself, thinking, "Old Burt will know his own writing then, won't he? I doubt if he'll know mine or old Roberts."

Then he said to Jamie, "That'll be OK by me then, as long as I get the letter back by dinner-time." He looked at Billy, "When's Jimmy goin' to the work shop then?"

"S'afternoon now, one a'clock, when d'you fink? Don'tcha know nuffink?"

Jamieson was beginning to get really cocky. "I'll have to cut him down to size," Peters thought to himself, giving Jamieson the letter.

On several of his appearances Peters had been taken to the court by himself, to listen and put in a plea to the charges put to him. On each occasion it seemed more charges were added. Each time his plea was 'Not Guilty' to all charges, even though his solicitor and barrister had advised against this course of action. He was playing for time and the barrister was finding it more difficult on each occasion to find a technical reason to argue for more time to prepare Peters' defence. Every time the defence team spoke to Peters about a new offence that he had been charged with he would argue that, except for the assault charge on a woman in her house many years ago and resisting arrest with intent, all the other charges were trumped up. The police were using the Commodores gang to tell lies about him. He told the barrister that he had never been a part of the gang although he knew some of the individual members and the other gangs. He had seen them on and around the docks.

"For crying out loud, I bloody work there. Saying it is my gang is ludicrous and a lie."

His barrister, Michael Simcock, nearly fell off of his chair when Peters said in a matter of fact tone. "Listen, Mr Simcock, I am an educated man and I would never ever be seen associating with the filthy rabble from the docks, or anywhere else for that matter. I, in fact, am employed as an undercover agent on the docks, checking ships and their crews for contraband, and have been doing so since arriving at the docks almost two years ago. I have never been involved in crime. Although I have admitted to assaulting that lady many years ago, that was because I was drunk. I was never charged then was I? So why now all of a sudden, eh?"

Simcock and his team left that interview, shaking their heads and wondering how on earth they would be able to defend such a Walter Mitty. They had to find a way of presenting a legally practical and honest argument to defend their client, even though everyone in the defence team knew Peters was as guilty as sin. He had even changed his plea from guilty to not guilty on the two charges he had previously admitted to.

Peters knew that the more time he was held on remand and went to the courts, the more likely he would have a chance of escaping from custody. The help he needed would have to come from outside. It wasn't too long in coming.

Peters' appearance for his trial was in Court Number 1 before Mr Nicholas Christian Harcourt-Jones, the presiding judge. The date was the 10th August 1914.

The newspapers had been full of the crimes the Commodores were accused of committing, although names had not been published: they would be in the Evening Chronicle later that day.

By nine-thirty that morning the public gallery was full of noisy Commodores gang supporters and family members. The press seats were full, along with one or two newspaper artists with sketch pads. This would be the biggest trial of its kind for years and everyone would want to know what these offenders looked like, whether they were found guilty or not.

Everyone who was to give evidence, including Jenkins, Roberts, Dai Jones, May Andrews and her Salvationist friend Jenny, and two men whose identity only Jenkins knew, sat patiently in the court waiting room, reading the books they'd brought with them or chatting.

At five minutes to ten, Peters was brought from the cells to the bottom of the dock stairs. Jeers and shouts of welcome greeted him from some of his supporters and enemies who could see him. An usher standing in the gallery called loudly, "Silence, be quiet!" A surge of angry raised voices was heard and directed at the usher, mainly from Peters' supporters. "Be quiet," repeated the usher, "or we'll clear the gallery!"

"You and whose army? You gutless toad. Come down here and try it." The usher thought it wiser to retreat, and, amid howls of laughter, disappeared through the gallery door.

Peters smiled at his two escorting prison warders, "Real characters ain't they, sir? Gonna be quite a day, ain't it sir?"

The remainder of the Commodores were being tried separately in other courts at the Assizes, starting that same morning. If any of the accused in those other courts were to be witnesses for the prosecution against Peters, an arrangement would be made for them to attend number 1 court at the convenience of the judges presiding over the other trials.

It had been decided by the prosecution council and police that the witnesses, other than the gang members, and forensic evidence that was available was enough to send Peters to the gallows, without risking the gang members tainting the prosecution evidence as most of them wanted to save their own skins from long terms of imprisonment or the rope.

Because of the nature of the Peters trial and the other courts being in session at the same time, extra prison warders and police were on duty in and around the area. That didn't stop mayhem breaking loose in Court Number 1.

Just as the clerk of the court stood up precisely at ten o'clock and said to a hushed court, "All rise" a portly figure in the red robes and long white wig of a senior judge appeared in the doorway behind the raised platform on which a large impressive carved wood and wine-coloured leather chair was situated. Placed in front of and matching the chair was a large desk which bore the papers, reference books and diary that would be used during the trial of one Gordon Arthur Peters.

The judge, Mr Paul Christian-Phillips, a circuit judge long used to sitting at murder trials, looked balefully through pince-nez perched on a large, unsightly, black spotted, bulbous nose at the murmuring, potentially, he thought, angry crowd. Not that that would worry him, he was used to giving orders and getting his own way.

He looked towards the prison warder at that moment standing alone in the dock, then to the clerk of the court in his black robes and wig. He nodded to the clerk who said to the guard in a clear precise voice, "Bring up the prisoner, officer."

The warder turned and called quietly down the stairs, "Bring him up, Joe."

Gordon Arthur Peters was almost unrecognisable as the man who worked in the Floating Harbour Master's Office on Bristol Docks. Or the man that was the self-crowned leader of the Commodore gang. Or the scruffy remand prisoner who thought he was a cut above the rest.

He appeared a tall man, about six feet three inches, clean shaven, well cut, long, collar–length, brushed back dark hair, with a few grey streaks running through it. He wore a white shirt with dark blue, almost black, tie, matching the well-cut expensive suit and highly polished black boots. His dark blue eyes were sunk into a now starved-looking thin white face, his thin, long, aquiline nose making those facial features imposing and stark.

Arriving at the top of the stairs he turned towards the public gallery, hoping that a few of his friends and supporters might be there. The one he most hoped for waived to him, gave him the thumbs up and grinned.

Peters turned to face the judge. The clerk of the court began by saying, "Are you Gordon Arthur Peters?"

At that, as if it was a signal, Don Haxton, his friend from the railway lost property office, turned to the man on the right sitting next to him, spat in his face and punched him full in the mouth. The man, well built, in his forties, completely bald headed with bulging eyes and biceps, stood up, grinned at Haxton and back-handed him across the mouth, sending him tumbling into the two men sitting in the row in front and across a man on his left. Those three turned on their seated neighbours and laid into them. From then on it was a free for all. Some of the men climbed over the front of the gallery and dropped to the floor, eight feet down, as if to get away from the mêlée. One man dropped into the dock itself.

One of the warders motioned to his counterpart to take Peters down to the cells, whilst he tried to prevent the man getting to Peters. Whatever the man's intentions were, the warder was big and good enough to prevent it happening until another rioter got into the dock. The warder escorting Peters down the stairs, seeing what was happening, shoved Peters down the stairs and went back to the dock to help his colleague.

The cells warder pushed Peters into the nearest empty cell, ordering, "Stay there until I get back!" He closed the cell door, hearing the click of the lock as it banged against the door jamb but not realising the door had bounced off the heel of Peters' boot. The door wasn't locked. Drawing his truncheon, the warder rushed up the stairs to help the other warders.

Police and prison warders were arriving in the court from every direction, the frightened legal fraternity cowering towards the front in and around the judge's rostrum. The press reporters and artists were busily taking notes and making sketches as the fighting spilled over into the centre of the court. The jury hadn't yet been selected so the potential jurors stayed in the jury room.

Peters, realising luck might be on his side as the cell door was not locked, slipped out and checked the cells on either side of the corridor leading to the rear entrance. They were all empty, the prisoners all standing in the docks of the other courts which were now in session. Checking quickly around he found the cell keys and other door keys hanging on a board in the small warders' office.

Taking all the keys from the board and a warder's cap and jacket from a locker along with a truncheon, Peters decided to cause as much distraction as possible. He locked the door at the bottom of the stairs to the court room, then found a bin of waste paper and half a dozen old newspapers, magazines and some spare shirts which he ripped up, then threw the lot on the floor near the door to the court room stairs and set it on fire. Finally he piled three or four wooden chairs and a desk on to the top of the fire, making a burning barricade.

Watching the flames catch and the smoke drawn under the stairs' door and up into the court, he laughed out loud. "Get through that, you dopey bastards," he yelled, although with the noise of the fighting in the court at the top of the stairs, he didn't think anyone heard him. Then he heard the shout "Fire!"

He picked the correct key to the cells corridor back door, unlocked it and, after a careful look around, walked out of the building, locking the door behind him. As he did so he heard a fire alarm ringing and he laughed till tears ran down his face. At a distance and with the cap and jacket, he could easily been have mistaken for a prison warder. His dark blue suit trousers and boots weren't out of place either.

He could hear the noise of the mayhem in Court 1 and kept walking quietly as if patrolling the building. The rear entrance to the courts was at the end of a cul-de-sac leading from a narrow side road, not far from Bristol City Centre. Parked in the cul-de-sac was a police van used for transporting prisoners to court. The police driver was running towards the front entrance of the courts shouting to someone to get a move on. He disappeared into the courts without a backward glance. It seemed that all the courts were having trouble; police and guards were running from one court to another, then back from where they came. The confusion had to be seen to be believed.

Peters smiled to himself, walked to the van and climbed into the driver's seat. He sat there for a minute, familiarising himself with the vehicle's brakes, steering, gears and accelerator. He remembered his first three driving experiences and decided it wasn't going to be too difficult to drive this van. He hopped out, swung the starting handle, jumped back in and with a crunching, screeching sound put it into gear. Without too much thought about what was happening around him, he let out the clutch and drove off. Changing gears was more difficult than he first thought but after the first half mile he didn't worry too much about that.

There wasn't a lot of traffic on the roads in those days, only a few wealthy people had cars and horse-drawn carriages, so there was nothing to worry or bother him.

In two or three minutes the court buildings were out of sight and he was driving towards familiar ground, the docks area.

He didn't know it but he or the van wouldn't be discovered missing for at least twenty minutes after the fighting and fire had been brought under control. When the prisoner and the van were both found to be missing, all hell broke loose again, the police and prison authorities blaming each other for not gaining control of the situation quickly enough.

It gave Peters a form of hero worship from the other prisoners, and a pathological hatred from those who were supposed to be guarding him. If he was ever captured he would find it to be the worst day of his life when returned to the prison and then to the court.

Peters was never captured, although a two months later his body was found in the Floating Harbour, badly beaten and severely damaged.

A pathologist's report stated it looked as though he had been beaten with a hard object, something like a club, but not killed, and then had fallen or was pushed from a great height on to hard ground and then into mud and water. He may have been brought up-river on the tide from under the Clifton Bridge. He might have even jumped from the bridge as some people had.

Some people suspected that Jenkins might have something to do with Peters' demise. When Peters escaped, Jenkins swore to Mr Roberts and Dai Jones that if he ever saw the man again, he wouldn't live long enough to stand trial. Ever.

No one was in the slightest bit concerned anyway. Not with the war just starting. Hazelton, who hadn't seen Peters' body, said, "Good riddance to another evil bastard." He told himself he would rather have seen Peters dangling from a rope, just to make sure in his own mind that Peters had gone, even though it went against his own personal views.

Three of the Commodores gang, Billy, Jimmy and Jameson, were hanged a few months after Peters' body was found, for the murders of Jenkins' sister, her husband and their daughter and the other man and a woman found in the house after the explosion and fire. They were implicated on their own admission that they had been at 31 Guinea Street and convicted on the forensic evidence found at the house and also on Peters' written statement to the police and those of the remainder of the gang who had turned King's Evidence.

The unfortunate Anson who had been wrongly convicted of Peters' crime was pardoned and eventually reunited with his wife and children. It turned out Peters and Anson had different mothers but the same father. From an old picture, their fathers' facial features could be identified in both half brothers. The features of the two sons couldn't be denied, they were almost identical.

Cyril Roberts couldn't go back to the Floating Harbour Master's Office, the thought of the murders were too traumatic for him. When he did go to collect documents and personal things he thought he saw the ghosts of Worrell and Edwards. Jenkins, who had accompanied Roberts on that first visit, tried to put his mind at rest by showing him there was nothing left to see or worry about. But he couldn't convince his deeply traumatised friend.

His wife and May Andrews also tried to help him through the memory of the callous killing of Worrell and Edwards. For the first few months he broke down in tears every time the men or the event were mentioned. He was never the usual friendly, jovial man he once was. Friends said that Peters had caused another death when Cyril Roberts passed away three days before his fifty-fifth birthday.

Later, as a sign of respect for the murdered men, it was decided by the Docks Management Board to demolish the building and rebuild it further along the dock, nearer to the entrance to the Floating Harbour. A plaque on a marble plinth was erected in the murdered men's memory on the exact spot of the old FHMO.

During those last few months after Joe Worrell died, May and Jenkins had decided they should marry as soon as possible. There didn't seem to be any reason to put it off any longer; they knew that they loved each other and nothing would ever come in the way of their feelings for each other.

May asked if he minded being married in the Citadel in St Paul's Road just before Christmas. A registered Salvation Army Officer, qualified to perform the marriage, would conduct the ceremony.

May asked Jenkins if he would mind very much if she wore her Salvation Army uniform.

"You still have your replacement reservist uniform, don't you?" she asked. Jenkins had been kitted out with a new uniform just after leaving hospital because he had three years to do on the army reserve list. It had been packed in a kit bag, placed in a wooden trunk and forgotten about.

"All right, love, when the time comes I'll unpack it and sort it out."

"That'll be lovely, won't it, Jenks love? Two soldiers joining together into one army."

Jenkins gave her a worried look. "I hope the Captain won't be giving too many orders," he thought to himself.

The wedding wasn't to take place. Not then anyway.

While all of these events were taking place, on the 4th of August 1914 the British Government declared war on Germany.

The British Government had promised to support Belgium and France if Germany attacked either country. Hundreds of thousands of men volunteered for service in the armed forces, among them many dock workers and seamen from the West Country and South Wales.

Dai Jones volunteered and enlisted in the Royal Navy as a stoker. Captain Redone, being a Reserve Officer joined the Royal Navy as a Lieutenant RNR, kept his ship and had it converted into a coastal patrol and supply ship, fitted with new engines, Lewis machine guns and a crew of six. Redone asked for Dai Jones to be assigned to *Welsh Lass*, renamed *HMS Welsh Coaster*. Dai jumped at the chance, even though he had to salute Redone, stand to attention and call him 'sir'. Mind you it took some training and patience to get him to do that.

Jenkins was called up in November. After a full medical inspection he was declared fit, A2.

Before the three of them left to join their chosen service, they held a party in a quiet pub near the Roberts' home. It was meant to be a small party but there were several surprising arrivals.

Dai Jones' parents made the journey from Swansea, Inspector Hazelton and several of his detective squad, and friends of May Andrews, all came to wish them well.

Cyril Roberts and his family were last to arrive. He was still very upset, even more so when he heard that Jenkins had been called to the Colours. He was so angry at the turn of events that he rarely spoke except to say over and over, "Good luck, Taff. Keep safe, come back to us, eh! Come back to us!"

Mabel, his wife, took him by the arm, "Come on Cyril, you're supposed to cheer him up. Come and have a drink, won't you?" Roberts followed her to the bar, shaking his head as if he couldn't understand or believe what was happening.

Redone brought his wife which surprised Dai. "Never thought you was married, skipper; you don't look the type, does 'e aye, Jenks?"

Redone scowled at Dai Jones, "Who blessed you with being able to think, Dai? Don't forget it's the RN we'll be in the day after tomorrow, and it'll be 'Aye, aye, sir. Aye Aye'!"

Everyone laughed as Jenkins said, "I told you, Dai, you should have joined the army, you only have to say 'Yes sir' once; with a brain like yours, you wouldn't get confused then would you?"

The party wasn't a very cheerful one, excuses were made early in the evening and it petered out so that only the three new service men and their families were left. They raised their glasses to each other and promised that "when this bloody war was over" they would meet here and get drunk.

May said, "And that'll be a promise, won't it, Jenks my love?"

Then they all shook hands, took their partners' hands and walked off quietly to their homes.

Now Lance-sergeant Jenkins, not fully fit enough because of his previous war wounds to go straight into battle, but fit enough to train men in discipline, drill, weapons training and close combat, was told to report to a holding centre in Bristol where he was made responsible for helping to organise the volunteers into sections, platoons and companies.

During the first six months of the war he was able to visit May a couple of times a week if he was lucky, and able to get a day or two's leave occasionally. His work didn't allow him too much time to himself but as those first few months went on he began to feel fit and confident again. When he couldn't go to see May he wrote to her, telling her of his feelings and what his daily routine had been.

He had only ever written a letter twice in his life during his first twenty years service. This time, he told himself, if he couldn't see May then he would write.

He did as well: there were never less than three letters a week during most of his service throughout the war, even whilst in hospital. There came a time when he couldn't write or receive her letters. When she found out why she could do nothing but forgive him.

In April 1915 Jenkins was posted to the Guards Depot in London. He was put in charge of a platoon of volunteer recruits, training them in fitness and for battle. Three months later the trainee soldiers were on their way to France, singing their hearts out and 'Fighting Fit and Fit to Fight' as one British general liked to put it, as they marched to their demise.

They were sent to replace the hundreds of thousands of soldiers of all nationalities who had fallen in battle. The casualties became so heavy that in 1916 Jenkins found himself training men and boys between eighteen and forty-one who were conscripted into the army, many not wanting to be trained as soldiers.

The Government, and General Staff of the Army, found that the casualty rate was so high that volunteers weren't enough to fill the gaps in the ranks of those already slaughtered. Amongst the French, Belgium and British Allies in the first ten months of the war over one million casualties had been sustained. It would have been impossible for the British war machine to go on had conscription into the army not taken place.

Chapter 7

Fighting Fit and Fit to Fight
France: the Western Front. The British, French, Belgium, Anzac and American sectors.

During November and December 1917, only the duels by the British, Allied and German guns, the artillery of each army, made the infantry soldiers, sappers and pioneers of both camps realise that there was a war still being fought and men on both sides being mortally wounded or killed where they stood or worked.

Soldiers dug out and repaired trenches and tried to drain the putrid water that lay in the bottom of almost every trench. The British faced the enemy along forty miles of the front line, the French with a much depleted army covered the left twenty mile section, and other allies, Anzacs and the Americans and many other nations, covered the British right flank. Soldiers of all nations worked like beavers after every attack or bombardment, unless they were buried in the mud, or carried to the rear dead or severely injured. Many managed to walk away to the field hospitals. Some walked but with other men guiding them; they were blind after being caught in a gas attack and were often seen walking one behind the other, eyes bandaged, hand on the man's shoulder in front, being led in groups by a medical orderly or someone who had a shoulder or arm injury but was still capable of guiding them to safety.

Troops moving up to their new positions in the line could only feel fear and anxiety as they marched along the swamp-like roads, trying to evade bogged-down trucks and horse-drawn guns.

Men from battalion pioneer companies at the rear of the front line troops worked frantically trying to fill the shell craters which kept re-appearing in the roads behind the lines. If a soldier slipped off the road or fell into a crater he was almost certain to drown in the muddy water or suffocate in the clinging, filthy, mud.

Although wet, cold and hungry, the British and their Allies were better clothed and fed than their German counter-parts. They also had better medical aid and facilities.

During the latter part of 1917 German bandages were being made of paper that when wet disintegrated into a porridge-like mass. If infection set-in to any of the enemy soldier's wounds, then gangrene would almost certainly follow, often resulting in amputation or death. Most of their medical supplies were almost useless or were exhausted.

In the winter months the British were building up huge amounts of food and equipment together with millions of rounds of ammunition for the artillery and infantry. Their storage areas and munition dumps covered thousands of acres of land, some of them a couple of miles to the rear of the front line to be easily accessible to the forward troops, some twenty-five to thirty miles in the rear as a reserve.

Both sides still suffered the same discomforts of weather, mud and cold. Both sides sent out reconnaissance patrols, or attacked a trench in the opposition's lines to capture prisoners for interrogation and to gain information for their commanders. Towards the end of December 1917, patrols and digging from both sides slowly petered out as the soldiers of both armies settled down to wait out a long cold winter, building their strength, re-supplying their lines and absorbing new young men as replacements for those lost in the conflict of the past four years.

More than 20,000 British
ldiers died on the first day of
the battle

General Harper KCB, who commanded One Division of the British Army, had never visited the front lines or seen his troops in action. But he knew of them well enough on his maps and in his plans. His regiments and battalions were numbered and inscribed on coloured pins placed in what he thought were strategic positions on his battle maps. Each pin representing a different division, brigade or regiment. He had only ever seen four or five regiments and battalions of his division marching past and saluting him when they were embarking on to the transport ships at Dover Docks.

"A smart bunch of lads these look, eh, Devonshire Light Infantry, Manchester Regiment, the Somerset Light Infantry. My! They look fit – 'Fighting Fit and Fit to Fight' – eh!"

That quote became his password. He, in fact, was an imposing figure of a man, six foot three, very well built, but beginning to run to fat, with a florid ruddy complexion: his passion for the best port was renowned. Although only in his middle fifties, with dark greying hair and a large dark grey moustache, he thought that he was still in his prime and young enough to be promoted to Field Marshal, especially after the war.

In his sector of the line the war had gone very well. He had been told of, and congratulated many times on, his troops' outstanding achievements.

He was unmarried, the army was his life and he saw no reason for any woman to interfere with it. The Officers Mess was his home and the officers his family. His only actual military training had been at Sandhurst Military Academy when he joined the army thirty years before. At that time he was recognised as a brilliant military historian and an excellent orator, so he was kept at the Staff College and trained in the art of planning and managing troops in battle, later conducting the strategy of battles and their consequences.

He had watched and been involved in campaigns and battles in India and against the Boers and the Zulus but he never had to fire a weapon in anger. Because of his status and rank there was always someone to protect him. Now, during this war, he had a platoon of soldiers to guard him, his officers and staff: not that he had too much interest in the administrative side of things, he had an adjutant to deal with everyday tasks and duties. He was too busy "fighting" a battle.

He wasn't a "Soldiers General", he was much too much of a Gentleman and Officer for that. He was a stern disciplinarian who kept himself to himself, except with his close senior colleagues. He had never had a conversation with an 'other rank', not even with his batman or his driver. He only gave them orders. His batman and driver preferred it that way as well, though!

The château was huge, covered in ivy on all sides, surrounded by ten acres of beautiful gardens, at least they were, until the military headquarters was set up in this wonderful quiet place. The château and gardens were set in the south of an area called Polygon Woods, in the Ypres sector. Much of the northern end of the woods had been damaged by shellfire. Broken branches and shell holes filled with mud and water littered the area. The château itself was out of range of even the biggest German howitzers, so there was never any panic when the enemy dropped their shells into the woods, searching for British units concealed amongst the shattered trees.

Pacing around the outside of the garden, around a track that had been worn through the woods, soldiers continuously patrolled guarding the Divisional Command building and its occupants. Those occupants, General Harper KGB and his officers, were often seen by those guarding them, sitting down to a dinner of pheasant or beef, cheeses and fine wines, whilst the soldiers had to make do with a thick potato soup, tinned corned beef, hard tack biscuits and, if they were lucky, a mug of tea with sweetened tinned milk: often, though, the tea was without sugar or milk.

Young soldiers in Number One Dress trousers and white jackets served the officers meals and attended to their requests. They had been transferred from their units and trained by the Officers Mess Sergeant in the duties of waiting on and serving these 'Gentlemen' their meals and wine. There were eight of them, together with two cooks and three kitchen helpers. One of the cooks had recently worked in the Savoy Hotel, in Mayfair, London.

The Sergeant of the Coldstream Guards, who looked strikingly like the General in poor light, had re-enlisted at the outbreak of war, but was considered almost 'over the hill' at nearly forty-two years old, even though he had twenty years of military service, much of it active service, on his record. If he hadn't been a reservist, he more than likely wouldn't have been conscripted into the army, as it wasn't until 1916 that anyone between the ages of eighteen and forty-one years were called up.

Whilst he had done his duty and on more than one occasion been wounded while in the trenches, as well as on his previous active service, he was now happy to be away from the barrages of shells, incoming or outgoing, the bullets, the mud, the stench of the dead, the cries and screams of the wounded and dying. He wished his wound had been a 'Blighty' one but because it wasn't he was extremely pleased to be doing the job he had been given, rather than going back to the trenches. Anyway he always said, "They'll probably shoot me first, at six feet three I'll be the biggest target, won't I?"

During the first weeks of his service in the trenches, he led his platoon 'over the top' on several occasions and they had been extremely lucky. Then his and their luck changed; he and half of the men in the platoon were hit by machine gun fire as they left the trenches to attack the German defences four hundred yards away. Sergeant Jenkins was hit in the right shoulder and quite badly injured. That day he and his young comrades lay out in the open, forty yards from the relative safety of the trenches, from sunrise at seven am until dusk at seven pm that evening. He listened to the moans and cries of the wounded and watched the men he thought had died, those he had led over the top, in case they were still alive. He had trained many of the men – boys he called them – and still felt responsible for them. He spoke and sometimes shouted instructions to them, trying to keep them from giving their positions away as German snipers took to taking pot shots at any movement.

As a reservist, he had been recalled at the outbreak of the war, then posted to battalion headquarters to help train some of the thousands of volunteers and conscripts. In May 1917 he was sent to France with a company of reserves where they worked behind the lines as a pioneer company, supporting the Guards battalions already forward in the trenches. They did this work for almost three months until they were considered ready to occupy the trenches. Then he and his young partly trained soldiers were called forward to take their turn to face the enemy bombardments, bullets and bayonets.

As he lay waiting for darkness and rescue he wondered how many were still alive. He kept whispering to the wounded soldiers nearest him to be quiet in case snipers located their positions and attempted to take shots at the wounded survivors. He knew how lucky he was to still be breathing.

A white flag of truce was all that enabled the company following up to pick up the dead and wounded before the next assault took place.

Whilst he was recovering from his injuries in a military hospital in the south of France a British and a French General with their entourages visited the wounded giving words of encouragement. They presented some of the men with medals for bravery and shook hands with many of the others.

Then the British General said something that made Jenkins go cold. He said, "If there are any of these men with wounds in their backs or feet, when they have recovered court-martial them and have them shot; we will not have cowards in our forces. They must face the enemy at all costs." His words were translated for the French General who nodded in agreement.

As the entourage moved away, an officer detached himself from the group. "Hello Sergeant, remember me? We met on that train all those months ago." He held out his hand, a large smile on his face.

Jenkins was amazed. "Christ almighty!" he blurted out. "Where did you spring from, sir?"

"Same place as you, retirement. Jenkins isn't it? And a sergeant I see." He glanced at the jacket hanging from Jenkins shoulder. He went on, "Blighty one is it?" He'd taken Jenkins left hand and shook it.

"Could be sir, don't really know yet. The MO says I might be lucky but I'll never get the full use back in my shoulder and arm, although if I work at it I might get three-quarters of its use back."

"So you may not be going back to the front then, will you Sergeant? So if not, how would you like to work for me?" the officer asked. He went on, not giving Jenkins time to answer, "Organising and running the Divisional Headquarters Officers Mess. Don't look so surprised, I've been looking for someone like you. I've already seen your service record, not that I was looking out for you especially. I've looked at a lot of sergeants' records. You see when I came here to the hospital, I had intended to look for and interview new staff for the new Divisional HQ which we will be moving up in a couple of weeks time. That's when the new General and his HQ will be arriving."

The major stopped, then went on, "Well, what do you think, Sergeant?" I know you were in charge of the Headquarters Battalion Officers Mess in 1913 before you left the army. It's in your record, so you do have some experience, don't you, even if it was only for six months. That's a lot more than the Lance-Corporal that they want to put in charge. How about it, Sergeant? I know you'll do a good job. I can't order you to do it, but I think we know each other well enough to understand that. I know I can trust you to carry out your duties and work without my having any worries."

"By the way, have you remembered my name yet? It's Richards! I didn't think you'd forgotten. Almost the same as your first name, isn't it?"

Jenkins thought, "Bloody hell he has seen my record, too."

On the tenth day of his treatment and convalescence at the Military Hospital, he was lying and dozing quietly on the ward veranda in the warm watery sunlight, half asleep and thinking of home and the woman he loved. He hadn't seen May since he had been posted to the training battalion in January 1916. He had kept every letter she'd written to him since he had re-enlisted on the orders of the Government. As a reservist it was his continuing duty to his country to do so.

He went to France with many others from the reserve forces. Later in 1917 all men, up to the age of forty–one, would be conscripted for the front; only ill health, or a work skill in such as the mining or steel industry, would save a man from being conscripted.

It wasn't Haig's 'England Needs You'

It was 'England is Taking You'.

He heard what seemed like a woman's light footsteps stop beside the couch and then a quiet gentle voice saying, "Hello, Jenks love!"

For a brief moment he thought that May had come to him in his dreams. Then he felt a soft hand take his. He opened his eyes as she bent over to kiss him on the cheek.

"Silly question this, Jenks my love, but what have you been up to? Didn't I tell you to stay out of trouble?"

He pulled her hand to his chest, "Bloody hell!" He almost shouted it out. "It's you my love, it's you! For crying out loud, May, you almost gave me a heart attack: can you feel it pounding, can you?"

"Yes I can Jenks, but it is me, really. They wouldn't let me wear my own uniform, so they gave me a Red Cross one instead. But I can wear my real uniform when I'm not on nursing duties, so we can be fighting our battles together, can't we?"

"I don't think I shall be fighting any more battles, at least not in the next few months. Perhaps the war will be over by then, eh?" He held her hand tighter, making sure it was really 'his' May.

They talked and talked about why she had joined the Nursing Service, what he had been doing up to the time that he was sent to the front then what had happened when he got there, how he came to be wounded and when.

May kissed his cheek, "You must have been terrified love, especially when you were left out in the mud and filth."

"I wasn't too worried about the mud or even the wound, it was those snipers, they would listen for anyone moaning in pain, locate him then shoot the poor sod; sorry, blighter. One lad nearly bit through his hand trying not to cry out and let the boche know where he was."

"We went 'over the top' at four-thirty in the morning, the attack ground to a halt about five, most of us having been hit in the first ten minutes. We weren't picked up until two o'clock the next morning under a flag of truce. Half of those who were wounded and survived the first half an hour died during the rest of the day and night. I was very lucky, I fell into a shell crater with another lad who in fact was a pacifist: one of the bravest men it has ever been my privilege to meet. They gave him the choice of going to prison or coming to the front as a stretcher bearer or nursing orderly. He chose the front. He was attached to our company and followed just behind us as we all went over the top. In fact, he wasn't more than five yards behind the advancing front rank. I was in the second rank twenty yards behind him."

"He was hit while he was dressing another soldier's wounds. A bullet hit his medical pack and struck his hip, yet he still managed to crawl from one wounded man to another, five or six in all, and get them into some sort of cover. He didn't have anything of much use left in his medical kit but managed to get hold of enough bandages and such like from the dead. Using the personal dressing packs of the wounded, he was able to dress their injuries and assist seven or eight of the lads."

"By the time he got to the shell hole that I was in, he was absolutely exhausted. A bit later, I was able to get him to bandage my shoulder and I helped him by dressing the wound in his hip. Even then, we had to use dressing packs from a couple of the dead from my platoon. We couldn't move back towards our own lines; any sort of movement was swamped with machine gun fire, by both sides."

"We had to share my water bottle because his, Mike was his name, had been shattered by a shrapnel. By the time other stretcher bearers got to us we had almost died of thirst and were frozen right through. Luckily our wounds had stopped bleeding but I bet young Mike doesn't sit down for a month or two."

"But it scares me to think that, if what that General said the other day is true, then people like Mike could be put against a wall and shot."

"Jenks, what did he say?"

"Well, if a man is found to be wounded in the back or the feet it means they have either shot themselves or been running away, their backs to the enemy. It shows you what lengths some officers will go to try and instil fear, not discipline, into the lads. I'm telling you, May, if that lad Mike doesn't get an award for outstanding bravery, then those in high places should come and do what he has done, to see what it is really like, to go 'over the top' unarmed, with just your guts and medical skills to rely on. I can't say that I would have been able to do it. Mike and his mates aren't the cowards that people like to call them and neither are the men that are so shell-shocked that they're almost paralysed and unable to move. Do you realise that at the start of a British assault on the German lines battlefield police stand in our trenches behind the soldiers going over the top and threaten to shoot anyone who doesn't obey the order to advance? It has been known for the field police to carry out their threat. Usually though, anyone that doesn't obey the order is arrested, taken to the rear and court marshalled, imprisoned and often 'shot at dawn'.

May held up her hand, shock and disbelief in her eyes, "Jenks, that can't be true, surely? Isn't there anything anyone can do about it?"

"Yes there is my love, but those in command are too frightened of Kitchener and Haig and their own futures to object. Discipline is the only thing that they think we understand, but that isn't true really. The truth is the soldiers are beginning to think for themselves and they don't agree with some of the orders that are given them. I think it's because older men are now being conscripted. They have always been used to thinking for themselves, so they find reasons to object and sometimes disobey orders that they see as senseless or plain madness. I don't like many of the orders that are given but it seems if we don't obey them we will be shot on the orders of our own generals and we could lose this war anyway.

"Come now, it's about time I stopped going on about me, isn't it? Haven't you heard enough? Now, May my love, let's talk about you and what made you come here and when you're going home, all right?"

"Well Jenks, after reading your letters, I decided I would be more use here than at home. When I read in the newspapers about the numbers of casualties, I couldn't believe what I was reading. How can anyone, no matter what side they are on, put so many to death? It is hideous, it is scandalous; there has to be other ways of settling these things. Politicians and generals always seem to get everything so wrong."

She was in tears, "How can all of you poor men stand this? Most of you won't go back to your families and neither will the Allies or the Germans. What will the wives and children do without fathers or brothers? I don't know what I shall do if you don't come back. I shall be devastated for the rest of my life."

He looked at her tearful face, longing to hug her and tell her he loved her but he knew it wasn't the right time. He knew that she loved him, he knew that before he rejoined the army when they had talked about marriage, just before the war broke out, even if she wouldn't tell him outright.

"Listen, my love, I know that your kindness and comfort to all of these wounded is appreciated by every single one of them, but I would feel happier if you went back to England and nursed the poor lads there. I know it will seem selfish but I want you to be safe with your own army, doing what you do best with the people that are going to need you. The orphans and widows will need and appreciate your help and kindness just as much as these lads do. I need to know that you are going to be safe and with the changing fortunes of this war anything might happen, so please, May love, go home as soon as you can, please!

"I know I won't be going back to the front again. They might even send me home. You never know, someone might give me another job somewhere. I hope not though, I'd rather be home near to you but you know about the army, don't you love? And only time will tell now, won't it?"

May continued to visit him every day for the next two weeks. During that time they became closer together than Jenkins ever thought possible with a woman. He had made plenty of friends in the army but this was an entirely new sort of friendship. He had known that when they were together in Bristol and realised what love actually meant. Before he hadn't realised what was meant to be in love. Now he really knew.

He also began to worry about her safety and changes in battles that might put her in danger. She thought that she was safe in the hospital and didn't realise just how quickly battles and situations could change.

He also knew that he should tell her about the Officers Mess job he had been offered, but couldn't bring himself to tell her in one breath that he loved her and in another that he wouldn't be going home for sometime because he was going to accept the new job. He waited until the day came two weeks later when May told him that she would be going back to Bristol the next day. She had waited until then because she found it difficult to make up her mind who would need her most.

When May came to his ward to say goodbye, Jenkins for the second time in his life was near to tears. They sat on a couch outside the ward looking over the French countryside. He realised then that he must tell her how he felt about her: he took her hand and watched her face as he told her how very much he loved her and would miss her while they were apart.

"Jenks! I already know that you love me and I'm sure you know how much I love you. I've known for a very long time how you felt, we women know these things, but please tell me everytime you write and everyday when we're together. We will be together, you know, for the rest of our lives and will love each other for ever."

Jenkins never forgot those words after she said, "Bye, Jenks, love."

He was now in overall charge of the Officers Mess and he had literally 'carte blanche' when he toured the local units and selected 'his' staff.

All the soldiers he had selected had jumped at the chance to work in the general's headquarters. He told each man whilst he was interviewing them that he would be RTU-ing them (return to unit) if they didn't conform to his ideas of discipline and duty. Every man was all too eager to agree to his instructions and orders. At the Officers Mess they were out of the front line, mud, starvation, decease, dysentery, shelling, fear and injury or death. At the very least they were guarded with the officers, fed decent rations and slept in a warm room, except when they were on call to serve the officers during the evenings. The hardest work they had each day was to serve meals and clear away, then, when all the officers had retired to their rooms or gone to their duties, clean the cutlery and glassware. They cleaned the dining room and the lounge, ensuring everything was spotless. Two of the waiters were available all day, in case they were called upon to take sandwiches or drinks to an officer's room or office. Two or three of them were also employed as batmen to various officers of the general's staff. The rest, while they waited for other work to do, polished cutlery and glasses and chatted about home and their friends and families they had left behind: it was as though the war wasn't happening for them. Nothing was too good for the general and his staff, nothing!

It was the beginning of January 1918 with chilling cold winds, snow, then rain sheeting down, soaking the sentries to the skin. The woollen gloves they wore whilst on their patrols were useless against the elements, so occasionally when the soldiers were close to the house, a waiter would take a chance and pass a mug of steaming tea to them. Once or twice a lad named Arthur James would invite them into the scullery, just behind the kitchen. He'd give them tea and sometimes a corned beef sandwich. Everyone was very careful. No one wanted to be sent back to the front, especially this time of the year, in fact not at all.

The Officers Mess staff usually heard when an attack was being planned or had happened, by the Allies or the enemy. After an unexpected particularly heavy counter-barrage by the enemy, casualties were extremely heavy. So until they could be transported to the rear, a large number were brought to the headquarters and laid in cellars and outbuildings in the grounds.

Many of the casualties would have been taken to the rear in trucks or on the narrow-gauge railway. The problem occurred when the German artillery found the range of the hidden railway line, managing to take out several miles of the line and a locomotive, disrupting the journeys of the Symplex armoured petrol engined locomotives for weeks.

Over two thousand miles of railway lines had been laid on the Western Front by the British and their allies during the First World War. These narrow gauge lines were laid, repaired and maintained by approximately six thousand sappers. The sappers too received many casualties keeping the lines serviceable and operating during many searching enemy actions.

The engines were normally very difficult to detect because of the specially made silencer built above the 40 horsepower petrol engine. Sparks, steam and smoke were not given off, therefore the enemy couldn't see or hear its movements, however spies and pilots of the German air force would often see the movement of these trains during daylight hours and report their positions. Therefore most of the ammunition, food and stores trains moved at night.

The General wasn't particularly keen on the idea of seeing the wounded in their shell-shocked, burnt and broken state, so he never visited them. He just wanted to get them to the hospital ships and then home – they were no use to him here – and their replacements sent up.

All he was really interested in was fit, young, fighting men singing their hearts out for their King and Country as they went forward to their demise.

Arthur and his mates tried their very best to help the wounded men at every opportunity. They asked the Mess Sergeant if two of them at a time could be relieved of the mess duties and allowed to help the Medical Corps staff to tend the wounded. The sergeant, after consulting the adjutant, agreed. "This ain't permanent, mind you! Don't forget where your duties really are!"

Albert Baxter and his mate Arthur Corbett were the first to report to the medical orderly corporal. They got the biggest shock almost anyone could have experienced: gassed, burned, blinded and broken soldiers. One or two who were less hurt than the others were as pleased as punch.

"I 'ad some real luck," one of them said: he had a bullet hole in his right hand and half of his forefinger shot away. "This is a Blighty one, mate, you won't see me back again. I'm off to dear old Geordie land, land of kings!"

Soldiers who were severely wounded, but the injury wasn't life threatening, often called their wound a 'Blighty one' because they would be sent home as soon as it was considered they were fit to travel and transport was available. The severity of the injury didn't matter to some of them, they were going home to their families and homes.

As Albert and Arthur moved around the wounded men, helping to give some a drink of water, lighting a cigarette or pipe for those that couldn't do so for themselves, they noticed a couple of younger men, boys really, sitting on the cold damp floor in a darkened corner of the cellar.

As Arthur approached them they both cringed away from him; it seemed as if they were trying to crawl into the darkness and protection of the wall.

"Don't go near them, or you'll be in real trouble, lads!" The warning came from a medical orderly who had come with them to show Albert and Arthur what was needed and what had to be done in assisting those who required their attention.

"What's wrong with them, mate? They look scared as hell. Why are they in shackles? What have they done? Are they injured? Who has ordered them to be cuffed up like that?"

"I can't tell you really," said the orderly. "The medical officers are calling it shell shock, the psychiatrists are saying that anyway, but the General Staff Officers are calling them cowards because they can't get up and go 'over the top', when the order is given to attack.

Their names were Edwards and Johnson; both were seventeen years old. It was their first month in the trenches and during the last week of that month they had been ordered 'over the top' with their battalion four times. Each time the casualties were so heavy, that by the end of that week the battalion had been decimated. Ninety per cent of the battalion, six hundred men, were wiped out. The remaining sixty or seventy soldiers who survived the slaughter and were still on their feet and able to return to their trenches were seconded to the support battalion which had taken over and occupied those trenches that the survivors had left that morning. The battalion had made four abortive attacks during that dreadful week with most of the casualties being left where they fell. On their arrival at the front these young conscripts, for that was what they were, came under constant counter-barrage from the German heavy howitzers firing from up to fifteen kilometres away. That first three weeks was spent burrowing into the sides of their trenches, before what was left of them were sent 'over the top' in a vain attempt to assault the German trenches three hundred yards away, across barbed wire strewn, broken, flooded, shell pitted open ground. The only cover from numerous machine guns and rifles, flaying the attackers with thousands of bullets, were the water-filled shell craters which claimed the lives of many wounded victims, as their wounds were so serious they couldn't prevent themselves slipping into the mud and slime at the bottom of the craters. So besides being seriously injured it was sometimes months before their drowned bodies were found.

The fifth time, the day after joining the new battalion, Johnson and Edwards were ordered 'over the top' again to advance in the most atrocious, almost impossible, conditions. These two lads did climb the ladders and went over the top again but a salvo of German shells literally blew the platoon they'd been attached to apart. After about four hours lying in a shell crater, they crawled back to their trenches. Neither was injured but both were almost deaf and some said they were suffering shell shock.

The orderly continued the account: "Then some bastard battlefield police comes along and threatens to shoot anyone that wouldn't go 'over the top' or came back before the assault was finished to the satisfaction of the commanders. The police said that the attack had not finished until two hours later. They were lucky the police didn't shoot them there and then.

"So now they're stuck here, because the MO cannot say whether or not they are fit or malingering cowards. If he or the other medical officers pronounce them fit, there will probable be a court-martial and if they are found guilty, they will be taken out and shot."

"What's a psychiatrist? Who the hell will shoot them?" Arthur demanded to know.

The orderly replied, "A psychiatrist is a doctor who deals with mental illnesses; they're the ones who diagnose shell shock. They say it's an injury to the mental state of someone but there are only about three psychiatrists in the whole army, here in France, so these two lads will be left for our medical officers to deal with. They have the same thoughts as the other officers: if the man can walk and hold a rifle, get him to the front. 'They are cowardly malingerers, make them stand and fight' is the stock answer as your sergeant will tell you," the medical orderly went on. "Usually it's their mates who form a firing squad, lads from the same platoon or company, if any are left alive after the assault. Otherwise names of the firing squads are drawn by lot, it could be anyone except senior officers and people like me in the medical units. Just imagine if they've done nothing wrong and they are absolutely petrified, literally frozen with fear. Now! What would you do with or to them, eh? What will you do if you get picked to shoot them, eh?"

Then the orderly shocked them even more. "Do you realise that when the general and his officers want to impose discipline and encourage men to go 'over the top' they will tell the commanding officer of one of the battalions that he, the general, thinks that particular battalion isn't carrying out the attack sufficiently aggressively and finally enough, and that the CO is to select men, two or three at a time, to be drawn out of the hat and have them executed by firing squad. In some cases men, including soldiers and NCOs who have been in the front line for over two years and been involved in numerous attacks on the enemy lines and escaped without a scratch and been decorated for leadership and bravery, are drawn out of the hat and shot, sometimes without a court-martial. This is to encourage soldiers from other battalions and regiments to show more verve and courage when attacking the enemy. It is also supposed to install a higher discipline throughout 1 Corps. Who are the soldiers more afraid of? The Germans or their own officers?"

Arthur or Albert, when it was their turn to help the wounded, would go out of their way to talk to, feed and try to comfort the two youngsters. They got them dry clothing and straw mattresses and a couple of blankets each.

Whilst there was no artillery barrages they would stay fairly calm. Usually they were quiet but withdrawn into their own thoughts.

They tried to thank Albert and Arthur, but could only stammer the words, half expecting to be struck or shouted at as had been normal when they were in the trenches, or being dragged by the MPs to the aid tent or shelters.

After a week or so the wounded were taken away to field hospitals at the rear and then to England, a long tiring journey on which many would succumb to their wounds.

Privates Johnson and Edwards, as the two lads later were able to identify themselves, remained in the cellar by themselves. The waiters continued to visit them and assist them with their needs until towards the end of January an artillery barrage began, which it was thought was to be the beginning of another attack. When Arthur and Alfie went to see how they were getting on, Edwards was almost dead; he had beaten his head against the cellar wall, fracturing his scull so severely that he almost bled to death. His friend Johnson was curled in the foetal position, sobbing as each shell exploded even though it was over a mile away. They didn't know that the barrage was concentrated on the British front, not on Polygon Woods. Afterwards a medical officer went to the cellar to examine them both. Thinking the MO was there to help, Johnson tried to overcome his fear and tell the doctor what his feelings and thoughts were.

The MO made a few notes and said to the guard on his way out, "Give him a few more days rest and he'll be fine. If the other one dies send out to the mortuary collectors." That was it.

The next morning two MPs arrived at the cellar, grabbed Johnson by the arms and legs, dragged him to a waiting truck and threw him in the back. He fell on the floor and began moaning and crying but nobody took the slightest bit of notice of him. They put Edwards on a stretcher and loaded him into the back of the truck, ignoring Albert's protests.

"Shut your mouth or you'll be going with him," one of the MPs shouted. "Get back to your work!"

They drove off and the only people to see them go were Arthur and Albert. They went back and told their friends what had happened but there was nothing they could do about it. They never expected to see them again.

On the 21st February 1918, the Officers Mess Sergeant called his staff to parade in front of the château with their Lee Enfield .303 rifles. Once there, they began to wonder what was going on. They had only paraded once before, when they had formed a guard of honour for a visiting French general. They couldn't imagine that he had been very impressed because none of them had done much in the way of ceremonial duties since they had joined they army.

As they stood on parade in front of the sergeant, they were aware of the stern, set way of his eyes and general appearance. He brought the squad to attention.

"Now listen very carefully to what I have to say, remember you are first of all trained soldiers, all infantry men!" He went on, "If I hadn't selected you all, you might well have been wounded and on your way home if you were lucky. It could have been even worse, you could have been blown to bits by the kraut guns or blasted away when you were sent 'over the top' on some crazy assault. So remember that when you've heard what I'm about to say next.

"In a day or two's time you will be paraded as a firing squad. No if's or buts, no questions or arguments, otherwise you may end up at the wrong end of one yourselves. Do you all understand!"

None of them could speak, most went pale with shock and a couple froze unable to speak.

"Do you all understand?"

The most they could do was nod and whisper, "Yes, sergeant."

"Right! Let's go through the drill! OK. Don't look so worried my lucky lads, remember how I explained to you a few weeks ago that when a firing squad was needed, his mates would draw lots to see who was to be in the squad. Otherwise they would be detailed off by their officer or platoon sergeant. Well I'm very sorry to say that there are two men who have been found guilty of cowardice by a court-martial. They haven't got any platoon, company or regimental comrades left. Their regiment has been withdrawn from the line as most of it has been wiped out. The wounded have been sent back to England, those who survived unscathed have been sent to other regiments or battalions: no one else can be spared." He paused letting what he'd just said sink in.

"So it's up to us, my brave lads, to carry out the court-martial sentence. First though we'll have to rehearse what the procedure will be and how we will have to carry out our duty. You mustn't worry about anything, just imagine it's target practice on the range. Don't look at anything but the target, usually a circular white patch. You've all done that, haven't you? Aimed at a white patch on a target? OK, lets get on with it. I'll let you all know when the execution will take place."

When he said 'execution' the youngest member of the waiters fainted. The remainder of the squad were marched off by the sergeant to the place where the soldiers were to be executed.

One of the cooks who had been watching the little parade came out of the château's kitchen and brought the young lad around. After ascertaining that the lad was better, the cook pointed him in the direction the squad had taken and sent him to join it. A couple of minutes later the squad was going through the drills that would eventually affect them for the rest of their lives.

The next day they were paraded again and marched into the woods to a place that had been a garden. It was about fifty yards square. A tree trunk without branches grew on one side of the garden. Four metal rings, two at shoulder height and two at knee height, had been screwed into the sides of the tree. Next to it a post had been driven into the ground. There was a small brick building behind the tree, probably a gardener's shed. Other than that there was nothing to show it was anything other than an unattended garden.

The eight waiters who had been detailed were marched in file to a position twenty-five yards from the tree. They were lined up in a single rank facing the tree then ordered to stand easy. They all stared ahead, faces frozen with fear when they realised with stark reality what they were about to do. They tried to control their shaking limbs and nerves, but the longer they waited the more nervous they became.

At last a group of a dozen or so staff officers, with their red hat bands and red collar patches which denoted their positions on the General Headquarters staff, arrived and stood about twenty yards behind the firing squad, to the right rear, allowing the officers to observe the execution without being endangered themselves. When they had all taken up their positions, a group of six uniformed people appeared from a side entrance of the garden.

Two MPs supported and half dragged a small whimpering figure to the tree. An army padre walked alongside a sobbing young man, talking quietly to him and saying comforting prayers to him, or so the padre hoped. The cowards, as they were to be called, didn't seem to be taking any notice of the padre at all.

When they arrived at the tree, the two MPs took one young man's arms and handcuffed him to the upper rings and then did the same to his ankles. Finally they passed a rope around his waist and tied him securely to the tree, preventing him slipping down. They then repeated the procedure with the other young man who seemed to find great difficulty in standing unaided.

The padre accompanying the prisoners went to each one in turn and said a prayer and a few words of comfort. He was in the same mind as most other officers, who all thought that all so called cowards should be dealt with in the same way, especially if found guilty.

A young lieutenantwho had accompanied the party, took a white circular patch and pinned it over the heart of each prisoner. He said something to the prisoners, but there was no reply and no recognition of what the officer was saying. As the officer turned away, the most able of the two prisoners looked up at the watching group of staff officers and said in a clear, defiant voice:

"I hope when your turns come you will receive the most slow, agonizing and painful deaths that can ever be imagined or devised and when that time comes, remember this day, that I will be cursing you and your families forever."

He looked towards the lads in the firing squad, "Help us out boys! Make sure of your aim, we know it's not your fault that the cowards behind you make you do this because they're too gutless to do it themselves. You've nothing to fear or berate yourselves for. We don't have to forgive you for this terrible crime these officers are ordering you to do. Don't worry yourselves about it, just do a good job. Otherwise they will put you in the same position that we are in now. If there is a God let him forgive you and let them rot in hell."

Arthur and Albert, who had been trying hard not to look at the young prisoners, suddenly realised who they were – Johnson and Edwards.

Arthur almost fainted; Albert said afterwards, "My legs went to jelly, I could hardly stand, I was so frightened."

At that moment the sergeant who had also realised who the prisoners were, walked quietly along behind the rank of riflemen. "Steady boys, we're not here to hurt the poor sods but to put them out of their misery and suffering. It's these bloody officers that are killing them, the evil bastards."

At that the lieutenant in charge of the execution began to read out the charges against Johnson:

"167298 Private Johnson, Peter, you have been charged with cowardice in the face of the enemy, in that you on the 17th November 1917 refused an order by Captain R Francis (now deceased) to leave your trench and go over the top to attack the enemy. You have been found guilty by general court-martial held on 20th February 1918. Signed, C R Harper KCB Officer Commanding 1 Division. The sentence has been confirmed by General Sir Douglas Haig KCB.

He then looked at Johnson and said, "Have you anything else to say Johnson?"

The condemned man ignored him and looked towards the firing squad; his eyes were dull and vacant, without a glimmer of hope.

The officer then, after reading out exactly the same charges in exactly the same wording, except for changing the name to 167333 Private Alan John Edwards, took two white pillowcases from his pocket and placed them over each of the prisoners' heads.

There was no sign of movement from Edwards. The padre said a few more words to Johnson, turned and nodded to the officer. The officer walked to one side, drew his sword and held it above and resting on his shoulder. Both MPs took up positions behind the rank of the firing squad and drew their revolvers, holding them down to their sides.

The lads, the firing squad, had been dreading this moment. The sergeant gave the order, "Shun! Port arms! Load! Ready! Aim!" Then, "Make it good," he hissed.

The officer's sword slashed down.

"Fire!"

Eight fingers squeezed their rifle triggers, eight .303 bullets sped to their target.

The waiters all stared in frozen horror at the 'targets'. Johnson slumped forward, the rope and handcuffs stopped him from falling to the ground. Edwards' knees gave way and he collapsed on to the ropes holding him up.

The next order was, "Port arms, unload." Rifle bolts were drawn back and flicked out eight empty cartridge cases. The sergeant walked along behind each man and checked each rifle was properly cleared.

"Shoulder arms, right turn, quick march!"

Tears welled up in Albert's eyes; Arthur's hands shook so much he almost dropped his rifle.

They heard the sergeant's voice that came through the mists of anger that swept over them. "Come on lads, it's over, we have to get back to the mess and our duties. You can have a good cry and moan about it later on, OK? Come on, left, right, left, right, pick it up boys! Don't let these supercilious bastards see how you feel. Surely their days will come. When it does, I for one won't grieve for any of them."

The sergeant was as angry and upset as the waiters; he was almost beside himself with grief. He couldn't tell the lads his secret, but it was tearing him up inside; hate and revenge was all he could think about.

As they marched away, they heard a single revolver shot, then another.

One of the other waiters said sadly, "My God, that bastard's just shot them in the head." They all turned their heads to see the lieutenant turning away from Johnson's body and holstering his revolver. That was the last they saw of the horrific scene as they marched away.

A telegram was received by the parents of Private Peter Johnson at their farm in Builth Wells. A brusque one line message:

'Your son died of his wounds on 22 February 1918. Please accept my condolences.
'Signed J J Wallace Jackson. Colonel. Army Records.'

A similar message was received by the sister of Private Alan Edwards at his home in Surrey.

At four-forty am on the morning of the 21st March 1918 the German High Command, having been able to disengage from the Russians on the Eastern Front, set in motion its final offensive, a devastating, massive attack on the British and Allied front lines.

A huge rolling barrage by six thousand artillery pieces, that the German Artillery Corps had amassed during the winter, was unleashed against the British and French, Belgium, Anzac and American lines. Following up close to the fall of the shells, the German infantry battalions fought, killed or captured and overwhelmed the totally surprised and shell-shocked defenders.

The Allied lines were broken in two places, to the left and right of its centre causing a huge salient to be formed in 1 Corps' area. That part of the line and its rear was eventually held because the New Zealand troops, known, along with the Australians, as the Anzacs, and with newly arrived Indian and Canadian re-enforcements, who were being rested in the second-line trenches and further back in the Polygon Wood area, were pushed forward into the huge gaps that began to appear, with only the advancing Germans trying to fill the voids.

The New Zealand Division was the only complete division left to be thrown into the huge gaps appearing in that part of the Allied lines, counter-attacking with the use of thirteen pounder 'Royal Horse Artillery' guns, firing at point blank range, supported by heavy fire from Maxim, Lewis and Vickers machine guns.

New Zealand and Australian battalions, the Anzacs, along with Indian, Gurka and Canadian reserve units, made rifle and bayonet counter-attacks, recapturing much of the lost ground.

The New Zealand Division fought the enemy at Serre on the Somme and held the Germans from the strategic centre of Armeins, despite heavy losses from German bombardments. Massive casualties were sustained by both armies. The New Zealand Division, alone, lost over three thousand casualties during this so-called quiet winter period.

Not before the German advance troops had reached the stores and food depots, accumulated over the winter period by the British and French, did their advance begin to slow.

The attacking German soldiers were amazed at the wealth and standard of food and medical equipment that they themselves lacked. Due to their tiredness and lack of re-enforcements and support, their advance came to a halt after five days. They had fought themselves and the British and French Allies to a standstill. The German infantry then had to abandon its new positions because there were not enough re-enforcements to push forward and consolidate its hard-won gains.

The British, French and the remainder of the Allied Forces on the Western Front had a large, strong, active reserve force. When these reserves were pushed forward into the action, they began to drive the attackers back on a long arduous retreat and by the end of the seventh day the Germans had reached and returned to their own lines, digging in and awaiting the inevitable counter-attacks by the Allies.

During that 'push' thousands of troops on both sides had perished, been wounded, lost or captured and General Harper KCB wanted to know why.

Why? Because the General Staff were barbaric, incompetent and confused, especially at Loos where in the confusion companies and battalions were directed to fire on each other. The Allied guns, firing from their lines ten kilometres behind, were hitting the *Allied* trenches with high explosives and gas shells.

There was no co-ordination between the generals and their staffs and the battalion commanding officers, many of whom were killed or died in the confusion. Companies of men were literally wiped out within minutes of going 'over the top' as they were ordered to do.

All the generals would do is say, "Fill those gaps and send them over again." They had no idea what was actually happening at the front. With the gas drifting back over the Allied troops and the smoke haze from exploding shells, it was left to the company commanders, be they majors, captains or even lieutenants, to direct any of the troops available and in their vicinity. Often where their officers had become casualties, company sergeant majors and sergeants had taken charge. In one company the only surviving NCO was a corporal who took command of the remaining six fit men of the company which at the start of the day been one hundred and thirty strong.

In his château twelve miles behind the front lines General Harper and his headquarters were protected now by a company of infantry which had been taken out of the line from the position where the main part of the Axis assault had taken place.

That company was one of the most battle-hardened and experienced in the whole front line of the 1st Corps. It had been replaced by a company of newly arrived replacements from England.

These men had only arrived in their trenches two days before and few had ever heard a shot fired in anger.

General Harper was furious, pacing around his map room and lounge like a demented tiger. "I want answers, answers!" he shouted at his staff officers. "Heads will roll. Get those gutless, cowardly, commanding officers here! In front of me. I will reduce to the ranks any officer I think has failed me, his men, or his duty. I will have any coward shot. Get them here!" he ranted. "I will discipline the rabble. There will be 'Discipline with a Bullet!'"

He kept his word too. During the next two weeks several battalion and regimental commanders were court-martialled. Young soldiers who had never seen or been in a battle before were punished by imprisonment for so called crimes they had never committed. Some were 'shot at dawn'."

Others had their names drawn out of a hat and were charged under King's Rules and Regulations paragraph 'so and so' of conduct prejudicial to good order and military discipline.

Junior battalion and regimental officers were demoted.

Two young lieutenants, platoon commanders, both wounded, ordered their remaining men to retreat from the overwhelming machine gun and rifle fire of the German attackers and were shot for cowardice. They, as the senior officers in charge of their platoons, did not continue to counter-attack the enemy as ordered by their company commander, even though they each had only half a section (four men) left standing from a platoon of thirty-five soldiers. They were found guilty even though the company commander had died as he left the trench at the start of the assault, and couldn't give evidence.

"Somebody is to blame," Harper kept shouting. "I'll get to the bottom of this." He was so angry, he sent three of his staff officers to take command of three battalions of infantry.

"Sort the buggers out," he ordered as they left the château. "Send me a daily report on the situation in your areas and the standard and suitability of your officers and NCOs. I want to know!

"I'll give them discipline, with a bullet!"

During the weeks after the 21st March 1918 all sorts of movements, re-enforcements, transport of wounded, re-supply of medical and food stores and artillery ammunition, which had been lost or destroyed during the German attack, was taking place on the roads near the château.

These movements included prisoners being transported to camps miles back in the rear. Most of the time they were transported in empty trucks returning to storage areas for new supplies but it was not unusual to see two or three hundred prisoners, escorted by perhaps ten or twelve British soldiers, marching to the rear or even working on damaged roads. The guards and their prisoners often looked relaxed and some quite cheerful as they realised they were out of the line and perhaps danger. As prisoners they had been told no harm would come to them, their wounds and injuries would be treated and they would be fed proper rations. One or two knew it to be the true as they had been captured before, but escaped, taking valuable information back to their High Command security services.

One of them, Hauptmann Klaus Grüber, had deliberately allowed himself and most of his men to be captured during the assault of the 21st until 28th March 1918 (with the approval of the German High Command).

Klaus Grüber was a typical Prussian-trained German army officer of his day – tall, square jawed, with cropped hair and wearing a monocle. His spear pointed helmet, greatcoat and boots, looked as though they belonged on a parade ground. With an Iron Cross pinned on his coat, he was typical of a German officer seen on the war posters in Germany. But no one would have thought that he was a German officer had they seen him at that time. He was dressed as an unteroffizier (a senior corporal).

The company which Grüber commanded was in fact a Kommando unit which had followed up the initial assault. After their 'capture' on the third day, thirty German prisoners, with an escort of what seemed to be eight Allied infantrymen commanded by a sergeant marched in a somewhat bedraggled pitiful group to the rear echelons of the Allied lines.

All of the escorting infantrymen wearing the shoulder flashes on their uniform of the New Zealand Rifle Brigade were German soldiers who spoke excellent English. Each uniform had been taken from a New Zealand POW or dead body, roughly cleaned, repaired and fitted to the man requiring it. Webbing, boots, gaiters, packs, pouches and weapons were standard New Zealand issue. Except for shoulder flashes everything was identical to the British uniforms. Even the identification tags they wore were authentic as they came from the Anzac casualties of an attack in 1917. They also had the pay books of those same soldiers. They would stand up to any inspection and those acting the part had a potted history of their characters off by heart.

The 'prisoners' were kept in a barbed wire enclosure for five days, a couple of old sheds was their only accommodation, but they were issued with blankets and food and allowed to light fires in the sheds. They stayed quiet not upsetting anyone or attracting unnecessary attention: they just waited patiently and rested. Their escorts stayed in billets just outside the little camp providing sentries and security until the Provost Companies could take control. So many Axis prisoners had been taken after the abortive assault, it would take weeks to sort them all out.

This is what the Hauptmann had hoped for in his planning. In the confusion and uncertainty he and his men could move closer to their objective without too much notice from any casual observer. Anyone getting too close and inquisitive could be silenced quietly and very efficiently.

The order given to the 'escort' sergeant from the local provost company commander was that they were to move to a new camp back past the Somme from where they would be sent on to the main prison camps, perhaps even to England.

There were so many Axis prisoners it was very difficult for the provosts to account for them all. Up to that time the British and Dominion Forces had captured over 188,700 prisoners. The rest of the Allies, French, Belgium and American, could account for just 7,800 prisoners.

It was what Grüber was relying on. From his previous experience as a prisoner the route they were given would take them almost to the place of his operation. Every man in the column knew exactly what his role in this task would be. Each man had concealed on him parts of weapons – pistols, rifles and explosives with detonators and cord. Also they had the weapons held by their 'escort'. The 'escort' had brought the hidden weapons through the lines, because they were never suspected or searched.

They had studied and committed to memory every map and feature of the area they were about to visit. Between them they would be able to traverse the whole area without getting lost. Just in case, though, several of the 'prisoners' had copies of the sector maps drawn on the inside of their shirt sleeves and very unlikely to be seen.

It had taken them almost a week to be moved to a position where, without suspicion, they could move along to the Allied rear to complete their task.

Theirs was a most valuable and informative plan, sublime in it's simplicity and, hopefully, bloodless in its action. But that wasn't to be!

They arrived in the north-eastern side of the Polygon Wood area and as a German barrage opened up on that part of the woods, moved rapidly through the forest across in a south-westerly direction for about ten kilometres. At that point Grüber estimated the group to be about six kilometres from the château and sent out some of his best men to reconnoitre the route there.

On their return it was decided to eliminate the three two-man patrols around the gardens and the three standing sentries that had been spotted. "Try to despatch them quietly," Grüber ordered.

His scouts had seen a sandbagged machine gun nest on the front porch, manned by only one man. There was also one at the back of the château, set in some cellar steps. It wasn't manned at the time. There was nothing at the sides of the building or on the roof.

A narrow road ran through the forest about three kilometres from the garden, which was approached by an even narrower track, just wide enough to allow a small lorry to drive through and up to two large ornamental wrought iron gates. There was a sentry box just inside the left hand side of the gate. It was occupied by the ordinary Allied soldier's worst enemy, a military policeman.

"We should be able to manage him," Grüber told his unteroffizier. "He must have a partner somewhere close by though. When we attack we shall just have to find him as soon as possible. I shall leave a couple of men to deal with him. Two of our 'escort' can do that in case anyone approaches to relieve them. They will be able to deal with them as well. We will attack the château when the officers sit down for dinner: in the meantime we rest and watch."

At the château that evening the adjutant decided that as the assault in March had been defeated, the protection by the infantry company was no longer required and informed the company commander. A platoon would be sufficient to guard the château and its occupants. He could return with the remainder of his company to his own battalion, which was five miles away, and stand by in reserve. Although pleased to get away from the monotony of guard duties, the company commander was disappointed in not being invited to stay for what he knew would be an excellent dinner. He detailed a platoon commander to continue with the guard duties around the château and marched off with the remainder of his company.

At eight forty-five pm, the German Kommandos attacked. They eliminated the MPs at the gate first and replaced them with their own British-uniformed men. Next the Germans removed and replaced the three two-man and three individual standing patrols, again with men wearing British uniforms.

Then unexpectedly a stroke of luck occurred for the attackers. Three two-man patrols came out to relieve the patrols who had been on duty for three hours: their watch was normally four hours but it had been decided to relieve them an hour early.

These six men were also eliminated. A total of seventeen men had been removed in fifteen minutes. The Hauptmann and his men couldn't believe their luck.

Now using all of his British uniformed men and a dozen in German uniform, including himself, Grüber deployed the Kommando into the grounds of the château.

As they approached the sandbagged pill box on the steps of the château, the Unterofficer shouted in English, "What time is it, mate? What's for supper?" He went close to the pillbox and pulled back the sleeve of his jacket saying to the sentry, "Look! my watch has stopped mate, what time is it?"

The sentry, seeing the British uniform, shone a torch on the sergeant's stripes, "Oh! its you Sarge." At that, a sharpened steel knife penetrated the sentry's throat.

The remainder of the platoon were found resting and having their supper in a brick outbuilding. Until then a shot hadn't been fired but on seeing a mixture of German and British uniformed soldiers all carrying weapons at the ready, some members of the platoon, being more awake than others, realised their predicament, grabbed their weapons and tried to open fire at the enemy soldiers.

They didn't stand a chance, there was no cover and the German's could fire from all sides through doors and windows. If a British soldier had a gun in his hand, he was killed. Out of the thirty- eight men of the platoon, only four survived uninjured. Of the remaining seventeen soldiers in the building, including the Lieutenant Commanding, two died and the remainder were injured.

The attack on the guard platoon had been a little premature. An Officers Mess cook heard the shooting first, looked out of the kitchen window and saw the flash of the rifles and pistols. They seemed to be about a hundred yards away.

"Christ! We're being attacked!" he shouted. Everyone in the mess heard him, then they heard the firing of small arms, including the general and his staff officers, none of whom were armed, most of their weapons being in their rooms.

"Destroy the maps and codes," cried the general. "Burn them, for God's sake, hurry!" He rushed out of the dining room towards his bedroom, throwing off his mess jacket, bow tie and cummerbund. As he disappeared into his room and the officers into the map room, several German uniformed troops rushed into the massive entrance hall, two or three of them fired their rifles and pistols into the ceiling.

"Halt! Hander Hoch," they shouted.

The mess waiters who had come into the hall obediently raised their hands and fell back, facing against the wall. The Germans, realising the waiters weren't a threat, went into the Map Room; seeing the staff officers trying to rip the maps off the walls and tables they began shooting the officers.

Hauptmann Grüber, hearing the shooting, rushed into the room, ordering his men: "Halt Machen. Halt immediately! You are destroying those who we came to get."

He began to look closely at the officers, dead, wounded and those alive. Out of the dozen staff officers working in 1 Division Command HQ, only a major and a captain had survived uninjured, two junior captains were only slightly hurt.

He pushed them all into a corner. "Where is the general? We know he was here, we saw him sitting down to dinner: where is he?"

He slapped the major hard across the face. "I can get someone to hit you harder if you do not tell me where he has gone. If you don't tell me I shall start shooting your wounded officers and then the kitchen staff and then you. Where is he?" he shouted.

None of the staff officers, nor any of the waiters, batmen, drivers or kitchen staff had seen the general disappear.

"OK!" Grüber shouted at his men. "Put these people in the cellar and guard them well. Shoot those injured officers, they won't be any use to us."

A major stepped forward. "Don't shoot them, they can't harm you; I'll tell you what you need to know, Hauptmann!" His German was almost as good as the Hauptmann's.

"All right, take them down to the cellars with these servants," was the reply. "Make sure they are secure," he told his sergeant and troops. "We do not want the alarm to be raised yet. Then tear this place apart! Get those wounded and captured soldiers from that hut into the cellars too."

The Officers Mess Sergeant, Jenkins, had been sleeping during the dinner. He knew that everything was in order and hoped he wasn't going to be needed that evening. He had decided to have an early night, knowing that if he was required someone would fetch him in a hurry.

His room was on the side of the house away from the attack on the guard platoon, so although he heard faint sounds of small arms fire he thought that it was the sound of a fire fight being carried on the night winds, which had often happened. Then realising the sounds of the weapons were a little too close he opened the door of his room and peered out into and along the corridor. There was no sign of anyone. Hearing shots and shouts in English and German he guessed that an attack was taking place on the château. Although only half-dressed, he ran past the staff officers' accommodation to the general's room, twenty yards away at the end of the corridor.

When he got to the general's room the door was partly open. Out of habit, he knocked on the door. "Sir," he began, "we are being att…" He didn't finish what he had meant to say.

The large picture window in the room was wide open: there was no sign of the general. Deciding capture wasn't the done thing, he headed for the window, but as he was about to climb through with one leg over the window sill, he heard a snarling shout:

"Halt Machen! Handa Hoch! Herr General."

"Herr Hauptman, we have him, we have him!"

Not understanding a word that was being said or what was happening to him, the sergeant gritted his teeth and climbed back into the room saying nothing. He raised his hands in surrender and was pushed and shoved along the hall to the waiting raiding party.

To his surprise the Hauptmann saluted him and said, "Herr General, you are my prisoner."

The prisoner, seeing the staff officers had been blindfolded, said, "It's all right gentlemen, all safe and well, all safe and well. Conduct yourselves as gentlemen and the fine officers that you are and no harm shall come to us."

The waiters, including Arthur and Albert, facing the entrance hall walls couldn't see what was happening behind them. They were all shaking with fear as they were herded down the cellar steps and tied and shackled to the rings embedded in the cellar walls. It was going to be sometime before they would break out of this prison. The cooks, their helpers, eight waiters and three wounded officers were the only personnel from the Divisional Headquarters staff left alive to be put into the cellar after the attack.

The injured and uninjured soldiers from the guard platoon were placed in another room of the huge cellar under the château and securely bound and shackled.

In the meantime, the two senior staff officers, Major Berry and Capt Rogers, had been taken to the Map Room and were being interrogated about the dispositions of troop placements as shown on the maps.

Suspecting the prisoner who was thought to be the general was being evasive and awkward, Hauptmann Grüber cursed the British officer class and demanded answers. He was met with a stony silence. He turned to Major Berry for the answers, who began a long rigmarole of what-was-what and who-was-who.

Then a voice from behind the officers said angrily, "Major, if you or any other officer give the enemy any further information you will be court-martialled in captivity after the war."

The Hauptmann looked at the major, waiting for his reply.

The officers all realised then that they had to give away as little about the British and Allied positions as possible. They had to be as divisive and inventive with the Allied, and especially the British, positions as possible. The officers had to make sure their 'stories' tallied: this was not an exercise that had gone wrong, it was real. Each officer linked his fingers behind his head and faced the wall.

At that the Hauptmann said, "Enough! let us get of here and return to our own lines. Gentlemen, we will extract further information and translate these maps after we have interrogated you further. Don't be misled, you will talk because your lives will depend on it."

With that the five officers were marched out to two trucks that had brought the guard platoon to the estate. They were given German overcoats, caps and boots, gagged and tied up. Two of the officers were thrown in the back of the first truck. Protesting vehemently, Jenkins played the part of an indignant General Officer as well as he could as he and the remaining two officers, dressed as German private soldiers, were thrown into the back of the second truck and covered with a tarpaulin.

One of the enemy soldiers sat on each prisoner with a Luger pistol jammed into his neck with orders to shoot him if they were discovered or tried to escape as they made their way to their rendezvous, at their 'jumping off point'.

Before moving off the German Kommando conducted a thorough search of the château and grounds, at least as thorough as could happen in the darkness and damage of the surrounding area.

The Kommando drove off: they had only suffered one casualty, one man with a slight arm wound. The Hauptmann congratulated his men on a most successful raid. He had intended to fire the château, but that would have only drawn attention to themselves. Now the British would never believe what had happened under their noses. Now the only thing they had to worry about was getting back to their own lines.

The trucks were driven down the track to the gates and Grüber's sentries picked up, then off into the darkness on a pre-planned escape route. The 'general' and his staff officers were trussed up like mummies to prevent any attempt at all to escape.

The trucks were driven at convoy speed along roads leading to the front, the German drivers even having the nerve to join Allied convoys on the way. Grüber's two vehicles tagged on behind three different British convoys without being noticed until they arrived at their 'jumping off point' between the French and British front lines in the early hours of the morning of the next night. They had been extremely lucky and the raid very well planned.

They hid all day in disused front line trenches. At a pre-arranged time a signal flares were fired into the night sky. Using damaged, disused and unguarded mining tunnels, which had been declared unsafe by the miners from both armies, they blasted their way back through the 'wall' which separated the Allied and Axis mining tunnels into their own Axis lines.

The tunnels were an ongoing part of both sides' trench warfare system. By tunnelling under the opposition's lines, making a cavern under the enemy's most fortified defences and filling the cavern with tons of high explosives, a 'mine' would be formed. If the tunnel and mine were undiscovered, when it detonated it caused maximum damage and casualties to the enemy troops and defences. At the start of the Battle of Messines, for example, 19 large mines were detonated under the German defensive lines, enabling the New Zealand division to capture the area in two days.

The tunnel that Grüber had selected had been unusable, and for a few months was deserted except for a 'listening party' who were trying to hear if their counterparts on the other side of the wall of clay were digging towards them. It was also partly flooded. Nothing had been heard of the Allied miners for weeks so it was thought to be abandoned. With the aid of German mining engineers and listening posts it was decided that the wall of clay was just thick enough to blow out on a prearranged signal, in one detonation. As long as Grüber and his party were in a secure safe proximity to the detonation, then at the right time the whole party could be through the tunnel before the British knew what was happening. It was unlikely that they would ever know what really happened. The German engineers would collapse the tunnel on their side as soon as the escaping party had got through to their own lines therefore making that particular tunnel even more unusable and dangerous.

Four red flares at the start of a rolling barrage by the Axis artillery into the Allied lines was the signal for the tunnel escape to start. It went exactly to plan. Within half an hour of the barrage starting the raiding party was back in its own lines and Hauptmann was receiving the congratulations of the commanding generals.

The captured officers were immediately taken to the German High Command Special Interrogation Unit where the questioning began immediately.

The staff officers held out for over thirty-six hours before they began to explain the details of the maps and troop dispositions, knowing that the attack on the château would have been discovered and the battle maps and plans would all have been completely changed. Orders would have been given to the effect that every German prisoner was to be thoroughly searched and interrogated immediately on capture, no matter how long it took and what rank the prisoner happened to be.

The 'general' was taken and sent to one of the various secure chalets in Germany which held high ranking officers until the end of the war. He would be held in solitary confinement for some months until after hostilities, albeit in a beautiful house in the Bavarian Mountains. There weren't any other senior officers of equivalent or equal rank to positively identify him. The only two people in the house with him were a captured soldier from the West Indian Regiment, who was employed as his batman-servant-gardener, and a French prisoner employed as a chef. He was guarded by a platoon of a German Home Defence unit day and night until some months after the Armistice was signed.

Meanwhile the Staff Officers had given what information they could remember knowing it was no longer valid and was no use at all to the Germans because all the information on the maps and in the code books had been changed as soon as the raid had been discovered, eighteen hours after the abduction had occurred.

Thirty hours after that a frightened dirty figure emerged from the priest hole in the floor of a built-in bedroom wardrobe. He had hidden there for almost forty-eight hours, shaking and mumbling to himself. He had never felt so lonely, thirsty or hungry in his life. He went looking for food and water of which there was plenty in the taps, but nothing to eat except dried bread on the floor on which rats were gnawing. He started to shake with fear when he realised that the headquarters had been abandoned and he was completely alone.

"I shall have to go and find help," he reasoned. "But where shall I start?" He decided to search the house from top to bottom, then he realised the house was deserted. The attack on the château had been discovered twenty-four hours earlier before the escaping soldier emerged from the priest hole which had been his hiding place. All the captured soldiers, dead and wounded, had been removed from the cellars and outbuildings twelve hours before the soldier climbed out from his hiding place. The building was abandoned.

It began to get dark outside and he was too frightened to turn any lights on. He knew that a road ran past the château about a mile away, so he decided his best plan would be to get to the road and flag down any passing vehicle and have the driver get him to a safe place. He was a good planner, he thought.

He put on the largest overcoat he could find and picked up a tin helmet that the soldiers had left in the hallway. When he reached the gates of the château he became more confident and went through and continued on down to the road. He had almost reached the road junction when four figures dressed in British army battledress stepped out on the track in front of him. He was tired, dishevelled and covered in mud and dust.

Seeing stripes on a soldier's arm, he said, "Sergeant, am I pleased to see you! I've had a terrible last few hours. Can you help me please?"

The patrol wore the arm bands of the Military Police and was led by a sergeant.

"Where do you think you're off to then?" the sergeant demanded. "On the run, eh! Who are you? One of the yellow buggers from the front, eh?"

The fugitive broke down and almost began to whimper. "I'm sorry I'm not well and I'm starving, I haven't eaten for over two days."

"Don't give me that you scum. Stand up. What's up, got a bit of shell-shock, eh?" the sergeant shouted, then he turned to the other MPs. "Did you hear that lads? He says he's not well and he's hungry; look at the state of him! You're a bloody yellow deserter, ain't you?"

"No! I'm not sergeant, I'm an officer. I've had to hide in the cellar when the Germans came and attacked the headquarters two days ago."

The fugitive didn't want to tell the MPs exactly who he was in case they were Germans disguised as military policemen. It was a ruse often used by both sides to gain information about the enemy.

"That's a good un ain't it, best I've heard yet. Why didn't you fight like those other poor sods that were killed?"

"I didn't have a gun, I was hiding." Then it dawned on him what he had just said.

"Hiding? While the poor bastards were fighting for their lives? You were hiding?" The sergeant was almost screaming. "And you an officer? What happened to the general and his staff? Was he killed or captured, what happened?"

"I don't know. I couldn't see, I had to hide in the cellar."

"So you've been in the cellar all this time? You're a bleeding liar! The whole house was searched from top to bottom. All the officers and soldiers were accounted for. The general and four of his staff officers were captured and taken away more than two days ago. So where the hell were you, eh? Was the shelling too much for you? You gutless swine."

Turning to the other MPs, "Him an officer? A bloody liar I reckon, aye! He'll say he don't know who he is next!" They all laughed.

"Nearly got us, didn't he?" another MP chortled. "He'll have us court-martialled next, the lying toad."

"OK," said the Sergeant. "Let's see if he knows what General Harper's orders are concerning cowards and deserters. Come on you, tell us what the general's Standing Orders are about deserters. Come on let's have it, I'm getting fed up waiting."

"They are all to be shot on sight!" stammered the fugitive. "But I am not a deserter, I escaped when the Germans attacked the HQ, I can prove it. He reached into the pockets of his coat, and came out with the Officers Mess Sergeant's pay book and identity discs. Sergeant Jenkins never wore the discs whilst he was in the mess, and had kept the pay book in his overcoat pocket so that he knew where to find it if he had to leave the building in a hurry.

The fugitive started to stammer when he realised it wasn't his own overcoat that he wore. "Look there's been a big mistake, I'm not a deserter, really! I am General Harper, your Commander."

"General Harper has been captured as I've already told you. Do you think I'm Princess Alexandra? You barmy bastard," shouted the sergeant. "Listen you, you're beginning to get up my nose; first you say you're an officer, now you've got a sergeant's pay book and ID discs, next you'll be a Corporal in the Horse Guards, then a private in the Pioneer Battalion. You are a liar, you are mad and you are a deserter, whichever way you look at it! Any of you blokes ever seen anyone like this sergeant before?"

Two of the junior NCOs shook their heads. "I thought I did once," said the third man.

"Where?"

"When we had to go to the front to pick up one of those yellow bastards that wouldn't go 'over the top'."

"Is this the man you saw then?"

"No Sarge, he don't look anything like him."

"That's it then, take the bastard away. The bloody Germans killed our mates who were guarding this hole for the general and for this bastard. Take him away: the cowardly swine should be shot for desertion and cowardice – General Harper's Standing Orders. We'll let the CO know when and if we get back. Tell you what, take him to that old garden out the back, you know where we did that execution a few weeks back."

The man couldn't believe his ears. "You can't do this! I demand to see your Commanding Officer, he will know who I am." He was beginning to get really frightened. "This is illegal, the orders are to execute the deserter or the coward after a court has sentenced them, not before."

"He knows King's R and R, don't he? He'll say he wrote them next. You've had your say, let's get on with it!" retorted the MP. "The orders General Harper gave in writing was all deserters to be shot on sight. You're deserting and in my sight. You will be shot. That is final."

Then he said to the other MPs, "Our CO only arrived out here last week from Blighty and hasn't had a chance to see anything except Jerry prisoners. I doubt it if he would know what to do with one deserter from the next, he's so green. We're so bloody snowed under with those prisoners, he won't be bothered with a deserter telling stupid lies. So now, sergeant, what's your name?" There was no reply.

The MP said to the prisoner, "We're your court-martial, and we find you guilty of cowardice in the face of the enemy and deserting your post. Right lads? And it don't look as if you are going to be missed, matey!" The three junior NCOs nodded in agreement. "So don't say another word, you yellow bugger!"

Turning to the other MPs he said, "Take him away and when you've done him, put him in with those other yellow bastards that were put against the wall last time we came. You know, those other little shits; they're in that disused cesspit, you can chuck him in it too, there'll be plenty of room and it'll be easier to cover him up there."

"No, no, no!" the fugitive 'sergeant' screamed as he turned and began to run into the woods. Four .38 revolvers appeared as if by magic and three rounds from each weapon were fired at the fleeing figure.

A couple of days after the mess waiters, cooks and wounded officers and men had been released, a search party found the other casualties. They found the officers who had been shot by the raiding party and the bodies of the guard platoon and also the general's batman and his driver. They had all been taken and dumped in the shed in the garden where Privates Johnson and Edwards had been executed.

No one could give any information about the general to the search party. None of them knew what had happened to him. The search party couldn't find any sign of Sergeant Jenkins either. One of the injured officers said he might have escaped, because no one in the château had seen him during or since the attack.

Later in the day a provost officer came and questioned the released captives on the whereabouts of Sergeant Jenkins as he wished to inform him that his nephew Private Peter Johnson had died. He'd been shot at dawn a week or so ago. When he turns up would they please inform the provosts, so that the sergeant could be informed of his nephew's demise.

On the evening of the next day the same provost officer returned and informed them that Sergeant Jenkins been shot trying to escape the German attack. He had been found in the old garden area with the bodies of the soldiers who had been killed as they patrolled the general's headquarters.

The investigation after the event showed that the German infiltration and attack on the Divisional Headquarters had captured General Harper and four of his staff officers. The blame rested firmly on the shoulders of General Harper and his staff officers.

After the war Major, now Colonel, Berry and Captain, now Lieutenent Colonel, Rogers met at the Berliner Hotel in Berlin whilst on holiday from their regiments during the occupation in Germany in 1921. The discussion turned to the time they were captured and imprisoned.

Berry said, "I wonder what happened to that fellow Jenkins from the Coldstreams?"

Rogers replied, "Didn't you know, sir? Some say he was shot whilst attempting to escape the attack and some say he was shot while he attempted to desert. Don't you remember, he bore an uncanny likeness to General Harper, that's why that fellow Richards, the Lord something or other, chose him to run the Officers Mess. Perhaps it was to use the fellow as a decoy or double: jolly good wheeze, what?"

As spoke he heard the voice of the maître d', "Good evening, General."

Berry and Rogers both turned towards the sound of the voice and saw a tall, stooping, white haired man with a large drooping white moustache passing their table.

"Good evening gentlemen, how are you both? Goodness me, you both looked quite shocked! Is there something the matter?" He went on, "The last time we saw each other was on that dreadful day when the Germans took us captive and away for interrogation." Neither officer could think of anything to say. They just stared at the tall figure smiling at them. "You know I almost escaped them but they were a bit too clever for me, still, never mind. All safe and well, eh!"

He smiled at one of his favourite comments. "Yes, all safe and well. Yes, still Fighting Fit and Fit to Fight, eh! Yes, Gentlemen, it is a long time since I last saw you or any of my erstwhile companions during those dreadful years. The army has since retired and pensioned me off on half pay. Shame the war didn't continue for a few more years; I'd have been a Field Marshal by now, eh! But it was a jolly good show, wasn't it gentlemen?" Berry and Rogers waited until the general paused for a breath but both were too slow.

"Did you know the bloody Boche refused to repatriate me until last year? After the Treaty of Versailles in June 1919 the swine kept me until they thought I would be no longer any use to our military masters."

He went on, "Do you know the Harz Mountains? A very beautiful area but it was an awfully boring place to stay – unless you can ski or like to climb. Anyway, I decided to stay there, I've nothing in England to go home to, so I think I'll be better off in these beautiful mountains. Better to know and keep close to your enemy, don't you think? Otherwise they will nearly always win."

He waited for a reply but there was none from either of the almost dumb-struck officers.

"Well, gentlemen, I must pop off now, things to do, you know." Turning to his accompanying entourage, and speaking in German, he said, "Come Ladies and Gentlemen, we shall be late for that party that the Mayor is giving!" Turning back to the officers he winked, "Gute Nacht, Berry, Rogers."

At that he disappeared through the hotel revolving door.

Rogers turned to Berry, "My God, was that really the general?" he blurted.

"Your guess is as good as mine," Berry replied: he was still pale with shock at the thought of what might have occurred.

A few weeks later the tall white-haired gentleman suddenly disappeared from a well-known hotel in the Harz mountains, Germany. The German Police were informed and the gentleman was identified by the hotel owner as General C R Harper KCB (retired), former Commander of 1 Corps in France during the First World War. He was renowned for the discipline he imposed on his troops and the execution of those who did not reach his required standards. The most infamous order he gave was: "Discipline them. With a bullet!"

There was nothing left in his suite to identify him except a small red and gold chocolate tin left in a chest of drawers. It was identified as one of those issued to private soldiers fighting in the South African war by Queen Victoria. Painted on the inside lid in silver was the inscription, 'Presented by Queen Alexandra, Malta 1907'. Scratched on the inside of the lid was '31 Guinea St. Bristol', and in tiny almost unreadable letters, 'Captain M Andrews, The Salvation Army, The Citadel, Bristol, Somerset'.

The local police chief, in an act of kindness to the unknown captain, sent the box to May Andrews with a note explaining the sad circumstances in which it had been found.

When a report of the general's disappearance reached London and the Army's High Command there were one or two raised eyebrows and the report quietly filed away: neither he nor the report was never mentioned again.

It was reported to have been said by an officer promoted in his place, "Strange the old boy stayed with the boche, must have picked up with some old 'frau' and was probable enjoying the Wiener schnitzel and beer too much to come home. At the very least there'll never have to be an investigation into the way he commanded his men and the way he fought that last battle. By all accounts he should have stayed at Staff College, he was very good at fighting battles on a blackboard, eh?"

Colonel Berry and Lt Colonel Rogers turned to the Brigadier General and Berry said, "Which was the battalion that you commanded for him, then sir?"

"Oh! I wasn't commanding a battalion at the time of his capture. I was kept at Staff College throughout the war, teaching the art of commanding men and fighting battles to the young gentlemen, the volunteers and conscripted, who I can categorically say, almost, all went to the Front with plenty of confidence, knowledge and not a little nerve. Brave young officers! Oh yes," he added as an afterthought. "I did volunteer to go to France, but those above thought I would be more use at Staff College, more's the pity," he added lamely.

"It's a pity that he's not hear to explain himself, sir," Berry replied. Berry actually detested General Harper, but he couldn't allow this untested, cynical, know-all of a college brigadier, who had barely reached thirty-five years of age, besmirch the reputation of a man who couldn't defend himself, no matter what faults he had.

"Whilst we were under his command as staff officers, up to and during the time of his and our capture, he was always hard on his troops and officers but he never ever once talked about his battalion and regimental commanders behind their backs, as we never would."

He raised his glass, "General Harper!" Roger's emptied his glass to the toast. They turned their backs on the brigadier and without another word left the room.

There was never any trace of General Harper after his disappearance and the investigation never closed.

A year later a bent, aged looking, bushy bearded, white haired man, dressed in a shabby suit with scuffed, worn black shoes and wearing a bowler hat, knocked on the door of the Salvation Army Meeting Room near Bristol Docks. It was opened by a young Salvation Army Officer, "Hello, I'm Jenny. Can I help?"

"I hope so, is Captain Andrews in today? If so would you be kind enough to tell her an old friend has arrived?"

Then her eyes widened as she recognised the stranger. She turned and ran back into the hall crying, "May, May! It's for you!"

May Andrews, who didn't look a day older than she had at their last meeting in the Military Hospital in France, came to the door, hesitating for a few moments before she realised who was standing there.

She stepped forward and took her man by the shoulders, looked him directly in the eyes and said quietly, "I've been waiting for you my love, where have you been? Oh! I knew you'd be back, Jenks, I knew you would. Come on, come on in."

Taking him by the hand she led him into the privacy of her small comfortable office. As she did so, May slid her other hand into her skirt pocket and grasped hold of a small tin box: she had received it through the post almost a year before. She had carried it with her for all that time, in hope that her man would return.

Then she whispered to Jenkins, "Thank God you're home, Jenks, where have you been?" She paused and then said, "I've been waiting to return this to you." She handed him his Queen Victoria's tin chocolate box. His face crumpled and tears welled up in his tired eyes but he couldn't speak.

May said it for him. "It's all right my love, you're home now and we're together again as we always will be," as she took him in her arms and hugged him to her. She saw Jenny peeking through the partly open door, tears running down her cheeks. Smiling at her and still holding on to Jenkins, May gently pushed the door closed, knowing that he wouldn't ever be taken away from her again.

Printed in the United Kingdom
by Lightning Source UK Ltd.
122363UK00001B/208-225/A